I0639557

A. A. Jameson

Shark People

the urge to submerge

Copyright © A. A. Jameson, 2004
Published by A.A. Jameson in 2011, reprinted 2021
defduf@gmail.com
ISBN 978-0-9568675-0-6
Available from Lulu.com

All rights reserved, including the right to reproduce this book,
or any part thereof, in any form, without the written
permission of the author.

References to Frank Zappa and quotes from his titles or works
are by express written permission of the Zappa Family Trust
and no reproduction rights or any other kind are implied by
any use herein. Selected lyrics from the following songs are
reproduced:

Cheap Thrills, Fountain of Love, Stuff Up The Cracks, Anything**,
I'm Not Satisfied, Later That Night,* and *The Duke of Prunes.* All
lyrics by FZ except *FZ & Ray Collins/**Ray Collins. All songs
copyrighted for the world by Frank Zappa except * ** by Frank
Zappa Music & Ray Collins Music. All rights reserved.

Susan, with heartfelt thanks

1. Birchwood not by Klimt

A sweating, bearded face condensed from a green-blue backdrop swimming with fishes: Stanley Blackster, locked away from distraction, staring at his mirror. Guitars, drums and synthesizers filled the room with a slowly pulsing, melancholy wash of noise. He took a towel and wiped away the sweat. He'd drifted off. It happened. Where? He was covered in sweat, so he knew where. But the past ten minutes were effectively a blank. Reaching down he snatched up his whisky and took a hefty pull. From the wall a silver barracuda studied him with a cold black eye. Always watching.

Steadying himself, Stan sucked in a deep breath and stared shakily into the mirror. He'd be all right in a couple of minutes. His temperature would return to normal and his guts would untwist. He just had to wait it out. The fishes would help. And The Balvenie of course. Another smoothly burning mouthful. Through the mirror and beyond himself, he closed his focus on the powder-blue surgeonfish, plump and soothingly blue, yellow fins, smart white collar and pouting black face, emanating serenity in gentle waves like a fishy Bhudda. Immediately he felt composure feeding back into his system. And the soothing turquoise walls of this small, safe room - turquoise was a reliable pool of harmony in the occasionally clashing seas of Blackster family life. And The Balvenie, a cultural pinnacle.

The sad, dreamy music surged and receded, surged again. Durutti Column. No human voice, no words. Another measured gulp, and the tide of heat and blurred impressions was ebbing fast: music, fishes and alcohol had restored him. An invincible combination.

Composed once more - he'd overlook the occasional uncoordinated lurch in his internals - he gnawed at a forefinger and contemplated a face on the slide towards middle age: black hair, shorter now, fell either side of a ragged line somewhere near the middle of his head, while his beard, trimmed ruthlessly while the mind was absent, had been reduced to fashion stubble. But surely the discerning eye could still pick out the ghost of the old Blackster imperial, the heavy, downcurving black moustache and the square of chin beard? The grand old days!

His gaze wandered to the parrotfish, a lemon, lilac and turquoise lesson in irrepressibility, and he smiled. Intoxication flooded

4

his mind and he thought of Liza, his own Black Barracuda, fierce patroller of the perimeters of his life. Parrotfish were quite different, easy-going givers and takers.

'What lies ahead for the Blacksters?' he asked, or thought he asked the mirror. There were certain problems, true, which were by no means insurmountable. In fact just now it was hard to recall with precision just what these so-called problems were. He was fully restored, and practised his thoughtful frown, his companionable nod.

As the music wound down there was an abrupt and startling hammering at the door, and a muffled shouting. Difficult to distinguish meaning in the din, but had he picked out the word *pathetic*? Possibly. A very short silence ensued, then more reasonable tones:

'Why don't you just fill up the bath and spend the night in it? Go on Stan, be true to yourself, live the life. Bugger us out here, eh? When are you going to bloody grow up?'

A violent thud, then another. Was she about to burn her way in with those eyes? Another unintelligible roar, some receding thumps.

Ah. Why did she allow herself to say such things – whatever they were? It saddened him. Mrs. Blackster. Liza. The Barracuda. He'd forgotten, they'd had a row, and now she'd reminded him. Nothing important, or it would have lodged in his memory, but he would need to make amends. Further intoxicant was required. He poured a nicely-judged shot of The Balvenie, and rinsed away the litter of bristles. He disliked untidiness.

'Unfettered wanderers in the oceans of the world.' He swallowed the smooth, smooth whisky, feeling at his most pelagic. The Balvenie - so easy to drink, and no doubt as to its restorative powers, but ... possibly lacking a little in terms of bite, now he applied considered judgement. In terms of lunge. Perhaps he had simply achieved a rapid tolerance to the marque, whereby shots subsequent to the first had no additional effect. It happened. He would search out alternatives, in that uniquely human quest for knowledge - knowledge for its own sake - just as soon as he'd finished the bottle. Dear Liza. He called up her image, so easy to do. There could be only one. An outstanding woman, really. Woman? No, a new word was called for. Sometimes, true, a distressingly primitive aggression troubled the glittering surface, as had just now been the case, but he could not hold her responsible for the occasional forays of an elemental something which lived deep within her. And liked a drink. She surely knew by now that aggression, whatever it may achieve in other areas of her life, achieved nothing with him. He was obdurate. Rock-ribbed. She'd had that one glass too many. Two, probably. It was understandable. In his mind, pleasingly bleary with fumes, emotion and hypnotic colour, he held her strong and beautiful black face, and felt only love undying. And his dear son, Gram, so young and unworn, life stretching away before him. What would become of Gram? There were too many people out there already, hordes of them, armies of them, swarming antheaps of them, all scheming and scrabbling for a living in this overcrowded and exhausted world. Liza and Gram, he loved them both utterly, and they must depend on his love. They were his world. And the noble hound, of course. The tears had started, and he let them run, appreciating them in the mirror. He would emerge now, march straight upstairs and rouse them, reassure them of his love, insist in the strongest terms that we three will prevail. Four, with the noble hound. Who was the captain of this ship? From now on, life would be different for the Blacksters. He would chart a new course. Start anew. Accept - no, seize - his responsibilities. One further mouthful of The Balvenie. Yes, he would seek out a fierier distillation. And Liza - hoo! Ferocious, on occasion. His own black Barracuda, she would hover there, watchful, and then, sooner or later, as inevitably as … he couldn't think of anything inevitable enough.

In the mirror he fleetingly glimpsed another face, settled blurrily on his own, an odd, feral little face he had once thought ugly. Just a flash, gone before it was there. Gone. Like its owner, poor little Kim. Another poor kid, now lost somewhere out in the endless world.

The music had stopped. His progress to the cassette player involved a painless rebound from the edge of the bath. Out with Durutti Column. Doleful, and no longer appropriate. Let them have something elevating and refined. On convivial evenings such as this he never felt alone. Not something to dwell on perhaps, but there was no apparent shortage of company. So, music to send them striding through life in style. Or at least, up the Blackster stairs. Zappa, *Bogus Pomp*. He turned up the sound a notch and went to stand before the giant sleepy shark, *Nebrius ferrugineus*, an old and valued friend.

This bathroom was his rightful place, his natural setting. Houses had characters, good and not so, and within them there would be a place where this was concentrated, or where it sprang from. He would often pass the odd evening hour in here, when life outside became disagreeable. More so recently. But there was a perfectly adequate, if smaller, second room upstairs, and any complaints were unjustified. His needs were few: music, a selection of fishes, the means for a harmless degree of inebriation, the sympathetic and generally unquestioning face, the turquoise tranquillity.

'Now,' he told the mirror solemnly, 'It has been a pleasant evening, but now it is time to re-enter inshore waters, attuned to currents and shallows, alert for predators.' Or for one in particular. 'So then!' He nodded along to a few stately bars, eyes closed, then reluctantly hit the stop button and gathered himself to make his exit. He was a man with responsibilities.

Two big, ragged birds swooped and tussled against a cold grey sky, above a bleak and wintry expanse of New Forest heath and scattered woodland.

'Buzzards.' With one of her challenging looks - come on, have a go then.

Heavy-duty ethnic headgear, woven from multicoloured Tibetan yaks, was jammed down over her ears and held in place with a red cord tied off under the chin. Bundled up in all this outdoor gear, broad-shoulders on a level with his own, she strode along like a man. A strong man. Amazon in the New Forest.

'Correct.' Let her have it. Stan didn't feel safe identifying anything right at this moment. There were an awful lot of specks whirling around out there. This was Gram's job, identifying birds. Those eyes were still on him. He did his best. 'Too big for crows.' A shrewd guess. Best to think in short, coherent bursts. His head wasn't just thumping. The inside of it was sucking in and out, and he was feeling desperately demersal.

'See!' The Barracuda poked out her normally luscious pink tongue, which just now looked threatening. So muscular and confident, and so pink. Glistening. But the eyes were off him. 'Tell Gram his old mother's a bird-lady.' Their son was the one absorbed in all aspects of the natural world, in his quiet way. Quiet was Gram's middle name. Gram Quiet Blackster.

They sat on a cold, algal-green wooden bench planted at the edge of the silent heath. In a minute he'd know whether it was better to stay still or keep on the move. This trip hadn't been his idea. Meanwhile, he made a show of looking around.

Hard to believe they once used to make the journey out here for nothing more rewarding than pleasure, to wallow around in aimless drugged and drunken afternoons in the sun. Had it really been them, or was he getting mixed up with some film, or a book? He was staring, and his mouth hung open, and he'd forgotten to keep on breathing. The Barracuda was cooing at the noble hound.

From a comfortable spot in the dead heather the hound watched them intently, alert for any signs of action. Kato was one of those big, soft golden retrievers, maybe not the brightest chocolate drop in the box, often puzzled but keen as you like, and without a mean bone in his body. And a smiler. Kato was always smiling, apart from the rare occasions when he had something on his mind. And everyone likes a smiler, don't they? Stan smiled too, crookedly, couldn't help it. He could see properly again, more or less. The buzzards, unquestionably buzzards, separated at last, wheeling away on broad, upswept wings.

'Interesting to see it at this time of year though, isn't it?' The Barracuda could be a forceful optimist, sometimes. 'I mean, with all the colours drained away like this, so austere. Deserted. Abandoned. Too bloody cold to paint though. I was just thinking, it's hard to believe we came out here with Alice and dear Julius all those times, isn't it? I bet you were thinking the same, right? Ally and me doing arty things, you drinking and smoking and blathering? Whenever you weren't dragging me off into the bushes, that is. And dear Julius, hunting for helpless little creatures to persecute? God, we were so young then, Stanley, weren't we?' She nudged closer and pushed an arm firmly through his. The New Forest slopped gently from side to side.

'We're not quite ready for the boneyard yet,' he managed. She'd messed up his vision again.

'Well, I know I'm not. Not so sure about you though. What's happened to you? You're like one of those broken-down old greyhounds these days, the ones they take out into the fields at night with a gun.'

'Yeah.' He'd been savouring a lubricious blast of fragmented sunlight and thrashing shadow, pulverized plant-life, panting, grappling brown limbs, sweat and alcohol. He remembered the bushes all right, but who'd been doing the dragging? Had he once possessed such awesome strength and determination?

'Hey, just look at the fat blackie.'

On the neighbouring bench some kindly old dear had put out birdseed, and a blackbird had hopped up to inspect it, one beady eye trained on the noble hound. A loud chirp would be enough to get Kato worried, but it wasn't to know that. Liza delved in her pocket and passed him half of something called a salmon wrap from the supermarket.

'That Kate Winslet's got a right hoot on her, hasn't she? You'd not want me hooting like that, would you Stan?'

This threw him.

'It was good though. I liked the models in their fantasy land, and De*borah*.'

Ah. They'd watched *Heavenly Creatures*. Kate Winslet had been hooting. He was expected to say something. 'Fat bugger.' He meant the blackie. The sad shreds of salmon were cold and dry, and didn't want to go down. They needed a drink badly. And where the hell did she keep the paracetamol these days? He'd turned the bathroom upside down – his bathroom – and couldn't find the bloody things anywhere. She'd hidden them. Well, he wasn't going to ask. He could pop into the first chemist's, on a pretext, treats for the noble hound or something, anything, just until they got to the pub.

The Barracuda was gurgling, showing off those unchallengeable teeth, those lightly inflated pink lips, the tip of that confident tongue. The alarming eyes were preparing to power up. 'Yeah, right. Fat bugger. Once we came here to party, now we've moved on and we've developed conversation, right?'

'I meant the blackie.'

She stared. Kato looked from one to the other. Noble hounds were sensitive, known for it.   'Yes, good film. Peter Jackson.' He couldn't come up with any more on that one.

'Penetrating.'

OK. He waved his salmon wrap. 'To wind up in a wrap, eh, after no life at all.'

Two pairs of eyes stared. The Barracuda lips had formed an ominous round pink 'O'.

'All the PCBs and heavy metals they cram into these poor old farmed salmon, you'd think they'd taste of something, wouldn't you?' He tossed the remaining chunk to Kato, who choffed it down.

The Barracuda was nodding slowly, unsmiling. 'Fish. I don't want to talk about fish, Stanley.'

Pity. Julian Pettifer had just fronted a BBC investigation into salmon farming. Tragic. 'Julian Pettifer's programme on salmon farming – '

'I said. Not fish.'

They gazed off over the drab, rolling heathland. No sign of the buzzards.

'What then?'

She sighed. 'Oh, I don't know, the new US president, is he legitimate? How many patients did Shipman really kill? Blair son of Thatcher. The fuel protests, the Dome closing, no, not that, I'm sick of that. England's new foreign football manager then. The Russian space station. There's loads of things. Just not fish.'

Two pairs of eyes stared.

'They've perfected this potato. When it needs watering it glows. Green.'

'Oh really?'

Kato sighed.

'Best you can do? Something closer to home then, let's see ... how about ... hang on, did you not go to a convention of weirdos, just last night? That was you, wasn't it? Not the most appealing topic, but you getting out at all is a major event.' She spoke like this to her students. 'Selected gossip please, and you know what I mean. How's my friend dear old Charlie, for instance? And your friend Ray? Got that new liver yet? Anyone given him a good thump lately? Lost his job yet? Stuff like that. Harmless chit-chat.'

Ah. Removing her arm, which felt like a girder, he delved about with gloved hands in both pockets, fished out a flat pack and fiddled a small cigar into his mouth, then delved again for matches, striving grimly to keep his head still and at the same time resist a throbbing command to bite into the cigar and swallow it. He got the thing lit, drew in hot smoke and blew it out through his teeth. Did he feel better, worse, or just as bad in a different way? There had to be progress, down at the cellular level. A creeping resurgence, just awaiting the first pint.

Stan rarely bothered with these conventions any more, but this had been on the doorstep, at Southampton Guildhall, and Ray had pressured him. There had been the usual knot of hard-core *Insidiator* fans, already wearing the new T-shirts. Liza had even provided her expertise to do the drawing for the gaping, anatomically correct tiger shark jaws to go on the back, very generously considering she hated the show. The little symbol on the left breast showed one stylised shark shape chasing another. Stylish, as sharks inevitably and invariably were. No words. It was a cult, after all, so they said, and there was no need for words. Cultists liked things to stay obscure and exclusive. They recognised each other by signs. Ray had come down from London for the day. He was a regular, even now, five years on. Charlie, star of the show, couldn't stay away either, and appeared in character. He was keeping his chin up, despite an obvious decline. No Kim, of course, but she'd been heavily in the air. He gulped in air and smoke, a convulsive action which brought on a bout of coughing. He'd forgotten to breathe again and his eyes were watering.

Stan had done his bit, mingled, had a drink or two, then made off with a few free T-shirts, one for Gram. The fanatics still sounded as though they could keep it up forever, and Ray marshalled proceedings with gusto. It even seemed that, far from getting the boot, Ray had extended his little empire in TV programme-making, and was promising the cognoscenti that *Insidiator* would be on their screens again soon, and then, then … a new series, which was like tossing them chunks of meat. But these people weren't representative of the viewing public, as they'd learned the hard way. They were odd folk, these. Deluded even. Sad. But Ray was an optimist, and with a following wind he was sometimes unstoppable. The fans had torn into his news and wolfed it down.

He was being jostled, and there was a distant sigh.

'In your own time Stanley.'

'Ray's fine, sends his best.' His voice surprised him. 'Still in his job, doing well in fact, wants us to go up to London for a weekend, visit the galleries and so on. T-shirts went well. The fanatics are getting less and less diluted.' He didn't mention the Kims, and she didn't ask. These were fans of Kim, rather than the show itself, and they were boycotting these little gatherings. They bore a grudge. He must make sure the name Kim didn't pop out. 'Charlie was there, of course, fully in character. Sends you his deepest salaams.'

'Poor old Charlie.' Like most people, or most women, the Barracuda had a soft spot for Charles Chinchard. 'If anyone ever needed a good woman … ' she petered out. Charlie used to have one. 'I hope you invited him over. Stanley?'

'Mmm.' The effort had wiped his mind clean. He pulled a face at the noble hound, who tensed in expectation.

Liza was giving him a firm look, on the edge of a low-grade glower, at odds with the jaunty headgear. 'Your attention please, Stanley. Ask him over for the weekend. Where's he living now anyway? Did he not move out to the countryside, Dorset or somewhere? He'll be lonely, I know Charlie. He went to pieces, and it's not fair. There's not many real gentlemen left, take my word for it. He should never have got mixed up with you and Ray in the first place. You should have seen what was happening to him. Stan?'

'Ah.' It would have to be straight to the drink now. Paracets were too slow.

'I see. Exhausted your squiddy little brain, did it, that? And going up to London to see Ray? Visit the galleries? Ray, in a gallery? It'll mean propping up a selection of his favourite bars, rushing through the nearest gallery, maybe, if there's time, then more propping. See me doing that? No, you've put that in. I expect Ray's as out of it as you are this morning. But he'll be back in the Bloody Pub by now.'

Bastard.

'Well, at least Charlie will have enjoyed it, a bit of appreciative company, evening out with a bit of an audience, chance to perform. I can't stand the thought of him living all on his own. I hope you and Ray looked after him. Meaning you. I know what Ray's like.'

An elderly couple of dachshund walkers stopped to admire the noble hound, how old was he, what a lovely dog, what's his name, the usual things. The Barracuda could deal with it.

The car park was almost empty. Out on the dead stretch of heathland, with its straggling copses of skinny trees and scratchy clumps of gorse, nothing moved. And why would it? A sign read No Smirking Beyond This Point. And wasn't that absolutely bloody typical? This was exactly the sort of country where people were paid to … no, hang on. That was No Parking. His eyes. Bloody things. Never been the same since he got back from the atoll all those years ago. They'd become erratic, and he'd learned not to trust them, but he kept forgetting. The morning after the night before too, and some moving parts may have been temporarily shut down, as a precaution, just until the pub. Did rods and cones move though? Rods did, cones didn't. Rods moved up and down. Cones just sat there. Or was that pistons? He studied the cigar between his gloved fingers. His blood had become sluggish, leaving his brain short. Another coughing spasm, barely choked down, but the Barracuda had decided to get on with life and was fulminating about work, the various oppressions, scandals and power-struggles at Hardwicke's Sixth Form College, which he found irritating. All right, she'd had enough, like all teachers, but was she saying she wanted to pack it in, leave altogether, or what? He must gather his resources and focus, concentrate on her words, and above all he must not snap at her. Because then she would snap back, and she could be savage. Grinding his teeth seemed to help, so he ground his teeth.

She loved teaching art to kids. Loved the art, loved the teaching, even loved some of the kids. In her she-wolf way. No, she'd never pack it in, surely. But try as he might, the gist of what she'd been saying, the meaning of it all, floated away with the cigar smoke. His mind was a throbbing wasteland.

He'd had one of those turbulent nights, sweating and hectic. Bad dreams. He wasn't sure any more whether the drink helped or made it worse. This time the gist of it had stayed with him. He'd been trapped in choking blackness, trapped inside something with hard, slippery sides, sliding around in there in the dark, no air, slipping and sliding in a slimy, reeking fluid, breathing the bloody stuff. Then the darkness was sucked away, and he was blinded by the sun. Heat had pounded, crashing like colossal cymbals. He could feel it now, a pulse of heat somewhere inside, a faint gnawing sensation in his guts, a tiny wriggling. It all revolved around that damned place, which never left his mind for long. Of course drink helped. Absurd to think otherwise. Drink. Soon. The thought cheered him: he caught glimpses of a serene life adrift, out of sight of land and scrutiny, rolling on gentle waves, on an endless journey, his simple needs attended to …

A gloved hand came into focus, holding a smouldering cigar, and beyond it a big, blond beast grinning around a long, pink tongue. The noblest of hounds. At the edge of his vision a bulky figure in an outlandish cap, red tassel dangling on a red cord, retying a scarf.

'Well Stanley, if you've quite run out of things to say, I want a bit of a walk. We need to keep fit. I'm putting on weight, and so are you. Then I'll be ready for a drink and a sit in the warm. The Bloody Pub. All in favour? Kato's a yes.'

Good for the Barracuda. His brain had been allowed sufficient time to catch up with its unspooling, an essential task left incomplete the night before. It had been a bad night for unspooling. The Barracuda's eyes were on him, and he must rally himself. A deep breath brought a hitch on the intake where all the tar and other crap collected, interfering with vital oxygen exchange mechanisms. He dropped the cigar and ground it out. The Bloody Pub!

'The Bloody Pub! An admirable proposal, unanimously approved!' He sprang carefully to his feet.

The blackbird flopped down out of the way into a tangle of brambles. Kato, who took no notice, was on his feet smiling, tail flailing away, ready for anything.

Stan was hardly in the mood for a walk, but he would cope. After all, in another life he used to walk for miles, out in the blazing heat all day … another life, another Stanley Blackster. Right, he would put his back into this walk, pull out all the stops, make it a walk to remember. In the distance a full pint glass shone like the Promised Land.

The woods were silent, the trees leafless. The noble hound went on ahead, pathfinder general, panting, tongue lolling, looking back anxiously every so often to make sure they were keeping up. His old hind legs were beginning to lurch a bit these days, a characteristic of the breed according to a colleague of the Barracuda's.

Roll on springtime. Already he was finding it hard to stay cheerful. The silence irritated him. So did his breathing, whistling away in his nose like a football match. He'd try breathing through his mouth. Winter in Britain, sniffles all round. Grey clouds hurried across a grimy grey sky. Underfoot, half-frozen mud crunched and squelched. Liza was humming to herself, arm hooked through his. Everything irritated him, all of it, but he wouldn't let it show. He was quite determined on this, and would regard it as a minor challenge. He could hang on until the pub, easily. The only good thing about the British winter was getting in out of it.

'Warming up now then, Barra?' This was his name for her, after the muscular, gleaming fish with all the teeth. She'd never objected.

'God, look Kato. The Bloody Pub's livened him up, and he's not even in it yet. Never fails. Don't you ever get bored with it?' Her grip tightened. She was smiling her voracious smile. 'I seem to remember a fit outdoor type, dashing footballer and field biologist. Where did he get to? Even the football fan, he had a bit of go. Now look at you. I don't know Stan, you seem to have lost a dimension somehow. If it wasn't for the hound dragging you out you'd be stuck inside all the time, in the pub, in the workroom – we'll have to think of a new name for that - or in the bloody bathroom. And what happened to all those cutting-edge conferences and things you used to go to?'

Dimensions? He could write a book. Page One opened in his head – *The Lost Dimension*. Nonsense. He hadn't lost a dimension, how could she say that? A response was called for, but he was feeling far too demersal just now. He squeezed her arm. It was theoretically possible one dimension may have started to fold over. A small one. As it matured.

They came to a short cut which took them off the track. This had been the way in to one of their hidden places, but Liza gave no sign of recognition, and he didn't point it out. Besides, at this time of year, without the greenery, it looked quite different. The noble hound was momentarily flummoxed, then bounded past them to regain the lead and keep a lookout for squirrels, which made him nervous. The trees grew denser here, towering above stiff, dead spikes of bracken and barbed-wire tangles of bramble. They picked their way through. Not exactly easy going, but it wasn't far back to the car park, and even Kato should be able to find that. The air among the black trees was lifeless and gloomy.

'Birchwood by Klimt,' pronounced the art teacher. 'Minus the colour.'

'Took the words out of my mouth.' Mud and bloody thorns, more like, with the occasional log to trip over. Memories of hours spent wading through knee-deep mud crept towards Stan's mind, and he pushed them away. That mud had been warm, and for a giddy instant he felt it squeezing up between his toes, and shuddered. Two or three birds at last began calling somewhere off among the trees, small echoing sounds in the stillness. Even so, his whistling nose was louder.

The noble hound had come to a halt, waiting for them. He had on his perplexed frown.

'What's up then, Flash?' Stan leaned down in stages to give the broad back a gentle slap. 'Lost the way? Come on, we depend on you dogs for this sort of thing, you're supposed to be good at it.' Kato didn't respond, which was unusual.

The bird sounds were nearer, louder, and there were more of them.

'What is it Stan?'

Chek-chek-chek-chek. Lots of other little scolding sounds. Moving slowly through the trees.

'Birds. I don't know. Just … birds.'

She stood beside him, squinting into the gloom. 'What's the matter with them? They sound really pissed off.'

They did. 'Found something they don't like. An owl, maybe, or a fox.' They'd seen foxes here before. He wanted to get on, but Kato didn't budge.

The noise was very loud now, and seemed to have come to a halt fifty yards away. Shadowy little bird-shapes could be seen buzzing about in some kind of evergreen thicket.

'Stan, look at Kato!'

15

The poor dog was trembling, eyes rolling around showing lots of white. He turned to Stan, staring up at him, and began to whimper.

It was eerie. *Chek-chek-chek-chek. Tak-tak-tak-tak.* The din went on and on. A pair of crows were there now, perched on low branches, black bodies pumping up and down as they shouted the odds at whatever it was. Must be a whole gang of foxes. A pride? No, that was lions. With foxes it was a gang.

Should he go over there, flush out whatever it was? But the birds were on the move again, flitting from branch to branch, the gloomy woodland ringing with their furious calls. There must be fifty of them now. No, more. Lots more.

'Stan ... '

Kato leaped up to plant his feet on Stan's chest, almost knocking him over, his whimpering now a frantic yelping, terrified bulging eyes locked on Stan's, desperate to find escape. The birds were yards away now, Liza was crushing his arm, and the dog, the noise - it was overwhelming, unbearable, and the birds were all around them, fluttering and shrieking, oblivious, not like birds at all, screaming at something, screaming at what? There was nothing to see. Then came a sudden heady waft of organic decay, of sulphurous mud, of corrupted fish and rotting vegetation. Stan's mind recognised it and mumbled no, this is an English wood, an English winter, before the thought was gone.

Then the birds were past, moving away into the Forest, their sounds slowly fading into the shadows.

With a heave at Stan's chest, Kato climbed down. Liza bent over to reassure the shivering retriever. 'It's OK boy, it's OK. The nasty birds have gone, there there.' She stroked him soothingly, holding him gently under the chin with one hand, running the other slowly down the length of his broad, trembling back. 'Yes. They're bullies. Nasty birds. They come from dinosaurs. Ask your uncle Gram. That's all they are Kato, nasty little dinosaurs, nasty, nasty. There there, good boy. You can have chicken tonight, how's that? Get your own back, yes.' She looked up. 'What did you make of that, for God's sake? That's the way he gets with the fireworks on bonfire night. All those birds. And that smell, did you get that? It was a bit weird there for a minute, wasn't it?'

Stan was already shrugging, but he was very confused. Air wheezed in his chest, he coughed and his nose whistled. 'Beats me, Barra. There must have been something. Everyone could see it except you and me. Some restless New Forest spirit maybe, doing the rounds.'

She was right. It had been weird there for a minute. She'd smelt it too. Hadn't he woken with it in his mouth this morning? Could he still taste it? An atoll moment. In the New Forest. Best to be decisive. 'Forward now! To the Bloody Pub.'

The noble hound, fully restored, resumed his trailblazing role, blond tail waving like a flag, looking back now and then to make sure they were safe.

The urge to get out of the Forest and make for the sea was irresistible. Liza did the driving, radio tuned to 5 Live and the football, neither saying much, until they hit the coast near Lymington and turned west. There was the sea, grey and choppy, deserted but for a couple of yachts and the odd gull. In the circumstances Stan was prepared to accept an untried pub and soon spotted the *Dolphin*. He'd passed it a few times and wondered.

Liza settled the noble hound then caught up with him at the doorway, where he stood, despite the inner urge, filling his lungs with this particular version of that smothering airborne brew which lived in and owned places like this. No two were the same. Sometimes you could even see it, moving about. He pulled it in deep and held it there, letting the thick mix do its work: beer and ashtrays, late nights and early starts, humanity and hair of the dog, bawling noise and silence. Stray beams of daylight, heavily filtered by immovable curtains, wandered through the teeming dust. All told, first impressions were favourable, an agreeably shabby vision, rounded out by the poised barman and two proper handpumps. He stepped over the threshold.

Ringwood Best was a local favourite, if falling perhaps just short of the pantheon, and he paid full attention to the slow, assured pouring, the whirl of bubbles in rich, dark beer, the negligible overflow into the sink below the pump, the careful setting of the glass on the bar towel. He was salivating. The Barracuda's tonic water, fizzing with ice and lemon beside it, came from the land of glowing potatoes. He lifted, relishing the impending religious experience, and swallowed.

An everyday marvel, available to all. Another slow swallow, and the dust began to settle. Forget the birds, and especially forget the smell. He'd been hungover, perceptions were inclined to get scrambled. There was a condition, wasn't there, where you smelled sounds, heard colours and so on. Saw tastes, probably. Synasthaesia. He had a mild and intermittent case of synasthaesia, which was nothing to worry about. To be reviewed when necessary.

At their table Liza wrestled clear of her outdoor clothes, shook free that gorgeous sheet of glossy black hair, and filled the room: dazzling smile, gulp of tonic water, jostling about on her seat in the customary unrestrained manner until she'd made it comfortable. Quite marvellous, now that he was ready and able to admire such things.

'Come on then Stanley. Seriously, I don't want Gore Vidal, for Christ's sake. Just give me some distraction. Speak. You can manage that.'

Indeed he could. The Ringwood Best, was in fact somewhat on the chilly side, and not outstandingly clear, but he'd overlook it. His indulgent smile, first of the day.

'The convention then. Nothing out of the ordinary, no breakdowns, suicides or death threats. Raymond assures us he's at last persuaded the powers to show the thing again, he'll give me a call, etcetera. And he says he's been polishing up his contacts in independent film production. Again. Yes, I know.' Ray always said this. It was part of the routine. Even the Barracuda, reliably galvanised by the smell of money, didn't react. She'd heard it all before. Also, her main objective was to make sure Kim hadn't accomplished an unlikely re-surfacing, but this was something she'd have to work up to. There'd be some circling first. Half his pint was gone already and he was thinking about the next. Should he stick with the Ringwood?

She set down her glass with a look of distaste, but she was the driver in the family. 'So, nothing dramatic then. And you and Ray went on to continue your discussions in the pub.'

'One or two things to iron out.'

'I hope you mean money.'

'That's the plan. He's pretty definite this time – ' he ignored the snort ' - and Ray has a new project, there could be an opening ...' Let it hang in the air.

'As a writer.'

'Yep.'

'A series? Steady work?'

'That's the idea.'

'What about Delyth?'

Delyth was Ray's second in command, who was trying to depose him. Quite enchanting, was Delyth, but she had no time for Stanley Blackster. Not these days anyway.

'Ray's in charge.'

Another snort. She was studying her glass, long brown fingers on its base, working it slowly round and round. Eyes down, long black lashes, smooth brown face easier to look at from the side, bursting pink lips.

'Same again then, eh Barra?'

The barman broke off his conversation with the bar-proppers and took Stan's glass without a word. At a nearby table locals were chuntering loudly about the fuel protests, all strongly in favour. The protests seemed to have caught the government off guard, and Tony Blair and co. were looking shaky. The barman grinned at Stan and raised his eyebrows, encouraging comment. Stan though had become conscious of the Barracuda's eyes powering up, piercing the silty air, tracking him, following him back.

'No news of you-know-who then, your little friend with the teeth? You'd have said though, wouldn't you?'

Her eyes were full on now, high-beam. Stan looked off across the bar, drew out the process of swallowing beer and arranging his breathing. It was murky out there, in the bar, with fishing knicknacks dangling from the ceiling, beermats pinned alongside a few muddy naval paintings and framed brown and white photos of the old ocean liners and massed crowds in Southampton harbour. Troops embarking for D-Day. The handful of locals were still chuntering, exactly as locals should, the barman was leaning on the bar analysing the weather with a couple of pipe-smoking old boys - a proper pub, being itself. What more could you ask? But he had to concentrate. Kim.

'Nope, nothing. And yes, I would have said.' A straightforward lie, as she well understood. 'No one's heard anything since she left, and that's - what? - three or four years ago now?' Breezily, a thing of no concern to him. 'Probably happily married with kids somewhere by now.' Hardly likely. Impossible to guess what would become of someone like Kim. Not that anyone was.

Liza's fingers worked at the base of her glass. 'Headlining at some circus or zoo somewhere, more like.' A direct stare, pink lips not quite concealing square white tooth-tips.

Stan said nothing, unhurriedly taking on more fuel, faculties humming confidently now, watching those fingers work at the glass. Eventually he felt her eyes leave him.

'Hmm. Stan, when we were in the Forest, did you find yourself thinking about Easterhouse? Especially with those weird pissed off birds? I bet you did.'

'Not especially, no.'

19

Julius Archibald Francis Easterhouse, frozen-faced research scientist and torturer of small animals, ex-wild man, ex-colleague and ex-friend, sort of, had become a recluse, incarcerating himself in the ancestral pile of Easter House to no-one's obvious regret.

'He used to spy on us, don't forget, in the Forest. I think about it sometimes. He liked to watch. Creep.'

'So you said. Well, he was a scientist. Enquiring mind and all that.' How he despised Easterhouse.

'He did Stanley! You never would believe anything bad about him back then, but Ally told me things ... anyway, I told you all this back then, but you weren't interested. He was a borderline psycho, no really Stan.'

'Still is, I expect. And if he did watch, it doesn't bother you now, does it?'

She frowned, pushing out her lower lip, an expression guaranteed to get the males at Hardwicke's Sixth Form College going.

'It's more the way he was with Ally, you know?'

'Yeah. Strange that, I'd have thought Alice would have kept in touch with you, and vice-versa. Thelma and Louise, all that.' Alice was the customary long-suffering girlfriend.

'Yeah. Thelma and Louise. I really liked Ally.' She frowned again. 'You're right. I've been lazy, got sidetracked. Same for her, maybe. Far as I know she's still in South Africa. I'll find out where she is, drop her a line. Make sure she really did get out before he buried her in that creepy mausoleum alongside him.'

'If you like, I could give the Prof a ring. He'll have kept in touch.' Stan had liked Alice too, but Ray had liked her better. And the Prof did share a university department with Easterhouse.

On his way to the bar Stan thought fondly of Professor Dalyell, a large and imposing character from the atoll days, old now, a solid and eccentric figure in academic circles, who liked a drink. He'd been good to Stan, at a time when he'd needed it.

Exchanging weather-related small talk with the barman, who now called him squire - an unfortunate jarring note - Stan basked in the tranquillity. The pipe-smokers had gone, turned to smoke. He and the barman then gazed together at the Barracuda, who had covered half the room in three strides and was inspecting one of the naval paintings. She'd recently complained of feeling old, and had had her hair cut at the front into a ragged fringe, an expensive machete effect which of course fitted perfectly. There was something essentially savage about the Barracuda. Feeling old? Wrinkles just couldn't get started on that perfect brown skin - it was impervious, too full of health, simply bounced them off. Just standing there in this dingy pub she flickered with vitality, brushing a finger over the paintwork, tapping a foot slowly on the sticky carpet, eyes probing the nicotine veneer. How on earth had he managed to entrap such a creature? How on earth did he manage to hang on to her? Why ever did she let him? Stanley Blackster was a singular character, granted, but even so ... he pushed away the thought that Gram had become vital to them.

At such moments he would think of *Jaws*, of her grabbing him with a small female sound, halfway between a gasp and a shriek, quite un-Barracuda-like, when Ben Gardner's green head popped out of the hole in his shark-wrecked boat. Yes. His mind wandered on ... rushing along the sandy sea-bottom, over beds of waving sea-grass, tasting the water, searching, hunting ... in over the reef, corals and fish shoals ... the light fading ... His thigh ached. There'd been some sort of altercation last night, when he got in late. Had she hit him? He couldn't remember.

'Have you told Gram about the match yet?' She had advanced, and made him jump. He'd glazed over.

Gram. Big Gram, who he liked to think was conceived in the New Forest, maybe in that thicket earlier today. Now he was their glue. A southern son of northern parents, with the voice and accent to go with it. Everyone liked Gram, a strong and gentle Blackster, whose natural expression was a gap-toothed half-smile. An elsewhere sort of smile. He still hadn't given up hope that one day Gram would move on from a very worthy - admirable in fact - intuitive feeling for the natural world around him into something more focused and, well, refined. Revolving around the eternal fascination of fishes. It was never too late, and he was a dutiful father. Gram didn't so much study nature as accept it, identify with it. Feel for it. Certainly he didn't like being called a biologist by his mum. My son the biologist, going off soon to study environmental science, going to make his mark on this planet. But Gram had the messy and muddled passions all teenagers should have. Some of them, anyway. He didn't, for a start, want to go to university, but Liza didn't know that.

Meanwhile the pub locals watched, some more obviously than others, as she strode beside him back to their table. They wouldn't have seen anything like the Barracuda round here before.

Sheffield Wednesday had been drawn to play Southampton at

the Dell in the FA Cup, and something had made him realize he needed to take his son to a football match. How long had it been since they went to watch Wednesday together? Gram would know. How long since he went to watch Gram play? Maybe Liza was right - he'd let things slide.

'Yep, Gram's up for it, as they say. We're meeting up with the Sheffield contingent at the pub.' The Sheffield contingent was Shanny, Stan's oldest pal and Gram's sort-of uncle.

Gram was sixteen now, big and handsome like his mother, with an easy-going, dreamy manner which Stan admired. Sometimes he showed a streak of his mother's stubbornness, but the Barracuda's capacity for instant aggression was entirely absent. A career in football had beckoned at one time, but it wasn't important enough to him, or to his father. Stan had stood next to screaming parents on the touchline and wondered what was wrong with them. How on earth could they get so worked up? One of them was the Barracuda. There'd been some minty exchanges with other parents, which had embarrassed Gram. The lad had the ability, and the physique, but who would employ a smiling centre-back? Not dedicated enough was the general verdict. The Barracuda could have turned out for Leeds United in their shin-kicking heyday. They'd have made her captain.

Stan lit up a cigar, watched the smoke coiling lazily, drifting, dissolving, slowly slowly. This was better. A pint, a cigar, a bit of peace. Why was that so much to ask? Poor Liza, working so hard every day. And not even able to have a good drink on her day out. She must be tired, but you wouldn't know it.

'Never mind Barra. Just think of the hols – boat rides, picnics, painting, pub meals, swimming, sunbathing ...'

The eyes fixed him, glass arrested halfway to her lips. 'We had all this out last night Stan. Don't tell me you can't remember? I am not going to the bloody Scillies again.'

He hadn't been concentrating. He liked the Scillies. No, Scilly. They didn't like you to say Scillies, the folk who lived out there.

'Scilly Barra. They don't like you to say Scillies.'

A snort.

He loved all the salty chugging about in little boats instead of cars. Bracing. Liza liked that too, he knew she did, as long as the trips didn't go on too long and she wasn't sick. Pubs in Hughtown were busy, full of boaty people of all grades, beer not too bad considering, fish names chalked on the board every day: mackerel, bass, gurnard, garfish. Last time a big sunfish, old *Mola mola*, had come alongside the boat while he and Gram had been out on *Sapphire* on a pelagic trip. Six feet across, carried up on the Gulf Stream, along with its jellyfish prey. You wouldn't know you were still in Britain - exotic plants all over, especially on Tresco, white beaches, even the odd palm tree, the early flower season ... but the weather was basically British Atlantic, the wind never gave up, and swimming was a challenge. And it wasn't exactly inexpensive ... but the noble hound was looking forward to it.

'The noble hound – '

She snorted again, like a horse. 'Yeah, I know, I know. The noble hound. Bloody hell Stan, we both know it'll be dismal, lousy weather, stuck in the bloody Mermaid while you do your fishermen's groupie bit. Great for you. All that feudal Duchy of Cornwall stuff, and it's not even as if it's cheap. And ... '

She was about to say, *without Gram* ... A sombre prospect. Gram had always gone away with them before, albeit with a fair amount of cajoling in recent years. Last time he'd said no more - or rather no more thanks, if you don't mind dad, mum ... And Liza had her sights set beyond the lovely Isles of Scilly, even though it meant leaving Kato out of it. It had been building up for a while, and they had apparently discussed it in full last night.

'Anyway, look, Stan. We went through all this – you really can't remember, can you? Christ! - my old bones? Tropical sun on my old bones? Liza's a tropical person?' She sagged theatrically in her chair, then drew herself up. 'Come on Stanley! Time for my Gauguin phase, get myself alive again. I want the sun, see some real colours before I dry up and blow away, not this watery stuff we get round here. I want to feel the heat on me, for chrissake!' Her colleagues were going off all over the place, and she worked harder than any of them. They had managed the Med once, Lesvos, but the noble hound had been stressed in kennels, and she wasn't talking about the Med.

Stan swallowed Ringwood Best. He knew precisely where this was heading.

'Stan. It's now or never, I told you last night.'

She might well have done.

'Gram would go for the Indian Ocean, you know he would! You used to promise him. You need to do it for him, for him and you, not just me, you pillock! Come on Stanley, no more dodging about. Get us booked in for the bloody Papalinas. I can get time off if we need it.'

'Time? Time we gotta.'

'Come on, we can afford it, bloody hell! If we need a bit more, we'll just have to get it. No holiday at all next year. Come on come on come on!'

There was nowhere to hide. He was the last bluefin tuna in a swimming pool, Japs circling.

'We can find someone to look after Kato. He'll not mind, he'll cope. Come on Stan. A baking sun, a real one! And a real suntan, for chrissake! Come on, I feel pallid! Real beaches, a sea you can swim in, not the sort where your heart stops with the cold. I'll never want to come out! You and Gram off diving. Together. Your son, remember him? Fish, Stan! Tropical fish! Barbecues, Stan, more fish! Cold beer on the veranda watching the sun go down. Cocktails. All those normal things. I work hard, now I want to enjoy, like other people! You used to promise me as well, you know, one day, your old stomping ground. It's time to deliver! God, it might even put some fire back in your belly! Stan - think of all those fishes! And you did promise Gram - diving in the Indian Ocean with his dad, on a real coral reef! Not like Lesvos. It's his dream! Or it used to be – he's given up on it. Show him his dad's not a goner ... You can't say no, Stanley!'

The idiot's grin had got onto his face, he could feel it. When she got going she was a force of nature. It was intoxicating just being dragged along, and the biggest part of it was that no-one else ever saw this side of her, this side of such a sleek and powerful animal, which felt the need for him to make the decision. A flaw, almost, a weakness. And decisions were hardly a problem to the hero of the hot and decaying world of *Insidiator*. He felt at ease as the master. Aggro was a million miles away, or at least two drinks. He pulled on his cigar.

In fact finances were constrained, more than Liza realised. Work had dried up lately, and a couple of commissions hadn't paid up – one had been rejected in fact, and the editor seemed to be stalling on the other. He'd allowed her to think he was doing better than he was. His accountant would be calling soon. Liza's income as overworked and under-rewarded art teacher kept the Blacksters going. And the sun-kissed islands of the Papalinas? He smiled. Some bad memories certainly – Easterhouse, all the so-called voodoo stuff - but wouldn't it be a charge to see Old Papa again? To show it off to Liza and Gram?

'Stanley? Come on, make a decision for chrissake! Your mouth's opening and closing, I want to hear words, not bubbles.'

He could feel something barrelling up on a tide of Ringwood Best: The Decision.

'The final foray of the Blacksters *en famille*, before the young gallant forsakes us? Leave it to me.'

Classic Boscanion. Act now, think later.

The Barracuda was nodding vehemently, cheeks bulging with tonic, those great brown eyes wide and shining. She swallowed too fast, coughed and laughed, wiped her mouth, crushed him with a hug. Her hero.

'Brilliant! Bloody brilliant! I'll hold you to it now Stan, no matter what. Why could you not say that last night, and save all the aggro? Well, I suppose the Bloody Pub's got some uses. I can just about face Monday now.' She banged down her glass. 'I've had enough of this bloody fizzy sugar water. Stanley - further intoxicant?' A playful thump. Only euphoria could have prompted this allusion to *Insidiator*. 'Hey, those weird birds? What are those tormenting things?'

Nothing sprang to mind.

'Harpies? They were harpies, tormenting Easterhouse, nature getting its own back. He's dead, must be, sentenced to roam the New Forest for all eternity as a bad smell.'

He certainly kept cropping up like one. That was enough Easterhouse for one day.

Off she marched, freeing Stan to bask. Who said all of life was grief and woe? He breathed a long sigh, gnawing at a finger. Way off on the distant shore and growing gradually smaller, the noble hound, clearly perplexed even at this great range, smile faltering, tail drooping … where are you going? ... take me with you ...

Liza was getting involved with the locals over at their table, the kind of thing she did. He had to keep an eye on her - sometimes it led to difficulties. She generally meant well, more or less, until she happened to spot someone she decided she didn't like the look of, usually based on facial expressions. But she'd been on tonic water, so he relaxed. For a time he tuned in to his blood, humming around the intricacies of his internals now, performing at a peak of excellence. Absently reaching for his pint, he drained it and stared, the world blurring once more into a swimming blue-green. Were the harpies still chasing a bad smell through the New Forest? He shivered. A strange episode, certainly, but not particularly disturbing. Why should people expect to understand everything they saw? Or smelled. Especially with synasthaesia rife in the land. But the Barracuda had smelled it. And Kato? Whatever it was that damp and noble nose had detected, he hadn't liked it. The face of Easterhouse began to form, white and

typically devoid of expression. Bugger. But he could blot these things
out straight away now, as a result of long practice. He'd think about it
all later, when he wasn't enjoying himself. For now, better to resume
this pleasing drift, not -

'Hey, Professor! You're needed over here.'

A large gin and tonic was almost gone, just a couple of gulps
for her, while his pint stood on the bar, settled and clear in the dusty
light. Liza sat at a table, hunkering forward, dominant, opposite three
men with the usual easy air of locals. Stan picked up his glass, braced
himself and went over. Two locals nodded a guarded welcome.

'Stanley, these guys are fishermen, right? They're winding me
up, trying to tell me, right, they get sharks as big as Jaws round here.'
She was in familiar, first-drink-combative mode. 'Stan here's an expert,
specially sharks, right?'

Thanks for that. His feelings towards sharks were complex, but
he didn't like the word expert, as she well knew. Without actually
staring he looked the threesome over. Two were reasonably Saturday-
afternoon drunk, one a few pints beyond. Shouldn't be any problem,
but he knew from long experience that the Barracuda sometimes took
entirely the wrong track, and just kept on going. She missed the signs
or, more often, ignored or wilfully misinterpreted them. The three were
smiling too much, not knowing quite what to make of this big, black,
forthright woman with the loud northern voice. You could only
sympathise.

'Bigger,' managed one of them, in a voice thick with drink and
Hampshire. 'Bigger than Jaws.'

Basking Sharks, obviously. He'd seen them on the crossing to
Scilly, on the *Scillonian*. So had Liza. She must have forgotten, or she
was just playing along. Stan took his new pint from the barman, who
called him squire again, and was more likely the landlord. He raised it
before swallowing. 'Baskers eh? Cheers.'

'Aye. Makos too, mind, out in the deep. Near enough great
whites, they are. And porgies. And blues. But the basking sharks, aye.
Big, mind. Bigger than Jaws.'

'How big?' demanded Liza. 'Twenty feet, twenty five? That was
Hooper and whatsisname in *Jaws*, remember? You're gonna need a
bigger boat?' A loud, gurgling laugh. The locals continued grinning.

'Bigger, lady. Thirty feet, easy.' The others nodded.

'But you'd be safe lady, they only eat tiny little shrimpy things.
They'd swim right past, probably wouldn't even see you like.' This one

was called Greg. He winked at Stan as he spoke.

Stan sighed to himself and swallowed beer. The laughter was over-loud in the peaceful, dingy bar.

'It's Liza, not lady. And listen guys.' She was waving a long black finger, flashing those strong white teeth. She was up for it, as they said nowadays. 'These British sharks, they don't eat dark people. Too rich, you know? They might come over for a sniff, but they don't hang around. It's white people they want. Fact. Don't ask me why. Right Stanley?'

Off she went.

They were grinning again, or still. 'Didn't know that, did we lads?' mused the father-figure of the three, the one in the little faded denim boating cap. 'Round here they just stick to plankton, the baskers anyway.' He grinned pleasantly at Liza, looking at the same time just a little crazy, like Quint in the film.

The drunkest of them, so far silent but blearily watchful, pulled himself straight. 'There's real great whites out there.' The others pulled at their drinks. 'Everyone round here knows.' In contrast to his colleagues, his face was nearly white, presumably the drink, and his eyes were green. 'Tourists though. Don't want to frighten 'em off, do we?'

'Frighten 'em off?' declared Liza. 'Your very own Jaws? It would bring them running, wouldn't it Stan? Jaws cruises? They'd be queuing up to go down in those cages. Give 'em a mackerel each to wave about, you'd make a fortune!'

The green-eyed man made a throaty sound, beer on its way back up, and a thin line of foam appeared at his lips. He swallowed it down. 'They live out there. Breed out there. Found little 'uns, they have. Everyone round here knows. Down Cornwall way. They keep it quiet.' He licked his lips. 'Other things too, out there, in the sea ... not in any book ...'

'Not in your blessed book anyway.' The elder, Quint. 'Miller's got the I-Spy book of fishes on his boat, that right Miller?'

It was a start, but Miller could do better. He'd await a quiet moment and recommend the marvellous *Fishes of the British Isles, both freshwater and salt,* by J. Travis Jenkins. Over fifty years old now but still ... he'd missed the Barracuda ordering another round of drinks. This was how it went.

'I could take you now,' Miller was insisting, 'right now. You'd see for yourselves. Every year there's more. Where do they come from?

Nobody knows ... no blessed experts know ... Experts ... ' He attempted a Barracuda-style snort which got stuck.

'Global warming,' put in the landlord with proprietorial confidence. 'Sea levels going up, everything swirling around out there, nothing has its rightful place any more. Blessed weather's changing everywhere too, not just Hampshire. They say all manner of strange things are coming up from the south, right lads?'

Miller was trundling on. 'Sometimes, you wouldn't even think they were fish, some of 'em.' His brow furrowed. 'Well, they're not fish, not in this world.'

'Go on then,' urged Quint, with mock weariness, 'take the lady – sorry, Liza - and the gentleman out to have a look. Would you two like to go out on the water with Miller?'

Miller assumed a look of bleary despair. 'Can't. You know that. Blessed boat's out of the water, isn't it? Blessed boatyard.'

Stan shook himself. Great whites, breeding off Cornwall. He'd read about one 29 inches long being taken down there, but had been unable to find official confirmation. And he'd been about to say yes, let's go, we'll take a crate of beer, eh Miller? And go out on the water. Not at all sensible, but the pull was strong. Good job Miller didn't have a boat then.

'Listen, thanks Miller. We'll be back down in a couple of weeks, maybe you'll have your boat back in the water. We can call in again. I'd be up for a spot of fishing anytime.' Even he was up for things now. Time they were off. The noble hound would be fretting.

'The noble hound will be fretting Barra, time for the off.' He needed to expel some Ringwood first though. In the hallway-type pub entrance the wooden door to the Gents had a fist-sized hole in it at face height, stuffed with toilet paper. Inside the graffiti was unexceptional, the usual appalling Saints v Pompey exchanges, one LEEDS FC RULE which triggered an image of the Barracuda, all in white, surrounded by fallen opponents, screaming at the ref while Norman Hunter and Billy Bremner attempted restraint.

When he got back she'd moved on to a discussion of modern art. He lingered in the doorway. Quint wore his polite, mildly lunatic grin, Miller's green eyes had glazed over, Greg seemed to be paying attention, and events took a fairly predictable course.

'These days they don't use paint no more. They use crap.' Greg.

Liza was nodding, smiling like a predator. 'That's a guy called Chris Ofili. I know him. He uses different materials to make his paintings, it's still paint, but elephant dung too, sometimes.'

'Elephant dung. Oh, right, that's OK then,' Greg grinned back.

In fact Liza did know this chap Ofili, rather than just his work. Stan and Gram had been dragged along to the City art gallery in Southampton to be shown his first show. Gram had liked the smell.

'What sort of paintings do you like then Greg? These naval paintings?' She waved at the pub walls.

'They're all right. Better than bricks and crap, anyhow.'

Quint stepped in. 'Who was that picture by we were looking at just the other night … ? On the cover of that book of yours, Miller. Ghost stories. Midnight Stroll. Funny name, Grim something. We all liked that.'

'Oh, right. Grimshaw. Atkinson Grimshaw. I know Grimshaw.'

'Course she does,' muttered someone, but she was talking and didn't hear.

'Walk it is, not stroll . So. You go for the moody stuff.'

Quint nodded affably. 'We liked it. There's the man, at midnight, strolling. Clear. The moonlight, trees. It felt cold, didn't it lads? A good painting can do that. You're looking, but you can feel.'

Miller nodded solemnly, cheeks bulging with beer.

'If it is a man, mind.' This was the barman stroke landlord. 'We couldn't decide. And is he coming or is he going?'

'Liza will tell us.' Greg again. It was hard to tell how far gone Greg really was.

The Barracuda was amused. 'I think it's for you decide.'

'We have. And we prefer it to elephant crap. That's all we're saying.'

The Barracuda was nodding, slowly and deliberately, and she had Greg fixed with the look.

'We all like different things, don't we?'

Greg held her stare for ten seconds - not bad - then looked away and muttered something to Quint, who frowned and shook his head.

'What was that Greg?' Liza leaned forward, gathering herself. 'I didn't catch it.'

Stan took a step forward from the doorway, but the three fishermen had fallen into a conversation of their own and, but for a meaningful glance from beneath the denim cap, Liza was left out. She wouldn't like that.

Stan went over and applied gentle pressure to her rigid

shoulders.

'Be there in a minute, Stanley. Just finishing my drink.' Still she hadn't released Greg from her stare, which tracked him as he got up and made for the Gents. Stan brought across an armful of coats while the watchful landlord came over to hold open the door and wish them a safe journey. He heard a loudly whispered *Bye Liza*.

Outside it was still cold, the air still murky and lifeless. She handed her coat and hat back to him. 'Just better nip to the loo, get rid of some G & T. It's a long drive. Won't be a tick.'

'Barra – '

After a minute or two he was not surprised to hear a muffled exchange followed by a moan. The door flew open and out she marched.

'Barra. There was no call for that.' She reached for her coat.

'For what?' Eyes front. Light, panting breaths.

'You know what.' He had to march too to keep up with her. 'Weedy little bloke like that, not even in your division. And he was leathered.'

She was pulling on her gloves. 'I was just finishing a conversation.' Her right hand flexed, once, twice.

'And?'

'No-one speaks to me like that Stanley, you know that.'

'Like what? Poor little twerp never said anything.'

'Not out loud.'

That's right. But those eyes had looked into Greg and seen something they didn't like, whether it was really there or not. How he got tired of this. Now, or as soon as his thoughts settled, Greg would be wondering what on earth had just happened to him. There he'd been, minding his own business, getting pleasantly bladdered in his own pub with his mates, just the way he did every Saturday lunchtime after a hard week pulling up crab pots, when the door bangs open and in marches -

He caught her arm, feeling furious muscle beneath the fabric. 'OK, maybe he did get a bit snotty, but it was hardly - ' He was being towed along. 'Hey! I'm not one of the bloody Grimshaw strollers, dammit!'

One of her snorts, eyes still front, muscles powering down, forward momentum slowing.

'Look, we've had a good day, haven't we?' The Drummer in the Deep was starting up again, somewhere around where the spine joined the skull. Not enough beer. Press on. 'I don't know how we've crammed it all in. Nice stroll – sorry, ramble – down memory lane, bracing hound walk.' Speak in bursts, around the thumps. 'Hitchcock moment with the birds. The Bloody Pub ... ' What else? 'Expedition planning, stimulating local research. Final workout.' More needed. 'Winding drive home for tea, nice bottle of wine.' Press on. 'You're all recharged for the week. And you say we never do anything. Christ, we're living the lives of five people each here!'

She had stopped. 'Yeah. How do we cope?' A small smile. 'Sometimes though, I don't know, I just want to scream and smash things, break out of this fog ...' Her fists were raised and clenched. 'What's happened to this bloody country? It's so frantic, no time. And the bloody weather! It didn't used to be like this. Is it just us? It's as if we're only half alive these days Stanley, muddling along in grime and half-light, no-one can see straight, the light bloody strangled to death! Half the time we can't even see each other properly, it's like a dream. Stan, I want to wake up! Now! Before it's too late!'

For a moment she looked desperate, and his heart went out to her. He held her, feeling the tension, waiting in vain for her muscles to relax. Weariness washed over him, and the backs of his eyeballs throbbed to the beat. He ground his teeth. A quiet evening in the bathroom suddenly had irresistible appeal. Flickering between the thumps, the image of a powder-blue surgeonfish projected soothing waves.

'Barra, you're exhausted, overworked ... look, before you know it you'll be on that beach with your pina colada working on your perspective. Who knows, maybe this country will sink while we're out there.' The rolling grey Atlantic, swallowing the North Sea. Jetsam tossing on the waves. Or was it flotsam? 'Then you'll miss it.'

'Not pina colada.'

'No. White port and lemon juice then?' An old joke, but she didn't respond.

Looking into his face, her eyes were slowly losing that ferocious intensity. 'Promise Stan? You have to promise. This can't be one of your leave it to me and nothing happens things, you know that? I've got this feeling ... that we need it, the three of us, you know? The sun. We need the sun. If we don't do it now, with Gram, I'm frightened about what might happen to us.' She glared back at the *Dolphin*, and he held her close, brought her face down to his shoulder, thinking he could feel her sag, just a little.

31

'We'll get the sun Barra. We'll colonise the bloody thing, take it over. Plant the Blackster banner.' The Blackster banner, flapping imperiously amidst the boiling gases – the Blackster crest, twin circling torpedo shapes, white on a red ground. Stylish, but she wouldn't approve. 'We will. Just leave it to me.'

She pulled away. 'Yeah, right.'

Not an expression of limitless confidence perhaps, but she was smiling again. Low wattage, but it would do.

There was a muffled yelping as the noble hound spotted them at last through a steamed-up window.

That night Stan lay slippery with sweat, mouth open, eyelids flickering. He was looking down from the simmering white equatorial glare at the centre of a bleached blue sky. Low over the sea, tracing the rim of an atoll, stood an ellipse of soft white clouds, bellies flushed with the greenish light of a lagoon. He moved closer. A rippling line of white birds crossed the vast, milky turquoise lens of water, lifting in a curve to clear the margin of dark mangrove, flying on over grey miles of scrub, riding the endless wind-stream to the sea. A distant thunder, surf on rock. He moved closer. A hunted flurry of silver fishes scrambled the glassy surface. He entered a winding tidal creek. Cloudy shallows flickered with turtles and cruising shark-shapes. Mangrove forest crowded in. A dark face peered from the edge of the glinting green forest, pale eyes fixed on the shallows, fixed on a thickset shadow moving shark-like through a silty haze. Wet inches on clustering, curving brown prop-roots marked the slow ebb of the tide. A naked, wood-brown man slipped from the forest, gliding over interwoven mangrove roots, gripping with large-toed brown feet. Brown crabs sidled away through stripes of sunlight and shade. Round eyes the colour of the lagoon bed's near-white sucking mud gazed into the thick, milk-brown water. Sea-sounds were very faint here, hardly more than a murmur. The undulating shadow in the water approached, angling upwards towards the reflected brown face. A forest bird called harshly as a snout broke the oily surface.

2. Blacksterdom

The Blacksters managed, but it was getting harder. For a time Stan's pseudo-science journalism had been the main earner, but these days it was Mrs Blackster's tireless efforts at her sixth-form college, Hardwicke's, over on the far side of Southampton Common, which really kept them afloat. The occasional large sums reeled in by Stan's more creative writings, which he perpetrated under the name of AB Defduf, had dried up. AB had hit his peak without realising it five years before when *Insidiator* was made into a four-part TV series by old chum Ray. *Insidiator* followed the meandering adventures of Boscanion, a would-be quixotic, self-dramatising character in the established tradition. It hadn't quite managed to set the world on fire, but for a while there had been the heady sensation of being at the centre of something, of riding the wave. Even the Barracuda had been pleased with that part. *Insidiator* had drawn a reasonable viewing share for the first episode, lost the fickle element - more than half - by week two, then hung on grimly to the rest until the end.

This had been a time of long and convivial lunches, parties at the smart houses of strangers, of travel and hotels, media chattering and fans. 'AB - where did you get the idea for the Aspidont?' One he never answered. Not directly anyway. 'AB – where will they resurface in series two?' Stan, as AB Defduf, had coped manfully with the demands. In fact, as someone who on the whole preferred fishes to people, Stan really had to be AB to do it. AB seemed to enjoy it. Follow-ups were discussed, *Further Adventures of*, other projects - a time of confidence and quiet determination. And then ... nothing. Confidence had ebbed, slowly slowly, determination with it, the two turning imperceptibly into something else. Ray steered odd bits of work his way when he could, but They didn't want to know about Boscanion any more. They wanted teen stuff, or that's what Ray told him and anyone else who cared to listen. And Ray should know. It was maddening, as well as bewildering. He had left Boscanion dangling in the required intriguing predicament. What happened next, for chrissake? He wanted to know himself.

As AB he'd tried other angles, different approaches, but even he could see this stuff lacked something – sureness, conviction – as if he was making it up. Which, curiously, he'd never felt with *Insidiator*. AB had settled into a gentle, planing descent, disappearing from view for long periods. The Barracuda had stopped asking about AB, not that she'd ever been happy with this business of a working alias, finding it shifty. She agreed with his mother, old Vera: what was wrong with the good, honest family name of Blackster?

Before all this Stan had managed his zoology degree, if not his doctorate, basically because he did have a genuine if lop-sided interest in the natural world. His interest wasn't precisely scientific, but it was consistent. As Professor Dalyell had put it, the interest was there, undoubtedly, but wasn't applied at quite the right angle. The Prof been proved right during the ill-advised shark study on Tsaramaso Atoll, and he had gladly departed the academic life for fame as a fantasist. From there he had drifted into writing about science for the uninformed masses. As The Media expanded relentlessly, so did the hunger, the craving, for matter to fill all those screens, all those pages, and as long as folk out there were willing to suck it all in - well, going with the flow was something Stan could do.

Meanwhile, after an up-and-down period of trying to make money from her artwork, the Barracuda had found, to the surprise of them both, an aptitude for teaching older kids, ones with an interest. For a while things were OK – no, better than OK, when he thought back: life with Mrs B. and a growing son, not to mention the noble hound, had been mostly agreeable. Even the nights hadn't been too bad.

Then he found himself becoming more easily irritated by editorial restrictions on what he wrote, and, especially recently, had allowed himself to stray from the rigid route march of straightforward science reporting. It was more interesting. More stimulating. Yes, he could provide the necessary pre-mastication and re-moulding of dry science, within the guidelines, readying it for consumption at a gulp. But how much more rewarding to take the worthy but inert base metal of this revelation or that - possibly the product of several lifetimes' fanatical dedication and sacrifice - and transform it into a glittering confection of challenging thought and speculation. It wasn't always easy, even for him. Especially given the need to retain something of the notional purpose of the piece, as defined by some remote editorial figure.

During the days of plenty he'd tried a quiet sideline in gambling, under the tutelage of an expert: Harak the headman from *Episode One – The Aspidont*. This had been a mistake, a near-disaster in fact, successfully concealed from the Barracuda, but only just, and he was still paying off the debt. And he'd felt so sure. In the pub Harak had seemed such good value, and so convincing.

There were occasions, more and more, when it was difficult to fight off a sense of dissatisfaction, of having been cheated somehow. Why couldn't he just be outstandingly, unequivocally good at one universally-admired thing? If only he'd tried harder at an academic career, shown some guts, he'd be cloistered now within a great library among books and like minds. The pleasing weight of knowledge, undisturbed contemplation … all a romantic daydream of course, since he knew perfectly well he found rigour and application tiresome. No, the pragmatic, essential daydream, the Getout Stakes, remained *Boscanion – The Movie*: a full-throttle, Hollywood SFX extravaganza stuffed with big names. As with all the best daydreams, he kept this to himself. Easy to imagine the snorting response of the Barracuda, and as for Ray … Ray despised Hollywood and all its works.

Stan yawned. He didn't really like to go out much any more - she was right again. Working at home was fine, as long as she was far away and Gram out or upstairs in his room. The noble hound was permitted. At one time he used to show Gram the results, his plausible pseudo-science along with some of AB's less earthbound efforts. Gram used to have some good ideas, good suggestions, but he didn't talk much these days. He'd always rated Boscanion though, no doubt about that. Gram wanted to know what happened next too. It had been so good, looking back on it now, making *Insidiator*. Gram had loved it. And then there was Kim.

He stared at the computer screen, hands flat on the desk either side of the keyboard. The dozing machine displayed *Acanthurus leucosternon*, the powder-blue surgeonfish, the old favourite, with its most restful disposition of colours. Could he justify calling a fish smug? Admirably smug? He had expended hours over this, gazing at the screen, well knowing the temptation of likening fishes to people was unworthy. The reverse was unavoidable. Ichthyomorphism. Mrs B, gleaming, hovering, bulging with power, ever poised for the lunge. Ray's truculent bullhead. Silvery Delyth. Certainly the powder-blue gave every impression of being inordinately pleased with itself, and with life generally, and its image was conducive to restful staring and lateral thought.

Basically work had become tedious, unless something caught his fancy. Increasingly he found himself taking shortcuts, no longer troubling to track down primary sources for his articles, settling for re-mastication of the already masticated, aware there would be occasional comeback. As there had been, just the once so far, which only served to vindicate a healthy contempt for the providers of his income. A good part of each working day he now spent practising his staring, either at the soothing powder-blue or, less often, at the world as it struggled and clawed its way past the window. The conferences, seminars, lectures and meetings, not to mention straightforward reading, which used to be the bedrock of his work, had largely fallen away, and he didn't miss it. He was finding it harder to reassure the toiling Barracuda that he now had all the contacts, that thanks to the electronic revolution there was no need to go tearing about the place, and so on and so forth, and fortunately she was generally too tired to pursue it with her old tenacity.

The noble hound ambled in, thumped to the floor and looked up, tongue lolling, forepaws neatly crossed.

'You great softie Kato.' How could you not pat that soft, noble head? How could you not give him some encouragement? Here was the benign element in the Blacksters' domestic situation. The essential buffer. He played with the large, soft ears, muttering gibberish. Kato panted with anticipation and lowered a large drool onto the carpet. 'It's age Kato. It's having a go at all of us.' The noble hound whined. 'Later, hound.' With a sigh Stan spun back to his screen.

Through the normal process of first noticing it in a distant corner of his mind, then spiralling slowly downwards while holding it in blurry peripheral vision, not looking directly at it until it could no longer be avoided, he was able to return to the work in hand. Here it was: he had to put something together on dire scientific warnings of a developing global 'pest and weed' environment. Researchers from America, Britain and Africa were suggesting in the Proceedings of the National Academy of Sciences that the Earth is entering a new geological time period, the Homogene, in which all parts of the planet will come to resemble one another. Up to 30,000 of Earth's estimated 10 million species were vanishing every year, an all-time record for the past 65 million years. The usual dizzying figures which no-one could grasp. Species able to flourish alongside man - rats, cockroaches, crows, the usual suspects - will be favoured by evolution. Stan had to try to point up the warning that evolutionary biologists should concentrate on working out how best to manage the planet's future instead of burying themselves in the fascinations of the past. We humans are, after all, the Guardians of the Biosphere, was the message.

The journal listed examples, species which were going or had already gone. Gone. The final word, the door slammed. Birds, insects, amphibians, plants - you name it. His heart went out to the alabama sturgeon, teetering there on the brink due to overfishing and loss of habitat. He could see a good ole' boy now, in his dungarees, waddling down to the waterhole with his hickory stick to get him a sturgeon. Over the generations they'd worn a path. Dynamite had replaced hickory sticks, and now the waterhole was a car-park.

Even worse, what was this about the tragic charco palma pupfish? Extinguished. In 1994. What had this little chap looked like? He intuitively felt it was - had been - little. Presumably there had once been thousands - no, hundreds of thousands - of pupfish, shoals of them in every pool and stream, quietly living out their lives day by day down the millennia, troubling no-one but for a few freshwater molluscs and invertebrates (it seemed unlikely such a fish would restrict itself to vegetable matter), never dreaming that the day would arrive - in 1994 - when just fifty of them remained, anxiously confined to one small spring in Charco Palma, Mexico. And then? That exact bit of water was needed - for a carwash, who knows? - and fifty pupfish were left flapping in the mud, the Mexican sun beating down, crows and dogs moving in, the sun going down, rats and roaches on the move, cats ... adios pupfish.

He would track down a picture of this gallant little Mexican victim of the Guardians of the Biosphere, and the fighting pupfish would not be forgotten. He would see to that. Guardians of the Biosphere? Surely Kleptocrats was the word, if the dictionary still had any meaning.

After a respectful period he pushed away from the desk on his executive wheelie chair - a functional gift from the Barracuda - hit the play button and poured a drink, the round eyes of the noble hound on him all the way. Louisiana Red began to lament as Stan leaned back in his chair to run a snatch of *Boscanion - the Movie* through his head: Antonio Banderas as Boscanion, flashing eyes and dashing black imperial, grappled with a full-grown male Jactator in a cloud of dust and flying slaver. And there was Kim, black-eyed in the background, watching the battle, small body poised in that familiar way, tilted forward from the waist, ready for action. He felt a pang. Who would take her place in the movie? He tried a succession of actresses, but their features wouldn't stick. That strange, feral face would not yield. And

Banderas wasn't right either. Too much machismo, short on nuance and sensitivity.

Reluctantly his mind noticed a large and imminent expense. The Papalinas. How was he going to pay for it? There was nothing in the pipeline, despite what he may have allowed the Barracuda to believe. Even he knew better than to pay any attention to Ray's dreams. It really was time the mercurial AB Defduf shook himself out of it and came up with something.

'Money, Kato old dab. Money. Any ideas?'

The noble hound tensed, staring hard at Stan, tongue lolling.

'Well?'

Kato shuddered, half rose, held the position and whined.

'Later.'

The capacious bar-restaurant-whatever was already full, burbling with busy media people. *Mulciber's* was their type of place - bright, modern, expensive, and decorated in a way which might have been unsettling if the babble, bodies and harsh lighting hadn't half-stunned him already. Ray had booked a table for lunch, and he only had to cope for an hour or two.

'What's it to be then?' Ray was rubbing his pudgy hands together, scanning the long, laboratory-like roomful of faces. The surrounding Angels and Devils theme to the mirrored walls multiplied the crowd by an unknown factor. Ray, a beer fiend with a double-figure membership number in CAMRA and shares in at least two breweries, had been cultivating one of the owners of this unlikely place, and considered the beer acceptable.

'Stanley, you'll have a pint of Timothy Taylor Landlord, naturally. Delyth? Imperial Russian Stout, as brewed for Catherine the Great? I should warn you the bottles are on the small side.'

'No doubt. Cranberry J2O please, Ray. With ice. Thank you so much.'

Delyth maintained a distinction between work and relaxation, unlike Ray. This was work. She was his thrusting deputy, approaching peak thrust in her late twenties. Pulling out a silvery cigarette packet she selected one with her red snapper nails and placed it between red snapper lips. She didn't offer Stan one and he didn't offer a light. They both knew they didn't get along, although he'd like to bet his feelings on the subject were more complicated than hers. Delyth watched Ray barrelling his way off to the bar, then her lighter snapped and she blew smoke.

'You know, I'm surprised our brave leader doesn't get himself into more trouble than he does. Holding meetings in the pub like this … so retro and unprofessional. It wastes so much time. And it certainly won't impress Diodary - ' she shot a glance at a steely wristwatch '- he's got far better things to do with his time.'

Smoking was a redeeming feature in Delyth, in Stan's estimation - the only one, apart from her manicured Welsh loveliness. He admired the businesslike way she dealt with the whole smoking process, without even a hint of the smallest scintilla of pleasure. Pure addiction. Sometimes, if you were lucky, she would expel smoke in twin streams from that delicate white nose, in the grand old film-star manner. Already, people nearby were casting peeved glances her way. No smoking in *Mulciber's*.

'Stanley. Are you with us darling?'

'Yes, Delyth. Sorry.' What did she mean, pub? 'Well, how many Rays are there? Isn't it a wonder to actually know the only one? A privilege just to see him function, really. He feels more creative in this setting, natural environment and so forth. And we do like a pint, don't we?' He managed one of his charming smiles then leaned back to stare at the twitching whirl of faces and working mouths. Teeth, wings, horns. Did anyone ever dare get drunk in this place? 'And nobody in his right mind would mistake this for a pub, Delyth.'

Delyth looked aggressively blank, tilting her head to direct smoke at the low ceiling. It was a fine, immaculately groomed head, no signs yet of the weariness and stress which would get her later, with any luck, when she'd finally grabbed Ray's job and the one after that. She favoured smart business suits, usually of an arresting colour - although today's was a sober midnight blue - which served to emphasize her trim figure and long, silken legs.

'You don't like *Mulciber's* Stan? Not *ee-bah-gum* enough for you? As a matter of fact, and despite what I just said, you might benefit from a bit more jostling at the watering hole with us media folk. You do depend on us, after all, and it might sharpen you up. I only say this for your own benefit, you understand.'

Hard to believe now that she'd once made a silvery lunge. Or it might have been him, in a self-sacrificial moment. Drink had played its usual part, but he was almost certain it had really happened. Ninety per cent. And he couldn't imagine that Delyth was ever drunk.

He gnawed at a forefinger. 'Who's Diodary?'

But Ray was back, setting down the drinks, directing his boyish, first-pint grin at them, subsiding heavily into his chair. He'd always been the same, bulling along through life, leaving bruises and long memories in his wake. Ray was Stan's age but looked older, with thick black hair cut sensibly in the unchanging Ray style, heavy black Clark Kent specs jammed on a pasty face, permanent blue jowls and fleshy pink lips. This look had seen him through babyhood, childhood, studenthood and everything since. One side of his face was pockmarked where glass fragments had burrowed before slowly working their way out, a memento of amateur chemistry attempts to perfect the eerie green light effect eventually put to use in the opening sequence of *Insidiator*. Ray had been a research chemist at one time. He used to carry a rattling Swan Vesta box in his jacket pocket - whatever the occasion, whatever the weather, Ray always wore a Mr Bean-type jacket, shirt, tie and dark trousers, always with black, shiny shoes - and whenever he fiddled a glass chip free he would pop it into the box.

'Cheers.' Ray grinned again. Even his mother would agree Ray's expression was basically surly, but the grin as he raised a pint glass to eager pink lips changed that. Ray was reliably foul in the mornings, jovial in the afternoons, and liable to fly off the handle at any time. The three of them - Ray, Stan and Julius Easterhouse - had been at university together. This had been a trio so odd that Stan cringed now at the image: Lord Snooty in a goatee with his chums - Clark Kent's short, porky brother and a refugee from the Mothers of Invention. That was Stan. There'd been a few bust-ups with Ray over the years, but Ray always bounced back. Julius though ... had he ever really been part of it all? Looking back, it was as if he'd been playing some sort of game.

Ray had drawn himself up to deliver a pronouncement. 'I shan't beat about the bush. Confirmation at last, Stan. As promised.' Pause for effect, glass poised. '*Insidiator* is to go ahead after all. All last-minute obstacles have been overcome.' He smirked at Delyth and swallowed beer with gusto.

They'd all heard this before from Ray, usually at the conventions, but this seemed different. Stan felt a gentle pulse of shock, mild confusion, then spreading relief. Here was something to wave at the Barracuda. She would snort, but an announcement in front of the staff, that made it official. And a re-run meant money. He swallowed Landlord, offering up a silent prayer of thanksgiving for this acme of the brewer's art. They could skip off to the Papalinas, no problem now. Certain memories would re-surface, certain feelings, but hallelujah, he'd worry about that if and when. Hadn't he said leave it to him?

'You wore them away, Ray,' he managed. 'They never stood a chance.' Would memories be the only items to re-surface? He was apprehensive now. 'When?' More Landlord.

'Oh, very soon, don't worry, I'll let you know. It was set up ages ago of course, but there have been a few trifling complications, and I needed to be sure before telling you. But it's sorted now, no turning back.' Ray was outstanding when it came to looking pleased with himself, and he had, after all, thrown himself into *Insidiator* from the outset as producer, pushing for it, pulling strings, attempting to interfere constantly with the script, and ever since push-push-pushing to get it back on. He'd never come to terms with the lack of critical and popular success, and he felt cheated. Ray's grand plan was to get an independent production company to make the thing into a film, and a TV re-run was part of his strategy.

'What Ray's trying to say is that not everyone thinks it's a particularly sensible thing to be doing.' Delyth smiled sweetly. She was a fundamentalist sceptic who thought the whole thing had been a self-indulgent and rather juvenile waste of time, effort and a limited amount of money. Write it off and move on. There were viewers out there for the grabbing and careers to be made. Ray and Stan were wilfully out of touch, and she failed to comprehend why any more time should be wasted on their foolishness. She had a lovely speaking voice, with the gentle rise and fall of West Wales, delicious against the hoarse, babbling backdrop. Very persuasive.

Ray put down his glass. 'A piece of work like *Insidiator* is always going to whiz over people's heads first time round. I think we all knew that.' He gave every impression of believing this. 'For goodness' sake, look at *Doctor Who*. The quality of the production was our responsibility, not the quality of the sodding viewers.'

Sometimes Ray didn't sound like a TV executive at all, even Stan could see that. But he hadn't finished.

'They're ready for it now. Its time has come. They'll be baying for a new series. When you look at all the American teenytwaddle pulling big figures now ... '

Delyth uncrossed her legs, and Stan realized he'd been staring at them. She leaned forward, raising her voice clear of the increasing din. 'Ray's lack of appreciation for all the *Star Trek* spin-offs, *Buffy*, *Roswell High*, *Farscape* and so on is not generally shared. Sorry Stanley - you do watch television from time to time, don't you? There's a bigger market than ever, of course there is, but that isn't who you're going to get. Re-runs are cheap, granted, but it's only been five years. And there's far more competition. You'll get exactly the same viewers, or rather some of them - they'll just be five years older. It won't lead anywhere, and there'll be no new series. You can carry on with your conventions, certainly. Sell the merchandise, if you can,' staring pointedly at Stan's T-shirt, 'set up a fascinating website, or do you have one already? Oh, well done. Just don't expect to make a TV show. Your production values need to be right up there now, and this kind of thing just won't attract the money.' A delicate huff of amusement, or disbelief. 'You need a cast people can like, or envy, or lust after - young and good-looking, or young and winningly whimsical - and it does help if your story is intelligible. Capital letters, big print. It has to travel. Viewers don't tune in to be made to work, they want to be entertained. Pretty basic stuff.'

Ray and Stan attended to their beer. More smartly dressed figures squeezed into *Mulciber's*, all talking, upping the volume as they pressed into the roar, shouting into mobiles, waving, gurning. How could they have so much to talk about before they'd even got to the bar? No, you got to the bar, took your drink somewhere agreeable, or if not exactly agreeable, somewhere you could shut things out, then after a couple of leisurely swallows, *then* topics of conversation welled up. A natural sequence.

'Americans,' sniffed Ray. Despite his job he held narrow-minded views. He admired such vintage wonders as *Blake's Seven, Sapphire and Steel, Catweazle, Adam Adamant, Worzel Gummidge, Quatermass* (especially *and the Pit*) and the *Andromedas*, not to mention *Captain Scarlet and the Mysterons*. All old stuff, stretching back into the sixties. US imports, symbolised by *Buffy the Vampire Slayer*, did not measure up. Better not to mention *Buffy* while Ray was around. Above all, Ray admired - though not uncritically - *Doctor Who*, with which he had been involved towards the end, and the resurrection of which was another project dear to his heart. Stan could see a monologue coming.

Delyth recognized the signs too. 'The shortcomings of *Insidiator* are well-established,' she announced firmly, ticking them off on red-tipped white fingers. Her pleasing voice was appealingly husky from all the cigarettes. 'Storyline obscure or invisible. Viewers did not relate to the fragments they could understand. Ending highly unsatisfactory, far too abrupt.'

'That's right,' huffed Ray. 'Straight lines and signposts, little pink bows at regular intervals with a big one at the end. All these so-called reviewers, their sole aim in life is to slither off to Hollywood. Anything requiring original thought, anything with true dramatic or literary merit, even if it *is* a failure, which this isn't -'

'*Y- e- s.*' Delyth made it a Paxman yes. 'So. Let's just stick to disposable fantasy TV, shall we? To continue - production values ... low, shall we say - you were restricted Ray, I know. Sets and design straight out of art-college. Narrative voice heavily over-used. Acting poor to grotesquely poor - I except Charles Chinchard, naturally. Critics did point out the derivativeness of the style, the lack of originality, but that's not really my field - sorry Stanley. But most of all, who was it for? Niche marketing, rule one. There was no clear target audience. Far too obscure for kids, too juvenile for adults - sorry Stanley. Pure self-indulgence.'

Stan was roused. 'Hell Del, anyone would think you didn't enjoy it.'

The sweet red snapper smile. She didn't like Del. 'It's not as if I've invented any of this. I'm quoting, more or less. I'm not saying it didn't have a certain following - '

'Still has,' interjected Ray vehemently. 'Steady turnout at the conventions, plenty of hits on the site.' He lurched forward as the gabbling mass behind made a surge. 'Just look at the bloody Kims. It made its mark.' Mobiles chimed and trilled.

A small number of fans had become obsessed with Kim, who had played the hero's bizarre sidekick, Anakim. This was what Delyth meant by grotesquely poor acting. Kim had been unorthodox, certainly. A little unsettling, disturbing even. Stan and Ray had decided, perhaps not immediately, that she was perfect. Charles Chinchard, playing Boscanion, felt the same, as did the Kims. And she had got better, markedly. Stan chewed at his finger, examining his newly-arrived plate: Lemon Sole, *Microstomus kitt*. A fine fish, with a certain understated style, albeit irredeemably demersal. A re-run would stir up the Kims, no doubt about that.

Ray was attacking a meaty heap of lasagne, muttering about Buffy.

'Let's get to the point,' shouted Delyth, shifting her chair forward as the noise in *Mulciber's* continued to swell, 'before Diodary arrives, Stanley leaves us, and we get down to business.' She checked her watch again and looked over at the door before fixing Stan with the direct blue-eyed gaze he had always found disquieting. Cosmetic skills had enhanced an inherent laser-like capability to the point where it was hardly fair. She must be near-invincible in these power meetings: Delyth was in essence a substantial pike, *Esox lucius* - all the big pike were females - natural environment a cold, deep lake. Ray's heroically overgrown bullhead's only real chance was to stick to the bottom and make use of natural cover. But that wasn't Ray's way.

He took over. 'Right. Stanley, our Delyth isn't in favour of a re-run. She has her own views on the type of show we should be putting out, but she's not in charge. So let's think ahead: we assume *Insidiator* clicks this time, and we have to be ready to go. We need to be able to tell them there's more in the pipeline. You roughed out a follow-up at the time, so we'll polish it up. Dig it out and we'll get cracking.'

'No prob Raymondo.' Which was taking a leaf out of Liza's book of aggressive optimism. Had he really roughed out a follow-up?

Ray lurched forward as the scrum flexed. 'Bloody racket. Right. I expect you've been looking at your tapes every now and then, should be easy to bring it all back together.' He chortled and rubbed his hands together. 'Just think what we'll be able to do with proper resources!'

Stan gnawed at a forefinger. His tapes had disappeared. He was guessing the Barracuda had chucked them, burned them in the dead of night maybe, but he wasn't about to ask. Nodding thoughtfully, he realized he'd been staring again at what bit he could see of Delyth's fine Pembrokeshire legs. Or was it Cardiganshire? Fabulous red snapper shoes. She really was a streamlined beast, was our Delyth, every scale in place and gleaming.

Ray's specs fixed on him. 'The other thing, Stan, is Kim. This just might flush her out from wherever she bolted to. She'll come to you, odds on. Are you prepared for that?'

Which was just what he'd been trying to avoid thinking about. Didn't they ever turn down the heating in this damned place? Every punter was emitting clouds of the stuff. Delyth's blue lasers were boring into him. His T-shirt was unbearably heavy and sticky with sweat. His insides gave a small wriggle. All around him the din withdrew, like surf running back down the beach, sucking at the pebbles. He had to break out.

'Back in a minute.'

He was up and pushing into the sea of mouthing faces, altering course whenever he hit horns or wings, slanting red eyes, a halo, then he was outside. A black cab was rolling away, the driver shouting out of the window. Shouting at him. He'd overshot into the road. He pulled off his T-shirt and took in deep lungsful of fumes and cold, gritty city air. A pigeon poked about in the gutter at his feet, tiny iridescent feathers in the turquoise neck patch flexing with each restless thrust of the head. It looked mechanical. Soon he was shivering.

When he got back Ray was scowling at his surroundings. There was no sign of Delyth.

'Stan? You look bloody lousy. So she still gets to you, eh?'

Two fresh pints were on the table. It was cooler. *Mulciber's* was half empty. They'd pumped people out and air in.

'Just the usual Ray, the old hot sweats.'

'Yeah yeah, the old curse of the tropics, I remember, if that's your story.'

Stan sucked down Timothy Taylor's Landlord, the stuff of life, cooling down various inflamed internals. It never lasted long. Already he felt better. Change the subject. 'Where's our Del then? Off filing her teeth?' More beer eased its way down. Yes. 'You've got the cellarman trained up Ray.'

'Not bad is it?' He held up his glass for them both to admire. 'He's coming on.'

'And our Del?'

Ray chuckled, getting in the mood now, and waved at the door.

'Back to work. Poor old Delyth was under a misapprehension, all set for a power lunch, hadn't prepared herself for a civilized booze-up. When the penny dropped that Diodary wasn't going to show, well, she decided she had pressing matters, etcetera etcetera.' Another satisfied chuckle.

'Who's Diodary?'

'Just someone our Del was hoping to involve in her little war games. Nothing to worry about, just another tale of the old greasy pole, not a part of your life Stanley. What were those things old Easterhouse had, those traps, when he was terrorising the local wildlife?'

'Pitfall traps.'

'Yeah, pitfall traps.' He sighed. 'Easterhouse. Whatever became of him - no, I couldn't give a toss. Anyway, I was supposed to go blundering into a pitfall trap today, but I got a bit of pre-emptive in before I left the office. She's good, Stan, but she's up against the Master.'

As in *Dr Who*, he meant. Stan decided he didn't want to know any more. 'Right. Good. What about you though Ray? I mean, don't you have, well, work to be doing?'

'It can wait. I expect you clocked the red eclipse?'

The image of a huge red moon. But that had happened in his head one night, hadn't it, not out in the world? How the bloody hell had Ray managed to see it?

'No? Awesome Stanley. The Earth's atmosphere, bending and discolouring the light, turning a run-of-the-mill full eclipse into an *Excalibur* backdrop. Or *Insidiator* come to that. Awesome.' He gurgled into his pint. 'You ought to get out more.'

The clientele had really thinned out now, and, strangely enough, so had the Angels and Devils. There couldn't possibly have been so many bodies in here after all. It had been some kind of illusion.

Ray took down beer in a long series of measured gulps, beaming now, perfectly at ease.

The shark angled off to begin a patient circling at eye-level in the sun-dappled, green-blue haze. Five feet long, an adult blacktip reef shark, *Carcharhinus melanopterus*, a sleek torpedo of brown and creamy-white muscle swinging rhythmically from side to side shark-style, neither dawdling nor hurrying. A long, sweeping uppertail drove the body down, wing-like pectorals and the flattened ventral surface of the head generated lift, the body's elevated mid-section induced drag and provided a fulcrum for movement, while braking and turning power were achieved through fins, which also prevented pitch and yaw - a symphony of complementary forces in perfect balance, evolved for a lifetime's cruising. The shark form had been perfected millions of years ago, no need for further evolutionary change. This was a familiar and unnerving situation: to keep turning in the water like this, shark stick extended to keep it at bay, not able to move fast enough, not able to keep up. The shark was lost for giddying seconds, accelerating out of vision, then it was back, sliding abruptly into place, feet away and closer, black eye unmoving between coppery lids, expressing neither excitement nor fear, interest nor disinterest. Expressing nothing. And the shark circled, closer yet, harder still to keep up. Gone again. Then back. Or was this a second shark? Gone again.

Stan blinked in the mirror. He wiped away sweat. Just a stray scene from Tsaramaso, a fragment of his life. It had always been nervy whenever a second shark turned up, impossible to follow both at once. But blacktips were lagoon sharks, fish-eaters, and usually, after half a dozen inspection circuits, they would lose interest and move on. Always moving. He could still sense the dwindling feeling inside which always hit him at that point, whenever the shark finally turned and swam away. The dwindling of adrenaline and fear, but why should it leave him feeling flat, even sad? Abandoned.

On Tsaramaso Atoll he'd finally rebelled over the shark work, and refused to carry on with it. Most of it was all right: catching, measuring, tagging and tracking had been interesting – no, totally absorbing. Stanley admired all fishes, although there was more to it, especially with sharks. Hooking them hadn't been so bad - they'd used barbless hooks which could be removed - but dragging them into the boat to kill them, all the clouting, stabbing and hacking, all the blood and guts, then the inspection and removal of whichever bits they were after - chiefly baby sharks - and the tossing back of what was left ... no. Naturally Easterhouse had not been able to sympathise with this squeamishness, which threatened The Study. Pull yourself together Stanley, at least try to pretend you're a biologist. Before long everyone on the research station knew about it - hardly surprising in the tiny and overheated community which existed at Tsaramaso in those days. He knew the other western researchers were talking about him, scoffing at Blackster the delicate Yorkshireman. Nowadays they'd call him a wimp, but they didn't have the word back then. Middle class, by and large. Outwardly confident and ambitious, like Easterhouse, but he'd soon seen through that. Julius had been the exception. The local workers, the Papalinois, clearly disapproved of the killing, but it was only what they had come to expect from these ignorant foreigners. And speaking out wasn't their way. They would see no contradiction in despising Stan for refusing to continue. His behaviour was unmanly.

It crept into his mind that the face of Roland, their patriarch, had begun to haunt recent dreams and driftings: dark and bearded, primeval, a wood carving with round pale eyes that never closed, it had emerged unexpectedly from the buried memories of Tsaramaso. Not by choice, certainly. He blinked. The evening face blinked.

He poured himself another Bushmills, which he was finding agreeable, stabbed the play button, gulped and faced up to the mirror. Zappa. *Strictly Genteel.* Keyboards, brass, crashing drums, stately and doleful. Apt.

'All here present salute the gallant pupfish! Gone but not forgotten.'

With brimming eyes he raised his glass to the forever absent pupfish's silent comrades hovering all around: parrotfish, angelfish, bonito, soldierfish, surgeonfish, barracuda. He was proud of the article, a minor triumph of advocacy, and would e-mail it through in the morning. Gram would be impressed. Murmuring along with the fading music *dum di dum di dum Bah Bah Bah*, he ran a hand over the cool turquoise wall. Dear Liza had designed and produced this marvellous, fish-filled wallpaper – hardly an adequate word – especially and exclusively for him. This had been some time ago, true, but it provided an enduring and potent symbol of the essential harmony underlying daily affairs in the Blackster household. A salute then, to life's finest partner.

And Delyth really ought to wear longer skirts, at her age. But she knew what she was doing. All part of her streamlined plan.

Stan took up the scissors, held them poised. Staring at the mirror face helped him think, or helped him not to. The full beard had been Liza's idea. The old arrangement had made him look like a downmarket version of a prominent American musician, according to her, which had sort of been the idea – not the downmarket bit - but never mind. She wanted an upmarket Ricky Villa, the Argentinian who used to play for Spurs. She wanted South Yorkshire's white Marvin Gaye. And, apparently, a full beard made him look less unbalanced. That's what she said, less unbalanced. Certainly there was less maintenance. Looking after the old imperial – heavy black, drooping moustache and a necessarily neat square of black bristles under the lower lip, not to mention the sideboards - had been quite demanding. The face grimaced.

Snip. He'd bequeathed the imperial to Boscanion, the well-known TV hero, who made much better use of it. And now he had some good news for the Barracuda, a rare situation, something to savour. Now the financing of their tropical adventure could be achieved. Not that he'd ever doubted that something would turn up, as was only proper. But he had to be careful. The sight of Kim on screen, or even that aspect of his news, could send the Barracuda straight into super-aggressive mode. He had to get his timing right.

A startling series of hammer blows on the bathroom door brought him back with a jump, snipping an earlobe on the way. He made a sound of acknowledgement, and waited.

Significantly there were no words from the Barracuda, just The Knock. He thought about a final jolt, but decided no. This Bushmills was excellent, really fine, but he could now see it fell just short. Possibly he'd been drinking it without due attention. He should try having just one small glass, and savouring it. The face in the mirror held a red-smeared white wad to its ear. His own blood. Hundreds of shocked corpuscles bidding farewell to the travelling life.

He'd wait until nearer the time, when there was no possibility of a humiliating reversal. They'd been here before. It would have to be a last-minute surprise, breaking the news with fingers crossed. He'd really like to tell Gram now – Gram was going through a phase of some sort, hard to say when it had started, but for a while now he had failed to note the old unquestioning attention to his father's words. He'd have to do something. Gram loved *Insidiator*, and admired Boscanion. But telling Gram and not the Barracuda would be asking for trouble. He would tell them both, when the time was right. His nervousness wasn't just to do with the Barracuda – *Insidiator* was his high watermark, and Delyth's lovely voice had summarised its perceived drawbacks. But what did he - and Ray – care for popularity? No, he must stop pretending. Of course he wanted success, he wanted to bask again in the glow of the Barracuda's admiration. Even more, he wanted things to be the way they used to be with Gram. And yes, he wanted something to happen to him, again. There had been Tsaramaso, then there had been *Insidiator*, then there had been nothing. Kim's distorted, mesmerising little face lived on in his head, and with it a fitful, circling presence impossible to bring into focus.

Perhaps one last small Bushmills, to which he would devote full and undivided attention, then he would make his exit to resume familial responsibilities. The snoring string bass and muted wah wah of Zappa's *Twenty Small Cigars* was perfectly in tune with setting and occasion.

3. The Barracuda

The cab-driver's rapid-fire Asian-Hampshire was too fast. From the passenger seat Stan gave the occasional grunt of encouragement while musing on his calendar's Fish of the Month: *Barbus barbus*. The barbel, a stolid, powerful, bottom-hugging creature. A drawn-out, whiskery face which had seen it all before. The accumulated knowledge of life on the bottom, not dramatically bright as freshwater fishes go, not as bright as, say, a roach or a chub, or even a rudd. Rudd actually gave the impression of being quite lazy, in an enviable sort of manner. The barbel wasn't lazy, far from it. Sluggish, possibly, but that was different, a combination of physique and environment. Highly popular with the angling fraternity in the local rivers, especially the Avon, due to its impressive size (rod-caught record 14 lb 6 oz) and a resolute resistance to the prospect of unfiltered daylight and so-called fresh air. A handsome fish, as the text had it, with scales of gold-bronze and pink-red fins, a native of the rivers of eastern England from Yorkshire down to the Thames. More widespread now, thanks to anglers, and the Royalty Fishery on the Avon at Christchurch was pre-eminent. Hold a big pink worm on the bottom in the strong current for which the barbel was so excellently adapted, perhaps let it trundle slowly along … long ago he'd reluctantly stopped fishing for sport, glorious though it was. Gram was dead against – putting an animal through pain and stress, maybe even death, just to make you feel better? Fishing for food, for your own consumption, was permissible. Which meant it was a long, long time since Stan had cast a line. Now he thought about it, the introduction of this handsome barbel from the Kennet to the Hampshire Avon had not been good news for the native chub, roach and dace quietly minding their own business: as well as competing for food, especially with the chub (another magnificent, bullet-headed green-bronze creature which could bring to mind some of the duller parrotfishes), the barbel had brought a little hitch-hiker, a parasitic hookworm. Julius had relished the story. The larvae lived out their tiny lives in the blood systems of shrimps; that was their world. And shrimps were of course created solely to feed fishes, etcetera, etcetera.

The cab had pulled up and the driver was rooting about for change, so Stan told him to forget it. Southampton's pleasingly wooded

Common helped keep the snarling city traffic at bay and gave the urban wildlife a foothold. From the tall, leafless trees drifted snatches of watery birdsong, faltering and stopping, starting up again ... every time he heard a bird now he heard the Forest harpies, *chek-chek-chek*, and felt a gust of unease. An over-ambitious intake hitched on webs of mucus down in his respiratory recesses. He hawked and spat, sending a lump spinning into the washed out greenery. Winter. Easy to believe it would last forever here, like Narnia with murk instead of snow. Summer was an unreliable possibility, not something to count on, which would be over in no time anyway. Britain was expected to emerge soon from its wintry half-life, but these things no longer felt inevitable. Everyone was resigned to global warming, even on a day like this. Those who thought about it anyway. Maybe we did it, but it will sort itself out, and even if it doesn't, nothing will happen for ages. Guardians of the Biosphere. Straight ahead was Hardwicke's College, focus of the Barracuda's working life.

This was an open day, when the art students showed their work, and Stan always came along. She liked him to, and he really did relish the proximity of youth, as long as it didn't go on too long. And they were younger every year. At the door a cute little girl greeted him, shy smile, blonde hair in what they probably didn't call a pageboy any more, offering red or white. He took a glass of Chilean merlot over to look at the work, arranged along walls, on folding screens and tables or hanging from the ceiling. Small clusters of friends and relatives were engaged in mostly hushed conversation, which meant the wine hadn't got to work yet, so he wasn't late. And there she was: Liza waved from one of the groups, ignited a smile and strode over.

'Well done, Stanley.' Peck on the cheek. 'I see you've found the drink.'

He stood back to look at her, slowly, up and down. Then again. He'd been unconscious when she'd set off this morning, as he usually was. She wore a slinky, calf-length, sleeveless black silk dress with a deep neckline, and a simple design - one of her own - printed in turquoise along the hem, along with the necklace of lapis lazuli he'd given her one New Year's Eve. Shining brown skin glowed against black silk like polished mangrove. In three-inch heels she was as tall as he was. Taller. Some teacher.

'Mrs. Blackster.' He was dazzled, all over again. How could this magnificent creature possibly be his? All around other members of staff blended in with the mums and dads. It was no surprise she got herself into situations, the only film star on the books. He felt a wash of shame. Just a wash. He hadn't always done the right thing by her, although fortunately she was unaware, by and large. But that was behind him. Henceforth he would behave in proper Boscanion fashion.

Not for the first time he fantasised her into Boscanion's world: the Queen of Zebrasoma, crazed ruler of fanatical and statuesque black women warriors, sworn enemy of the Ruahari, and, come to that, of men in general; given to highly specific modes of torture, strung out over several episodes, as she and her Impi became fabulously drunk on palm wine, eating male delicacies fattened by lengthy and appropriate diet. Jactators, slingjaws, almighty Ang himself – all would cross the street to avoid an altercation. She could do it too. He preferred non-professionals, for the surprise element. These Hollywood actors, going through their paces in yet another movie – who cared, really? Anyway, an unrealized fantasy it would remain. The Barracuda had plenty of chutzpah, but she would never go for it. Follow in Kim's sturdy footsteps?

His thoughts turned to Hardwicke's College and its down to earth gallery of characters. It was a steamy situation, really. The Barracuda wasn't one to tone herself down, and the college was awash with hormones. Not just the kids either. He'd heard stories, not all of them from Liza. But most of her colleagues didn't have the nerve.

She laughed now, throaty and loud, not a full-throttle laugh, but good to hear, nice and relaxed, didn't happen too often these days. Sweet, winey breath. Yes, he was glad he'd come.

'Having any stalker trouble these days then Barra? Point them out.'

'Round here? As if. You're the scriptwriter, Stanley. Dish me up a leading man. Denzel Washington-type please, no quirky little habits ... ' she was keeping an eye on the door, and fired off a smile at someone.

'No tantrums, no breakdowns?' This was often a theatrical occasion, at least behind the scenes. 'Not even a moody cigarette up on the roof?' She often got sucked into her students' dramas. She liked to be involved.

'All quiet, fingers crossed.'

'I'll mingle then.'

'OK. There's some good work. I'm hoping the local press will show up – they've been invited. The management want to put a stop to these little events, and we're the only art department in Southampton still making the effort.'

Stan scanned the room, wondering idly which young faces matched up with the desperate characters in Liza's home from work stories. What will become of them all? They were so young, so tentative and innocent. With not the slightest notion of what lies in wait for them once they filter eagerly out into the predatory world. He tugged out a tissue and dabbed at his eyes. These lights, far too bright. He always felt oddly paternal at these affairs. So easy to see why she got such a kick out of it, or at least, why she used to. A dozen of her colleagues, maybe more, were leaving at the end of the year, giving up on a lifetime's toil in some cases, while the remainder hung on grimly for their pensions, hoping for early retirement or yet another slice of downsizing. They'd be replaced with younger, cheaper folk. No-one got a kick out of it any more. In Liza's department half the staff were now expected to deal with twice the number of students. There were no secretaries, the paperwork was endless, and they all cut corners. Because she would have to carry out an official investigation if a student's attendance fell below 85%, and she didn't have the time, Liza made sure this didn't happen. So did everyone else. It was understood. Just a matter of a mark in a column, and attendance at Hardwicke's was exemplary. The management knew perfectly well what was going on, but it was the only way their system would work. Management was efficient, doing a good job. Liza had become so disillusioned, so worn down, that she was actually contemplating joining the enemy, leaving the teaching, the art and the kids, and moving in with them, the managers. She hadn't said so, but he could tell. There had been approaches, and hers would be a conversion to celebrate. Even the Barracuda was weakening. She wanted a shot at the good life now that it was clear Stan wouldn't be providing it.

He watched her go, that athletic stride, the focal point of wherever she was, effortlessly capable. And manage she would, with or without Stanley Blackster. He knew that.

Approaching with his empty glass he gave the girl his encouraging smile, to put her at her ease. He learned her name was Karen.

'Are you really Mrs Blackster's husband?'

'That would be me.' A winning smile. 'What were you expecting, Muhammad Ali?'

Her own smile went vague. She'd no idea what he was talking about.

'Lennox Lewis then. Mike Tyson?'

The smile was fixed now. She was looking over his shoulder, where someone else waited to be served.

Toby, a colleague of the Barracuda's, was addressing a band of relatives: '... really quite dramatic impact of her African trip ... ' Stan and Toby nodded to one another. The students called him Tobe, whereas he knew the Barracuda favoured a greater degree of formality, and, no doubt occasionally, fear. There had been fallings out with Tobe, and he'd come off much the worse, but Liza had managed to fall out with most of the staff at one time or another, and Stan wouldn't have heard the half of it. He came to rest at a collection of paintings, photographs, and combinations of the two, illustrating the city's electric jungle night: essentially traffic, transformed from a heap of snarling metalwork into a silent whirl of lighted points and blackness. He stared. With sound absent like this it needn't be a city at all, hardly even earthly. Restful. Conducive. He deliberately slowed his breathing, no hitches now, slowly in, pause, slowly slowly out, pause, time and motion easing down to the perfect, eternal rhythm. Kim had shown him this way of breathing, as a form of meditation. As he lost awareness of his breathing, his vision slowly expanded, intensified. The works became bluer, larger, acquiring silent depths...

A muffled, grating, underwater sound tugged him round. A throat being cleared, a voluntary exercise of the relevant muscles in order to displace accumulated mucus a millimetre or two, for social effect. He was blocking someone's view.

His glass was empty so he returned to Karen, her welcoming smile now uncertain.

'Mr Blackster, same again?'

'Yes please Karen. And call me Stan.'

She took his glass without meeting his eye. His mind went blank, and he just couldn't think of a single thing to say.

Next he studied a congregation of contorted miniature monster-figures, fashioned in clay, which he found crude, powerful and disturbing. Some were blue, some bloody red, others mottled and barred with both colours, and although each figure was distinct - some unmistakably reptilian, others grotesquely bird-like, bat-winged or simian - it was somehow clear they were all the same elemental thing. Which was quite impressive. Liza had described this young man well enough, an awkward sort, disturbed even, but talented and ambitious, heading for the stage, television, film, presumably by way of advertising. Stan turned and casually searched the room, trying to pick him out: the Nick Cave lookalike in the charity shop black suit over there, who had Tobe backed into a corner? The shaven-headed scrum forward glowering from the shadows? The same impression struck him every time he came - how uncomfortable and rather silly the boys looked, and how charming the girls. Take little Karen. Was she one of Liza's? He didn't recall the name. Was any of this her work? He should ask, put her at her ease. So much appealing blankness, so much scope. Her pretty little face, so symmetrical, lacking the stamp of personality. A face destined to fade from his mind within hours. Unlike Kim's, with its over-dominant jaws, those tantalisingly blank black eyes in which it was all too easy to read stupidity ...

He wandered on. They should turn down the heating in here, but he'd step outside presently, just as soon as he got one last refill from little Karen. College wine glasses were undersized, presumably to put the brakes on the students. He came upon several differing interpretations of a single fairly hefty female model; a wall of Warhol faces; an attractive deckchair. And here were the pictures made by the girl who'd gone to Africa, each bursting with the colours of the sun. What would Liza's Indian Ocean paintings be like? She'd stopped painting, he couldn't remember how long ago. He leafed through the girl's workbook, Rashila Khan, smiling at her earnest description of a visit to Tate Modern, taken there by Mrs Blackster. One of the artists she admired was Chris Ofili, he of the elephant dung, not the artist of choice along the Hampshire coast. He recalled Miller's drunken, green-eyed face. Miller, who had wanted to take them out on the water. What would he have had to show them? He wouldn't have minded going back, going out on the water with Miller, but the Barracuda's decisive action had put that out of the question.

Most of the art students were girls, lots of them with fine-featured Asian faces. The Barracuda had told him which ones came from the big crime families. Rashila's workbook confirmed Tobe's words: prior to her African awakening the sketches weren't exactly dull, but even he could see the marks of teaching. Now she dashed them off and the pages burst open with colour, colour that ate up the paper. This was what Liza needed. And he would provide it! Resolve pounded through him.

En-route to his refill, he became aware of Liza's erect black figure, alone now, sipping red wine, watching. He waved and gave a thumbs up as he presented little Karen with his glass.

'Some good work Karen, any of it yours?'

She shook her head. 'I'm Media Studies, just helping out.'

Media Studies. An easy opening there, but he could still feel the eyes on his back so he smiled and moved away, crossing the room towards Mrs. B, nodding at one or two half-familiar faces, yes, excellent show, talented youngsters. She had this way of subjecting him to guilt. Time spent encouraging fine young ladies like Karen could hardly be described as misdirected. Liza could rely on his lifelong support, and she should know that. And that he really did understand and appreciate what she had dedicated her life to. He prepared his smile, but a determined, burly and bullet-headed figure brushed past to plant itself squarely in front of her - the glowering rugby type. Stan came to a halt, watching and waiting, prepared for some sort of uproar, but after a short-lived mumbling the burly young man shambled away.

'All under control, Barra? What was that about? An admirer?'

She was radiant, in her hands a plate bearing a large, heart-shaped chocolate cake. Blue-green icing traced out a rather lurid series of unintelligible symbols surrounding the words *Black Star*.

She could not stop smiling, and this was the real full-throttle beam, not for him but for the cake and its presenter. 'It's from all of them, all my students. Sometimes they call me that, between themselves.'

Stan, suddenly finding this sea of youth overwhelming, had to look away, eyes watering. Wasn't there something marvellous and sad about it all? They didn't feel it, they were too young. All the little fishes, filtering out into the ocean. Not many to survive intact, some not at all. He felt an overwhelming relief. This was why he should come out, engage with the world. Occasions such as this were essential, to provide assurance that he must really like people after all. Just as long as they came at him one at a time. When they started getting together of course, things changed.

Perhaps there was time for one last top-up from Karen. He slipped a proud arm about the Barracuda's taut waist, squeezed and kissed her ear softly, but before he could speak she said, 'Right, time to knock off. Time for the Bloody Pub.'

Even better.

The *World Afloat*, cannily placed a stroll away on the edge of the Common, was known to all as the Boat, short for teachers' lifeboat. Because of its location and an easy-going style it was always busy, and the beer was reliable. Also due to its location it had hosted some dramas over the years, one or two involving or starring the Barracuda, but she had never been barred.

Stan sat, staring at the excited mass around him, quietly weighing up the buoyancy of the Barracuda's post-exhibition mood, judging currents, shoals, hazardous rocks and undertow. Not to mention the state of the tide. He had news for her. It was the end of term, and the place was packed with teachers knocking it back. They'd made it through another segment of the great ordeal, and Liza was in full and forceful flow. Having just learned that the college's senior management were to be whisked off to a luxury cruise-liner in Southampton Dock, where a suite had been booked for a back-slapping banquet, she was fired up. She'd actually been invited, at the last minute, part of the buttering-up process, and had loudly declined. Arvind, who Stan would have to keep a particular eye on, had done the inviting. Arvind seemed to have been given the task of converting Mrs Blackster to the dark side.

'And I wonder how the bill for that little shindig will show up in the bloody accounts!' She had engulfed a plate of whitebait and two glasses of Chianti. 'While the rest of us, the people who actually do the work, who maintain the place's reputation, have to scrounge and beg for materials. Bloody scandalous!'

Standard stuff. Sharma eased into the seat beside her, with a perfunctory grimace for Stan.

'Sharma! Have you heard about Sir Keith's bloody banquet?' Sir Keith was the college principal. Why they called her that he'd no idea.

Sharma taught maths, computer skills and so forth, and she'd made it clear from the beginning that she didn't much care for Stan. In fact she'd once observed him misbehaving, and reported him to the Barracuda, back in the days when he used to go out more. At the time he'd tried his customary laconic approach, which didn't work, so ever since he'd just looked right through her and out the other side. Another handsome woman too, if built on a less robust scale than the Barracuda, but too serious, with severe spectacles and censorious lips. The Barracuda was nodding in vigorous agreement as Sharma's beringed, red-nailed fingers gestured off towards Tobe and a self-conscious little band of students. Stan checked for the glowering, cake-presenting hulk, but he wasn't there. He heard the name Arvind, and the two women laughed. Free of scrutiny for the time being, he could afford to relax and observe. These two made an exotic pair. Sharma was almost a fellow barracuda. Almost. Predatory, certainly, with the capacity for a sudden dash and grab, but from cover rather than open water. More calculating, less impulsive, she did a lot of watching with those cold, bespectacled eyes. Not a barracuda. One of the more flamboyant morays, perhaps. A honeycomb moray, *Gymnothorax flavagineus*. Large adults were known to be aggressive.

A girl over at the bar caught his attention, a student presumably, slim with long black hair and a skimpy red dress. He preferred black hair, and there were so many artificial blondes now. The Barracuda's mane took some beating, although she did have to work at it. This girl seemed to be on her own in the press of teachers and students. He swallowed Ringwood Best, waiting for her to turn around. Acceptable but past its peak, time the barrel was changed. Was there something familiar about her? Not one of the Barracuda's little shoal, anyway, he'd have noticed her before.

'Too young Stan, even for you.'

There'd been no let-up in her conversation with Sharma, but she'd noticed. She had this thing, this jealousy of his admiration for the young. Why he would never know, but he'd seen it often enough now. She should feel impregnable, above such pettiness.

He realized he was on the lookout for distraction again, keen to allow things to be put off, but he would tell her about the re-run in a minute, at the end of this mediocre pint. Again he felt uneasy. Life had flowed onwards for the five years since it was on TV. Not smoothly, but onwards. Five years ago was a bygone era. Mussels and Ringwood Best slid around in his gut. Was it going to look ridiculous now? Ray might think its time had come, that they would ride a wave rising out of this sea of bland, over-produced American youth fashion-fodder - it was Ray's job to know about this sort of thing - but how convincing was Ray, really, when you looked at the sleek Welsh blue laser-pike? He pictured Ray, out on the streets in his anorak, uncomfortably easy to do. Were they way out of their depth? Push that thought away! Liza gossiped on, fabulous teeth outmatching even Sharma's. The Blacksters needed the money, end of story.

The pub cat, kipper-coloured and overweight, was sliding through a forest of busy legs. Abruptly it froze, staring straight at him. The muffled rushing sound in his head, like wind in a forest, or distant surf, was so faint it might have been there for years. Cat. He recalled another cat, quite a different cat, a tough and scrawny feral brute with a scruffy black pelt, lips drawn back from chipped yellow-brown incisors blunted on a diet of crabs, rats and turtle hatchlings, dead now, buzzing with flies in the steaming mangrove forest where something had dragged it, festering in the tropical heat, raw red where stomach contents and muscle had been torn away, hermit crabs clustering wherever there was blood. Tsaramaso.

They never did work out what could have done it. The few feral cats were themselves the only sizeable terrestrial predators at large on the atoll. Roland or one of his minions gathering raw materials for voodoo had been the favoured theory, but the Linois guides had shaken their heads, quietly amused. *Well, I cannot say.* He could remember their words: *Voodoo? Here in Papalinas? No, there is no voodoo here in Papa. This is for old people, and for the Malgaches.* All Linois seemed to view the inhabitants of Madagascar, well to the south, with a curious mixture of contempt and fear. And although it was all a great joke around the research station, he knew that by that stage most of the researchers must have seen things they preferred to pretend they hadn't, especially to themselves. Moonlit beach strolls were a thing of the past, and the old settlement after dark had become a no-go area. And it was the mangrove's rotting smell which had wafted past with the rushing harpies of the New Forest.

With a start he realized that he was the subject of the Barracuda's predatory brown stare. Sharma had gone. He must have been asked a question of some sort. Managing a sound of general encouragement, he wiped away sweat with a sleeve and reached for his drink, sensing excitement, agitation. In fact, as he tuned back in, the whole place was agitated, the room-filling babble now lapping at the edges of hysteria. School was definitely out. He couldn't see the girl in red. The cat was gone.

Tobe's gang of students edged closer in a mass shift, which distracted Liza, making her watchful, and Stan directed her attention towards the tropics. She sighed, stretched, closing her eyes with a wide, lazy, pressure-off show of teeth. 'Stanley, I can smell it now. Sand, salt, those coconuts, fish on the barbecue. The little beach bar near the fabulous, fabulous five-star beach hotel. Peace. I'll draw, take the oilsticks … ' Her eyes flew open. 'Stan, did you see the colours in Rashila's work, the girl who went to Tanzania?' Her eyes closed again. 'That's for me. And this will be the last time away with our little boy, Stan.' Eyes open again, serious. 'How do you think he's going to cope, Stan, at university, our little Grammy? He's so vulnerable. He'll not stand up for himself, grab what's going. It's your fault. It's you he gets it from.'

'Oh, cheers'. He'd heard all this before. 'Well, if you're that worried, we can send Kato instead. He'll cope.'

'Hah!' Then a hoot. 'Kato's even worse. In fact how on earth do I put up with the three of you?' She reached across for a playful punch to his arm. 'If it wasn't for me, where would we be? And when are you going to understand, Stanley? Kato only pretends to be bright. It's an act.'

Sad but true. 'He'd handle Media Studies.'

The Barracuda was smiling politely, not a natural expression. Her head of department and arch-enemy, one of Sir Keith's henchwomen, was doing the rounds. 'Here it is!' she hissed, hanging on to the smile. 'Showing its face for five minutes before dashing off to cram its snout in the trough next to Sir Keith and the rest.'

The two nodded grimly at one another. 'Grnnngh,' hissed Liza through her teeth at the retreating back. 'Next term. Next term, matey. If I come back.'

It was the end of term after all, hence the courtesy, and she was on only her third glass. The proximity of Tobe and the students helped dampen things down too.

She returned her gaze briefly to her drink, then fixed him. 'Seriously Stan – tell me what you think, about Gram and uni. He never talks about it. Has he said anything to you? No, of course not, stupid question.'

Gram had no intention of going to university. He knew that much, and there'd be hell to pay when Liza found out. He should have straightened this out, had a good talk with Gram, but there never seemed to be the opportunity somehow ... 'University would do him good Barra, in some ways.' Deep breath. 'Have you ever thought though ... there's something to be said these days for taking a gap year, going off and doing something else before diving straight back into formal education, you know? Lots of kids do it now – well, why am I telling you? Employers like it, initiative ... out there ... '

'Doing something else? Like what?'

She'd gone to full alert. This was her, easy-going, tipsy banter to full-on confrontation at the flick of a switch. It always caught him cold, even when he was half-expecting it.

'What aren't you telling me Stanley? He *has* told you something, hasn't he? Come on.'

'He hasn't told me anything. Just calm down.'

Her eyes flashed a warning. She hated that, being told to calm down.

'No, really Liza, he hasn't.' Those eyes drilled through him. 'I can tell he's just going through ... he's just a bit unsure. Idealistic. It's normal, isn't it? Jesus, I've heard enough stories about your lot. Even I remember how confused you feel when you're sixteen. He's just thinking things out for himself, that's all. Needs some space.'

'Right. Space. And you don't have to tell me about being sixteen, Stanley, thank you very much. That's my working day. That's *working* day.' She sprang to her feet, reaching for the empties, leaning down with a fierce flash of teeth. 'We don't want Gram ending up as a bit of bloody driftwood like his father, do we? Do we?' She leaned closer. Winey breath. Huge eyes. 'One day, one day Stan, you're going to get such a bloody shock. It'll bloody floor you.' She set off for the bar, parting the crowd easily.

What did that mean? Probably nothing. Melodrama, slight hysteria, the place was seething with it. A mild epidemic arising from creative overload and release from oppression. Understandable. But driftwood? It had come to something when ... most men in the room watched her go, he noticed, either surreptitiously or not. And it was a big room. And most of the watchers were teachers, colleagues who knew her, saw her every, yes, working day. He wondered again how many of them had tried it on, just how many had the nerve? He'd had the nerve. He belched softly, tasting hops, garlic and mussels. No fishes on the board today. Mussels were perfectly acceptable of course, when there was no fish. Driftwood? Absurd. She'd soon see. His internal situation yearned for further intoxicant.

The Barracuda was delayed for an age somewhere in the mass of teachers, and by the time she made it back the driftwood was history. This was how it was. She rattled on about Hardwicke's College again, the further machinations of management. Stan took a long, grateful pull at his beer – they'd changed the barrel - made sure he was seen to be listening carefully, pushed what had happened to the back of his mind, aware it was getting pretty cluttered back there.

Another long swallow and his blood was rushing, he could feel it, his blood was on the charge. He waited for indications of a lull, then sidetracked her neatly into a show of admiration for the chocolate cake on the table between them, then for the impulsive generosity of youth, then:

'Barra, I had a meeting with Ray. It's on again. They're definitely showing it again. No, really. It's going ahead Liza, no ifs and buts this time.' He'd stopped breathing. Another miscalculation?

Those great eyes, he thought, not for the first time, how was it they were always so wide-open? Hardly human eyes at all, when you looked really closely. Not that you did, when they were on full beam. Hungry eyes. Eyes that see too much. Eyes that see things which aren't necessarily there.

She was sipping wine relentlessly, and nodding to herself.

'Oh, fancy that. Searching my feeble old memory now, but I've a vague idea I might have heard that before somewhere.'

'Yeah, I know.' It wasn't going too badly. 'What can I say? This time there's no doubt, Delyth was there. It'll pay our way Barra, handsomely. But you can believe it when you see it, how's that?'

She leaned forward. 'Look, what do you want me to say? I hope you're right, of course I do, but even if you don't get the sorry-there's-been-a-change-of-plan call and it does go ahead, it's not going to bring back the happiest memories of our life together, is it? Don't expect me to dance on the table. And don't give me that hurt look. Life's moved on, we've moved on, haven't we? I have anyway. Don't expect me to watch or anything, but it's in the past, the little witch-bitch is history, so I'll just be pleased for you and hope it gives you a kick up the arse, you never know.'

She smiled and thrust forward her glass. 'Believe it when we see it, OK. But whether it happens or not, the countdown to the Indian Ocean has started, right? To the Papalinas!'

They clinked, and her face softened. When her eyes went like this, when the fire went out, when they looked deep into him, he found her as irresistible as he always had. Still the raucous, gangly Sheffield schoolgirl who could never blend in, never stay quiet and never steer clear of upset.

'It is going to do the trick for us Stan, isn't it? We are going to be all right?'

'What man will stop us?'

She smiled her glorious smile, but the softness, which never lasted long, had gone already.

Stan sat once more in his workroom, thinking about work. He was staring at the powder-blue surgeonfish, references open next to the keyboard, noble hound dozing on the floor beside him.

Sharks were back in the news with three attacks off northwestern Australia, a great white they thought, and he was to knock out a piece on shark attacks and protection measures, in the popular style. At least, that had been his starting point. He'd been side-tracked into more engrossing but nevertheless legitimate research: bringing up to date his inventory of the recorded stomach contents of tiger sharks. Since his time on Tsaramaso this had always been a name to send his blood on its way with a bit more zip. The tiger shark, *Galeocerdo cuvier,* was called the maneater of the tropics, for which there was undeniable justification: whereas in more temperate waters the demonised great white certainly killed people, it didn't as a rule eat them. It had flourished, on the evolutionary time-scale, alongside marine mammals such as dolphins, elephant seals and sea-lions, and these were its preferred prey. The tiger, on the other hand, would eat almost anything, as was illustrated effectively enough in *Jaws.* What was it Chief Brodie said, when the car licence-plate (an item on his list) came clattering out on a smoking tide of digestive fluid, about the rest of the car being in there? Small tigers had a liking for sea-snakes; but they didn't stay small. This dusky-barred, square-snouted brute, with its rows of oddly shaped and ever-ready teeth able to slice through turtle shell and shark hide, grew reliably to five and a half metres in length, although the usual selection of chilling tales had them bigger. This was the species which had fascinated Stan most during the shark studies with Easterhouse on Tsaramaso. They hadn't seen many, none of them less than ten feet long, but he'd never been able to get as close as he somehow felt he ought to. They seemed so detached, so implacable, so dedicated to the task of being tiger sharks ... and when they got up towards twenty feet long, over a ton in weight, they'd passed beyond being fishes. Or perhaps they'd become *the* fish. He'd seen enormous whale sharks in Papalinas waters - magnificent, majestic, larger than any tiger could ever dream of being, but they didn't have the same effect. Tigers had been among the sharks recently discovered lying perfectly still (still!) on the floor of submarine caverns in the Gulf of Mexico, apparently enjoying the narcotic effect of seawater abnormally low in salinity. This was his kind of fish. At night on Tsara he'd taken to going out to the nearest lagoon channel, Passe Femme, with a torch, even wading out into the rushing waters, searching for a wide-based dorsal fin, a tall, sweeping tail, a silent grey bulk ... tigers came into the lagoon after dark, hunting for turtles, rays, other sharks. This was their time.

Eventually he circled reluctantly back down towards the place where his work was waiting, and there was the powder-blue. Perhaps he should put a tiger on his screen, instead of this soothing, herbivorous reef fish. It would provide stimulation. With a sigh he clicked his way back to where he was supposed to be. The shark fossil record was three times as long as that for the big box-office dinosaurs, one hundred times as long as that for man, Guardian of the Biosphere. This meant they were fairly solidly here first. One estimate of many suggested that for every Guardian killed by sharks, the Guardians wasted anything up to two million sharks – most of these were harmless little would-be sharks, dogfish and so on, but it was pretty one-sided. His article was taking shape. Checking a list of references his eye inevitably strayed, and there it was: Easterhouse, J.A.F. (1986) *Life cycle of sharks at Tsaramaso Atoll, Indian Ocean.* No mention of Blackster, S. Even after all this time he could feel himself getting worked up.

He and Julius had designed the study between them, under the Prof's supervision, and he had done half the work, to start with anyway. Time and again he'd set out in a five metre boat with local boatman and guide and all their gear, into never-ending wind and saltwater, out in often alarming seas - forget health and safety - involved in several near-misses the Director never heard about, always at the very least getting soaked and chilled, then parboiled when the sun got up, and exhausted … and then, after too many such trips, he couldn't cope with the killing any more. There had been other things going on too. It had never been an easy situation down there, even at the best of times, with a clutch of disparate but – Stan apart – ambitious young post-graduates, including a couple of women whose civilising influence had been negligible, all struggling to get along on this harshest and most remote of atolls. Whatever else might be happening around them, their one imperative was The Study: the atoll's geological history, its rainfall and weather patterns; the structure of its vegetation; the hydrodynamics of its lagoon system; the biology and ecology of the giant tortoise, the dominant terrestrial animal; the phenology of its flowering plants; the breeding biology of its seabirds; the distribution of its insects; the ecology and impact of the feral goats. The life cycles of its sharks.

Even at the time he'd often found himself thinking, what are we doing here for christ's sake? It was grotesque. And heaven only knew what the native Linois staff made of it all. These Linois were native in the sense that they were citizens of the Papalinas, born and bred on the main islands hundreds of miles to the north, mostly Margaritifer and Dragonet. They had been sent down to Tsaramaso by the authorities to work for a set period of time. Roland was the exception, as he was to so much else. When he was drunk – which was often, despite station regulations – he would boast that he had been born on the atoll, that his family had always, always lived on Tsaramaso. And they would never, never leave.

It had been a peculiar and extremely volatile situation, which some had handled better than others. Weeks of daily routine would go by with nothing more than the usual overheated bickering of immature academics, then perhaps one night the innocent feet of a newcomer, out for a stroll or a sulk, would lead him down the wrong path. There would be a sighting, a half-sighting, a dizzying glimpse, of a scene which would turn perspective inside out. If a report were made – even if it were taken seriously – the Director would make no impression on Roland's obduracy. Fresh new faces would gradually realize that the balance of power at Tsaramaso was not what it seemed, not quite what had been described to them back home. The intermittent flare-ups, feuds and drunken fights between the Linois, with the occasional stabbing, provided the daily background to station life. Disputes were always settled in favour of Roland and his closest henchmen, who were all relatives. The Director was a pragmatist: the research station functioned, the assigned work was completed, the reports were produced; he would deal with problems among the research staff, Roland would look after the locals. They respected Roland. The Director's term of duty would come to an end, and Roland's dark stone-face, eyes too round and too pale and too close together, would watch him go. Roland, or one of his men, was always watching. Watching, judging, but never pronouncing, in the glaring heat, while palm leaves clattered faintly in the breeze.

Stan squirmed convulsively in his chair as an ant skittered lightly down his back. No, no ants in the British winter. Sweat. He should drag his mind back.

He'd had to leave Tsaramaso prematurely; not that he'd been the first, and presumably not the last, but even after all these years his feelings were of failure, of having been judged and found wanting; of having been expelled. Easterhouse had stayed on to complete the work with someone press-ganged from another project, and had published as sole author. Stan was relegated to the acknowledgements, 'for valuable assistance during the initial stages'. The Barracuda had urged him to have it out with Easterhouse, but what was the point? He had failed, and there was no way round it; and besides, there was a little more to it than she needed to know. Julius had unwaveringly pursued his academic self-interest, and Stan had retired injured from serious scientific endeavour, limping off into more imaginative and demanding areas. Come to think of it, he hadn't come across the name Easterhouse in the scientific literature for some time. It seemed unlikely that such a spotless *ubermensch* would ever hit the rocks, but you could always hope. Julius had never tanned, never sweated and he never - but never - got dirty. Impossible but true. He could see him now, thin lips unsmiling, cold grey eyes in the white Easterhouse face, the incongruously jaunty African hat sitting there like a joke. How he'd longed, back then, to see Julius go sprawling full-length in the mangrove mud, just once. But he never had. It seemed wildly surreal now that Julius had ever undergone a juvenile phase, a brief period of drink, drugs, jazz (incredible) and outlandish dress, of which the multicoloured hat was the sole reminder.

His eye, roving freely now, came to rest on the framed photo of himself with the Barracuda and a young Gram, taken by Shanny outside Hillsborough, all three of them kitted out in Owls colours, blue and white, Liza looking posed and exotic, like a model on location. In the ground she'd always given as good as she'd got from the usual handful of idiots, but he and Shanny had had to get involved more and more, and in the end she'd packed in going. In fact this photo recorded it, the day of her last visit. Grimsby Town at home. The Town fans were waving their blow-up harry haddocks, which perhaps looked more like a hovering flock of psychedelic cod, but he'd tried hard to buy one. They wouldn't give up their haddocks. And they had the best badge, a trawler cruising above three haddocks rampant. How had the Blacksters ended up in Sheffield, so far from the sea? The Original Blackster must have swum up the Humber, surged into the Trent and battled up the Don with the determination of a salmon.

Well, Liza wasn't missing much these days. Wednesday were struggling, as they liked to put it, at the bottom of Division One, which since the reshuffle meant Division Two. They'd been in the almighty Premiership – their rightful place, everyone agreed - not long back, and now Division Two loomed, which was really Division Three. Division Three. Shanny had called to confirm that he'd got tickets for the Southampton game. Shanny had always been the real Owls fan, Stan more the armchair sort. Next to the Hillsborough photo was one of

Gram and Kato in Riverside Park, comparing gormless smiles. *Pink Panther and the Grievous Angel* had been scrawled across it in felt-tip by the Barracuda. She liked the films, with Burt Kwouk as the inept manservant, and she'd had a thing about Gram Parsons. Next to it was a more curious object - the yellowing skull of a ferret. It had been given to him by Kim one day with no explanation, just one of her quick grimaces, a small gift, the kind of thing she did. He frowned at the memory. They'd been close then. Too close, maybe. She'd been like ... no, not a daughter, it was hard to say what, and he didn't want to think about it. He brushed awkwardly at another runnel of sweat, and tried to re-direct his thoughts, but Kim had rippled through them and was gone, and he was left with a momentarily overwhelming sense of loss.

A good luck charm, he'd told the Barracuda at the time. A ferret's skull? What sort of good luck is a ferret's skull going to bring anyone? He stared at the powder-blue surgeonfish again floating on the computer screen, at the keyboard, scanner, printer, calculator, power-pack, phone/fax, photocopier, discs, files, reports, papers and reference texts, all fairly neatly in order. Further along sat a heap of pads, pencils, pens, tippex, stapler, loose leaves, folders, music and video tapes surrounding a big, black ghetto blaster – this was the setting for the activities of his more creative other half, AB Defduf. A bottle was tucked away there, and a nicely-weighted shot glass. The wastepaper bin was overflowing. Stan felt more comfortable over there. He wanted to go over there now. His technical writing was becoming less rigorous and more ... creative. To hold his interest there had to be more than a straight version of events. Most people felt the same these days. It was a natural development. They wanted more, an insight, something to give the facts a lift.

He pushed off in the executive chair and the noble hound jerked out of his slumbers and looked up, tail thumping the floor.

'You know very well it's too early Flash. Don't try it on.'

Gram was moving around upstairs. In the past he would come down for a chat, to see how his old dad was getting on, discuss whatever topic he was working on. These days he stayed out of the way. He'd thought he'd found the interruptions tedious, but he missed them. Reaching the blaster, he rummaged for a tape and pushed it in, dug out bottle and shot glass and poured pale blended BNJ - Baillie, Nichol, Jarvie. Roy Estrada's clacking bass, the ambling rise and fall of a 3-note piano line, then Ray Collins' deeply sincere 50s croon: *For you I could do anything, for your love, my heart cries.* The Mothers, from *Cruisin' with Ruben and the Jets.*

The noble hound heaved a sigh. He knew this one. A song Liza used to help out with, singing the *Take my loves* and *La la lalas* behind Shanny up on the pub's music room stage, swaying Motown style. *Take my heart, my love, my everything. For so long, I've needed your love.* Glorious. But as the sax came in and he gnawed at a finger it was Kim he was trying not to think of.

The tape clicked. He held an empty glass.

Rubbing his face, he snapped off the player and towed himself back across to the computer screen. There was work to be done. He settled himself, cleared the powder-blue, and applied himself once more to sharks.

Fatality rates - the percentage of those people attacked who died - were strikingly higher off Natal than off California or the Eastern Cape, due it was thought to the different species involved: tigers and bull sharks in the warmer waters off Natal, man-biting great whites further from the tropics. In fact Natal beaches had been extensively protected by nets from the mid-1960s, and attacks there had been virtually eliminated. Sydney beaches were netted earlier, and in the two years preceding World War Two fifteen hundred sharks were killed there, including 900 'potential maneaters'. Sheer slaughter. And it went without saying the nets didn't kill only sharks. A more reasonable argument could be advanced for encouraging the public to accept the very remote possibility of shark attack as a natural if prickly part of the whole sun, sand 'n' surf package, while leaving the persecuted sharks to go about their sharkly business as they had been doing without complaint for the previous 100 million years, before the Guardians of the Biosphere finally evolved and showed up.

He would recommend that the magazine conducted a poll, to establish the number of modern-day risk-takers among its readership. This was the kind of thing they would go for, the kind of thing news agencies were likely to pick up. But his attention was already exhausted, and he eased off down a more interesting sidestream: northwestern American Indians believed a woman carried off by a shark then returned as one. And here, the same belief, that a person could be re-incarnated as a shark, but this time with the duties of guarding relatives and family resources on the reef. He liked that, the family thing. Sustainable. That should go in. But a question occurred to him: would a shark, stylish by definition, necessarily make a stylish person? Solomon Islanders told of a woman giving birth to a shark.

Wouldn't the reverse be more intriguing? His musings were interrupted by a thumping sound.

The tail of the noble hound was signalling an urgent need for activity.

Stan roused himself and clicked the powder-blue away, then reached down to tug at the grinning hound's ears. 'You want something, don't you, Flash? I can tell. You want it now. You don't know what, but you don't care, it doesn't matter. Anything, eh, as long as it's now.' Kato yipped, and made a great production of struggling to his feet. He seemed to stiffen up these days after the long spells lying down which made up the bulk of his life. 'Come on then old feller, let's go for a cruise, eh?' Stan put his lips to a soft, hairy ear. 'You'll be seeing your old friend Kim tonight, old dab, how about that?' *Episode One – The Aspidont* loomed at last. Kato yipped and pulled free. He never had liked her.

'Yep, that's Kim right enough. No half-measures.'

The noble hound sat at the door, huffing desperately, staring up at the handle.

Stan sat alongside the Barracuda on the settee, sunk well down. She was going to watch after all, or at least try, for his sake. The noble hound was in position at their feet. Gram had come down from his room and sat alongside in a chair, sulking. He and his father had been discussing world affairs.

Gram had been following the saga of the wretched Chagos islanders, and had a copy of a recent *Hansard*: an article in the *Times* by Matthew Parris had described how the UK government had pretended there was no native population so they could be expelled to allow the Americans in. Everyone knew this already, but Gram's disgust, and bewilderment, were aimed at his father's lack of agitation. He'd been out there, he'd worked out there, for God's sake! Chagos was a thousand miles away from the Papalinas, but it was near enough. He knew the people, he had friends out there, he liked them, what about Bernard, he admired Bernard, used to talk about him a lot, and they were the same people, Creoles, all those islands lumped together, the British Indian Ocean Territories, why aren't you involved, why aren't you helping them, you're a journalist, you could have helped.

This was how the Barracuda gene showed itself in Gram. Forceful. Passionate. Aggressive even, when it was something he cared about. He explained his position, that this is what humans did, this is what they've always done. Humans took. They took from everything, including each other. 'Growth' was the word they used, a concept requiring no justification, the most fundamental right. Consequently they always had to have MORE. It was like objecting to the colour of the sea. Gram had heard it all before. There was more to it than that, you had to believe something could be done, and it was up to people with concerns and insight, like Stan, to do it.

He would learn, but for now they sat in silence. At least he was here.

Apart from the dull glow of the screen the room was in darkness, leaving the four of them to their various thoughts. In two minutes Boscanion would begin his adventures for the second time. He would meet the Aspidont. Liza had decided that to ignore and avoid this major event in their lives would be childish and disloyal. It wasn't easy for Stan either, and it was better she didn't realize that. A couple of shots of BNJ had been sent down to quell his wriggling stomach and he was already uncomfortably warm, even in an equatorial weight T-shirt. Here came AB Defduf's big moment; which should have been a dismal thought after five fruitless, drifting years, but he was tingling. He'd put a lot into this, maybe too much. His youth. His confidence. And they told him it hadn't worked. The Barracuda had never really got over it either, despite what she might say – after all, she'd believed all his guff, swallowed the lot. It had taken a large bite out of her youth too, if not her confidence. He felt a spurt of resentment of his own - he'd believed all Ray's guff. No, he couldn't say that. He'd believed himself. It was just a TV show, dozens of them on every day. He needed to calm himself down. Further intoxicant was regrettably out of reach in the flickering dark. He tried to hold the image of a powder-blue surgeonfish, but it was as though he'd been rushed back through the past five years.

Kim really had been an unanticipated complication. How could anyone have anticipated Kim? Sometimes, when he was feeling at his most demersal, he tried to recall how the story of *Insidiator* had evolved, how and why it had changed, how it had become an attempt to replay awkwardness and a thousand missed connections - failure, really - as some sort of gentle, if weird, romance. Hard to believe it had all come out of his head. Because it hadn't started out like that.

Easy enough to remember its beginnings on the page, the light-hearted and harmless goings on in the life of an absurd and hardly original figure called Boscanion – typical biology student stuff. A young Barracuda and her friend Alice, both artists, had done the illustrations, Ray and Julius (Jules at that stage) had looked it over and offered suggestions. Ray, even then a hopeless SF and Fantasy bore and amateur film-maker, had later abandoned a career in chemistry and barged his way into the world of radio, where at length he'd managed to get a heavily-edited 60-minute version of a Boscanion escapade broadcast. This was a laugh, everyone agreed, and some money had rolled into the newly-invented AB Defduf's bank account. Ray had surged unstoppably onwards into TV drama, and Stan had been dragged along. Ray was a believer. He encouraged Stan to write more, although his continual attempts to grab the steering wheel had to be firmly resisted. Ray was soon manoeuvring for a screen version, and eventually got his way. Easterhouse meanwhile had abruptly grown up, and had long since withdrawn into the academic world, but Alice still sometimes put in an appearance. One day during pre-production Alice brought with her a curious little would-be actress friend called Kim.

The storyline developed, changed, and Boscanion was propelled into a decaying equatorial world, appropriately populated, and *Insidiator* became a dream-like story told by a book which, or who, besides maintaining a narrative, delved regularly into the airy recesses of Boscanion's mind to express a hero's deepest hopes and fears. Ray had marshalled smoke, mirrors and stirring sound effects to augment a handful of actors and flimsy sets, all in the grand *Doctor Who* manner. The result was a tour-de-force, or such was the consensus of those involved. The Book's voice, learned and sonorous, generally mournful, with outbursts of *Blake's Seven's* Orac-style peevishness, was provided by ace thespian Charles Chinchard, who had soon perfected a suitable cod-Arabic accent. Charles naturally also took the part of the hero, Boscanion himself, with, even the critics agreed, consummate aplomb. Charlie had been another one to get too involved though, another one to put in too much of himself.

The Barracuda's strong brown hand held his in a fierce grip. He wondered what was going through Gram's mind, what memories were surfacing for him as he sat there in the dark staring at the screen. Or was he still sulking? Gram had loved Boscanion, right from the start, even though he'd only been ten or eleven years old when it was all going on. Boscanion had been part of the family, for a while, and Gram had looked up to him, admired him, if that was the right word for a ten year old. Maybe they should have aimed it at ten year olds. And Kim seemed very – not fond, you couldn't say that – interested in Gram, still not quite the right word, but Gram never mentioned her. Gram was very sensitive to his mother's feelings, and she hadn't kept them to herself when it came to Kim.

He wanted to rip off this T-shirt, badly wanted to get up for a BNJ, but it was too late: the eerie music, brimming with memories, crept into the darkened room. They were being taken slowly along a gloomy corridor echoing to a single set of footfalls; glimmering greenish light issued from a series of glass spheres set high along the walls, each containing an imprisoned fire-drake; there were scuttling sounds and ambiguous shadows. The music ebbed. Slowly down stone steps, into the suggestion of a vast room, where a lone fire-drake illuminated a marble table set with a single, high-backed chair. At the dim edge of the green light, rank upon rank, row upon row of books led away into the dark. In place, before the chair, lay a great red book. The chair scraped back, creaked with a settling weight. The book's cover, wine-red, glossy and supple, bore at either side a heavy brass clasp and, in relief, a slumbering face. Overfull, curving red lips twitched, red eyes slowly opened. The face frowned ponderously, and a reedy voice spoke the old Malagasy word, the invitation to enter:

'Mandroso.'

The red brow furrowed, the red face assumed an expression of concentration. The brass clasps fell open, the cover lifted vertically to reveal a title page.

INSIDIATOR

Liza abruptly released his hand, got to her feet and left the room. Kato struggled up and padded after her. Stan sneaked a look at Gram's staring, flickering face, fixed on the screen.

The title page drifted up and to the side, and here began the text, neat lines of bold, unidentifiable marks and symbols. An image slowly took form over it, of a dim, dark forest. Speaking very distinctly, in a rich and world-weary voice which echoed very faintly only at the outset, The Book began its translation …

4. The Aspidont

On the forest floor sprawled a lanky figure, long black hair in disarray, the unconscious face strikingly adorned with downcurving black moustache and small black beard. At the edge of the glade shadows moved purposefully in the gloom. Groaning, the man pushed himself slowly to his feet and looked groggily about.

'Urnngh. Ah.' Then: 'And what place is this?' His full, deep voice resounded in the rustling quiet of the forest. More quietly: 'Some form of alcoholic delirium, no doubt temporary. Still, it would be imprudent to ignore a pressing sense of unease. Onward then.'

For three hours Boscanion walked, aware of snickerings and half sounds at his back, occasionally closer and off to the side, and of flickers of movement in the blur of dark and ancient tree trunks. And still his hair stood stiffly at attention, despite his best attempts to bring it back under some control. With a snort he pulled from his pack a wide-brimmed hat of a dusty, wine-red colour.

'I hear you!' he announced presently. 'I hear you, lurkers in the shadows. Now, observe - I am protected!' While causing his eyes to bulge in threatening fashion he flung wide both arms without breaking stride, making a series of meaningful passes in the air, to no obvious effect. The snickerings were stilled, nonetheless. Boscanion smirked in grim satisfaction. 'Such bamboozling will not hold them for long,' he muttered. 'Darkness will make them bolder.' He threw up a glance. The skies, heavy with cloud, were illuminated by a dramatic but perceptibly fading purple light. Boscanion turned, bared large white teeth in an actorly grimace, then resumed his long-legged striding.

Waning sunlight filtering through the lichen-dripping trees, coupled with an annoying series of sibilant but increasingly intrusive whispers at the edge of hearing, marked the passage of time. At length Boscanion came upon a story-book cottage in a clearing, welcoming orange lights aglow. Bothersome crepuscular insect life was beginning to make itself known as he made his way through damp, knee-length herbage and pushed with some difficulty through a belt of heavier air which glowed briefly at his passage. Inside the barrier were none of the disagreeable night-fliers and he ceased beating with his wine-red hat.

He turned to look back. An improbably large and ragged black shape flapped and swooped over the forest. Boscanion stroked at his hair with minimal effect, then gnawed absently at a forefinger as he considered his prospects.

'Greetings to all within!' he eventually boomed.

The heavy door, bearing a crudely worked and weathered flying bird, possibly of the crow tribe, drew silently open.

'I see you.'

The voice was quiet, as though speaking from a far place, the speaker concealed from view.

'I am, as you will recognize, a lone but not unsophisticated traveller,' Boscanion purred, beaming his best actor's smile, 'presently seeking shelter from the prowlers of the forest night.'

'Jactators. Whiptails. Knifejaws. Terrops. Simple creatures, with simple cravings. Inside you will not be molested. Enter.'

Boscanion flexed his long, angular frame to pass the threshold, finding himself in an oddly large and bare room. His host regarded him from what seemed an unlikely distance. He - it was clearly a male voice - was tall and concealed within flowing garments of green, white and yellow, exactly the colours of sunlight on forest leaves. In the blank green face, startling white circles around the eyes contained impenetrable silver-green discs; the leaf-green skull was disconcertingly tall above these non-eyes, and squared off at the top; the mouth was a thin line of darker green.

So much could Boscanion discern, but there was a curious lack of clarity about this green face: he blinked to clear his vision but was still unable to register detail. 'Ahem. It is most hospitable of you to admit me. No doubt I would have got the better of these simple creatures, but as I always say, no matter how tall and secure the tree – '

'You are not at risk here. You will sleep,' announced the thin olive mouth in its thin, precise way, which was rather at odds with the overall summery tone. 'Tomorrow, you may continue on your way with renewed vigour and purpose.'

'Ah. Yes. There you hit upon a strange thing. I seem unable to quite remember just what, or where, my way is. An inconvenient truncation of the recent memory ...' Boscanion pronounced the words grandly, rolling his r's apparently out of habit. On the bare stone wall hung a highly polished metal plate, copper perhaps, possibly an outsize cooking implement of some sort. Moving towards it, which seemed to involve too many strides, he examined his appearance, and gasped. 'I really must apologise for this outlandish hair arrangement. I understand now the timidity of those ruffians in the trees. Jactators, did

I hear you say, and one or two other unsavoury types … ?'

'You have experienced some excitements,' observed his host. 'This can be a slippery place for the unwary, for those not fully alert. An aggressive hairstyle is insufficient protection.'

'Well,' considered Boscanion, who was beginning to detect the faintest whiff of mockery, 'as a newcomer I am naturally eager to acquire such local knowledge as will ease my path. Excitements? Yes, quite possibly. I remember the forest, your charming residence, and before that … ' He inspected his reflection: the customarily dramatic black moustache and chin beard, which together he liked to term 'imperial', were in sore need of attention.

The tall green figure made a sound which may have been a sigh. 'You have been removed from your accustomed and most appropriate location, and deposited here. Do not be overly concerned. You will inevitably be drawn back to your native place. I fully expect you to awake with purpose. Tomorrow.'

'Ah. Yes, I do have a sense of … dislocation. Your predictions are most reassuring. I have no recollection of events leading me to this gloomy forest, but my mind clings to an image, of a circle, set in blue. The circle is incomplete. And the sensation of having been ejected - physically spat out, as it were - hangs over me like a cloud. Most peculiar.'

'Perhaps. I have learned that at certain points in the world material is continually drawn in for re-configuration and eventual expulsion. It may be that you drew too near such a node.'

The figure had moved silently behind Boscanion, but induced no image in the polished metal. The tall green head gave a slow nod, perhaps of encouragement. Boscanion felt almost sure he could now discern a glint, or glimmer, deep within each of the silver-green eye-discs inside their bizarre white eye-circles, this by employing his keen peripheral vision.

'Ah.' he nodded wearily. 'Are you saying I have been re-configured? It all sounds rather demanding, and I'm sure you're right, but I am unable to apply my proper focus just now. And perhaps an imposing weapon of some type would add weight to my prospects. I shall inspect a selection in the morning. It would be of some comfort to me though, in addition to the courtesy you have shown me already, if you could provide more detailed guidance. Then we may sit down together and take our evening refreshment. Possibly your cellar boasts a variety of intoxicating beverages … ?'

Just then the green lips spoke certain words. Boscanion's eyes glazed and he swayed, collapsing gently into a deep blue darkness which folded comfortably around him.

Next morning a pale orange sun suggested itself over the forest to the east as Boscanion opened the door and peered out. He was refreshed and had evidently eaten and slept well, but was quite unable to recall details, or in fact anything. He was a traveller, so much he knew, and should thank the master of this homely house, but there was no-one to be found. The interior seemed little more than a single, surprisingly large room, uncluttered with indications as to the nature of its occupant. Still, he had found facilities to bathe and attend to his moustache and beard, in which it would be perverse not to take pride. His hair though … still it framed his emphatic features with a wild black corona.

Now he looked out over the glade, silvery with dew, and produced the class of smile he privately considered forceful, even charismatic.

'I thank the master of this house for his hospitality to a traveller here in the forest. If one day by chance our paths should cross again, I shall doubly repay the courtesy.' Some black birds, quietly foraging in a far corner, took to the air with irritable croaks. 'So, now I fare forth!'

Pulling on his wide-brimmed red hat and taking up his pack, he left the cottage and pushed once more through the springy resistance of reinforced atmosphere where two substantial heaps of grey-white ash lay, smoking gently.

'Boscanion is once more on his way!' he called, to no-one in particular. His sturdy, air-cushioned boots, burnished to a somewhat meaty gloss at some point during the night, carried him without hesitation into the looming forest and off down the narrow trail towards the low, molten glow of the new day's sun.

The day passed uneventfully enough, and the dreary black trees eventually thinned and fell behind. Boscanion halted at a broad but shallow stream coursing out onto an expanse of red plain pocked with granitic outcrops and boulders. Here, by dint of concealment and careful observation, he caught and killed a cautious but slow-moving crab-like creature possessing two pairs of formidable, pincer-style claws, fortunately all deployed forwards, which when cracked open provided a rich meat with only the briefest whiff of ammonia. Nearby grew watercress. As he lay drowsing, Boscanion discovered that the utterances necessary to erect a sphere of safety for the night lay within his brain.

Next morning a small column of men with beasts appeared, a caravan picking its way carefully along the edge of the forest. They paused to water the fretful, camel-like pack animals close to the point Boscanion had reached, and eyed him warily across the rippling grey waters: six men, bearing a miscellany of crude but threatening weaponry. Opening a shouted conversation with them proved difficult, owing to taciturnity and feigned deafness, so, grumbling, Boscanion waded across.

'Good day to you! I am Boscanion, a traveller in the world, delighted to find fellow wayfarers out on this dreary plain, forlorn and wild, and to see that you move with such evident purpose.'

The headman had unsettling golden eyes and rather complicated headgear which involved curving earflaps, a row of brassy discs, and a dried, boxlike spiny fish fixed somehow to the top. He grunted. The others said nothing: they too had eyes of the same, lion-like colour.

'Why do you trouble us?' asked the headman eventually. His face, in common with those behind him, was heavy-featured, grim, burned the colour of cooked crabshell and bearded with unkempt, straw-like bristles. Boscanion was encouraged to see he had a drinker's nose.

'I seek only stimulation, good company, the unfettered hospitality of the open road, a degree of harmless and possibly inspirational intoxication around the evening campfire ... in short, I should like to join your caravan for a period.'

'What do you offer?' Already, members of the band were busy tugging and kicking at the guzzling pack animals, which were crouching on queerly angled forelegs, hindquarters raised; they clearly preferred to be left in peace, and raised a ponderous, hooting outcry.

Boscanion considered. What could he offer?

'Deft and far-ranging conversation. Untold hours of anecdotes and droll tales. As conviviality proceeds, I might perform a small drama for the company, recite poetry ... '

'Angs?' The headman eyed Boscanion's pack, clearly sceptical. 'Have you angs?'

'Angs, you say? Not presently, but at my destination I anticipate - '

But the headman turned away, taking up a heavy shaft topped with various slicing, stabbing and gouging projections. The group formed a shambling column and moved sullenly off, the pack beasts with much foot-dragging and angry hooting.

'Also, I am a fully accomplished wizard!' shouted Boscanion, projecting his actor's voice through air now thick with dust, the jingling sounds of harness and the chunterings of man and beast. 'I can house you in utter safety from the brigands and beasts of the night!'

The last pink and gold light faded to lavender, then quickly through grey to black, as the caravan set up camp and prepared food in practised fashion. Boscanion sat by the spluttering branches of the fire, sucking reflectively on a long bone ridged either side with cartilaginous protrusions which proved quite impervious to human teeth, even his own. He had been given to understand by the headman, Harak, the only one so far to address him, that he was present under sufferance, and would be given food and water but no more for the duration of the three day march to the coast, at which point the caravan would have reached its destination and the relationship would be dissolved. In return, Boscanion would assume full responsibility for camp security. A cloudy and evidently fiercely potent beer was, exasperatingly, strictly reserved for original members of the expedition.

The night sky was brilliant with stars. Boscanion pondered their configurations, and experienced a confusing surge of emotion. 'Starry, starry night,' he muttered, puzzled, then again, 'Starry, starry night.' A lazy sound wound up out of the darkness, to him like the sound of a ping-pong ball bounced repeatedly on a table, the tempo increasing over several seconds, then silence, then the same again. Boscanion's curiosity was pricked, and not just by the sound. A ping-pong ball? A term without meaning. He experienced an urge to leave the camp and seek out the source of the sound, but felt this would not be wise. Something small and dark - a night bird? - flitted at the furthest edge of the flickering firelight.

Eventually the sound, repeated over and over, became maddening, and Boscanion drifted into fitful unconsciousness. At some point he was roused by a ripping sound as something tried to gain entry, followed by the brief illumination of his fence and a softly explosive *whoosh!* Boscanion nodded dreamily but was too weary to investigate.

After three days without significant event - fights among group members, apparently over angs, were watched by Boscanion from a respectful distance - the coast was achieved: a narrow, hazy blue line grew in thickness, the curling white stripes of breakers came into focus and their soft whispering became a muffled thunder as the air assumed invigorating properties, lifting all their spirits. Harak became voluble, although not to Boscanion, and even the beasts ceased their complaints.

The township of Kilwa, home to the caravaners, proved to be sprawling, run-down and seriously underpopulated, the poor houses evidently constructed via robbery of existing buildings, which in turn had been put together utilising the shells of earlier, more worthy structures. Boscanion found somewhere to replenish himself. Once an inn, a title could still be discerned, possibly *Pwason Ba*, chiselled into the masonry of an ancient wall.

'Very quiet today,' he offered to the sullen figure serving his meal, a form of soup in which greyish items were adrift - prime Doubleheader, he was assured. Intoxicating beverages were, depressingly, off today's menu. 'Where is everyone?'

The man's dull golden eyes showed no interest in conversation. 'Where I should be myself.' He made to shamble off.

'Ah. If I have inconvenienced you ... and where is it you would rather be?'

The man paused reluctantly. He had the tall, powerful physique of all Kilwans, with the addition of a heavy paunch, and the same drab, animal-skin clothing. 'It is the hour at which we gather to observe the feeding of the Aspidont.'

Boscanion made a sound of understanding. A negligent flourish of his empty hand left a brassy, red-gold disc on the crusted table: an ang, one scale of a mightily-armoured marine creature, itself called Ang, deified by the Kilwans. The owner of these rare tideline scales, for which all Kilwans hunted and fought, had by all accounts never been seen. At least, never as such.

This unsuspected ability to produce local coin from thin air Boscanion had incorporated without difficulty into his repertoire.

The following day, after a morning's inspection of the sights of Kilwa, Boscanion fell in with the general movement towards the seaward edge of town, there to witness the feeding of the Aspidont. The town's full muster was barely fifty, with no evidence of children. A further half-dozen, of strikingly un-Kilwan appearance, did not leave a small compound on the outskirts except to perform agricultural labour, for which they were solely responsible. These individuals did not speak, and appeared drugged or entranced.

Boscanion arrived to find the Aspidont had already emerged - or more likely been forced - from its crude, stone-walled shelter, or cage, into a small and squalid sunken arena. He saw a form basically human, with the size and proportions of a youth, greyish-pink in colour and without clothing. Prominent ribs were further emphasized by dusky shading. Long, strangely stiff hair of indeterminate colour fanned back in an impressive crest from an oddly shaped head. The features of a female, though poorly formed, were there for all to see, despite the best efforts of the Aspidont to conceal them. It walked upright, torso tilted slightly forward, clearly aware of an expected pattern of behaviour. There was a general murmuring from the crowd, in the terse local manner, with an occasional shouted comment:

'Down! Down on all fours, where you rightly belong!'

The Aspidont made no response.

'What is the creature's history?' enquired Boscanion of a lion-eyed onlooker. No response. Perhaps, above the murmuration, he could not be heard. He coughed loudly. 'My good Kilwan, pray enlighten an ignorant traveller.' The man looked round, reluctantly. Boscanion deployed his most ingratiating smile. 'I sense a certain ill-will towards this outwardly pitiful, naked creature. Why so?'

'It is not a pitiful creature. It is an Aspidont,' came the firm declaration. 'That is sufficient.'

Boscanion already suspected the women of the town to be less truculent than the men. One now stepped forward.

'She - it - lived among us, took our food. Harak himself it chose. In time he made his discovery. Now the disguise falls away.' A sour, aromatic reek accompanied this information. Boscanion took a fastidious step backwards. 'Aha.'

Harak, towering over the mass by virtue of his puff-fish-topped headgear, had moved to the edge of the shallow pit. From an assistant he took rope and lifted high a small, brown and black goat kid. Large, mangy-looking scavenging birds watched from a nearby rooftop. Beside them crouched a small, wiry black man, birdlike himself and no larger than the birds, apparently naked, gazing intently at events in the pit. A black crow sporting a bold white chest landed nearby to set up a furious croaking, directed at either the crouching man, his vulturine companions, or all of them together. Odd, thought Boscanion, but the chief of the Kilwans was declaiming:

'Ang of the Awesome Deep, who causes the oceans to rise up! Observe the preparation of true believers for your night to come!'

Harak was an imposing fellow. For the event, evidently the high point of a dismal Kilwan day, he had donned the jaws of some fearsome beast, wearing them on his chest. Boscanion was familiar enough with the headman's occasional outbursts of bombast, usually drink-fuelled as now, and had been studying the Aspidont. Despite the dusky skin-tone, a certain undeniable thickness at the joints and a shortness of neck, which restricted general flexibility, and the unfortunate face, the creature was to all outward appearances human. As though sensing his attention it lifted its head. Boscanion was shocked by the gaze which held his. The eyes were of the required golden, but of a very dim intensity, like lights guttering in darkness. The face was feral and the expression withdrawn. The jaws were unkindly exaggerated, thrusting forward the face in grotesque fashion.

'Do you know me?' muttered Boscanion. 'How can you know me?'

'Here creature!' bellowed Harak for the benefit of all. 'As a counterfeit Kilwan you have abused the open-hearted goodness of a noble and innocent folk. Now, you will serve our needs. Feed!'

The goat kid hit the floor in a bleating flurry of struggling limbs, and the Aspidont moved forward. The change was instantaneous and profound: from a detached and diffident being the Aspidont abruptly metamorphosed into an arrow of frighteningly focused ferocity, hurling itself in one movement to throw the terrified animal down, hold apart chin and breast and rip out the exposed throat in a display of savagery which left Boscanion clutching the fence.

'No!'

'Yes! Now the Aspidont drops its disguise!' crowed his reeking neighbour.

The crowd exulted in a mixture of emotions with which Boscanion could not identify and which left him uncomfortable. The Aspidont had satisfied its immediate needs and was towing the limp corpse to its squalid place of concealment. Again the creature sought him out, the brutish lower half of its face now red. He thought to see a yearning in the flat, dark gold eyes.

'Who are you?' he murmured.

The crouching man on the rooftop had gone. Only the scavengers waited there.

Two days later as Boscanion, now fully rested, prepared for his departure, he again found himself drawn to the seaward edge of town. Surf boomed in the background and huge black, sickle-winged pirate-birds wheeled overhead. Again he watched, fascinated, as the Aspidont killed and dragged off its meal, this time a large, flapping fish fresh from the sea. He learned from the evil-smelling crone Hamrur that the good folk of Kilwa would shortly present the Aspidont in sacrifice to almighty Ang, the feared deity of the depths who, at his whim, provided or withheld fish and currency, took or spared the lives of seafarers, lifted up or withdrew the very sea itself. It was the firm belief of all Kilwans that Ang had found reason for dissatisfaction with the people of the world, and was sending the waters to cleanse the land. Only they, the faithful Kilwans, were to be spared, on the understanding a proper gratitude be demonstrated and maintained. Ang himself, often in the form of a pirate-bird, was apt to visit Kilwa unexpectedly to seek reassurance on such matters. Fish was the mandatory final meal preceding such events, which custom dictated should take place at highest tide under the full moon. Hamrur, in delivering this glut of information to a stranger, was clearly becoming, or remaining, unpopular with her neighbours, and Boscanion moved off before difficulties arose.

'Some say the Aspidont lurks unseen in many folk,' reflected the crone, as her audience slipped away. Then, to herself. 'Even among true Kilwans. And in the final days we shall learn the truth.'

The Aspidont had paused in its tearing and gulping at the entrance to its den to watch Boscanion, as he abruptly became aware. Golden flecks glimmered in the flat, black eyes down there in the pit, like coins in a pool, tugging at his memory. He fretted.

'Why do you study me so? While I would agree you seem to have been harshly dealt with, this is the world's way, and there is nothing I can do to ease your situation.'

The eyes stared, looking deep into Boscanion.

'No,' he said definitely, a modicum of projection throwing his words into the pit. 'I do not know you, nor you me.'

Certain Kilwans had observed this largely inaudible discourse, and muttered together.

'I must depart,' he announced more carefully, 'lest I become your replacement in the pit.'

That night, his last in Kilwa, Boscanion slept badly, innards burbling with sour local beer, haunted by a feral, black-eyed face at once fearsome and pleading. Finally he arose, to wash, dress, attempt something with his hair, prepare his pack and make an early departure. He would pause at an agreeable spot on the road to take his breakfast. But ... on the road to where? The question of his destination nagged at him. How far? In what direction? Was he to simply keep walking until something unmistakable occurred? He was uncomfortable with this arrangement. However his excellent air-cushioned boots appeared eminently trustworthy. They had never let him down, insofar as he could recall. Now he considered them, he felt sure they had carried him with a certain quiet style through the latter stages of his presently obscure mature life. Yes, his excellent boots would find the way, and he had already lingered too long in this cheerless, inward-looking shanty-town.

The moon rode full and high, silvering the trampled byways of the town, which were deserted. Distant night sounds out on the plain could now and then be distinguished through the ceaseless surf booming, louder now with the surge of the peak tides. Boscanion became aware of a commotion and tracked it to the sunken pen. This, it now transpired, had been so constructed as to fill with seawater at higher tides by the simple lifting of a submerged sluice gate. Appropriate scattering of offal, fish guts and so forth would quickly attract predatory creatures accustomed to patrolling the marine shallows at night - not to say dusk and dawn - for town waste or, if fortunate, an unwary town-dweller or item of livestock. The traditional scheme was for one or more such brutes to travel the channel - at several hundred yards in length an insurmountable barrier to escape - lured by the flavours flowing forth, enter the pen and devour its occupant. All townsfolk had gathered to enjoy the occasion, able easily to view proceedings in full, stark moonlight. Only now, something was amiss.

Boscanion, ignoring a succession of hostile glances, sought out his informant Hamrur, trusting her to be at least as tipsy as was the broad mass about them. Harak the headman was readily identified, issuing loud instructions to an untidy team lowering ladders to the brimming, milky waters on which floated all manner of repulsive debris. Men descended carefully to prod with long, saw-tipped poles.

'A mishap?' hissed Boscanion.

'The Aspidont cannot be found,' declared the crone. 'They search for it now. It may have enshrouded a pocket of air below, surviving there. It will cling to life!'

There came a loud exclamation as a large, dark fin entered by way of the flooded subterranean channel, and the pole-wielders smartly ascended their ladders. The fin, trailed by the sideways sweep of a mighty tail, moved in unhurried fashion, patrolling methodically around the pool. All eyes, including Boscanion's, followed its progress intently.

'The Aspidont is no more!' cried Harak authoritatively at last, the man-eater having satisfied itself of the thin pickings available in the pool and, after a sluggish ingestion of floating offal - allowing onlookers at least a churning view of white underside, pink maw a-bristle with far too many teeth, and a disinterested round black eye - departed as it had appeared, with a final sweep of its tall, notched tail.

'Without doubt the vile creature attempted a desperate escape along the tunnel, and there met its end,' concluded Harak.

The crowd considered this, the low-level hubbub carrying unmistakable overtones of disappointment, even resentment. Harak held high a ceremonial hoop threaded with coconut half-shells.

'Ang is thus assured of the merit and obedience of his chosen people.' He fingered the jaws at his chest, which Boscanion now saw to closely resemble those so recently active in the pit. 'So may outsiders contribute to the best interests of all Kilwans!'

The headman seemed to be searching those gathered around, and Boscanion chose the moment to slip discreetly into the shadows.

It was some time before Boscanion felt reasonably safe from pursuit. He had at one point to whisk the night air into a shimmering curtain to deter a being of uncertain description lurking among a tumble of ancient boulders. Striding on after this demonstration and basking in a new sense of invulnerability, Boscanion shouted words of encouragement to his tirelessly marching boots.

The coastal vista of silver, black and steely grey became slowly suffused with colour as the sun made its appearance. Boscanion, or his boots, had decided to strike off to the north, keeping the glittering ocean at his right hand. Ahead stretched an endless coastal strip of white beach, outcrops of black rock and, set some way inland, a succession of low dunes mottled with coarse grasses, sheltering dark groves and thickets. Heat and glare were mounting, and he now donned his dusty red hat. His hair in recent days did appear at last to be responding to natural laws, falling gracefully around his shoulders in a more regal and appropriate arrangement.

For some time he had been aware of a figure keeping pace with him, maintaining its distance at around two hundred yards and making no real attempt at concealment. Its bearing, upright but tilted forward from the hips, which produced a slightly stiff, tottering gait, was familiar to him. He turned now and projected his voice through the noise of the breakers.

'My friend! The trail is long and the sun will soon be high. I am about to take pause for refreshment and rest. You are most welcome to join me, if you so wish!'

The figure was no longer in view, and Boscanion sat down on the lip of a large, shallow crater in the sand, from which the deep-dug tracks of some heavy sea-creature led a short distance to a smoothly shining strip of beach where waves had wiped the slate clean. With a flourish he took out a lump of cured fish and his trusty water bottle. Undulating lines of large white birds filed out to sea, low and occasionally close enough for the rush of air through long, stiffly held wings to be heard above the surf. Further out a party of glistening bodies, each with its hooked fin, broke the surface at intervals. Boscanion pulled off his indefatigable boots with some theatrical sighing, then wriggled his toes in the gritty white sand. The air tingled.

'A glorious affair,' he called out, aware now of his follower's approach. 'Life!' He slowly turned his head. 'Surely you find yourself in full agreement?'

The Aspidont stood a few paces off, resting lightly on the sand, upper body tilted slightly forward, arms akimbo, as though preparing to spring at him.

'Yes,' murmured Boscanion, taking in the startling face, with its look of immanent ferocity masking something more subtle. Then louder: 'Yes. You, especially, will surely savour this day.'

A crude leather garment of Kilwan style now covered the small female body.

'Please. Sit with me.' Boscanion made an easy gesture to the crater lip. 'Will you take some cured fish? Poor stuff, granted, but the finest to be had in the unfortunate township of Kilwa.'

He placed a curling brown segment carefully on his broad-brimmed hat, beside him on the sand, and pushed it forward. The Aspidont snatched, swallowed at a gulp, eyes never leaving his face. Boscanion next offered his bottle, but the Aspidont slid down into the crater and, burrowing with both hands, presently brought forth a number of round, white eggs. These it consumed whole, proffering one which Boscanion graciously declined.

He studied the intent features, the outsize, working jaws. The Aspidont's stiff crest of hair was darker now: oily - lustrous, one might almost say - and speckled with shining water droplets. Here was a fine day for hair! And those jaws were prodigious!

'My dear, I feel we know one another somehow, and yet I have no name for you. You must forgive me. My memory has of late been playing me small tricks. I am Boscanion.' He knew he must be wary, and flexed his fingers in the warm sand.

'My name is Boscanion.'

The voice was a surprise, low and husky, the words pronounced with some difficulty. For a long moment the jaws stopped and the wide-set black eyes regarded him. No glimmers of Kilwan gold there now. Yolk on the thin-lipped mouth was a startling orange-yellow.

Boscanion stroked his handsome black moustache, gnawed at a long forefinger.

'Aha. I am pleased to know you, although you cannot, I am afraid, be Boscanion. That is myself, and there can be only one. I feel though, that our futures are somehow entwined. Do you sense this also?'

There was the slightest of nods.

'Where you go?' The voice was thick, as though forcing its way through a congested windpipe.

'Ah. Hmm. You will be surprised, but I am currently unable to answer your perfectly sensible question. I can say only that my boots follow the correct path, of this I am certain.' He decided to try an encouraging smile.

The answering smile was quite unexpected, or perhaps it was a grimace, affording Boscanion a brief view of sharp pink tongue, somewhat pointed white teeth and masticated egg. The face immediately resumed its customary feral demeanour, but for a moment a girlish creature had stood before him, unquestionably. Fascinating. He must remain alert. Still …

'Will you accompany me for a while? I feel that we, a pair of outsiders, might benefit from the alliance. I have some small skills in the magic arts, allied to a probing intellect, a fund of amusing tales, and a keen interest in the human condition, ah, in all its myriad manifestations. You will find me irrepressible. For your part, you are clearly an adept in the essential art of survival in this curious world, and I expect you will prove an engaging companion, when you fully recover from your wretched recent past.' He cocked a thick, black eyebrow. 'Well, what is your response to my proposal? Will you unite your fortunes with mine, at least temporarily? And along the way, perhaps we can find you a name of your own.' Boscanion had on his broadest actor's smile, and was delighted to see again the quick, kittenish grimace.

'I come with you,' croaked the rusty voice.

'Splendid!' Boscanion shook sand from the rumpled red hat and pulled it on. He directed an intrepid gaze towards the way ahead, feeling absurdly pleased with himself.

The scene slowed and froze, began to dissolve into neat lines of glyphs. A vertical strip of red, figured in white with a stylized pair of circling sharks, formed at the centre. Pages fell soundlessly over this, the bookmark, and the fleshy red face slid back into place. Plump red lips yawned over red teeth, red lids lowered. The Book slept once more.

5. Shanny

The *Cunard* wasn't the nearest hostelry to the Dell, revered home of Southampton Football Club, but it was already busy, and only one blue and white shirt was showing in a scrum of red and white Saints fans.

'Now then Stanley, you old bugger. About bloody time. You're late. And where's your colours?' Shanny's abrupt Yorkshire bark boomed through the Hampshire burble. He folded his *Daily Mirror*. 'Want to know what bloody paper says? Reckons half our schoolkids think Adolf Hitler was a British Prime Minister. Every other kid, that is.'

The venerable Shanny, his old school chum, looked a good ten years older than his years. His short, muscular body, broad-shouldered and narrow-hipped, was topped off with a big, angry red face, made bigger and angrier now by retreating hairline, lifestyle and a multitude of aggravations; Shanny's scalp and jowls bristled and there were tattoos everywhere.

'Just half? Yeah, reassuring. You'll be ready for another then?'

No need to ask what Shanny was drinking. Shanny took nothing but Guinness, surely the most over-rated and overpriced drink going these days. The apotheosis of marketing, a giant con. He was looking old though, Shanny was. Old and mean.

FA Cup fourth round, and Wednesday had to fell Southampton who were somehow clinging on to life in the Premiership, or what folk like Shanny still called the First Division. The Owls were struggling, even though they still pulled the crowds, and an invigorating bit of giant-killing was just the ticket.

'Where's your lad then Stanley?' Shanny wiped away froth and rolled a cigarette, shoving the tin across the table.

Stan waved it away with a cigar. 'Not for me. You should move on to these, Shanny, give yourself a bit of class.' He applied a light. 'Gram'll be here' - he shot a look at his watch - 'in about forty minutes, give or take. He's not a drinker, our Gram.'

Shanny grunted, sucking away at the spindly roll-up. 'Aye. Not yet.'

They shouted at each other for a while about their chances, about recent injustices to come Wednesday's way, about the manager

Paul Jewell - on his way unless today saved him - then about dramas and doings back in Sheffield. Shanny had driven lorries long distance for the same local company since leaving school, but now they were in trouble and the recent fuel price rises meant anything could happen. Stan's old mum, Old Vera, up there in her little terraced house near Hillsborough wanted to know, why hadn't they been up to see her, Stan and Liza, with their Gram? Especially their Gram. Old Vera these days was a grey-haired, leather-lunged cackler who wore socks and slippers, still hated Tories, and always seemed to be watching snooker or *Coronation Street* on TV. Stan felt the pang of guilt, of course he did, and smiled at the memory, slightly shocking at the time, of the all-purpose, meaningless old-folk grin she'd developed on his last visit. She'd be stuck with it now - those grins never went away. And Vera had always been a scowler, known for her scowls. The grin meant exactly the same as the scowl, but it was a sign. Old Vera thought the world of Liza and Gram, naturally, and took every opportunity to berate him over his lack of appreciation. She'd told Shanny they should get themselves back up to Sheffield. Houses were cheaper up there. Life was cheaper up there. Cheaper and better. The invitation naturally included the noble hound, even though his visits left her with hairy carpets. She approved of Kato's manner, and the two of them got on very well.

Stan nodded, smiled, swallowed exemplary Pots ale, brewed here in Hampshire, blew smoke, shook his head, smiled and nodded. Into his mind had floated the image of Kim, looking up from the pit. Hell of an image. You didn't see images like that on TV now, did you?

More bodies thrust themselves into the packed and noisy pub. A small band of blue and whites had arrived, and stood in a tight cluster at the bar. Shanny nodded impassively across a roomful of smoke and bodies.

'Jeff Cairns and his lads,' he growled. 'Bloody nutters. They're after bother. Steer well clear.' He stood up, took their empties and burrowed off towards the opposite end of the long bar.

Stan drifted. Kim, or Anakim rather: it was an intriguing process, this evolution of the Aspidont. Well, not really evolution, in the normal sense. Adapting, reconfiguring through close association, to resemble the dominant - or admired? - form of life. Ever onwards, ever upwards. He couldn't quite recall how he'd come up with that. The marvels of the brain. Or more accurately the cerebrum, a double-edged weapon if ever there was one. Fishes had stopped short.

'Bloody Pots? What kind of a thing is that to be asking a barman for?' Shanny's muddy eyes were bulging, fish-style, lids lowering slowly as Guinness went down. He belched. 'Come on then Stanley, tell us how's your Liza?' Shanny was another fan, used to make a fuss of her in the old days, in the pub, at matches.

What could he say? 'Oh, same delicate little flower, you know. Had enough of work, reckons we're in a rut. You know.' He recited, ticking off on his fingers Liza-style: 'Never go to the theatre, never go to the cinema, never go to a restaurant - unless it's in a pub - never go to concerts, never go to exhibitions, not together ... '

Shanny grunted in sympathy. 'I get same from our lass, near enough. They don't understand, Stanley, they never will. It's not in 'em. Anyhow, if there's a restaurant in it, it's not a pub, is it? I mean.' He fixed Stan. 'She's all right though, your Liza?'

'Of course she is. You know Liza, unstoppable.'

'I don't know. She's not as tough as she makes out, maybe.'

'Pleased to hear it. No, she's tough Shanny. Needs a break, that's all. Bit of sun.'

'Weather in this bloody country? Bloody sick joke! Always the wettest this, the hottest that, windiest the bloody other.'

Shanny went off on a rant, and Stan found himself wondering again where Kim had gone all those years ago – five? – and why. Never even said goodbye, that was the worst of it. And while he was at it, what had happened to those five years? Where had they gone? Viewed from his chair here in the *Cunard*, it looked very like one long night's sleep. A comfortable one, in the main.

Shanny was peering intently through smoke, black pint poised and half of it gone. 'See that pillock Bush got in after all then, even though he had less votes. Bad news that, for all of us. The Florida Fix, they're calling it. Hanging Chads. First thing, cutting off aid to any international outfit involved with abortion ... ' He was off again.

Stan directed smoke towards the dingy ceiling and watched it go, slowly slowly. Bernard used to say that, back on Tsaramaso, when they were trying to catch something, an ibis or a heron for the ringing scheme, a wily old parrotfish for lunch, or a juvenile shark gliding through the sunlit shallows with that hypnotic sway. Slowly slowly. What was Bernard up to these days, assuming he'd stayed out of prison? Bernard had always made enemies too easily.

Shanny was onto the state of emergency in California following de-regulation of the electricity supply, an indication of what would be happening here before too long. A staunch lefty, he, Liza and Old Vera could keep egging each other on for hours. Soon he'd be having a go at New Labour. Stan deflected him towards Derek Malcolm's 100 best films, recently listed and described in the *Guardian*. Most were pre-1970, films now being made for kids not adults. Ever since *Star Wars*, which had just seemed innocent, spectacular fun at the time. He couldn't accept that *Jaws* had played any part in this dumbing down. That was educational. And now kids thought Hitler used to live in Downing Street.

Eventually Shanny gravitated back to the subject of Liza, who he sometimes tended to treat like a younger sister. In the old days he used to front a pub band back home, Shanny and the Sharks, great name, and he'd get her up there onstage to provide deep, breathy backing vocals. She'd been good at it, and of course she looked fantastic. Some gravelly blues, but more good old-fashioned rock 'n' roll and doo-wop. Stan had lent a hand too with the latter, on occasion, driven up there by a gallon of Darley's or Thorne's, arm round the Barracuda, belting it out with the best of 'em. He'd been selective mind, only his favourites, and at the fag-end of a demanding Saturday night the long hair and imperial had, he felt, brought a note of authenticity to proceedings. Happy days. He told Shanny about the proposed expedition to the Indian Ocean.

Shanny considered. 'Be expensive though Stanley? Papalinas?' He rolled his bulging eyes.

Well yes, but there was the TV re-run, which meant money filtering through. And the more he got used to the idea, the more clearly he saw that Liza was right – they needed this trip. The Blacksters needed this trip, for all kinds of reasons.

Shanny sniffed. He never had thought much of *Insidiator*, which at the time had come as a disappointment - Shanny had a romantic side under all the bluster. He had spotted the flaw:

'What about your Kato though?'

The noble hound. It had been nagging at him. Kato would assume he was going along, as usual. He wouldn't understand. They'd arrange something, but whatever it was he knew that nearer the time he wouldn't be able to meet the noble eye.

'Yeah. We'll have to sort something out for the old feller.'

'Aye, better. Papalinas. That's where you used to be, right, when you were off at college?'

'Yep. Not the touristy part, where we'll be going. Where I was, it wasn't for tourists.'

'But you know it, like. Know your way round.'

Stan nodded, his mouth full of Pots.

'Aye. Right. All right for some. Be too hot for me and our lass, anyhow. Palma'll do for us. Same hotel again this year. You know where you are and what's what, bar does a good drop of Guinness, you get your paper every day. Any twats, we sort 'em out ourselves. Talking of which, we won't be leaving our Kevin in charge of the house this time.'

Kevin was a little swine.

Shanny went on in gruff praise of Palma: it would do for him, German tourists and all. If they wouldn't let him be scattered at Hillsborough when he popped his clogs, Stanley could tip him out at Palma on a nice bit of beach right next to the bar. Mrs Shanny knew the spot.

Shanny's face, bulging with blood, was alarming until you got used to it. He still wore his little silver shark ear-ring, like Gram, Stan was pleased to see. Gifts from Stanley Blackster. Sharks all round.

'How's the old health then, Shanny? Still staggering along?' A ritual question.

'Ask me again at end of season. Bloody club ought to insure us, with what they put us through. Bastards! Nowt wrong wi' me Stanley, same as always.' He was staring moodily off across the crowded room, starting to get wound up. Football was too important to Shanny.

'Come on Shanny - we're due a cup run, aren't we? Bit of glamour? We should be able to get past this lot, eh?' There were a couple of hard glances over pint glasses from nearby Saints fans. Shanny mouthed his glass for a while, trying to lock eyes with one of them, then pushed his way off towards the Gents. Stan had forgotten just how wound up he got, as kick-off approached. He'd forgotten a lot of things, and for a moment the prospect of being at a match lost its appeal.

Freed from the need to pay attention, or appear to, he let the pub noise recede, and re-lived a few scenes: Harak, revered Headman of the Kilwans, cut a fine figure on the screen though, didn't he? With a puffer fish on his head? And those dazed, non-Kilwan workers kept in a cage, they'd been drugged with puffer-extract, zombie-style. He could have made that clearer though. He could have made a lot of things clearer, he could see that now. Part of Delyth's critique. And just when did he have the idea of a female sidekick, trailing in the wake of

Dr Who? TV demanded a sidekick of course, but he'd had a dynamic and faithful hound, able to converse reasonably sensibly, offer the necessary support, admiration and so on. Preferable. Easier to cope with. Like Lassie? No, not like Lassie, more along the lines of the two droids in *Silent Running*. In manner. Huey and Dewey. Shanny barked in his face:

'Aye. We can take Southampton. Who are they? Jumped up, soft fuckers ... ' He glared around but no-one chose to notice. The other group of Owls fans had upped the Yorkie volume and were waving for them to go over. For an unpleasant moment Shanny seemed to be considering it, but he turned back to the table. 'Anyhow Stanley, we know where you're going to plant me - where are we going to plant you?'

'Me?' He'd never thought about it, partly because it was so obvious. 'Burial at sea, Shanny. Re-cycle the old bones. Turn me into fishes.'

Shanny squeezed his red face, threatening to pop something. 'Nice. Hoovered up by doggies and crabs. Wouldn't fancy that, me. Anyhow, they're going the other way now, out into space. It was in the paper, some American paying to be buried in space, just shoved out the airlock. Reckons he'll last forever, floating about, up there. Preserved, like.'

No. Appalling thought. 'As if there isn't enough of our crap up there already.' A great heap of perma-litter – they'd even photographed the damned stuff. 'Space, the final frontier. And now you're having to dodge dead American millionaires.'

'Aye. Wouldn't fancy that, me.' Shanny had swiped up the glasses and was heading for the bar.

'Hang on Shanny, it's my round. Anyway I said we'd meet Gram.' He felt the same though - they'd just got comfortable. He missed this. But they'd make up for it later, after the match. The atmosphere in the pub was getting to him, alcohol, smoke and testosterone. He found he was praying for a result, for Shanny's sake.

They moved outside, onto the pavement where men were streaming in one direction as if sucked. Gram appeared on time, smiling his quiet smile, dressed in black from the ground up - boots, trousers, jacket, stretch cap jammed on over his long hair. The only spot of colour was a badge on his chest which said *Stop*. As they watched him approach he must have made way politely for other folk half a dozen times, despite the fact that Stan could tell he was worked up about something.

'Hi. Hi, uncle Shanny.'

'Bloody hell Stanley. Big lad you've got. Still playing central defender then Gram? You'll be able to knock 'em about a bit now, eh?'

It went without saying that a younger Shanny had dreamed of one day playing for Wednesday. In their outstandingly dirty and cynical local pub team, Shanny had been eye-catching.

'Not so much now, no.' Gram's voice was pitched low, husky and pleasant. He hadn't gone in for barbed-wire tattoos or face jewellery - the stylish little silver shark dangling from one ear looked fine and was all he needed.

'What's up Gram?'

'A bunch of Americans has put up the money to bale out Huntingdon, at the last minute.'

Huntingdon Life Sciences, a debatable title. They'd been under the cosh following revelations of abuse of test animals, intimidation of workers, cars being torched, shareholders pulling out. A Mark Avery, spokesman for SHAC, dedicated to shutting them down, had been on TV one night, leaving you in no doubt of their determination.

'They were on their knees! They owed 22 million quid!' He looked angry, but his voice remained pleasantly low.

'The government sees it as a test Gram, a challenge to 'em,' barked Shanny. 'I've just been reading about it. If they let this lot go under they think other companies will get scared. It's all about money.'

'Yeah. So what's Blair promised these Americans?' Gram had turned to Shanny.

'That the law will protect their interests.' Stan waited for his son's attention. 'Did they name these American investors?'

'No. But SHAC will find out.'

'Oh aye.' Shanny sounded unimpressed. 'The animal libbers. Oops - forgot summat.' He ducked back inside the pub.

'Did you see the video they shot inside the lab?' Gram stared at his father. 'I thought you'd be, well, pissed off about it, like me.'

'I am Gram, I am. Can't say I'm surprised though.'

Gram snorted and looked away. 'Be different if it was fish.'

'Come on. What's that got to do with it?'

At that moment Shanny barged out of the *Cunard* with a carrier bag, which he offered to Gram. 'Here, Gram lad. Happy Birthday. Bit late, like.'

Gram peered in and grinned. 'It's great.'

'The new away shirt. To be worn with pride.'

'I know. Thanks, uncle Shanny.' With a smile he reached out to shake Shanny's paw.

'Don't put it on just now,' muttered Stan, glancing back into the rapidly emptying pub, but Gram and Shanny had already set off.

The three of them joined the flow of marching feet, along into Archer's Road, to the waiting police with their coughing radios, day-glo coats, motorcycles and transit vans, enormous horses and circling helicopters. They all shared this compulsion to march. No-one dared stop. Again Stan felt a prickle of unease, and wondered whether it was a good idea after all to bring his son, but there was Gram, striding along beside his short, muscular uncle, nodding and smiling, and listening. Gram was a good listener.

They found their places in the away end, all seats these days, and settled into their buckets. With just over 15,000 punters packed in the Dell was full, supposedly giving the home side the edge they often seemed to need. A move to a new stadium was imminent, and fans were apprehensive. The sky was clear, the air had that crisp, wintry edge which sharpened the senses, and the two teams appeared to a rousing mixture of cheers and boos. For the first nine minutes the game went well. Then Davies got the ball in the net for Southampton and the sudden thunderous roar blocked out everything. Their own end was screaming abuse. Anyone but Davies. Davies had previously played for the gang down the road at Bramall Lane. Shanny looked and sounded as though he could kill Davies. If he behaved like that on the other side of the wall he'd be locked up, sharpish. But there were plenty like Shanny. Plenty.

The game resumed. Stan, a great pretender, was utterly detached from the gut feelings spilling out all around him. Where they were overcome with passion and bile he felt mild intimidation and slight embarrassment. He stole a glance at his perplexing, black-clad son: was Gram a pretender, like his father, or the real thing, like his uncle? He should know this, surely.

Shanny, who never had to pretend, was making his usual full contribution to the foul-mouthed abuse rolling down from the stands like a river; and it would carry on rolling for the full ninety minutes, aimed mainly at the referee, who at least was out on the pitch running around and couldn't hear the words, not until the chants started up, anyway. The linesman had to run up and down right in front of them:

'You fucking blind spazza!'

Saints players had to come over to take throw-ins:

'You useless wanker! You dirty cunt!'

Shanny had to keep it up. Whenever there was a lull he'd start up the chant:

'Ooo are yer? Ooo are yer? Ooo are yer?'

Just before half-time Stan and Shanny had to get quickly to the toilets, returning to light up and stamp around while the announcements and kids' matches went on. The queue in the bar would be too long. At 1-0 there was still hope. All around people were chatting, laughing, making calls, reading papers and programmes, listening to radios, eating hot dogs and sipping hot drinks. The club mascots were out on the pitch in their ridiculous costumes to rouse the crowd. Shanny reckoned he knew who was inside the lumbering, top-heavy blue and white owl. From a few rows back a loud female voice chastised them for smoking in a non-smoking area. Shanny stared hard at Stan for a long second, with a look of barely suppressed fury, but thankfully he didn't respond. Mellowing with age.

The teams reappeared and the shouting resumed.

'Get rid! Get rid! Fucker!'

Southampton proceeded to control the second half comfortably and the bucket seats were unyielding. After 66 minutes Andy Booth stunned everyone by sending a header in off a post, and they were level. A pent-up primal bellow vented from one great, roaring, steaming beast. Shanny was on his feet, screaming incoherently, pumping fists at the sky, red face bulging and berserk. Stan recalled the beast with a rush, in the old days, before there were seats to restrain it, when its power had been terrifying. Then he realized Gram was on his feet too, fists pumping, eyes wide and bright and empty, mouth slack. The inchoate roar steadied itself, became a triumphant, aggressive chant. Shanny was cramming everything into the moment, blood surely racing round at impossible, unbearable speed, winding itself up to burst out through his pores in a fine red mist, spray-painting his neighbours. Shanny and Gram grabbed at one another, both of them chanting, 'Ooo are yer? Ooo are yer? Ooo are yer?'

Shortly afterwards Southampton sent on a Norwegian secret weapon who immediately started causing problems on the right, and less than fifteen minutes later a free kick was handled in the Wednesday area, by the same Andy Booth. Dodd put the penalty away for Southampton. The dramatically more immense red and white resident beast bellowed again, and Shanny was reduced to futile snarling at the lonely figure of Booth, out there on the pitch quietly considering the shift in his fortunes.

'Oh when the Saints, Oh when the Saints, Oh when the Saints go marching in!'

'Crap fucking stadium,' gritted Shanny. 'Not a patch on Hillsborough.'

Beattie scored a third in injury time, and that was that. The Owls were free to concentrate on the league.

In memory of the good old days Stan took them for an Indian meal. To his pleasant surprise Gram came along too, badgered into it by Shanny. Although not really his uncle, Shanny wanted to know it all. What about girls then Gram? Why, what's wrong with meat? Why have you stopped playing football? What are you going to be doing at college?

Not that Shanny was really listening. They'd lost and Shanny was coiled up, listening only to a voice muttering inside, a mean voice saying mean things. He'd be back to normal in time for the next match, ready to go through it all over again, but for a while he'd be a ticking bomb. Stan watched his son, who was getting on with Shanny a lot better than he remembered or expected.

Gram listed recent and not so recent health-scares involving oppressed, abused hordes of cattle, sheep, pigs, chickens, salmon, standing up well to Shanny's meaty fundamentalist contempt. And Shanny looked to be coming out of it, prodded by hot food and alcohol. Gram was a vego, but even vegetarians had to be careful. Vegetables weren't all they seemed nowadays, often pseudo-vegetables, drained of nutritional value by selective breeding and NPK fertiliser. Don't even talk about GM. He was earnest, but all the while smiling his guileless Kato smile.

'They'd only have to show the way meat arrives on the shelf once on TV and half the country would turn vego. Especially chickens. And it's only a matter of time before the next disaster, you wait.'

'What the bloody hell are we supposed to get down us necks then Gram? Bloody fresh air?' Shanny hoisted a forkful of biriani towards his glistening red face.

'Not that easy to find.'

Stan's contributions had ceased, unless you could count the Mothers singing *Call any Vegetable* a long way off in his head. Seeing his TV child again had shaken him up. He'd been good, no question.

Which English character actress would make the best big-screen job of old Hamrur, the drunken and talkative Kilwan crone – Dame Judi? Kathy Burke? A minor part perhaps, but it could always be built up. She could run the village inn, the *Pwason Ba.* Maybe change the name to something jollier. Perhaps the *Magic Tench,* in honour of the great Jack Vance. This set him to contemplating the dense, dark-olive solidness of *Tinca tinca,* the fine if bottom-dwelling tench, physician fish of slow and still waters, sometimes a fat, buttery golden-yellow, sometimes almost black with glints of bronze bottle-green, the males with spade-like pectorals, fond of bread-paste and worms, the youngsters mystifyingly hard to find … He sensed a glower, and surfaced long enough to nudge Shanny off into an appraisal of the current standing and future prospects of his Kevin. He felt bloated, in the traditional manner: Kingfisher lager, hardly the first entry in the Golden Book.

That rather marvellous brute of a shark, swimming around the flooded pit in the moonlight, that hadn't looked bad at all. He couldn't remember it being that good - how had Ray managed it, and why couldn't he remember? Such strong images! It was as though they had all been banished from his mind. It all had such freshness, such power. Surely Gram had been impressed? He hadn't asked yet, been hoping his son would say something.

A big red face had appeared, inches from his own, waving an empty glass.

'Come on Stanley, get it down your neck. You having a pudding?'

No. He was full as an egg. 'No. I'm full as an egg.'

Stan called a cab to take Gram home and went outside with him to wait. Shanny had been unable to persuade him to carry on with them to the pub, thankfully. Gram was looking off into the city night as he spoke:

'Thanks dad, it was cool.'

They'd started saying cool again. And why was he so damned polite? These were almost the first words Gram had addressed directly to him all afternoon. He'd been doing all his talking to Shanny.

'Yep. They had a go, didn't they?' He couldn't say 'we'. 'They're just not up to it.' Which was not something you were likely to hear from Shanny's lips. Enough to make the lips of an adult Shanny turn white in fact, which they did when eggs were under guard. A small fish, but belligerent. 'Shanny's good value, eh Gram?'

'Sure. He is OK though isn't he?' At last he turned to face his father. 'He looks, I thought he was going to choke, have a heart attack or something, you know?'

'He's what they call a fan Gram. It's pathetic. The clubs depend on them, treat them like crap, and they keep coming back for more. Shanny stopped being miserable there for a good 5 minutes, when Booth's goal went in, and he knows that's as good as it's going to get. They're a big club on the slide.' He didn't say 'we' again, and maybe Gram noticed, but he was staring off into the distance again.

'Yeah. He cares.'

Gram sounded impatient or something.

'What?' No response. Right, when would Wednesday be coming down to play Portsmouth? He ought to know this. 'Listen, Gram, I'll have to find out when they come down to Fratton Park – would you fancy it?' He was having to suck in little gulps of air after each sentence. Kingfisher and biriani had inflated his innards, and it was hard to get anything else in.

'Sure. Taxi's late.'

Yes, he'd imagined it, Gram was OK, just ready to get off wherever he was going. He made a determined effort to belch, but nothing doing. This must be how deep water fishes felt, one minute quietly nibbling a fishy morsel at a sensible depth, the next choking on their own expanding swim bladders as the hook bit and the hauling began.

'You haven't said much about *Insidiator*.' Suck. 'Did it stand up?' He was surprised how keyed up he was about this, and annoyed at having to ask.

Gram seemed to consider, then gave a grunting nod.

'Boscanion stands up though, doesn't he? Gram?' Was that a nod? 'What did you think, seeing Kim again?'

'You can't expect mum to sit there and watch, you know?'

'Well, she didn't, did she? I don't think it really bothers her that much any more, it was all a long time ago. Didn't upset you as well, did it?' It still puzzled him that Gram had never mentioned Kim, even when they were on their own. 'Did seeing her again mean anything to you? I used to think you liked her. He nearly said she liked him. 'She … had a favourable view of you, I know.' What was this, Jane Austen? 'You did spend a lot of time together.' She liked you, I know. You spent a lot of time together.'

Gram from behind was tall and black. 'I can't remember. I was only a kid.'

Even Stan knew he should give it up. 'She started to think of you as her little brother.'

'Huh! She was weird.' Emphatic, dismissive. 'And Kato couldn't stand her.'

'True.' Quite unlike the noble hound, but true. The wolfish smile, perhaps. Hungry. 'There was no harm in her though, Gram. She was a good kid.' He felt fat and sentimental.

'And what if she shows up again, seeing it all on TV? That's what mum thinks, you know that?'

'She won't show up Gram, she's history, and your mother knows it.' Stan realized he didn't believe any of that, and it sounded like it.

The cab drew up and Gram made his move.

'Say thanks again to uncle Shanny for the shirt.'

Some years ago they'd visited a local 'sea world' to watch immaculate blacktip reef sharks endlessly patrolling twenty foot tanks, endlessly on the lookout for food that wasn't there until feeding time. Listless and diseased flatfish had formed a heap on the bottom, there were a few more colourful species stolen from tropical coral reefs, a layer of slimy gravel, rocks, bits of weed and the odd string of bubbles. Young Gram had dutifully learned the wonderful fishy names, including the scientific ones. Got him! Stan had thought at the time, a chip off the old block. But later he'd come to see that for Gram fishes were no more and no less fascinating than anything else in the natural world. Major disappointment. The Barracuda had never fancied these trips (Not fish Stanley, thankyou), but Kim had been keen. Might even have been her idea. They'd planned a raid to get the fishes out. But the fishes belonged on the other side of the world, where the sun burned down on a clear blue sea. A home they would never see again. Better to put poison in the tank, someone had suggested. But they'd only get more.

'Right. This'll do driver.'

Not the place Stan would have chosen at all, but Shanny was impatient for Guinness. The *Upward Man* was one of several big, refurbished drinking bunkers punctuating lines of shops in the city centre. It was bitterly cold now, the wind clattering litter down the street, and on the door of the club next door a pair of besuited bouncers wore gloves and Southampton FC stretch caps pulled down over their ears. One nodded to them as they entered the bunker. Immediately the atmosphere was thick with gloom and aggression, but by this time Shanny had marched to the bar and it was too late.

Stan studied the blackboard advertising the evening's two special offers, giving himself time to blend in. They could go for a cocktail called Red Lightning, full of ingredients, touched off with grenadine, two for a tenner, or for the same price they could have a Bucket of Bud with a Jumbo Bag of Crisps, delivered to your table by our lovely waitress. An initial scan registered a table swimming with drink, soggy crisps and fag ends, where half a dozen men knocked back Red Lightnings, grunting and occasionally bellowing at match highlights on a big screen up on the wall out of their reach. A couple of solitary drinkers round the edges and that was it. As she squeezed by them with a bucket, trying not to slop lager, the lovely waitress put on a brave face, grimacing around the bag of crisps clenched between her teeth. The *Upward Man* was right at one end of the mostly glorious pub spectrum.

Stan went for Greene King IPA on the grounds that it was better than nothing, and they drank quickly and in silence, apart from the odd Indian belch. He was willing Shanny not to warm up before they left and insist on taking off his leather. He just wasn't in the mood, but Shanny had never been one for blending in and life had just given him another kick. He soon began sending out hard-man stares over his Guinness. It was like watching goings on in a rock pool, minus the enjoyment.

A young couple came in, finding themselves at the bar and under scrutiny before realizing their mistake. The girl was dressed for dancing on a Caribbean beach and the comments soon started up, but at least it deflected attention from Shanny, who was now sucking angrily at a roll-up, muttering to himself, the words 'Fucking Booth', 'Bastards' and 'Fucking Jewell' prominent. Without asking Stan he went back up to the bar with his glass, ignoring the nervy smile of the new bloke.

They were shouting at something on the screen. Not the atmosphere for drifting. He still felt bloated and his beer had run out of flavour after a couple of gulps, but here came another.

Shanny swallowed half his pint straight down without removing his stare from the gang at the next table, who were exchanging loud remarks about the girl at the bar.

'Do you ever think back Stanley, to those times in the pub at home, those Friday nights, your Liza up on stage with us?' He was shaking his red face slowly, seeing it.

Stan nodded encouragement, but there was no more.

Shanny sighed. 'Come on then Stan, take us somewhere decent. Guinness is piss. And I can stop at home in Sheffield if I want to go in a fucking craphole like this.'

Outside the cold hit them hard. A noisy gang in blue and white were swapping banter with the two nightclub bouncers. Jeff Cairns and associates.

'You're going wrong way Shanny lad. Beer's in there.'

'Piss is in there more like. You'll get a good scrap though.'

Jeff rubbed his hands together and grinned at his mates. 'Right lads,' he called to the bouncers, 'no skiving off, you two.'

The Yorkies filed into the *Upward Man*.

A cab ride took them to a familiar, proper pub: the *Stargazer*, a big, bustling and reliable venue out near the university. One of those places that drew in folk who thought they were passing by. Inside the light was soft and smoky, more of a glow, and they were instantly wrapped up in the steaming beery warmth, cigarette smoke, shouted conversations and laughter of a well-run pub on a Saturday night. The opposite end of the spectrum. It was set back from the main road and not the sort of place you found by accident, unless you made out the glow on a winter's evening. More often than not Stan brought the Barracuda here on a Friday night to celebrate the end of the teaching week. And, mostly, they had a good time. There had been the odd flare-up, usually Blackster v Blackster, but the Barracuda had also gone for the occasional more or less innocent bystander. Then they would drop it for a few weeks, without having to discuss it, but they always came back.

They carried pints of Archer's Best and Guinness to a relatively quiet table just being vacated in a back corner.

'Aye, this is more like it,' conceded Shanny, unzipping his jacket and having a good look around. He seemed to have calmed down.

At nearby tables students were attacking great, heaped plates of fish and chips; beyond, a middle-aged party stood at the long bar in evening gowns and dinner jackets alongside two open champagne bottles; in a corner elderly regulars conversed solemnly in a haze of cigarette smoke. The swarming staff were all slim girls below the age of twenty, dressed in black, all smiling as they took orders, served drinks, delivered meals and cleared tables - students studying locally, trying to make ends meet. Liza knew one or two of them. High on a wall a TV with the volume turned down showed non-stop sport, and a muffled thud underpinning the chatter meant music somewhere.

Stan got out the cigars. 'Yep, it's OK in here. I let the old girl tow me in here sometimes, you know, whenever she's overwhelmed by the pub urge.'

Shanny nodded, even managed a quick grin. 'Where's your Liza tonight then, not coming to join us?' He definitely still had that soft spot for the Barracuda.

Stan blew smoke. 'Out on the razzle. Some of her gang from college.' The *Boat*, then Sharma's cave, apparently. Or the other way round. 'You know how it is for teachers. Up to their eyebrows in stress.'

'Bloody hell!' Shanny smoked the small cigar furiously, the way he smoked roll-ups. 'Stress! Don't tell me. They only invented it twenty years ago, now every bugger's got it.'

Shanny had problems of his own. The threat of redundancy had been hanging over him for a while now, a near thing during the fuel protests, and young Kevin was keeping the local police on their toes. And he might say his health was OK, but as Gram said, it didn't look it.

'She's bloody great though, your lass. And your Gram, good lad that ... talk about bloody lucky. Am I to take him back to Sheffield and send our Kevin down?'

'I'll think it over.' The Archer's was exceptional tonight, had to be a fresh barrel, the stuff of life. Yes, who could complain about Gram? Bright, fit, good-looking, everyone liked him, just enough of his mother's spark, a leavening soupcon of his father's ... what? Balance? Calm? Was wisdom too strong? And a certain kind of quiet élan, not always in evidence, but you only had to see it once ... He felt a spasm of unease. Gram had seemed, not evasive exactly, but not exactly looking for his father's company either. How long had it been going on? He couldn't think. Growing up. Old male young male. Same throughout the animal kingdom. Liza had noticed. She didn't miss much. Quite the opposite.

'You'll see her later Shanny. I expect she'll be in good form.'

'Aye. Maybe we can have a singsong.' He chuckled. 'And your Gram should never have packed in the football, never. I mean, these days, if you can stay on your feet for ninety minutes without breaking a metatarsal and kick the ball to someone in the same shirt they give you shedloads of money. And your Gram's a bloody natural.'

Shanny had made short work of the cigar and was rolling a cigarette. 'What about music then? We used to have it banging out all the time, didn't we? Now they jam bloody machines on their heads.' He started nodding, tapping at the table beside his pint glass and murmuring the words to *Desiree,* or possibly *Sharleena.* A stack of old tapes travelled the country with him in his cab. 'It's all crap now though - you should hear the stuff our Kevin listens to. Bloody trip trop summat, gangsters and crack addicts, all guns and bitches and stuff.'

'Gram? He plays this chill-out stuff sometimes – ' he was guessing ' - you know, nothing that's going to burst a blood vessel.' Gram spent hours in his room, but he couldn't remember hearing any music.

'Oh aye. Whales singing.' Shanny looked angry, but he wasn't. 'You should train him up, Stan. Get some rock and roll in there, some Led Zep, get some steaks down him.'

Stan swallowed beer, concentrated on its downward passage, seeing its tawny warmth mingling with and overwhelming the feeble, soulless stuff he'd had in the last place.

'Aye. Tell you what Stanley, I've listened and learned, me. Broccoli. No-one back home told me it had lost 75% of its calcium since 1940. From now on, it's out. Broccoli! When did broccoli first come in anyhow? We never had broccoli. Cabbage, we had. And sprouts.'

'Mmm.'

For a while they smoked, drank and stared. Stan saw Kim's fleeting, wolfish grimace-grin. Then Shanny started on about his son again. He was clearly worried.

'You want to get him away, Shanny. Get him out of it, away from his gang. Set him up somewhere where there's work.' It would cost a bit, but Shanny earned good money.

'Aye. Like here you mean?'

Ah. Kevin and Gram in close proximity? No, he didn't want Gram teaming up with Kevin. Old Vera said he'd become a snob, with his southern ways. He took the empties off to the bar, where one of the young girls asked after Liza. He'd been quietly cultivating this little girl, in a fatherly sort of way. Nice kid.

'She always looks so great, your wife. Like a model or something.'

Aya, her name was. Her small face had an attractively dusky,

Mediterranean tone, but her eyes were a greenish-blue and tilted up just like a little elf's, a rather fascinating combination which looked somehow unstable.

'I bet she designs her own clothes, doesn't she? And she must work out, does she?'

She certainly does, was the answer to that. Aya's ears weren't pointed, he'd checked. But she'd inflicted on this arresting little face a sparkly stud of nose jewellery, which made him wince.

'I wish I had her figure.' Aya was perhaps the slimmest of all the smiling girls in black. 'And her height. Is she a model, your wife?' Aya was concentrating on the rapidly filling glass, but glanced up at him with those angled, tropical ocean eyes.

'She's a lady boxer. The Black Barracuda. Not heard of her? '

Aya sighed and nodded to herself. 'I knew it. Showbiz.'

'She spars in here sometimes, Friday nights.'

'Come on mate,' someone growled.

At some point he'd have to talk to her about this nose jewellery, but there were people waiting to be served. He pushed his way back through the crowd gripping two hefty, vase-shaped glasses with difficulty, each full of cloudy yellowish beer and overflowing with thick white froth like toothpaste. He eased them down onto the table.

'What the bloody hell's this? Where's Guinness?'

'Here you go, Shanny. Live a little. You can drink all the Guinness you want back home. This is Hoegaarden. Wheat beer, from Belgium. That's how they like it. Clears out the pipes. You don't like proper bitter, so get this down. It cost enough.'

'Belgium?'

'Go ahead, won't kill you.'

'Fuck.'

For a while they stared at the sports screen, and eventually the goals from their match appeared, to one or two cheers, as well as Booth's handball, which predictably set Shanny off on a red-faced muttering rant. He was back on the Guinness, leaving Stan to take care of both vases of Hoegaarden. What had he been thinking?

'Anyhow Stanley. Your TV thing the other night. I did watch it, don't know why, with our lass and our Kevin.'

Stan worked his eyebrows. His mouth was full of white froth. This stuff was a bad move, but he wasn't going to say so. How could it be so fizzy? He felt like Mr Creosote looked just before he exploded in *The Meaning of Life.*

'Nah. Sorry Stanley. It were crap first time round, and it's still crap. You should have got a few Klingons in there, you know, some good baddies, like. And that Kim ... ' Naturally he took Liza's part in this. 'Can't act, looks like a bloody baboon ... you should have got some fit young lass in there, like that Buffy.'

Stan gulped back froth with a snort.

'What's up with Buffy? She's all right is Buffy. And she can act.'

As Shanny gazed up at the screen Stan inspected his oldest friend, the pumped-up, bristly red head puffing furiously away on a fag, the shiny blue and white football shirt, the stubby-fingered, tattooed, red right hand mechanically lifting and lowering the pint glass. He was a disturbing sight, really. You wouldn't sit down next to him on a bus, never mind in a pub. The tiny silver shark dangling at Shanny's ear seemed more friendly and familiar than Shanny himself. Hard to believe, but he would soon be back down there, gliding over a reef, with Gram beside him.

'Anyhow Stanley, like you say, it'll bring in some coin.'

'That's right. When it comes through.' And in fact Ray had been on, intimating in his confident, ask-no-questions manner that he might have more news for Stan soon, further *Insidiator*-related developments. Yes, he'd heard it all before, but Ray had been right about the re-run, hadn't he? Eventually? No point in mentioning it to the Barracuda, not yet. But he felt a flush of sudden confidence. Why shouldn't he take a leaf out of Ray's book of optimism? He'd earned it, all that hard work, all that straining of the imagination. It was Liza, she lacked confidence in him. She didn't believe. Well, we'll see about that. 'There tends to be a bit of a delay, before it comes through, but it already looks as though it'll lead to more work. Which I could do with, Shanny, to be honest. Passing through a lean spell.'

'Yeah. Anyhow.' Shanny belched, distracted again. 'Shit!'

There was plenty of time for one more, as long as they guzzled this one down right away, then there was the twenty minute walk to liven them up for a nightcap or two at Blackster Towers, where a bottle of BNJ waited. Shanny would be heading back to the People's Republic of South Yorkshire first thing in the morning.

Stan wanted to pick up again with little Aya, but there was the usual scrum at the bar so he let Shanny do it while he sat and drifted on a gentle swell of pub noise. After a time he noticed a small disturbance in the haze up near the ceiling, over in the far corner, small eddies in the cigarette smoke, caused by some sort of extractor fan in the wall over there. As he watched dreamily, faint wisps or tendrils appeared to flicker outwards through the air: intriguing, but no amount of squinting could quite bring it into focus. For some time now his vision hadn't quite been up to the mark, and a dismal attempt to read out the list of ingredients on a tin of something or other had alerted the Barracuda, who was nagging at him to go for an eye test. He wasn't keen. Spectacles were not in keeping with his image of himself, they were for characters like Ray. On the other hand the spectacled parrotfish *Chlorurus perspicillatus* seemed to manage perfectly well, as did the little spectacled filefish *Cantherhines somethingorother*. Perhaps the monocle breams provided a more elegant exemplar. Yes, Boscanion himself would approve of the *Nemipteridae*, small but self-possessed consumers of plankton and benthic invertebrates. He looked around: even some of the students wore spectacles. No, he'd just look ridiculous. It was suddenly very warm. Why did last orders always trigger a rise in temperature? He resisted the sudden urge to pull off his shirt, just fight his way out of it, rip the thing off, hurl it across the room.

There was a wavering track now, still at ceiling height, around twenty feet up, moving slowly closer, slightly opaque, with wisps and curls and tiny, glinting specks which came and went in slow-motion. His mouth was dry, his hand dead on the table next to his glass. Slowly it came on, uncertainly, the glints now like grains of sand drifting in the shallows where the tide is a whisper. There was a hold-up, the shifting air pausing, hovering overhead. He was staring straight up at the ceiling. Could he make something out there? If he looked off to the side, and then edged slowly closer, could he see the beginnings of a pattern? A rhythmic hushing far in the background. The faint smell of mud, of vegetation rotting. It was moving again, on towards the big window, quicker now, the nucleus gone, a dim and fading wake speckling the upper air with the dull glint of gold.

'Bastards!' Shanny was muttering to himself as he plonked down the drinks. 'Bastards!' He shook his head in angry bewilderment, fag dangling from his lips. 'Fuck 'em.' He lifted and drank.

Stan stared at the window for a while, just cigarette smoke there now, then helped himself to paper and tobacco, staring still as he made a cigarette.

'Smell anything, Shanny?'

Shanny was oblivious, chuntering away about Booth and

Jewell, then Dooley, then Blunkett, then Blair, and scarcely looked up. Another bit of weirdness. Another atoll moment, as they used to call them, to go with the birds in the Forest. He didn't like what he was feeling. That same smell. The old synasthaesia flaring up again? No, come on, it was necessary to consider whether these had been real events or uncompleted brain unspoolings from the night before, occurring only in his head. He had the queasy thought that if he asked the Barracuda and Kato, they might not remember the birds. Birds Stan? What birds? Kato's bewildered look. He shook himself mentally, filled with unease. Far better if he had imagined it. But Liza would remember – she'd called them harpies. She'd remember the harpies. The tobacco was strong, and he could feel moist brown smoke working its way into the linings of his lungs, turning pinks to shades of brown. Smuggled in, from Holland. Shanny had a standing order. He breathed some out, and it just looked like smoke.

Shanny's eyes were watering. 'Bloody Belgian piss! I can still taste it.' He belched around a gulp of Guinness. His face was redder, more congested than ever, and seemed to be working in small suppressed spasms, threatening again to spatter everyone with blood and Guinness, Mr Creosote-style.

Stan startled himself with another belch of his own. Biriani, Kingfisher and Hoegaarden – probably never been attempted before. He should have stuck to Archer's, what had he been thinking, wasting capacity like that? He'd had to get two of the damned things to go down, to avoid looking stupid. He rubbed his arms, his chest, where the sweat was chilling. Had that smell gone, if it had ever been there? Think about the Papalinas. Back to Papa. This too made him uneasy, but he pressed on. OK, a few bad memories, big deal. That was fifteen years ago, not last week, for Christ's sake, and they'd be in the soft, touristy main islands, seven hundred miles away from Tsaramaso. He needed a kick up the arse, even he knew that. And this was for poor, hard-working Liza, and for Gram. His family, dearer to him than anything. The noble hound though. He saw Kato grinning a frozen grin of reproach.

'We used to enjoy a bit of fishing, eh Stan? River Witham, River Trent. The bloody Don even, the times when it wasn't full of detergent suds and crap. Roach, bream. Aye, used to enjoy that, I did. They were good days, Stanley. Good days ...' Shanny had come out of it again and peered hopefully towards the bar, but time had been called.

The smiling, black-clad girls fanned out to clear up the debris.

At Blackster Towers all the lights were on. A prickle of apprehension rippled through Stan's cocoon of alcohol and bonhomie.

'Stan? Stan?' Liza was upstairs, her voice loud and urgent. Kato was making those panicky little yipping sounds.

'Liza?' He pounded up the stairs and she came out of their bedroom clutching a champagne bottle. Gram was behind her, looking worried. Kato bounded past them and jumped up, trying to plant his forepaws on Stan's chest, yelping, eyes rolling.

'Hey, take it easy old chap.' Stan eased him heavily to the floor. 'Barra. What's going on?'

She looked wild, snapping eyes jammed open, whites tinged pink, dark face shiny with sweat.

'There's been a guy snooping around. Up on the roof.' She spoke in a rush, breathless, waving at the ceiling with her free hand. 'You didn't see him? A little guy, up on the roof? Looking in the windows?'

'Where Liza? Which window?'

'Gram's! Gram's window, looking in! I said!'

'Bastard!' growled Shanny behind him.

Liza's fist clenched and unclenched on the neck of the heavy bottle.

'Gram?'

'I didn't see him, dad. I was in my room, then I heard Kato going mental, and mum came running up the stairs … '

'Right,' said Shanny. 'Am I to find him and hammer him, Stan? Where's your torch?'

'Table by the front door.'

He went to put an arm around her but she was too hyped up, too much adrenalin pumping round, and she backed away. The tang of gin hung in the air around her. She was well gone and wanted to hit someone. He'd seen her like this before. Try to calm her.

'How long ago, Liza?'

'Ten minutes, something like that. He'll still be around Stan!'

Gram was shaking his head. 'No mum, it was nearer an hour ago.'

She threw him a ferocious glance then turned back to Stan, fist squeezing rhythmically at the neck of the bottle.

'OK Liza, OK, let's hear it, from the beginning.'

She gave him a look of scorn, but steadied herself. 'I was just coming in. I saw something move on the roof, a cat, but it wasn't a cat, like a cat but too big, and I thought monkey, crazy, but then I saw it was a man, a skinny little guy, like I said.'

'On the roof, OK ... what was he doing up there?'

'I said! I said! Looking in Gram's window! Watching Gram!' She whirled to confront her son. 'You must have seen him! He looked like he'd been there for ages Gram!'

'I couldn't mum, really I couldn't. When you're inside, at night, with the lights on, you can't see much outside.'

'He's right Liza. What happened then?'

'Then? He was just ... I couldn't see him any more. What does it matter? He was up there, that's what matters!'

Those ferocious eyes were blazing now. She was sliding out of control again.

He tried to be gentle, but it had to be said. 'Liza - how would anyone get up on the roof? They'd have to fly up there.' None of it made sense. The champagne bottle gave a twitch. 'OK, maybe they could get up there. Maybe it was a kid. Burglar. There's been - '

'It wasn't a kid, Stan. I know a kid when I see one. And he wasn't trying to break in. He was just watching.' She looked from husband to son. 'So that's the way it is. Well, I don't give a toss! I know what I saw! How dare you humour me! You couple of bastards!' The bottle thudded to the carpet and rolled away as she made fists and lifted them.

Gram looked miserable. 'Mum, it's OK. Dad's only trying to help ... '

She ignored him. Her eyes had narrowed. 'You know something about this, don't you Stan, you bastard!' She spoke deliberately now, ominously, surging towards the threshold. Gram tensed behind her. 'This is something to do with her, isn't it? Your little friend. I can tell. Like in the Forest. It *smells* of her, just like it did then. She got to both of you. I knew, even back then. And she's here again, isn't she? That *creature*?'

On the word *creature* her face contorted with venom and ... fear? She'd gone beyond anything Stan had seen before. This was the worst ever. He was facing a stranger, a wild-eyed, snarling thing, tensing to spring. Jesus.

Gram lunged forward to grab her arms at precisely the right moment, and the two of them grappled her spitting and swiping, kneeing and raking, back onto the bed. Stan held her down, eyeball to mad eyeball, feeling her chest heave as she spat in his face, spat and screamed abuse at them both, screamed and gasped, gasped and panted, sobbed and shuddered. The sounds of Shanny blundering about downstairs distracted her, and when he thumped up the stairs she went limp, closed those terrible eyes and began to cry. On the landing Kato started to howl. Slowly Stan released his grip and she pushed him off, turning her face into the covers, body shaking in spasms of sobs. He left the room and closed the door.

Shanny looked shaken. He'd found nothing, and seemed bewildered. He'd never seen her like that, and there seemed to be some sort of unspoken accusation that it must somehow be Stan's fault. How could it be? Jesus, it was bad enough as it was. Had Shanny been there when she was ranting on about Kim? He couldn't remember, the last half hour was already a confusion of dreadful images. Where had it all come from? Completely out of the wide blue bloody nowhere. His head was banging.

'Come on Shanny, she's OK now, let's go down, leave her for a bit.'

'You sure about that Stan? She won't, do anything like?'

The two of them sat awkwardly downstairs for twenty minutes with a whisky, Kato on the floor between them, then Shanny went through to his mattress on the floor. He had an early start.

It was too soon for Stan. He slipped quietly outside with Kato for some air and a prowl round. He peered up into the orange city night to where the roof angled, overlooking Gram's room. There was a tree, there was a drainpipe. It wasn't impossible. Some kid, had to be, some local Kevin up to no good. Maybe a peeping tom, trying to get an eyeful of Liza, got the wrong room. He'd seen the looks, in the pub and at the college. Whatever she thought of him now, he had no doubt she'd seen someone. Something, anyway. Stop pretending, not even a squirrel could get up onto that roof.

Over the next few weeks he'd make a point of checking after dark, make sure she could see he was taking it seriously. Jesus, he hoped she'd sleep, hoped she'd wake up all right in the morning. The noble hound padded into the torchlight, tail wagging uncertainly, tongue lolling, looking for reassurance. Stan played the torch over the broad, blond back, careful to avoid his eyes.

'And what did you see then Flash, what's your version? What did you see Kato?' The Barracuda's wild state had spooked everyone. Hounds picked up on that kind of thing, especially this one. 'S'all right now chap.' He switched off the torch.

He slapped the broad back and the tail accelerated. She was like a bomb. Why did she get like that, why couldn't she control herself more? Not that he'd seen her that bad, well, not since the old days. Drink, unleashing the beast. Shanny had probably seen it before then, if he cared to remember. But the Barracuda wasn't the sort to be unduly agitated by a man on a roof. And why bring Kim into it? That damned TV showing, just the idea of it had stirred her up. And Kim had never smelled of anything in particular, had she?

Beneath the tree, on the ground, a leaf caught his eye. Again he looked up at the tree, a silver birch - not the sturdiest of climbing trees it had to be said. The trunk rose straight and pale in the night air, into a mesh of branches and twigs as yet leafless. No broken branches, no scuff marks. He bent to pick up the leaf, a pleasingly dark lozenge-shape with a smooth, veinless, bottle-green surface which caught the street-light as he turned it in his fingers. A laurel of some sort, like the famous takamaka of tropical memory, but botany had always been a weak point. He'd never been able to focus properly on plants, to generate any real interest. He didn't have the patience. Plants just sat there, growing. No style.

The light up above in their bedroom winked out, leaving them in darkness.

Stupefying heat shimmered in the mangrove forest, the sun an unfaceable white glare somewhere overhead. Distant surf murmured, a fish slapped water, a bird called. The network of curving brown prop-roots stretched away in geometric progression, darkening in the silent shallows of the half-drowned forest. Above the oily waterline crabs and snails clung to warm, brown wood; below, schooling juvenile fish swarmed in the vast nursery of interwoven roots anchoring the forest to the sucking white mud of the lagoon bed. A lemon shark, yellow in filtered sunlight, patrolled the cloudy green shallows; young turtles grazed, dim disc shapes. On a large mangrove root perched a wiry, bearded brown man, naked, long brown toes following the warm curve of the wood, peering intently at an approaching pattern of ripples, a succession of neat u-shapes broken up by the sluggish, side-to-side action of a sweeping tail. At the thicket of roots a snout appeared, then a head, then a cat-sized, grey-barred body hauled smoothly clear of the water. The brown man turned abruptly full-face, searching with round, close-set eyes the colour of sand.

Stan was on the floor in darkness next to the bed, covered in sweat, befuddled. His hands grappled out of habit for the headtorch he kept at the bedside. On the other side of the bed was a lump which droned in sleep and didn't move: Liza, gone with sleeping tablets. He was choking on thirst and his brain was on fire.

In the bathroom he gulped water, banged down paracetamols and towelled away sweat. The mirror-face was eerie under the headtorch's weak beam and reflected glare, fish-shapes shadowy on the walls around.

He looked eighty and felt worse. In his hand he held a crushed leaf. Memories had been unlocked and a rapid-fire sequence of images blazed through his brain: black night, the flaring light of a fire among the tall coconut trees by the beach, the smell of roasting meat - goats brought back from a field-trip. Ragged laughter, drunken shouting. After dark the settlement of the Papalinois workers was a no-go area, but here he was on the shining beach, driven from his bed by memories of disembowelled sharks, needing to walk, just walk and clear his head. Thump and suck of surf, a million stars, the fresh wet track of a turtle. He edged in towards the shadows of the beach-crest undergrowth and a nightjar whirled up in front of him, hunting moths, then returned to its invisible station amongst the coconut litter. The gutteral squabblings of fruit bats in the big indian almond tree mingled with hoarse shouts and laughter. The nightjar's weird, soft, popping call spiralled endlessly up out of the darkness. He walked on, away from the crude whitewashed houses, away from the noise. On the beach, in the moonlight, shone the wet prints of two sets of bare feet, leading out to the surf and back into the coconut shadows. Suddenly, there before him stood little Talma, of the direct stare and swinging hips, stopping him with her bold, distracting white smile, someone else making off unseen through the crackling swathe of dead coco leaves and husks. Talma said nothing, just kept smiling, encouraging. He approached, said something. Moments passed. They were being watched.

Stan worked the tap for more water. He was dying of thirst here. The water was ice in his throat, in his gut. A cold shower, that was the thing. But he couldn't stop remembering.

The following day he'd been told that Talma was unable to come to do the daily cleaning. She was ill and couldn't leave her house. In fact she was Roland's woman, it was Roland's house, and he'd locked her in it. Roland was much older than her, no-one knew how old, the head man of the twenty or so local workers and their families.

From that day on things became unpleasant, with stories circulating, hostile looks - not just from the locals - and word of threats overheard. He grew twitchy. The Linois all carried knives. In the end the Director had called him in. The staff were refusing to co-operate if *Black-stair* was involved. Sit down Stanley, I'd like to know what this is all about. I've heard certain stories about you and the cleaning woman, but have taken them all with a pinch of salt. However, I now have Easterhouse coming to me, most dissatisfied, saying you're refusing to carry out necessary work, and now we have these problems with the staff ... and what's this about wading out into the lagoon at night? No doubt you have good reason, but you should know by now how the staff are inclined to react. They're convinced you're up to no good out there - I know, I know, but it's part of my job to decide when to take these things seriously ... we need to think about the efficient and safe operation of the research station ... difficult situation for all of us ... have to consider everyone ... early signs of strain ... supply boat due in two weeks, perhaps it would be better all round if ... must inform Professor Dalyell ...

Those last two weeks had been an ordeal. At night, fired up by drink and by Roland, some of the younger, more volatile workers took to hanging around Stan's small corrugated house, making a great show of sharpening branches with their machetes. No good trying to talk to this gang, one of them presumably the lad Talma had been with that night. An oppressive atmosphere seemed to settle over his house, especially at night when he began to imagine he could hear something on the roof, a settling weight, a long, throaty sigh, the occasional scratch or click of a claw on the corrugated zinc. Every night he heard it, sooner or later. The first time, he'd gone out to look. There was no moon, and the black shadows of the swaying palms must have confused him. He didn't go out again.

The house began to smell bad, and he traced it to an oily patch or smear high up on a wall, in shadow under the roof's overhang. Nothing would rub the smell away. One morning he noticed fresh earth around the back of his house, disguised with strewn vegetation, and found a bottle a couple of feet down, half filled with a viscous black fluid in which he could make out plant seeds along with what looked like the long, hooked finger from a bat's wing, the jawbone of a small carnivore, nail clippings, God knows what else. He knew what that meant. Before it got too dark he hurled the bottle into the sea. He also asked the Director to put out the news that he was leaving. The dreadful pressure in the air had relented.

But there was one final field-trip to make. Easterhouse had no choice: the research programme demanded a trip to the most remote part of the lagoon, over twenty miles away, on the next spring tides, to measure and tag sharks and sample an area where juvenile sharks had previously been tagged. Unfortunately, only Blackster had the expertise to assist him. They would take a boatman and guide and supplies for four days. It was a notoriously difficult area. Roland, with unrivalled knowledge of the trails, tides, currents, channels and rocks, would be both boatman and guide, and he would take Alain to help. Stan couldn't say much - no-one would listen anyway - and his request for Bernard, who was more independent, less hostile and more experienced than Alain, was ignored.

He was history on the atoll, and he still had the Prof to face when he got back, but if he could just get through this one final trip he would soon be back in an impossibly remote Britain where he could forget all this, put it behind him like the bad dream which on balance it had to be. He'd miss the fishes.

'Stanley?'

He jumped. The light snapped on. A tall, animal-panting black woman stood there.

'Stan? What is it? What's going on? I heard, I don't know ... '

Liza. Liza, squinting and confused. Kato alongside.

There was a noise from downstairs and she grabbed at him. She looked muddled, uncertain, vulnerable, not a familiar version of herself, a million miles from the mad, screaming thing he now recalled with a jolt. Something was downstairs. He groped around in his memory.

'It's OK Barra. Just Shanny. He's staying the night, remember?'

He spoke softly to her, stroking the twisted black hair, guiding her back to the bedroom. Hell of an evening, one way and another. His head ... think about it all tomorrow. Sleep, desperately needed. Sleep. The noble hound flopped down in the doorway, on guard.

6. Legend of Xutha

The train journey from Southampton to Gatwick was a new one for Stan, and he found its meandering route quite agreeable, redolent of more gentle-paced times before the invention of stress. First they dawdled along the south coast, stopping at Hove and Chichester before swinging grudgingly northwards away from the sea. Almost at the outset he had eased into the half-dozing and welcome mindlessness he associated with long train journeys. So much better than travelling by car, where you were expected to remain alert at all times to avoid death or maiming or to pay attention to the Barracuda. She was the driver in the family, enjoyed it, working off surplus aggression while he held down the attentive passenger role. No, this was much more conducive. It was one of a string of identical bleak, grey days in the south of England as the realm underwent its annual struggle clear of winter and into early spring. The flat English sky filled with low grey stratus and wind-blown drizzle, the agricultural acres and truncated woodlands of Hampshire and Sussex constantly interrupted by uninspiring towns, villages and industrial sites: truly a vista of the demersal. Out there too they were fighting to control an outbreak of foot and mouth disease, discovered in February in twenty-odd pigs at an Essex abbatoir, now spreading all over the place - Wales and Scotland, even Northern Ireland. There'd been a near-daily horror show on TV, flaming mounds of livestock lighting up the nights of Essex, Devon and Northumberland, new cases being discovered all the time. Gram was appalled by it. Farmers had been assigned helplines and priests. Recent images - the pyres, men in overalls with guns, carcases swinging in crane grabs, weeping men and women, Gram's agitated face, a black hand kneading the neck of a green bottle - drifting together, forming vague patterns, drifting apart, as his brain completed the previous night's unspooling. Eventually his focus settled again on the three phone calls he'd received yesterday.

He rehashed the row he'd had with the magazine's commissioning editor over the Modern Mass Extinction article - or, more properly, the Fighting Pupfish article. It was highly unusual for the man to actually ring up, but it was almost as though he'd been spoiling for a fight. Firstly he'd provoked Stan by suggesting he'd missed the whole point of the scientific study by concentrating on one regrettable but minor aspect of it. And while Stan hadn't managed to get hold of a picture of the intrepid little creature, he carried in his head an image of a Churchillian pupfish, jaw jutting in defiance. Almost he could see the cigar, puffing. Minor aspect? 'The charco pup was hardly minor!' he seemed to recall shouting into the phone. 'The charco pup was a miniature evolutionary marvel. This is a tale of our times!' He'd held onto his temper and sense of proportion, despite the provocation. 'And now it's gone. Forever. Not just for a week or two. G. O. N. E. And why? Because some Mexicans wanted to wash their bloody cars!' Didn't this sum up the situation far better than a string of facts, figures and theories?

The man hadn't budged. He hadn't even demanded a re-write, which would have put him in a difficult position. Well, so be it. He would file the article under 'P' for future use. There were other publications, other editors, editors with larger minds, with some imagination, some vision. He would find a place for the pupfish.

Meanwhile, his current project was the great raft of new exhibits to go on show at the London Natural History Museum, the first instalment of an almighty heap of 22 million pickled oddments never before seen by the public. Plenty of fishes: a twelve foot oarfish found by a man walking his dog at Whitby in 1981 (the noble hound would still be running); the first pufferfish to be scientifically described (opening the door for the CIA to make their own zombies using Caribbean pufferfish extract, a useful snippet); groupers caught in the Pacific Marquesas by Captain Cook. Fishes galore. Curator of Fishes - now, there was a job. His eyes misted over at the thought. How many times had he told himself he should have stuck to one line of study? Why couldn't he just damn well stick to one thing, follow it through, get his head down and just do it? How many times? He lacked stamina. His whole life had been dogged by poorly-angled application. Too late now.

The next batch to go on show would include turtles and sharks. He'd take Gram along – he was bound to want to go – and spend the day there, then perhaps meet up with Ray for a refresher or two. Plenty of acceptable hostelries in those parts. On his wall calendar he'd ringed the date, beneath the fearsome, six-barbelled face of a Wels, or Danubian Catfish, *Silurus glanis,* current fish of the month. An inarguable brute, the Wels, getting up to a length of fifteen feet in Russia and weighing half as much as a cow. A spirited introduction to the English Home Counties at the beginning of the twentieth century, the Wels fairly epitomised the demersal, and its diet consisted of whatever it liked the look of. He must make sure this piece on the NHM collection would succeed where the Pupfish had, so far, failed.

Call number two had come from his accountant. There had followed a short and sombre exchange of views. Stanley's popular science writing was really flowing now, he felt, but income was not. It was time for AB Defduf, author and creator of *Insidiator*, to resume his contributions to the cause. He had forced himself to read one brief review of the first episode, but it had been written by some sort of raving teenager with no perspective and no experience of the world. Had this person - man or woman? boy or girl? - liked it or not? Impossible to say for sure. The review made no sense. He'd go with Ray's jubilant verdict. First episodes were always the most difficult, having to set scenes and grab attention. Episode Two was better, where Boscanion and Anakim meet the ridiculous Ruahari. Yes, anyone who got through Episode One would surely go for Episode Two. He'd steered well clear of the subject of Kim, naturally, since the man on the roof. He wasn't stupid. But surely Gram would have to say something about Kim, sooner or later. Maybe *Episode Two – The Ruahari* would do it.

A voice asked to see his ticket. He was on a train. Straight-edged fields of dull brown earth were rattling by, dotted black with a few lost-looking crows. The third of yesterday's phone calls had been quite, quite different, and had propelled him onto this train.

'Hi. Am I talking with AB Defduf?' a thin, high-pitched American voice had piped. 'Hi. This is Louis Vanderhorst.' Then a hissing pause.

Louis Vanderhorst, the Hollywood big-shot. Of course. It sounded like some kid trying out a funny voice.

'Oh, hello there Louis. How ya doin?' Ray. It was Ray.

'AB. You don't sound too surprised there. They told you I'd be calling, right?' piped the voice. There was a muffled comment to someone in the background, then: 'AB. I'm into London Gatwick tomorrow, no, tonight. You and me, we gotta meet. I'm a big fan, AB. Maybe the biggest. That's right. I'm buying the rights to your characters. Yeah. Hey, AB. We gotta make a movie! AB?'

Although Ray had never been famous for his funny voices. Or, come to that, his sense of humour. Stan started to feel dizzy.

'That's great news. Mr. Vanderhorst, sir, you, er … your voice sounds very faint. Could you speak up a bit?'

'Yeah, right. I'm in the jet, AB, way up, over Europe someplace.' Another muffled interjection. 'Yeah, Italy. AB. You meet me at the Gatwick Hilton tomorrow, say one pm local. Got that? Meet me in the lobby. I'm in room - ' a pause ' - yeah, room 101. Just so you know. You got that AB?'

'Got it Louis, I'll be there.' If only.

Two minutes later he'd convinced himself there was no way in this world it could have been Ray, and who else would bother? Maybe, maybe it was genuine. Jesus.

The window was steamed up. The train was at a standstill, out in the sticks somewhere. Black and white cows twice the size of danubian catfish stared and chewed. The railways were in a mess, on the news every night. He checked his watch. Mid-day? Some days it never really got light. The train lurched and clanked, stopped again. Over the public address a heavily distorted voice told them a suicide on the tracks up ahead was causing difficulties.

From Gatwick station Stan followed arrows to the Hilton along endless walkways, moving briskly through the travelling hordes. It was much brighter in here than it was outside but there was something wrong with the air, and sounds were distant. There was something not quite right with the whole situation, but what choice did he have? No amount of memory grabbing had produced anyone remotely capable of or interested in playing such an elaborate game, but did he seriously expect to be meeting a Hollywood bigshot in a few minutes time? Hardly. He hadn't told the Barracuda, so no-one else knew about this meeting, and if it was all some kind of weird mirage – well, he wouldn't have to do any explaining. Except to himself.

Then he was in the busy but somehow muted reception area of the Gatwick Hilton, as requested, wearing his *Insidiator* T-shirt with the tiger shark jaws for easy ID, moving in a relaxed but purposeful manner. He'd walk slowly through, then back again, have one last look around for form's sake, then off to *World of Whisky*. Or did you have to catch a plane for that?

Louis Vanderhorst, a figure familiar to anyone who looked at TV or leafed through magazines in waiting rooms, bounced into view.

'AB! Has to be you! Great T-shirt! Turn around! Yeah! I'll take a couple.' He made a dry scraping sound like a chuckle, pumped Stan's hand, clapped him on the shoulder and steered him towards the restaurant area. 'AB. Like I said, I'm your number one fan. I got a busy schedule, but I just had to fit you in. This is a great moment for me.'

Jesus, it wasn't a joke! While his head whirled Stan managed to be mildly shocked by Vanderhorst's youthfulness. Much younger than all those magazine photos. And small. Had his voice even broken? Louis had a doughy face with small blackcurrant-eyes, an American face with an on-off smile and little pearly teeth. It was evident straight away that when they weren't taken up with talking, his thin lips made a habit of pouting spasmodically. Most of the time they were taken up with talking.

'So then, AB.' Louis had managed to get an arm round his shoulder, even though he had to walk up on the toes of his black combat boots to do it. All his clothes were Gram-style black - baggy combat trousers, T-shirt, denim jacket, the shades pushed up onto the top of his head; the Vanderhorst hair was black and wild. Diners and guests round about were the audience.

A waiter escorted them to a table at the back and a man Stan had failed to spot sat down with them. This one was built to the same delicate scale as Louis but was older, wore a shiny grey suit and tie, had a skullcap of ginger hair and moved in short bursts like a rodent.

'AB. Like you to meet Milt Steinitz.' A perfunctory flap of a small, white Vanderhorst hand. 'Milt helps out with stuff.'

Stan nodded. 'Milt.'

Milt's slitty eyes flicked across for a second then returned to his boss, whose lips were twitching impatiently.

'Now, AB. Like I said before, we just gotta make this movie. I buy the rights, we really get the show on the road, but what do you say you and me get things moving right now?'

'Erm. Sounds great, Louis. I'm an admirer of yours, as it happens. *Legend of Xutha, Religion of the Trees, Faded Bliss ...*'

'Now. You just picked out some good examples there, AB. I kinda like to do one big studio movie, then use the bucks for something nearer my heart. You probably know that. Something a little more challenging. More personal. Don't get me wrong, still big bucks! But *Xutha, Trees* - that's the kind of thing we're talking about here. *Bliss,* that's the other sort, brings in the finance.'

'Yep. *Xutha's* my favourite. I rather like your portrayal of the marine world, especially the fishes. It lifts the film close to greatness, I think.'

'Yeah, the fishes are in there. What I was thinking - '

'*Legend of Xutha* must have put fishes into more minds than any film since *Jaws.*'

'Yeah. The fish ... they weren't really fish, AB. They were a little more complex than that - '

'They began as fishes.'

'OK, they started out as fish - '

'And they ended up as fishes.'

Vanderhorst's lips were puckering, unpuckering. 'Not really.'

'You didn't think so?' This was puzzling. 'Well, I've seen it three times, and it seemed to me - '

'Listen, AB, we don't have too much time here. Forget the fish.'

'Oh. Right.' Vanderhorst had a point. It could wait. 'Well, I expect you just saw the first part of *Insidiator* the other night on TV, right?'

Louis frowned, and waved the menu. 'You kidding? Some guy sent the whole thing to my office. On tape. I got it in my room upstairs, right now. It bombed on TV, I know - no offence, AB - but I see possibilities. Big possibilities. Why hasn't some guy over here made a movie already, like they did with *Doctor Who*? Hey! The guy was right, this show was ahead of its time.' He waved the menu again. 'Come on, let's eat guys. Time's a wastin'.'

The discreetly hovering waiter eased forward and Louis ordered concoctions of pasta, vegetables, exotic salad and fruit, which scarcely registered with Stan, who was distracted. What could Louis mean by 'not really fish'? He'd pin him down later - this had to be cleared up.

'AB. That OK? Milt, he don't eat. Hey! AB - you should try the Zinfandel - California wine. Blush. You know it?'

Louis Vanderhorst sketched in his vision. 'Digital effects now, they can create any place, any weird creature you like. You think it up, it's there, on the screen. *Lost in Space*? Forget it. That's like *Forbidden Planet* now. And *there's* a movie ready for a re-make. These guys now ... it costs, sure it does. Just as long as the power stays on, right Milt?' He aimed one of his curious, bone-dry chuckles at the unspeaking Milt.

Stan noticed he was the only one drinking the wine. Louis took quick, hummingbird-style sips at his mineral water, while Milt just sat there.

'OK. AB. Your show. Boscanion and the weird girl. Classy source material, no question. Now, we have to develop a script, use it to raise the finance to get things rolling, you know all this, right? Script is where you come in. Start thinking. We got guys can help you out. Motivation. Boscanion. The girl. This light thing they have. We build up these two characters of yours - well, better say ours now, and actually there'll be three, but we'll come to that later – but the story has to be big. We can handle that. I kinda like to produce my own work, you probably know that. You ever read Hermann Hesse, AB?'

Stan blinked.

'Yeah. He's kinda outta fashion now, hippies got their hooks in there. I'm thinking we go with the *Narziss and Goldmund* angle. Main guy's the shrivelled up, intellectual type - yeah, I know AB, we gotta make your guy more desiccated, dry him out a little, OK? A thinker. Right now he talks too much, too many words. Quaint's out. No. We go for the cloistered type, limited experience of life. So all the drinking, that's out. But this girl - she's just a wild, sensuous animal. But she wants to learn from this monk, this unworldly guru, she wants to improve her intellect. No! Not a buddy movie. Jesus! OK, she gets so far, makes so much progress, then something happens, between them, and she regresses, goes even further back, right to where she turns animal, goes all the way. She couldn't avoid her fate, you know? Then the guy, he realizes being a monk isn't the greatest thing in the world - she's changed him. One last meeting, but it's too late - they can't even communicate any more, and the guy, he kind of rebounds the other way, disappears into his own mind. But in a revelatory, *2001* kind of a way. OK, it's an old story, but we got three strong characters, we weave it in with an end of the world thriller kind of thing, great effects, but subtle, not so they detract - dynamite! What do you say, AB?'

'Ah.'

'Yeah. Just a few ideas. Think about it. Listen! Like I said, screenplay. We got writers, but we need you. It's your baby. You can handle that, AB? I guess you can. Brain power. You'll have to come out to the west coast, long as it takes. Gotta lady AB? Kids? They come too. No problem.'

Noble hounds?

The dusty chuckle. 'Matter of fact, way the unions are pushing, maybe we'll all be coming over here instead, right Milt?'

Stan was fired up. Who would be in *Boscanion - the Movie*? He had his own ideas, honed in private over the years, which very definitely did not include drying Boscanion, either up or out. But he'd tackle that later. 'Any thoughts about casting yet, Louis?'

'Depp,' piped Louis round a mouthful of mango. 'He'll love it. The girl ... we need someone with that animal quality, looks maybe a little disturbing. Lacey Chabert, the little girl out of *Lost in Space*. No!

Too old now. Better one of these bug-eyed oriental chicks, a complete unknown. Hey!' He smacked the table. 'That mean little streak in *Crouching Tiger*! Sensuous, but dangerous. You'd go with that AB? Your girl on the TV - yeew! *Planet of the Apes,* maybe. You guys were brave AB, no question, but you went too far with the latex, or whatever the hell you were using back then. That piece of casting cost you audience, no question. You'd never have got there in the States. We got ways of suggesting weirdness, without turning people off. People, they only take so much, you know, AB? And listen! We need a real, top-of-the-range badass in there too. A third character, gotta have some durability. I mean, where are the quality badasses in the movies these days? Go ahead, show me. Hannibal? OK, maybe Hannibal. That's one. Darth? To start with, not any more. Zachary Smith? Ming? Freddie Kruger? Jason? Add them all up, you still only got two dimensions. So, we need a badass people get fixed in their minds, they want to see him again, they pay. No-one pays to watch good guys. And. Your TV storylines, just a little too obscure, AB. Streamline things a little, make it bigger, more direct, load in a little more action, uh? More kablamm. What I'm thinking, apocalyptic, but with that nice light touch.'

'Ah ... '

Milt made some signal which Stan missed. Vanderhorst snatched up a napkin and patted his lips.

'OK! AB, gotta go now. Listen, I knew you'd be right behind this. What we've had has been a preliminary discussion, right? Just us, tossing ideas around while I was passing through, OK? Start thinking it over, flesh out the characters, and work up a real badass - we got guys can help you there, like I say. Milt here will send you a copy of *Xutha* - no, better make that *Trees* - and.the release form, so you can get into my style. Look at the leads, look at what motivates them, how I show it, the signals. Don't worry about story details right now. And maybe read some Hesse. OK?'

'Ah ... ' Each Vanderhorst pause took him by surprise. 'Yes, I think so. What about a contact number?'

'AB. Maybe lay low on this for a few weeks. Like I said, this is a preliminary. Just until the lawyers tie it up, uh? Milt here will give you a call, don't worry about it. This is just you and me, OK?'

And Milt, thought Stan, but Louis Vanderhorst was on the move, most of his meal still on the plate. Another tiptoe clap on the shoulder, another pumping handshake. Milt had melted away.

Stan's hand was dropped, Louis snapped off a mock salute,

piped *'Mandroso!'* switched the smile on, off, and marched away through the tables, firing off smiles at the other diners. Louis Vanderhorst was gone.

Stan poured out the last of the wine and took his time drinking it. He hadn't found an opportunity to clear up the misunderstanding about *Xutha's* fishes, but never mind. There would be plenty of time for that. The Zinfandel was pretty cloying this far in, as well as pink, and disappointingly unpotent. Presumably the way Californians liked it. To which view they were perfectly well entitled. Perfectly. It was a big world out there, and he had never exactly idolised conformity, had he?

He took out a cigar, feeling buoyant, pelagic in excelsis. The Getout Stakes had just come in. He drained the Zinfandel. Just wait till the dear old Barracuda heard about this: she'd be leaping about. Vanderhorst couldn't object to him telling his own wife. And, even more, it was something for Gram, something to make him just a little bit proud of his clever old dad. Restore the faith.

Who had sent Louis the tape though? He should have asked. Had to be Ray. But Ray wouldn't let the Louis Vanderhorsts of this world anywhere near it. In fact, Ray might be a problem. Worry about that later. He savoured the thought of Delyth's pike-like perfection shaken by the news. A minor bonus. It must have been a fan then, some discerning member of the great British Public. Well, whomsoever it might be, Boscanion would not fail him. Or her. He smiled benignly at the other diners on his way out.

The South Terminal shopping area was hot and stuffed with drained and tinny air. He felt light-headed, and put it down to success. Soon he found he was carrying a Gatwick bag containing a slinky silk dressing gown plastered with Gauguin women, fit for a Black Barracuda, as well as an expensive book on sharks and rays, mainly for its photographs, a gift for the excellent and outstanding Gram, and a squeaking plastic bone for the noble hound (the choice was limited). And for himself, a bottle of malt with a name he couldn't pronounce, from the top shelf. Lots of ds and bs and hs - he'd just pointed his credit-card. He deserved it. They all deserved it. He was overcome with admiration for his small, perfect family. And they would have the time of their lives out there in good old Papa, he would see to that. He must find a payphone and tell them.

Infuriatingly there was a queue, despite all the people standing around shouting into mobiles. Liza was forever telling him he should have one himself, but she wasn't serious. He was a free spirit, she knew that.

Then he was back on the train, bag safely beside him, drifting off again, the carriage swaying, pleasantly warm. How tense and weary everyone appeared, even the plane people – in fact they in particular looked itchy and out of place, with their tans and luggage, learning quickly how to tone themselves down again to fit back into this underlit grey world. People had to put up with a hell of a lot, when you thought about it. Life. Just staying human was a battle, wasn't it? How did they all cope, carve out little niches for themselves, gouge out a living, find a little slot to inhabit? He was soon lost in a fuzz of warm, comfortable, drifting admiration.

Nothing had happened since the atoll - no life with Liza, no Gram. No Kato. It had all been a dream. The atoll filled his mind: Julius, white-faced and patrician in his groovy hat, scarcely speaking to him now, quietly furious that the work was threatened; Roland's baleful, sandy stare; Alain's mixture of macho posturing, hostility and nervousness: Alain, who jumped when Roland spoke; Alain, who, whenever he wasn't curled up in a corner asleep, was usually smiling. But here a smile could mean many things. Bernard was even younger, impulsive and argumentative, the loner in the neat little moustache and flamboyant headscarf, always antagonizing the other Linois, always starting fights, once or twice leaving Stan little choice but to get involved himself. Bernard's periodic roaring binges, achieved through his beer allowance from the small atoll store topped up with illicit home-brewed lentils and jam, were followed without fail by lacerating, pink-eyed hangovers. Bernard's whisper … *when you cut your fingernail, your toenail, you must burn … your hair, when you cut, you must burn … not to leave for the woman who clean your house.*

There had been one trip, to measure rainfall at a rain-gauge in a remote part of the atoll: Stan had been abandoned by Alain, his so-called guide, out in the trackless miles of scrub, out in that deadly heat, under the weight of his back-pack for three hours, water gone and panic hovering. Wherever he looked the same parched scenery had faced him, shimmering in the heat - except way over there, where a dark belt of distant mangrove bordered the lagoon, marking the labyrinthine network of tidal creeks and pools. He had a choice: should he use his compass, cut directly across to the mangrove, hope he struck the one creek among dozens where the small boat, he knew, would wait only so long? Or should he spend precious time trying to re-locate the trail? He went for the mangrove. Which was the wrong choice, and he was in a fairly desperate state when Bernard found him. Saved him. Brought him back along an ancient trail cryptically marked with fragments of fossil coral which Stan's eyes could not see. Nor were they meant to. The trail wasn't there for people like him. They'd reached the boat just in time, while there was barely enough water to get out into the lagoon to make the crossing back to the Station. He remembered all too well how Roland and Alain had watched in silence as he and Bernard climbed in. No welcome, no questions, no concern. Roland's face showed nothing, not even disappointment.

A fuzzy, buzzing silence grew steadily louder, until he came to in an empty compartment. The train had stopped. Discarded newspapers, fizzy drink cans and crisp bags littered the aisle and the empty seats around him. Apart from the buzzing, which seemed to be coming from both outside and inside his head, there was no sound. The shadowy station sign read Portsmouth, the end of the line. He was clammy with sweat and he'd missed his stop. His Gatwick bag was nowhere to be seen.

Shopping. Had to be done. The Barracuda hated it as much as he did, or very nearly, but she was disciplined. Whenever too much space appeared in the cupboards and fridge she drove to an enclave of superstores and petrol filling stations planted out at Hedge End. Stan was there to help, which he did by staying out of the way, inspecting the drink section and the fish counter until the Barracuda rounded the corner with a laden trolley. She didn't like it, but she was efficient. It was a joyless, demersal affair, but he could be depended upon to make the best of it. Although eager to be involved, Kato had to wait out there in the city of cars: afterwards the Barracuda would drop the two of them off on Cobden Bridge and they would amble home through Riverside Park. Stan and the noble hound considered this last part a reward for the rest.

Stan was impressing himself with his ability to relegate the current headache by pushing it to the back. Mixed feelings here at the fish counter, inevitably, pondering the usual selection of kippers, mackerel, plaice, the cod and haddock which were scarce in the sea but not in the supermarkets, creamy-grey fillets of coalfish, a slab cut from a ling dragged up no doubt from the false security of an Atlantic wreck, the desperately sad farmed salmon, which had never really been alive, next to hunks of supremely pelagic tuna, a pile of identical bass from a Mediterranean farm, and a lone John Dory, *Zeus faber*, which looked out of place and down in the mouth. He was tempted by *Zeus*, but he and the Barracuda had promised the local fishmonger they'd stick with him. Fishes were in a tight spot, notwithstanding the immensity of the oceans, and so were fishmongers. On top of all the quotas already in place, a Euro-ban on cod fishing in parts of the North Sea had just been announced. Gram wanted them to stop eating fish altogether, as he had, before there were no fishes left to eat, but Stan could never contemplate that. He must eat them, marvellous creatures. As he'd told Shanny, one day he would return the favour.

Distractions made the news - salmon had been manipulated back into the Thames – but fishes were on the way out, as long as humans remained. All very well getting excited over Huntingdon Life Sciences, but what about Project 863? He could barely bring himself to consider it. In Project 863 the Chinese were genetically modifying fishes to promote faster growth, among other things. Some of these wretched Chinese fishes contained human genes. Beyond nightmare. And anything finding its way into the public domain was already years out of date and a fraction of the ghastly whole. He should move on to the drinks.

The shelves of spirits soothed him, the Grenadine with its anemonefish, the puffed-up Wild Turkey, the neat white feet of the Famous Grouse. He would take his time making his selection. The government had backed off from wiping out all the wildlife on Dartmoor, but foot and mouth was whipping through the flocks and herds. He thought of those peacefully grazing black and white beasts he'd seen through the train window - they couldn't burn them fast enough now, couldn't keep up with all the corpses. They were being shipped direct to the rendering plants. The Tories were calling for a state of emergency, the government insisted it was under control, and Britain was being spoken of as the Leper of Europe. Now they were going to slaughter another 300,000 sheep which were probably healthy, just in case.

Liza trundled imperiously up with the Blackster trolley and resumed her description of an exhibition she'd taken the kids to, which she'd started in the car just as he was putting in some work on his Badass. It was on at Southampton City Art Gallery, something to do with the history of the docks, and Stan had to go and see it. Immediately the headache shimmied forward. It was all about concentration: there was only so much, and he had to hold enough in reserve to keep a grip on things like headaches.

Mrs Blackster had taken some convincing over the Vanderhorst bombshell. She wanted to see something in writing. It wasn't quite the wholehearted, force-of-nature response he'd fondly anticipated, but then there had been disappointments before. Things between them hadn't yet fully recovered from the man on the roof, and those alarming eyes were more watchful than ever. However, she would see. Later that evening was Episode Two. He had been quietly hopeful that she would watch this one - the Ruahari after all were good value in their conceit and uselessness, and he must find a place for them in the movie, but she'd arranged to go out. To the *Boat* presumably, for a drink or two with Sharma and some of the others. If the moray's little gang tonight included Arvind, the persistent agent of management, so what? Something warned him he was under scrutiny.

'Where are we at with the holiday booking then, Stanley? I've left it all to you, with your local knowledge, and I expected to be wading through the brochures by now, picking out the flashiest hotel with the best beach. I've been looking at a map of the main island. Margaritifer, is that right? Gram's been asking too. Come on, what's to do?'

She was fingering South American red wines on the topmost, expensive shelf, new territory, and beneath the cheery veneer there was the brittle steeliness, the readiness to snap. It was exactly a week since the explosion of gin and adrenalin, but she'd never again mentioned the man on the roof, as though it had never been. She had recently taken to snoring like a bear, assuming bears snored, and he would lay beside her at night itching and clammy with sweat, listening to the drone, resisting the urge to shake, creeping off for a shot only when he had to.

Shanny had telephoned a couple of times to see how things were. As expected, it had shaken him up, and he still sounded faintly suspicious of Stan's part in it. He was expecting to be out of a job any day but didn't seem too concerned, anticipating a healthy redundancy package, far more worked up about Sheffield Wednesday, who were still sinking and had sacked Paul Jewell.

'No worries Barra. I'll have it sorted tomorrow.' She said she'd left it to him, so why didn't she leave it to him? If he could create sufficient negative pressure at the back of his skull, it would suck the headache straight out, like Ripley dumping her alien-relative at the end of – which one was it, *Alien* 3? It had clung on, fought and scrabbled, didn't want to go, but then *swish*, out into space. He'd sort it out.

Tomorrow. Just now he was looking for a spirit which left less of a mark the next day, without sacrificing power. Apocalyptic, but with that nice, light touch. He needed a Badass.

'Margaritifer, that's right.' A name sweltering with palms and white sand. 'The locals - the Linois - call it Marga.'

Liza nodded, flexing those teeth, and tried out the words. She had managed to negotiate extra time off after the official break, partly on the pretext of an artistic Hands Across The Oceans project, but he suspected she had given other, unspecified undertakings. Good for her.

'Stanley?'

Her tone made him try to concentrate. 'What?'

'I had a look on Gram's computer this morning.'

His eyebrows lifted. She didn't agree, loudly, with that kind of thing. Snooping.

She gestured. 'I've been worried about him. We both have, haven't we? All this sitting up there in his room, hardly going out, never bringing any mates round. And the girls should be queuing round the block.' A short, meaningful stare. 'Anyway, I went in there this morning. I'm his mother.'

Gram was downloading porn. It was about time. Hang on though - there was porn and there was porn. And the ordinary sort would hardly bother the Barracuda.

'You shouldn't have done that. He's sixteen, Barra. It's his room. We decided that.'

She ignored this. 'He's in contact with animal rights activists, Stan. The bad kind, you know. Direct action, baseball bats, firebombs through the letterbox and so on.'

Stan sighed. 'He's got his views, Liza, and we both know what they are. He doesn't like the way animals are treated here. Who does? Why shouldn't he want to do something about it? Come on, you're not really surprised, surely?'

'But firebombs, Stanley!' She lowered her voice to a hiss as shoals of shoppers cruised by. 'Addresses and names, the labs they work in, all over the country. Profiles, crime-sheets, so-called, even photos. He's right in there with them, Stan.'

'Not necessarily. You know how it works. If you're interested in something on the net you can wind up in all kinds of weird backwaters.' He spoke with authority. 'Googling. Done it myself. It doesn't mean he's involved.'

'You don't talk to him Stanley. How would you know? He's

your son for God's sake! He needs guidance, but he never gets it from you. You just plod along in your own exclusive little world. Just because he wouldn't drop everything for bloody fish - don't think I don't know! You've never treated him the way a normal father would. Gram might as well be a lodger. I've tried, but he needs a father.'

There was that hard look again. He could do without this, just now. He held up his hands. 'OK, OK. I'll come quietly. Jesus! Look, I hear what you're saying Liza, OK? Maybe I have let it slip a little, but we went to the match, didn't we? And it works both ways – he's changed, hasn't he? Growing up. Talking to him isn't so easy any more. But I'll tackle him about it, don't worry. It'll be nothing. He's just wandering about on the net, that's all it is, but I'll talk to him. Don't worry, yes, I'll see to it.' He could feel his temper slipping, had to hang onto it. A drink wouldn't hurt.

The Barracuda was jostled by a passing trolley and sent one of her glares after it. 'Hey! Lady! What do you think this is, a bloody motorway?'

'Come on, Liza. What's this, trolley rage?'

She looked at him deliberately, strong white teeth biting down on that soft pink lip. 'OK, you'll talk to him, father to son, and you'll get to the bottom of it? You'd better, Stanley, because quite frankly I don't like the way he ignores you these days - '

'He doesn't!'

'Take it from me. You're not exactly on the alert, or even in the same room with us half the time. He doesn't respect you the way he used to, the way he should.'

Nonsense. Utter nonsense. 'Gram – '

'Gram's not Kato. You've got to pull yourself together, see what's happening under your nose. Be told! Forget about bloody fish, forget about bloody drink – you've got a son who's slipping away from you! God, are you even human?'

His mouth opened and closed.

'Well, are you?'

Folk hurried by.

'By and large.'

Liza stared, slowly angling her head. Her eyes got bigger. Time ground to a halt. 'Yeah. Right.' Then she nodded. 'You'll see to it.'

He nodded back.

'Promise?'

He nodded.

She seemed to be considering something carefully, then quite suddenly the steeliness seemed to go out of her, the eyes dimmed, moistened. 'Everything is all right, isn't it Stan? I mean, everything?'

He was wary. What did she mean? Did she mean with him? With her? With Gram? With the whole wide world? When he pulled her to him she tensed up at first, then relaxed slowly, lowering her head to his shoulder. 'Is everything all right? Hardly. The world's about to go pop, Barra, and all the problems boil down to one - there's just too bloody many of us. No votes in chasing that one though.'

'You sound like Gram. I mean us. We'll be all right, won't we Stan, us? I'm stressed, that's all. We just need a break. We just need to get away for a while.'

But not from each other? This was most unlike her. There'd been a brittleness ever since the man on the roof; or perhaps it was age, and it had been developing for a while but he hadn't noticed. Maybe he had taken his eye off the ball, at some point.

'Shanny has an interesting theory about stress.'

She looked at him, lips pursed. 'Oh?'

'Yes. Shanny thinks they only invented it twenty years ago and now every bugger's got it.'

'Yeah, right.'

'That's the gist of it anyway.'

'Thanks. That would be every bugger except you.'

Unfair. He just concealed it so well. 'You wouldn't like me stressed, Barra.'

'I might. You should try me.'

He could see where this might lead, and pulled her gently to him.

'We're OK Barra.'

They kissed. He stroked her long, black, shining hair. She sighed into his shoulder, then tensed and mumbled something. Stan felt the need to divert their thoughts.

'For every yellowfin - '

A hand shot up. 'Not fish! Christ.'

Stan worked his tongue around the inside of his mouth. Thoughts would not come. He could hear teeth grinding.

She looked up and kissed his nose, then tapped it firmly with a forefinger. 'Not fish Stan.'

He was staring, he knew he was.

'OK then, this silk Gauguin dressing gown. Did you really buy me one? You were making it up, weren't you?'

'Yep. I mean nope. No, I really did.' Ninety nine per cent certain.

'Describe it.'

'All greens and yellows ... couple of his women ...' Better make that ninety. Wasn't there a vague animal image ... ? 'There was a fox, or something ... '

'That's male sexuality, the red dog.' She nuzzled his neck, made a growling noise in her throat.

Back to ninety-nine.

'And you left it on the train, right?'

'No. Some bugger nicked it. And the other stuff. I told you. Bastard's wearing it now.'

She kissed his neck, pulled gently away and studied him. How did she transmit such force through her eyes? Delyth could do the same thing, if not as powerfully, only in blue.

'You've done brilliantly well Stanley, at last, with this Louis character. I want you to know that. Maybe I've not told you properly. Not that I ever had any doubts, of course.' She reached for bottles, not from the top shelf. 'Don't forget I'm out tonight.'

'You have a good time Barra, you deserve it.' She would never stop hating Kim, and he wanted to say Kim was just another floundering kid, like one of yours at work. But she wasn't.

Liza had piled in half a dozen assorted Cab Sauvs, Malbecs and Merlots and a green litre of Gordon's. Stan hefted a Wild Turkey bottle, chewing a forefinger as he admired the bird. Of course Gram respected him. Wild Turkey then? Was this the spirit to suit the requirements of the moment? To play its due part in the creation of a stimulating imaginative landscape? Of course Gram respected him. Perhaps a quick nip, a sort of stage-setter, as the Blackster trolley trundled away towards the checkout.

Now, the noble hound was waiting.

There were new signs of natural life in Riverside Park now, yellow-green buds spotting the trees, a few more birds trying out their voices after months of frozen silence. Still damned cold though. Freed from his chain, Kato went bounding off across the grass, called a halt for an urgent sniff, bounded off again. After a coughing bout which shivered his fragile head, Stan set off too, pushing his hands deep into his coat pockets, deciding to stick to the path. At least here you could see the dog turds coming, whereas out in the grass it was a minefield. Even now the noble hound had adopted the posture, grinning like an idiot. Stan was supposed to clean up after him, as the Barracuda and Gram were always insisting, and even had the plastic carrier bags in his pockets for the purpose. It was the right thing to do, no question about it, but he looked the other way.

The perpetual game of park football was in stop-start motion. He and Kato usually paused here to watch for a while. It was somehow reassuring that such remarkably unathletic middle-aged men all over the country felt the urge to do this, and he liked to try to predict the first casualty. If Shanny trotted out onto the pitch now, Stan would have to make him favourite, odds-on. And then it would be off to Hillsborough, or failing that Palma, with the ashes. Or maybe, in the middle of one of his rants, after fifteen years of threatening, his head would finally burst. Out on the pitch two dreadnoughts collided and went down. Team-mates gathered round, hands on hips.

He congratulated himself on having resisted the urge to take another swig of Wild Turkey in the car before setting off with the noble hound. Prudent. The Barracuda would have noticed and had something to say, and he could do without it - he had two things to think about now: a Badass and Gram.

The path wound its way down to the River Itchen where shoals of minnows persisted among the supermarket trolleys and traffic cones. The noble hound, up ahead, had found a lookalike and was trying to mount her, or him - Kato had never been able to tell the difference. He went about it as though acting out some dim folk-memory.

'Kato! Get back here!'

On a bench by the river two girls sat with an older man. As he got closer, Stan could see that one of the girls wore her hair in a small, lacquered, fan-like arrangement, in the manner of Kim's old fans. He felt a shiver of anticipation. The second girl leaned forward, and she too sported the crest. He'd never seen them here before, hadn't seen the hairstyle out in the wild for years in fact, and this was presumably a result of the re-run. A good job the Barracuda wasn't here.

The noble hound reached the bench first and said his hellos, tail flagging away. The two girls – young women, really - stood up, kissed the man on the cheek and moved off along the path, arm-in-arm. Disappointment eased into resignation as he recognized Charlie Chin.

'Hello Charlie.'

'Stanley! Or, I should say, AB! My word! Here, do sit down, my dear chap. Is this the famous Molossian Hound? Magnificent beast! His name?'

'Kato.'

'Aha! To your Clousseau, yes of course. Here, Stanley, do join me ... '

Stan lowered himself to the bench, summoning inner reserves for a lengthy session. Maybe having a hangover would make this easier. He would let it flow over him. How long before the old boy asked for a loan? Well, here goes.

'This is a bit of a surprise, Charlie. What brings you to the big city?'

'Oh, you know me, Stanley. Life in the country is all very well, village greens and cock-crow and so forth, but I find it can become enervating. I felt the need to re-kindle my zest for life. At the convention I met some young friends - fans, if the truth be known - and they very kindly invited me to stay with them. Here I am. They seem to derive pleasure from escorting me to centres of culture and entertainment in this vibrant city of yours. It's most flattering.'

'Ah. I see.' Stan nodded, slowly, looking off along the river. Bankside trees, still leafless, flew fluttering plastic bags. 'Would they be the category of fan we know and love as Kims, Charlie?'

'Ahem. Yes, they would. And quite charming. They seem to think a great deal of me, Lord knows why, and I'm bound to confess that an old man finds the company and conversation invigorating. You can understand that, can't you Stanley? I say! These are heady days, what? To have the great adventure again on our screens? We have the remorseless Raymond to thank for this.'

Charles Chinchard was at his most fluent and had clearly been drinking, which came as something of a relief. At the convention he'd been lamenting the cruel hand life had dealt him, yearning eloquently for the hangovers he could no longer regularly afford. Stan carried out a discreet inspection: the long black coat and scarf smelled stale and ginny even in the cold and breezy outdoors, the foppish old red fedora on the bench beside him carried a whiff of desperation. He resembled more than ever an old and venerated English character actor playing a toff down on his luck, an illusion Charlie was perfectly happy to encourage. During the production of *Insidiator*, or just afterwards, his long-time marriage had collapsed, he had dived into the bottle, and work had dried up. He had cultivated his own version of the imperial moustache and beard and the long hair he had worn as the swashbuckling Boscanion, all now an improbable black; in addition, the veteran actor's face was obviously made up. His old eyes sparkled with the joy of life, in best Boscanion manner, but its source was a bottle of gin. Gin was Charlie's preferred drink, as Stan had reason to know. During production there had been some marathon sessions, with Ray usually at the helm and whoever else was around, in funds and in the mood happily on board. Harak the headman had been a particularly dedicated participant.

Now, who would play Harak in the movie? It would be a new story, but these characters were a part of the whole. Essential. He could work them in. Bernard Hill perhaps, or even Vinnie Jones; but someone less familiar would be better, someone with a powerful and commanding presence, demonstrably dim ... and he must get out of the habit of considering only British actors, he must think international, and there were any number of Americans suited to the part ... or, why not show some imagination, take a gamble with a non-pro, a star in some other area, let's say football. A strutting German mid-fielder, that Effenberg for instance ... No, maybe not. Play safe then. Bruce Willis would do, bit of challenging character work for him, or perhaps Kurt Russell. They were all small though, weren't they? But no American accents, absolutely not, he'd have to put his foot down there.

'There's talk of a film, Charlie ... '

He shouldn't have said that. He hadn't been concentrating.

Chinchard stared at him, eyes wide. 'A film,' he mumbled. Then, 'A film! And how overdue! More good work by Raymond? I wish to know the casting schedule! I must know everything Stanley! I must prepare! It was ordained. My new friends assured me we stood on the brink of great things! Wonders are in the air!'

In his head, Stan kicked himself. 'Hold on Charlie, hold on. There's nothing definite, and I can't say any more. In fact I'd appreciate it if you kept this to yourself. You'll have to - '

But tears were tracking through Chinchard's makeup, and he was making snuffling sounds. Kato, slumped on the path at their feet watching the world go by, looked up.

'Do you ever hear from her, Stanley? Truly, I mean? From Kim?'

'No Charlie.' He always asked this. 'No-one has. You know that.'

Chinchard nodded. The old boy was wheezing now. 'Yes. Of course. It was my fault you know, my fault she went off like that. She was so vulnerable, wasn't she? So lacking in the guile we are all supposed to have. I … I wanted her to go away with me, when we had completed our work. Somewhere hot. She was always so cold, wasn't she? I grew up in India, did you know? Foolish, foolish old man - that's what you're thinking. But we used to talk. You know how she was, pitifully eager to learn, almost desperate to improve her appreciation of the arts, of matters cultural. For a time, I was her tutor. I thought … foolish of me, yes, you're quite right of course. Excuse me Stanley … '

Chinchard pulled out a flat quarter bottle of Beefeater, took a tiny nip, popped it away with an attempt at Boscanion's dashing smile.

'I've talked with my friends about this actually, over and over. Of course, they think she was marvellous, and they say I've nothing to reproach myself for.'

'I know what they think. They think she was kept under lock and key and fed control drugs like Judy Garland. They blame Ray. Me too, I expect.'

Chinchard nodded, but he wasn't in the mood for listening. 'I feel better about it now. I used to think she looked to me as to … I don't know, a surrogate father I suppose, as well as a teacher.' He looked suddenly thoughtful. 'An odd thing. Between you and I Stanley, she simply didn't seem quite able to grasp abstractions, despite the intensity of her yearning. It was rather strange, but no doubt I have my shortcomings as a guru-figure. Anyway, I eventually came to realize it was you she wanted to be with, you she wanted to impress. How she envied dear Liza! Yes, to Kim you were always Boscanion, not I.'

Memories swirled up like disturbed sediment. 'It was all a long time ago, Charlie.' He seemed to be forever telling people that. 'We managed to get a decent show out of it, anyway.'

Chinchard brightened. 'It is very good, isn't it? Even now. Some of my finest work, Stanley, and thanks in no small part to yourself and Raymond. My Book, too, is a source of some satisfaction. There were certain technical obstacles to be surmounted, you know. All was not as straightforward as it may appear now – '

'I know Charlie. I was there.'

'I beg your pardon? Well, yes. Of course you were there, my dear chap. I can vouch for it. And tonight, the second instalment, wherein I encounter the bibulous and truculent Ruahari. A small company is to assemble for the occasion, at which I am to be guest of honour.'

Stan was preparing to make his escape.

'Must you go? It's been delightful to see you again, I was meaning to look you up. And so hale and hearty to boot!' Chinchard leaned over to whisper confidentially, 'And thank you for the news, AB. It shall go no further, you have my word.' A bout of loud throat-clearing followed. 'We must keep in touch, now that we share a city, so to speak. And I should so like to see the marvellous Liza again, a true nonpareil! My card.'

Stan took it, smiled his thanks and tucked it away.

'And Stanley, you will let me know of any *developments* … ?'

Chinchard had a trick, which he used now, of making his eyes bulge, the result of a stint as Rasputin early in his career. An inquisitive dog-walker accelerated smartly away in the wake of her labrador.

'Of course, Charlie. Just don't hold your breath. You know how these things are. And enjoy it tonight, right? Raise a glass.'

'I shall! And afterwards I am to visit your renowned international port. My friends are to bid farewell to a traveller. I anticipate a splendid evening!'

'Good luck Charlie.'

The noble hound had resumed his role of pathfinder, and stood looking back over his shoulder.

'Farewell, Kato!' called Chinchard, waving graciously.

Not far along the path Kato ploughed through the mud and plunged into the Itchen, floundering against the sluggish current, indicating that he should be thrown something to retrieve. The Barracuda would be furious.

7. The Ruahari

Stan sat with his son in the darkened room, warily glued to the luminous screen. He took a long pull of Wild Turkey as the fire-drakes glowed their green glow, unseen things scuttled in the shadows and his guts twisted. Another, better world. He shifted in his seat to gain Gram's attention, without success. Surely Gram felt the same spasm of anticipation? If not the same helplessness. The noble hound heaved a sigh. The red book awoke.

'Mandroso.'

The face of Boscanion stared out from the burnished brassy dish, eyes wide, handsome teeth fully on display.

'A face of character!' he congratulated himself in his rich, actor's voice. 'I read here an understated nobility, leavened with the ready humour of everyman, who takes what each day brings with a shrug and a smile.' Carefully he moved into place a blade to trim an edge of the imperious black moustache; with equal care he then struck a theatrical pose of despair, shoulders drooping, and addressed his image: 'You and I, we must maintain one another's resolve and spirit in difficult times. We are far from an unknown home, while futility and despair hover like predatory fishes.' He sighed, and his eyes filled. 'We are human men, you and I, subject to the full depth and range of human feeling.'

The blade moved on, to the black square of beard beneath the full lower lip, which now curved in a defiant smile. A soft, throaty laugh once more transformed the face in the dish. 'Aye. Humour and resilience are our preferred strategies when faced with the world and its ways - even such a perplexing world as that which now surrounds us.' He held up a long forefinger. 'Notice, always there is the quiet gleam of a keen and questing intellect. Always Boscanion thirsts for knowledge. We shall reach our goal, certainly, but what is it? What place in this world of curiosities is to be our final destination?'

The dish reflected only dimly the face of the figure behind him, a pale face with hair as black as Boscanion's own scraped back behind the head into a crest-like fan.

'I shall assist you, Boscanion.' This was his companion of recent miles, an Aspidont.

Boscanion considered this. 'Well said! And I am confident in the abilities of such a formidable survivor as yourself!' As yet, the Aspidont had no name. 'It is presently a cruel fact that my conscious life began just days ago when I found myself on the forest floor, and was required instantly to deploy the full array of Boscanion wits in order to elude determined pursuers bent on mischief. No doubt they were simply going about forest affairs in everyday fashion, but for newcomers it sets a bleak tone. Curious ...' He moved the blade fastidiously along the lower edge of the black square of bristles, where the long, clean-shaven chin bulged. 'I almost feel I was shot there, to the forest, from some giant gun-barrel or monstrous sling. But this seems unlikely.'

'Yet you have a name.' The Aspidont's voice was more assured than it had been at their first full acquaintance by the sea several days before.

'Naturally I have a name,' replied Boscanion waspishly. 'I have only to consult a reflective surface and there is Boscanion!' He went on more calmly. 'No, my dear, you are astute. It is my belief that when I reach my destination, where and whatever this may be, there I shall be made whole. And,' he attended now to the luxuriant side-whiskers, 'the name Boscanion, as you point out, is a small beacon in the darkness.' He glanced significantly down at his highly polished, air-cushioned boots. 'In addition, we may take heart in the belief that these admirable boots possess what I lack - a certainty in their course.'

The Aspidont smiled quickly, showing white teeth which were pointed and also slightly curved, so that the points angled away from the centre of the face. This, more than anything, gave the quick, grimacing smile its unique, and, increasingly for Boscanion, enchanting character.

'As you say. We shall be guided by the boots of Boscanion.'

'My fine new friend,' announced Boscanion, turning from his mirror in the crook of a leathery-trunked tree of the coast, 'I am encouraged to observe that your diction, enunciation and vocabulary have improved dramatically under my tutelage, during the brief period of our acquaintance.'

The Aspidont's extraordinary, feral face again glowed briefly with that fierce smile. Once lustreless hair, now almost as black and glossy as his own, had been brought to order in its severe, fan-like arrangement using Boscanion's fish-comb, and now topped a clean, if pallid face from which round, wide-spaced black eyes stared fixedly at him above the jut of outsize jaws.

'Your appearance too, refines itself ...' Boscanion coughed delicately and looked off along the marching lines of sand-dunes, their attendant groves of scrubby trees sheltering from ceaseless wind and sea-spray. 'Things are looking up for us, on all fronts. With your food-finding instincts allied to my own small skills and sense of destiny, we make a formidable team!'

Collecting his pack and battered red hat he took the Aspidont's somewhat inflexible arm and led her out along the beach-crest, where coarse, salt-tolerant vegetation knitted sand together and offered firm footing. The pale orange sun had begun its climb, washing colour into the bluest and most placid of seas and the red coastal plain with its dark and distant line of forest, the two held apart by the white belt of beach and dunes stretching straight ahead; above and all around in the hot blue sky, piled clouds of creamy white and lilac rode the wind from the sea. Boscanion's air-cushioned boots unhesitatingly set off northwards with a purposeful stride.

Later that morning they came upon the wreck of some sort of vessel, almost covered in drifting sand, constructed of an oddly flexible, silver-grey material which Boscanion failed to recognize. He could discern no trace of seams, junctions or fastenings; it seemed all of a piece.

'Curious,' mused Boscanion, removing his hat and craning his long neck to view a piece of the hull against the sky. 'The outer surface is scratched and weathered, but from inside it is translucent ... as though before calamity overtook it, the hull was clear as glass.' From the vessel's sides protruded a series of large and mystifying stumps. He straightened, grinning broadly. 'Consider, my friend: to travel in such a vessel, to view the fishes about their hidden lives, as they in turn view you. What an adventure!' He flourished the dusty red hat.

'Not only fishes, Boscanion. The hunting creatures. They also would look in.'

'Ah.'

Earlier they had witnessed a tremendous affray beyond the reef, a thrashing of finny limbs and flying water eventually stained red. He thought also of the foraging brute he had witnessed in the Aspidont's pit, and shuddered. 'To a degree one can admire their purposeful grace, so long as it directs them elsewhere.'

A tentative attempt on the hull with his blade made no

impression: in fact the strange material appeared almost to repel the blade in a manner both disturbing and hazardous.

'Who do you suppose constructed such a singular craft, my friend, and how came it to be wrecked here?'

His companion was not one of life's shruggers, he had noticed: her arms remained stiffly flexed, held out from her sides, the upper part of her torso leaning forward slightly. A quick gesture of the lips was perhaps the equivalent of a shrug, a brief tightening over the bulge of teeth. She pointed. 'See the marks.'

All but erased by wind and tide, the peaks of great parallel ridges could just be seen in the sand between vessel and sea.

'And here also'. She pointed again, to a shallow, half-obscured depression in the sand, well over twenty feet across. 'It was not long ago. When I came to you and you gave me the poor fish of Kilwa. Maybe then.'

Boscanion noticed she had not approached, and in fact viewed the thirty foot long structure with an impression hard to read. Apprehension? Distaste? At that instant her face was again the primitive, blood-chilling mask he recalled, suddenly, from the Kilwan pit. He must not forget. And how long had be been thinking of the Aspidont as 'her' and 'she'? He must stay alert.

Long before mid-day the sun became too fierce for travel, and Boscanion crawled beneath a beach tree which under the influence of salt winds had evolved the form of a fantastic heraldic beast galloping towards the sea, long leafy train flowing astern. He found other creatures sheltering there, reptiles with hard, shiny cases and hooded eyes, clustering together in a shimmering fog of insects. Fortunately these were not large and he was able to push them aside and otherwise discourage them; beating with his hat dispersed the greater part of the swarming insects, which appeared anyway to prefer cooler reptilian blood.

The Aspidont appeared towards evening with a brace of swallow-tailed vermilion fish bearing yellow spots, overlarge heads and countless, splinter-like teeth. She seemed able to procure fish or other items of edible wildlife - small rodents, crustaceans, large insects, myriapods, reptiles - not to mention water, whenever required, and while Boscanion baulked at one or two of the offerings, the Aspidont devoured all with equal relish.

Boscanion had started up a fire using sun-bleached branches shed by the extravagant tree, and was roasting a spitted fish, the burning wood bringing a pleasingly aromatic tang to the evening air. He had observed that his companion ate all her food raw - an occasionally distressing sight - but now she watched the flames with every appearance of interest. There. It was 'she' again.

'My friend. I cannot go on calling you simply 'my friend', accurate though I believe this to be. We will face unknown trials together, and I must know you by name. I - '

'I am Anakim.'

'Aha! Anakim. Yes. A fine name. A hunter's name.' He was nonplussed. Why had she not divulged her name before? And why was this name, perfectly well suited as he immediately saw it to be, vaguely familiar to him? He had heard this name recently, in connection with a form of meaty fish popular among the good folk of Kilwa - one of the predators, in fact. Anakim. Coincidence no doubt, or perhaps the first name to fly into that singular little skull. Boscanion became aware of round black eyes studying him as he chewed at a forefinger. He withdrew his hand and cleared his throat.

'Well then, Anakim. I have told you of myself, inasmuch as I am currently able. Now what of you? What of Anakim?' He had long wanted to ask. 'The adventures of the road bring us together, and I learn more each passing day. But I cannot yet see behind those fine black eyes of yours - you are in many ways still a stranger to me, and I would like to know you more. What is the history of Anakim?'

The thin lips tightened fleetingly in characteristic response. 'I must learn, that I become better. It seemed my path lay with the folk of Kilwa, a superior group. I was one of them. Then ... I learned I was not. Already it is a fading dream. Now I am here.'

'Ah,' murmured Boscanion, fascinated if little wiser. He himself had told her of dreams, apparently a novel concept. 'No cause for self-reproach there, my dear. I myself found the Kilwans an unsatisfactory advertisement for humankind. Take their beer ... well, undeniably potent, but otherwise falling woefully short of customary standards, I can assure you. You were not the first in their pit, nor will you be the last.'

Anakim's far-set eyes never wavered. 'Now, I wish only to learn from you, Boscanion. To be as you are. I will help to find your destination, if I can. That is all.'

Boscanion pondered. 'My dear, your words fill me with fortitude and conviction. But before your wretched time at Kilwa? What lies in your past?'

It was now dark, and the flames flickered in her black eyes. The swallow-tailed fish proved excellent, with a surprisingly intense flavour allied to a solid, springy texture. For the first time Anakim had taken her meal cooked. A luscious scent from the night flowers of the fantastic beach-tree mingled in the air with fragrant wood-smoke.

'Long ago, warm salt water. Feeding was good. The great world was outside. I was small. I was protected. After this, I was adrift. Then I found Boscanion.'

He was about to ask more, but at that moment a sound came from the darkness, muffled by surf and wind, a short sequence of gutteral coughs or barks, accompanied by a substantial rush of air.

'Aha!' Boscanion dropped the remains of his fish onto a palm leaf and jumped to his feet. 'This pestilential place! A night prowler approaches, and I have neglected our defences.'

A dark shape passed low overhead, to be followed shortly by sounds of a heavy settling and the unhurried arrangement of leathery wings. Presently a slightly luminous, fox-like face appeared at the edge of the flickering firelight, and perfectly round, honey-coloured eyes looked down from a height greater than Boscanion's own.

'Advance if you come in peace, begone if you intend harm!' intoned Boscanion hopefully.

A long, fleshy tongue licked hooked, yellow teeth as the creature made a sound of derision. Black wings, folded in the manner of a cloak, could now be discerned, and heavily clawed limbs.

'I give you fair warning, I am a mighty wizard! Advance at your peril!' Boscanion flourished an arm, producing fitful sparks in the air. The creature moved decisively forward. Its round eyes were enormous in the firelight.

'A spell, Boscanion,' suggested Anakim at his back. 'A spell to send the Jactator back into the night.'

Boscanion's features contorted as the fox-face towered over him. 'I don't seem ... '

'Hur!' The creature spoke with difficulty, but the word 'Wizard!' was ground out clearly enough. An arm shot forward to take Boscanion by the throat.

Boscanion threshed madly in its grip, feeling claws cutting, straining back his head and squeezing shut his eyes as the arm drew him close and the jaws angled for a decisive bite. The Jactator's breath was hot and foul.

'Ah ... n-o-o-o ...' Now was the instant to wake from this

terrifying dream!

Abruptly he was released, and fell to the ground. The creature had given vent to a tremendous rasping cough and now worked awkwardly in prone position, great black wings in disarray, as a result of deft strokes made by Anakim's blade behind the joint of each standing limb. Two more quick slicing movements disabled the grasping arms. The honey-coloured eyes, still perfectly round and expressionless, regarded this unanticipated tormentor. Wrinkling a black snout, the Jactator heaved a weary sigh and moved its head back and to the side. Anakim, already in a half-crouch, darted forward and sliced almost casually at the exposed throat.

Between them they dragged the carcase onto the beach, aware of clickings and scuttlings and shadowy shapes around them, then Boscanion with some difficulty constructed a proper defence and they settled for the night.

Some time later, though well before dawn, Boscanion roused: standing a short distance away and, distressingly, inside the defences, stood a dark figure with a tall, square-topped head, a blank black face, and below it, at the chest, a wedge of shining white, in shape like a downward-pointing triangle with each corner neatly nipped off. Boscanion slid his eyes to the side - no sign of Anakim - then back to his visitor.

'Welcome. No doubt you first called out to avoid startlement, and the depth of my slumber left me unaware. I am resting after a taxing evening. Please ... ' he gestured at the still glowing fire '... please, arrange yourself comfortably. It is a cold night.' He was aware of the hairs at the back of his neck standing to attention, and not only there. 'Clearly tonight I am not at my most irresistible, and my spells are less than fully effective.'

Still the figure had not moved, nor did it during the brief period it chose to remain in silent scrutiny - not, it seemed, of Boscanion himself, but of the empty depression in the sand beside him. Boscanion did not relax, but was able to carry out an inspection of his own: a lofty figure, black as night apart from the startling white gorget, wearing flat-topped headgear of some sort. He cleared his throat and spoke again, with an attempt at easy authority:

'Ahem. I am unable to overcome the sensation that you and I have met before.' No response. 'Just now I cannot recall the circumstances - forgive me - but perhaps you would enlighten me?' And again, no response. Indeed, the figure showed signs of insubstantiality, and within seconds was gone.

Attempts at further sleep were disrupted by unsettling visions and dreams, in which a broken ring in the sea loomed large, and, from the beach, sounds of clashing and tumult woven into the roar of the surf.

Anakim appeared shortly after the sun had risen, carrying by the legs a selection of rather gaudy, armour-plated crustaceans gathered from the rocks. Boscanion built up the fire.

He restricted himself to the usual pleasantries until they were well upon the trail. There were now occasional human footprints in the sand and, some way ahead, a rising trace of smoke which trailed off inland in lilac-grey wisps as it met the sea-breeze. The day was still young enough for one or two songbirds to warble brightly from the scrubby thickets, and the now-familiar shelled reptiles were already out cropping the coarse dune grasses.

'A fine morning, Anakim,' Boscanion announced, striding along at a comfortable pace. 'And it is in no small way due to yourself and your prompt actions that I am here to enjoy it.' He glanced at her, trundling along easily, to his side and a step or two behind. 'Please accept my sincerest thanks. For a moment my mind was an unhelpful blank, as that terrible creature - '

'Jactator.'

'Yes indeed. The Jactator. A daunting brute.' He fingered the parallel scratches at his throat. Well, you have ensured that Boscanion may persevere a while longer in the world, and I am in your debt.'

Anakim kept her eyes on the way ahead, but flashed her quick, fierce smile. She herself appeared quite splendid this morning, he noted. Look at her: vibrant, healthy, pacing along, eyes front, black crest rigid, her whole being flowing effortlessly forward in the wake of that thrusting jaw line ... rather magnificent, all in all.

They strode on. As before, white seabirds swept by on stiffly curved, black-tipped wings, making for the open sea in graceful single file. So had it been, so would it always be, mused Boscanion.

'In the early hours,' he finally resumed, 'we were host to a second visitor, differing somewhat from the first.'

Anakim trundled on, matching his pace perfectly, eyes front.

'You may have noticed him,' he tried again, 'although I admit you were not prominently in evidence at the time, and may somehow have stepped out for a moment through my secure perimeter?'

'I saw no-one. No visitor but the Jactator. You were much disturbed, Boscanion. Perhaps you dreamed.'

Was there a mocking note in the husky but increasingly nuanced voice? No. Surely not. 'This was no dream, Anakim. In fact, my memory of the recent past is flawless.' He thought it best to leave things there, for the time being.

At the next prominent dune they made an ascent, feet slipping in the soft, hot sand. From the summit an intoxicating panorama was revealed: to one side limitless and unmarked deep blue ocean, to the other the dusty red coastal plain, pocked with sporadic rocky outcrops and dotted with trees which grew thicker and less stunted as they stretched into the hazy distance, merging finally into the misty blue wall of the forest; ahead and behind, the marching dunes and narrow white strand, the gentle curve of an occasional palm. And, also ahead, a column of smoke, filmy white now against an eye-catching backdrop of terracotta and stonework, disappearing into the sky's blue-white glare.

'So then, Anakim. Fellow humans at last!' He looked at her keenly. Fellow humans? 'Ahem. We will anticipate a civilised and convivial reception, while at the same time preparing for withdrawal in the event of difficulty. I shall proceed to the headman's dwelling place and make my introductions. You will remain in hiding until we meet at a pre-arranged place and time. In the unlikely event that I fail to appear, you must contrive to assist my departure. What is your opinion of the plan?'

Anakim nodded, shielding her eyes from the sun, looking up at him. 'Can this be the place you seek, Boscanion?'

She looked so intent, and completely without guile, single-heartedly investing her full being in a future they now appeared to share. Boscanion took off his old red hat and settled it gently on her sleek black skull, the somewhat bizarre hairstyle - which he now found rather dashing - tilting the wide brim in comical fashion. 'No, I somehow think it unlikely. Not here. But perhaps here we will find an indicator, a sign of some sort.'

'I will come with you.'

He thought to detect an edge of anxiety in the husky voice, or was it an effect of the stiff breeze which blew steadily from the sea at this altitude? The round black eyes stared into his from the shade of the hat.

'I must not leave your side, even to the end of your journey, wherever this may be.' The thin lips pulled back into the fierce smile, which this time was slower to fade. The small tongue showed pink between those queerly angled white tooth-points. 'I am your companion.'

He threw back his head and laughed, a rich and heartfelt laugh whisked away on the salty wind. 'You are Anakim, you are! And no-one had a finer!' He gripped her across the narrow shoulders, feeling her tense, then relax. He realized anew that, for all appearances, what he gripped was solid sinew and muscle. 'And we must look out for one another in this strange and heartless world.'

Still the half-smile lingered, a wonderful sight to Boscanion who was suddenly almost overwhelmed by the notion that he had been alone for an eternity. He licked his lips, extending his tongue to the black moustache. 'Mmm. Sea salt. You must find us water once again, Anakim. We shall rest, and in the mid-afternoon, when the sun permits, we shall emerge to execute our plan.'

They descended the dune and entered the shade of the thicket at its base.

The township, run-down and sparsely populated as he had feared, almost a ghost-town, was known as Ruahar, and sat at the mouth of a wide, brown river, beyond whose outfall sat the dark bulk of a single large island. Outlying dwellings nearest the sea were abandoned and half-drowned. Styling themselves Ruahari, the inhabitants were wary to the point of truculence but not actively aggressive, and Boscanion was able to ingratiate himself with a few simple tricks. He managed to negotiate accommodation and food for two - 'My companion lags behind but will arrive soon' - plus further supplies and onward transport, in return for establishing permanent nocturnal protection for the whole of Ruahar, after the manner of a demonstration he agreed to perform that coming night. He then made his rendezvous with Anakim and brought her to the ramshackle village's outskirts. In contrast to the equally surly Kilwans, the Ruahari appeared to have been charred over the generations well beyond the colour of the most overcooked crab - in fact they were quite remarkably black, with in certain lights a striking indigo sheen or lustre. They exhibited generally handsome features, with woolly black hair cut short, and strong white teeth which were sparingly on view now as they watched the approach of the two travellers. Clothing consisted of loin-cloths in a variety of bright colours. Around every neck, wrist and ankle hung charms of beads, seashells, teeth, dried seeds and other less identifiable items, and at his throat each man carried a small, patterned pouch of animal-skin.

Boscanion conducted Anakim, her characteristic half-crouching trundle contrasting with his own erect, confident stride, along the dusty thoroughfare and out into an open area dominated by a very large, leafy, spreading tree. In its branches winged, fox-faced animals the size of small dogs clambered and squabbled over crimson, nut-like fruits. At the top perched an uneven row of the vulturine scavenging birds he recognized from Kilwa.

'Boscanion. Have you found an indicator?'

Boscanion looked about him at the poor hutments, the few scuffling pigs and mangy scavengers, and sniffed fastidiously. 'To date, no. And yet I am content that this is where I should be at this point. I shall make my enquiries in due course, in a manner best suited to the sensibilities of our hosts, which I am presently assessing. Indeed, I have grounds for optimism that intoxicating liquor, which infallibly has its place in even the meanest society, will be on hand this evening for our refreshment. It is then that our hosts will be at their most loquacious.'

In the shade of the great tree squatted the elders of the Ruahari, blending eerily into the shadows. The two visitors were virtually ignored.

'Our hosts conserve their capacity for merriment,' murmured Boscanion, 'and I have detected already a certain haughtiness in their regard for women. Better to be circumspect until assessment is complete.'

He had noted that, when caught unawares, the aloof Ruahari were in fact staring openly, not so much at himself as at his faithful companion. Anakim flashed him a quick look which he took for one of understanding. With a heavy, dusty flapping, two of the large scavenging birds left the crown of the tree to beat ponderously away over the rooftops; in the tree's shade insects buzzed and sang.

Boscanion halted, allowing his eyes time to adjust from the blinding glare. 'My friends. Here, as I promised, my companion Anakim. A keen hunter and fisher, honoured to make the acquaintance of such masters of the craft as yourselves.'

This was a line which had met with earlier success. He fixed his best grin while tapping gently with his boot at Anakim, who murmured politely but failed to lower those round black eyes.

The headman, who was Sarda, ignored her, and while his colleagues considered the ground or distant objects, addressed himself to Boscanion. 'We spoke. You sleep here tonight. Yes. We give you guidance on your path. You work strong magic for the protection and good fortune of the Ruahari. Yes.'

'A wise investment,' agreed Boscanion solemnly. 'I shall see to it presently, following a period of rest and refreshment. No doubt you have spiritous liquor - rum, wine, toddy or some such - for the delectation of valued guests? Aromatic liqueurs? ... beer then, or cider?'

'Before it is dark, you place your power around Ruahar. Then, the Ruahari will not need to guard against the night things. The Ruahari will eat and drink. You will be with the Ruahari. Now, you rest.'

The whites of Sarda's eyes were in fact largely pink as they rolled to indicate a circular building of mud and thatch. Boscanion bowed low, and smiled to see Anakim's doffing of the red hat, now her own. Again he noticed that the silent group of squatting village elders appeared to surreptitiously watch, not him, but Anakim as she walked in her accustomed place, at his side and slightly behind.

Boscanion slept soundly while Anakim kept a sharp lookout at the door.

That evening, fuelled by a cloudy local drink derived by all accounts in short order through the fixing of receptacles at the crowns of favoured palm trees and allowing the collected sap to ferment in the sun, the assembled Ruahari grew boastful.

'We are a mighty people,' declared Sarda. 'Yes. All other peoples fear the Ruahari. Yes. We are the greatest hunters. The greatest sailors. This is true. Yes.'

Pink-eyed faces nodded solemnly.

'I myself have heard this,' cut in Boscanion, raising his coconut shell politely. He would conduct his probing of local geographical knowledge in stages. The first mouthful of this bakka had been difficult to get down, but it seemed to improve. 'And what of the Kilwans to the south?'

There was a general snort of derision. 'The Glasseyes? They do not know how to hunt or fish. The Malbars also to the north. Yes. All but the Ruahari are afraid of the sea.'

At a peremptory gesture a lesser native ran forward to refill the shell in Sarda's pink-palmed hand. Each council member now displayed a pair of long, palm-fibre filaments, dyed pink and held at the sides of the head by a band of similar colour, possibly in a show of respect for some well thought-of local insect or crustacean. Sarda's antennae were longer and more brightly coloured than those of his colleagues, as was only fitting.

'It is well known,' offered a henchman, 'the women of these Glasseyes, they went with Jactators, long ago. Yes.' There was loud endorsement of this view and a general nodding of antennae.

'Yes, yes,' mused Boscanion, 'I can see this. So much is clear to the merest passer-by. But do you have dealings with them, or do they attempt to cause you disturbance in any way?'

Sarda was contemptuous. 'They dare not come here ... ' His eyes were bulging now, glistening as the bakka took him in its grip. 'Our great ancestors came here, from their lands in the sea. Yes.' He waved vaguely, 'many, many miles in the sea. The seas rose up and their lands were drowned. They came here, crossing the miles ... we took this place for our own. Yes. Because we are strong. But our homelands, they will rise again from the sea, and one day we will return. We are prepared. Yes.' He slapped at his leg.

Boscanion surveyed the squalid cluster of huts and teetering shelters, and could only nod. The gluey saltfish stew bristled with small bones and was not easy to consume in a dignified manner.

'I am something of an epicure,' he announced at length. 'And I declare this meal delicious! Your local brew, too, this bakka, I find quite acceptable.' Which was by now more or less true. Were the Boscanion eyes also pink and bulging, he wondered? Anakim was not present, since they were attending to men's business.

'All Ruahari men, they are good cooks,' stated a pink-eyed tribesman loftily. 'The Glasseyes, they eat the berries, they eat the small fish, this is all they can catch. They do not cook the small fish, they just eat, like that.' This man also slapped at his leg, then performed a small hopping, slapping dance, antennae waving madly.

'This reminds me,' Boscanion broke in. 'I have, fixed in my mind and in my dreams, an image of a broken ring, or not a ring precisely, since it is slightly flattened. I feel that in it, and around it, is a vast ocean.' All eyes were on him now. 'Does your great seafaring tradition enable you to interpret this for me?'

Even at the village, with a large and noisy fire flaring and spitting, the surf provided a background wash of sound, with irregular thumps as heavier rollers hit the beach. Nocturnal insects creaked and buzzed and rats of an impressive size wandered over from time to time, attracted by the smells of food, to watch, noses twitching, until someone hurled a stone or a fallen fruit.

'All Ruahari know of this place,' intoned Sarda, in a portentous voice. 'This is Lemperyal. Many, many miles at sea, sail for many, many days. Our ancestors, they knew this place. They have told us. A place of strong, strong magic. The most powerful ju-ju man lives there, and this is Mappa.' His voice dropped to a hoarse whisper. 'More powerful even than ... '

All antennae were stilled, and Sarda's mouth worked in silence, then he resumed in his customary, hectoring fashion. 'Yes. Lemperyal. The great world, it is the child of Lemperyal. And one day, this world, it will return back, into Lemperyal. Yes. All Ruahari know this.'

Boscanion leaned forward: a series of separate discussions had broken out, on various subjects, as the bakka was quaffed - indeed, one or two resembled arguments. Antennae waved furiously. 'Can you tell me,' he shouted, 'how my companion and I might secure passage to Lemperyal?'

Sarda's broad black skull jerked an emphatic negative. 'Is not possible.'

'Ah.' Boscanion shuffled closer. 'I see. In what manner of sense? It is perhaps too far?'

The headman wished to move on to a more agreeable subject. 'We have been supplied with the faulty materials. Our boats just now they are not good. Yes. We can easily sail there with the good boats. The Ruahari are the greatest sailors. One day we will return to the place of our ancestors.' He slapped his bare arm irritably.

Boscanion was not troubled by these silent, biting night-fliers, ascribing this to long sleeves, long, loose fitting trousers tucked securely into impregnable boots and his general aura of invulnerability.

The first fight had started up as Boscanion quietly slipped from the firelight. To clear his ringing head he took a short stroll, amused to note the occasional stumble, and stood for a while inside his invisible fence to watch the dark, restless sea perhaps two hundred yards distant. A heavy-set, crouching thing approached, to shamble back and forth, emitting an urgent snuffling, but sensed the defence and soon wandered off. On conducting a brief survey, Boscanion had earlier reached the conclusion that the township of Ruahar was unreasonably large, and had therefore decided on tactical rather than comprehensive defences. In consequence, but for a relatively small sector centred on his own dwelling, the village was not fully protected, or at all - something of a gamble, carrying the theoretical possibility of complaint in the morning. But now his head was aching, and he trudged off to his rest.

The following day Boscanion strolled around Ruahar, Anakim at his heels. The Ruahari had celebrated late, exhausting the stock of bakka, and now lay about unconscious in the shade or sat in silent groups staring pink-eyed at the ground, awaiting fermentation of the next batch. At the edge of the village two men laboured to repair the wall of a hut. Their skins were a dark tan rather than the blue-tinted black of the Ruahari, their features sharp and their oily black hair worn long and straight. Boscanion learned that the two were employed as builders and labourers in this village and others, but lived themselves some way to the north. Here then were the Ruahari's despised Malbars. Both chewed in mechanical fashion, eyed Anakim warily, and seemed content to be distracted from their work by affable conversation. This meandered along pleasantly until Boscanion guided it to its first point - the white-chested campfire apparition.

'This is Jaff.' They both nodded, but looked carefully around. 'It is better not to speak the name.'

'Ah.' Boscanion looked around also. 'I see. And what is the nature of Jaff – sorry, of this personage?'

'He is a wizard, a ju-ju man. He has some magic, he knows the special plants. He flies in the air. Possibly you saw a bird, a crow? The Ruahari fear him, but pretend they do not.' The Malbar slid a glance towards the distant group of recumbent black forms, some of whom could conceivably have been watching. Boscanion had detected during the night certain sounds - distant screams, and so forth - which caused him apprehension.

The two men from the north were uneasy, so Boscanion passed smoothly on to a further point of interest: 'I had hoped to procure transport here, by sea, to a destination offshore. But the headman assures me their supplier of materials has let them down, and that all craft are unseaworthy.'

The northerners exchanged knowing looks. 'We are these suppliers. I am Mugil, master boatbuilder. We build and repair all boats, since the Ruahari no longer recall how to do this. Their skills have been channelled into the production and consumption of a small selection of inebriants and narcotics, as you have seen.'

His companion continued. 'This allows the men to revel in visions of grandeur and achievement, while the women carry out what labour is needed for survival.'

'Ah. It also appears to affect their eyes, rendering normally white portions pink,' pointed out Boscanion. Anakim was monitoring the distant group.

'This is true.' Both Malbars displayed faultlessly white surrounds to a thin rim of muddy brown iris and abnormally large, black pupils. The attention of Mugil's colleague, who seemed the more alert - or nervous - of the two, switched constantly between Anakim and the distant Ruahari. 'In fact, the Ruahari boats are presently out of commission, due to an interruption in payment. Soon, stocks of saltfish will be gone, our payment will be resumed, the boats will be repaired, and the Ruahari will again eat fresh fish.'

'Tell me then, Mugil, I am curious: what form does your payment take?'

Mugil shrugged. 'We take fruit and vegetables, which are excellent and tended by the women. Also saltfish, and, oh, there is the Thymallus leaf, for which we have something of a fondness. It grows nowhere else. The women tend and harvest it, that the Ruahari men may hoard it for their own ends.'

Here his colleague indicated that talk had become too free.

Boscanion nodded. 'A full response, Mugil. Well, this is most interesting, if not of immediate benefit to our own prospects. Tell me, might there be some uncertainty as to the navigational expertise of our brave Ruahari seafarers … ?'

Mugil spat a green pellet against the Evil Eye and spoke with feeling. 'There is no uncertainty. They believe that if they venture beyond sight of land they are outside the protection of Jaff, and will be devoured by monsters. Nor do they dare to swim, even in the river, which they will not cross, knowing it is patrolled by predators.'

'Ah. This is not encouraging.' Boscanion's smile faded.

'Boscanion, we should depart now,' suggested Anakim, eyeing activity among the villagers beneath their tree. 'A fresh batch of intoxicant has been secured.'

Boscanion beamed at the northerners. 'As you say, Anakim. I thank you, gentlemen, for your most enlightening conversation, but now we are keeping you from your work, and we must be on our way.'

'You travel northwards?'

'It may be, it may be … this has yet to be decided. For instance, how to cross the river?'

'At low tide, at the widest part, the current is weakest. There is an old causeway. The waters rise daily, but it is still possible to make the crossing. The water is no more than chest-deep for a man - ' here Mugil spared Anakim a glance ' - and you are tall and have strength.'

'Ah. And the predators?'

Mugil's head wobbled, signifying nothing helpful, then he continued. 'In two days you will reach a village in good order. This is Terapon. Say there that Mugil and Mata are well. You may explain something of our situation.'

'Of course, this is the very least we can do ... should we choose a northwards track. Perhaps there we may secure passage to our destination ... ?'

'You will find no-one willing to undertake a long sea-journey at the present time. The oceans are in turmoil. Currents and drift can no longer be predicted, landmarks have become hidden reefs.'

'Boscanion, the Ruahari are rousing.'

It was true. Noise levels were rising steadily beneath the tree, and it seemed there was cause for agitation.

'Good-day, gentlemen. I leave you to your work, and trust payment will be secured in full. And what lies beyond your home town, should we in fact decide to try our luck to the north?'

'Two days beyond Terapon you will see the great city of Dar. You do not know of Dar? Very bad place. Something very bad is in the air, and in the earth. It is the custom at Dar for men to kill men. And it is said, not all are true men. Jaff is there. Better you track inland to clear Dar.'

A group of Ruahari, re-animated by drink and furious to learn of various nocturnal predations, pursued Boscanion and Anakim to the edge of the river, some of the more inflamed venturing into the shallows to brandish heavy cutlasses. All gave up presently and trudged noisily back, perhaps fearful of losing a share in the remaining bakka.

In mid-river the current was forceful and the footing uneven. Boscanion was carried away towards the rolling sea, but Anakim was an astonishingly powerful swimmer, seemingly impervious to the current, and he was brought safely to the far shore.

The scorching sun soon dried Boscanion's clothes. He found Anakim knee-deep at the river's edge, contemplating the small creatures which swarmed and flitted among the interlaced roots of the mangrove trees.

8. Julius

Onscreen the powder-blue surgeonfish, while Stan stared. From a position near his feet Kato watched, head on forepaws, brow furrowed. Stan was pondering Boscanion's doomed world. How real it had all been for a while. Doomed, but alive. At the centre of that world was Kim. He couldn't remember how, but she had made herself its centre. He couldn't remember, because he'd been on the inside. And now it felt more real, more vital than anything that had happened since. A movie was inevitable, and what if Ray was right? How could someone like Vanderhorst feel a part of that world? Consider Anakim. How could they possibly find someone else to be Anakim? Some film-star? Ah, he was having second thoughts now. He foresaw trespass and defilement. But the money. He could look on it as a challenge, regard it as something quite different from the reality in his head. Calming waves issued from the powder-blue. Yes, a new reality, without Kim. Kato heaved a long, weary sigh, then heard something and perked up, tongue lolling. He looked from the workroom door to Stan and back again, no response, then pushed himself to his feet and trotted off to investigate. Stan eventually followed.

Shanny had turned up with a couple of suitcases and the notorious Kevin. It transpired that Liza had talked him and Mrs. Shanny into it, bringing Kevin down here, get him a fresh start, plenty of work round here, get him away from the week-by-week stew of drink, drugs, fights, burglaries, disappearances, aggro with the neighbours, the police. Typical Liza, helping people, taking charge, and she hadn't mentioned it because she knew Stan would object. Sensible. They were just stopping in to say hello, grab a cup of tea, en-route to a nearby guest-house located, checked out and booked by Mrs Blackster.

She was living right up to Shanny's expectations.

So, here was Kevin. He'd inherited his father's broad shoulders, slightly bulging eyes, boiled-ham complexion and tattoos, but his all-too ready smile was disconcerting. He wore the usual logoed black stretch cap pulled down to eye-level and three rings in each ear. He looked a tough little nut, which of course he was. Kevin was another real world.

He grinned. 'Uncle Stan. Where's your Gram then?'

Thick accent, of course. The noble hound looked eagerly from face to face.

'Who's this then?' Kevin was down there, gripping jowls, jerking Kato's confused face from side to side. 'This your Kato is it? I've heard about you. You're all right you are Kato. We'll be mates then eh?'

'Hello Kevin. Yes, this is Kato. Gram's upstairs, in his room. No smoking in the house, OK?'

'Auntie Liza said.'

Between them Shanny and the Barracuda had managed to get Kevin signed up for training with P & O as a ship's steward. The long-threatened takeover of Shanny's haulage company had finally taken place, and he'd skipped off down the road with his payoff. Experienced long-distance lorry drivers were always in demand - his priority now was to get Kevin sorted out. Aggressive noise thudded from Gram's bedroom. Not whales singing.

'Stop worrying Stanley,' Shanny growled, waving his mug reassuringly. 'It's that trip trop step stuff. I'll make sure he leaves your Gram alone. Little bugger's in the army while I'm around. And if this doesn't work out, that's where he's liable to really land up.'

Shanny was settled in with his Guinness, his smuggled Dutch tobacco and his *Daily Mirror* when Stan arrived at the *Stargazer* that evening, and there was a freshly-pulled pint of Archer's for him, still hazy with the last shimmer of pinprick bubbles.

'That lass of yours is a diamond, Stanley. You know that. She got us fixed up right, got us some grub. Lad's got a couple of beers, she's watching telly with him for a bit. He starts on with P & O first thing tomorrow.' He tapped the folded paper. 'Foot and mouth. Bloody farmers infecting their own beasts now, for the compensation. And they've been moving stock all over t'shop when they shouldn't. Folk are turning against 'em. Had it easy for too long have farmers.'

Stan took a mouthful of Archer's Best, held it in his mouth, savouring the soothing, quietly exhilarating assemblage of zesty tangs and essences, extending the moment, swallowing reluctantly. Sensational. Wild Turkey had primed his taste buds to perfection.

'How many do you know then Shanny?'

'How many what?'

'Farmers.'

'Where am I going to meet bloody farmers?'

'Well then.'

'Anyhow, they're not farmers any more. They're countryside stewards.'

'Right. So how many countryside stewards do you know?'

'Countryside stewards?' He blew out red, stubbly cheeks. 'Where am I going to meet bloody countryside stewards?'

'Well then.'

'Rebranding Stanley. Like they changed Windscale to Sellafield, remember, because it got a bad name?'

'Right.'

'We'll see how long countryside stewards last.'

There was silence for a while. Shanny seemed to be considering something. 'All right Stanley, that bloody hoss-faced lass on telly, that Kim. I know Liza hates her guts, that's obvious, but I could never work out why she hates her so bloody much. What really happened Stanley? Tell us.'

Ah. Good question. Maybe the only question. 'Kim was like a child, Shanny. Very naïve. You've seen what she looked like – nice smile, but a bit odd. Different. Bit slow? She was one of those people who gets taken advantage of, you know?'

Shanny gave a sceptical grunt.

'Anyway, I felt sorry for her. She had nothing, just used to turn up, do the job, then go. I showed her around a bit, took her back to Blackster Towers, made her a bit of a family friend, why not? She thought the world of Liza, and Gram. And Liza liked her too at first, mothered her a bit, you know how she is with kids – look at your Kevin. Then for some reason she started feeling, I don't know, left out. She was at work, Gram and me and Kim used to go out places, nothing much - the docks, down to look across at the Isle of Wight, the Needles, the aquarium, she loved the sea did Kim, that kind of thing - but Liza got the idea we were getting too close, she was somehow being edged out, and she got a bit jealous.' *Got a reet munk on,* as his Old Vera put it. 'She's got a powerful imagination, has Liza.' As you've seen for yourself, he nearly said.

'Aye. But did you though? Get too close like?'

Stan sighed. This was verging on the disrespectful. Shanny could never understand, and he had to remind himself that this was his oldest friend. People really thought like this nowadays – read any newspaper, watch TV. It was the way the human mind worked.

'Not in that way Shanny, come on. She was just a kid, right?'

'Aye but – '

'No buts!'

'Aye.' Shanny backed off, motioned for Stan to continue.

'I suppose I felt responsible for her somehow. She was like one of these runty stray cats, but for a while back then she was like Gram's older sister. Gram was just a kid, remember. She used to spend a lot of time with him, just the two of them, up in his room.' Although he'd no idea what she'd found to talk to Gram about. He'd wondered at the time, but the most he'd ever been able to get out of Gram was *the sea, tells me about the sea.* 'They used to get on. They liked each other.'

'And your Liza wouldn't like that, I can see. And what does your Gram have to say about it all now?'

'Never mentions it Shanny. He was only ten or eleven, wasn't he, so I don't suppose she made much impression.' He couldn't believe that. 'And Liza thought … well, she thought it was a bit unhealthy, a bit morbid, Kim being with a little ten year old so much, on their own, while she was out at work. And I'm not denying Kim was a bit weird.' He swallowed some beer while Shanny waited. 'Well, Liza didn't like it, and we all know she's not someone to hide her feelings away.'

It had been a strange time, now he was forced to think about it, somehow infinitely less real than *Insidiator*. It was hard to pick it all apart, the reality and the dreams, the drink and the acting. Shanny was still waiting. 'So Kim was banned from the house. Then she upped sticks, cleared off to parts unknown, hasn't been seen or heard of since, end of story.' He reached for his cigars.

'Bloody good riddance. And that's it?'

Stan ignited a cigar and blew smoke. 'That's it. The TV has just stirred it all up again, that's all.' There was no more to say. 'Give us your glass.'

At the bar he chatted bar chat to the little barmaid Aya, just harmless banter, not really going anywhere, not meaning anything. She reminded him of Kim a little – small, slightly odd-looking. Vulnerable.

'So, Aya, have you been watching that weird TV series, *Insidiator*?'

'No, don't think so. What's it about?' An elfin smile of encouragement, nose jewellery aglint.

'It's very good, very imaginative. Bet you like love stories? It's a love story, but different. Stylish. Few monsters. You'd like it, you should give it a go. I don't know, it's uplifting somehow, makes you feel the world could be a better place. The heroine looks a bit like you.'

'Oh really? That's my ambition, to be an actress.'

She'd told him this before. She was studying drama. He hoped he hadn't spun her a yarn at some point about being a screenwriter, then forgotten. No, she would have reminded him. Not a bad idea though. He was, nearly.

'What was it called? I'll look out for it.'

'*Insidiator.*'

She tried out the word. 'What's it mean?'

'Oh.' He hadn't been asked this in a long while, and had to dip into his handful of stock answers. 'I think it means that what you see in the mirror isn't always the whole story, you know?'

Aya nodded uncertainly. He was putting her off now.

'There we are. One Archer's and one Guinness was it?'

'The next episode's really good, they say, very dramatic. Romantic too.'

His voice sounded far away and unconvincing, and now he thought about it the next episode was in fact not outstandingly uplifting. Boscanion's boots brought them to the ruined city of Dar, where men killed men. He remembered he'd wanted to keep the whole thing light-hearted - not for kids, certainly not, but nothing too demersal - but by that stage he hadn't been entirely in control, and ... Aya's smile had frozen. She was waiting for his money and there was chuntering behind him.

Stan stood with the drinks, swaying ever so slightly, orientating himself before heading back to the table. He'd had a quiet couple of Wild Turkeys with the noble hound in the afternoon, then a couple more in the bathroom with the fishes before setting off. Very convivial. The squad of girls in black were at full stretch and performing marvellously, weaving their way through the press, all still smiling as far as he could see. Enjoying their work. Smoke from his cigar wafted into his eyes, causing him to lower the drinks fairly messily onto a handy table while he composed himself. Students watched him, and he gave them a Boscanion smile. How many of them watched *Insidiator*? They should lap it up: enquiring young minds, first tentative steps on the path of life, the world stretching out before them.

But he wouldn't ask. Nodding and smiling his apologies, and squinting, he grabbed up the glasses and set off.

Shanny was staring at the face of Peter Shreeves, new potential hate figure, which filled the sports screen. Shreeves had taken over at Hillsborough after the 4-1 defeat at Gillingham. They were saying the club was 16 million quid in the red, and the chairman had stepped down.

'Fuckers! And we'll soon have best ground in fucking Conference League.' The programme moved on to golf before he could work himself into a real head-popper. 'When you off on this flash holiday then?' he barked at length. 'Your Liza was telling me about this Hollywood big-shot.'

Great. Now everyone knew. Only surprising the barmaid hadn't asked about a part. He waved his cigar vaguely.

Shanny nodded. 'Sounds like a right daft idea to me, but you're quids in mate, just what you needed.'

In fact Stan had yet to hear from Milt, much less the Boy Wonder himself. Perhaps he should give Ray a ring. No, bad idea. Who had sent the tapes to Vanderhorst? It was nagging at him. In his darkest demersal moments he wondered whether he'd dreamed the whole thing up.

'It's not definite, Shanny. Still has to be confirmed.'

'Oh aye. Any road, you can afford it now. Stop pretending you're skint. Tight bugger.'

'Cash flow Shanny.'

Shanny seemed to be smoking one roll-up every five minutes. The only time he wasn't puffing away was when he was rolling the next one or drinking. Forget breathing. In fact, look at that, he was actually rolling one now when he was only halfway down the one in his mouth. Stan looked off through the smoke. Aya was collecting glasses and gave him a smile. At this range and in low pub lighting the sparkle of nose jewellery looked exotic rather than disfiguring. The place was heaving. Where did they all come from? Where did they all live? Despite the din, a student had passed out, face down on a table, and been abandoned by his mates. A girl in black cleared away the debris of plates and glasses around the heap of hair.

'Cash flow be buggered. Give us your glass, you poor sod.' Shanny barged off into the crowd, leaving Stan to drift. The slapping mosquito-dance of the Ruahari, he liked that. And the antennae. And the way that, for all his shortcomings, Boscanion never let himself down. Or his companion. Aya would see this, Boscanion's reliability amidst the ruination of Dar. Perhaps he would let drop that he, Stanley Blackster, was in fact AB Defduf, the creator. Later, when she was hooked.

A face was staring into his. A dark face. Its mouth moved. Skimpy beard, like tightly coiled black wire. Stan stared back, paralysed.

'That sea, man. That sea.'

Dreadlocks. OK, OK. Probably a student then. Stan shook his head, mumbled no. He was drenched in sweat and his stomach had twisted. For a giddying second he'd thought he was back on Tsaramaso Atoll. The face scowled and retreated into the crowd. Stan got to his feet, had to cool off.

Outside it was near freezing. He could see his breath. Orange city sky, only a few stars strong enough to show. Traffic rumbled, beasts of the city night. He took in a cold, soothing lungful, then another, willing his heart to slow down. Jesus, he must have been miles away, bloke gave him a start, thought it was one of Roland's atoll gang, stupid. Just some student, looking for ... the sea? In a pub? Equilibrium was returning. He needed a drink.

Stan eased back into the hot mass of bodies, noise and smoke. When he flopped back into his chair Shanny was halfway through his next Guinness.

'OK then Stanley?'

'Fine. Breath of air.' He sat down and gulped Archer's. 'Nice evening out there.'

'Why didn't you let poor bugger take the chair then? We expecting somebody?'

Ah. Seat then. Not sea. Bloke had only been looking for a seat. He could see him now, propped against a wall with his drink. 'You never know.' Get a grip. The seat was still there, still empty. He tried to catch the bloke's eye, but he was looking the other way.

All afternoon he'd been sitting at AB's creative end of the work-room with Kato and appropriate soundscapes - Durutti Column, Beefheart, *Jazz from Hell* - pen in hand, trying to summon up this damned Badass. Not an obvious, boringly evil type, better make him (or her, a *Blake's Seven* Servalan-type? Or it?) more subtle, or com*plex* as Louis would have it. A lisping quoter of poetry perhaps, say Spenser, Traherne, Izaak Walton – good opportunity for some telling fish lines – throw in a nursery rhyme now and then, one of the sinister ones, *Ring-a-ring of Roses* and so on. He, she or it would naturally be stylish, have one or two esoteric interests and a range of nasty habits. Antony Sher would do a good job, or if need be Joaquin Phoenix. English accent, or perhaps Central European, Bela Lugosi-style. No, far too obvious. Charles Gray was dead now wasn't he? If it was to be a he. Already he could see he'd have to smuggle things in, past Vanderhorst. An evil hound wouldn't work, since no-one would believe it. An obvious option would be to make the Badass an unusually resourceful and ambitious fish. With a grudge against humanity. It could be done, as Vanderhorst himself had shown with *Xutha*, even if he didn't seem to realize it. Odd, that. He would have to keep an eye on the way the production developed. Would a stylish shark necessarily make a stylish person? Not the first time he had asked himself this question. Of course the answer was yes. Who said he wouldn't enjoy this movie-making? He'd feel better when he heard from Vanderhorst, or at least his sidekick Milt.

A middle-aged chap came over from the next table and asked about the chair, but he managed to stop Shanny giving him it. The black student was still up against the wall, watching. It would just have to stay empty. Shanny shrugged. He was rambling on in negative fashion about the early days of England's new Swedish football supremo, Sven Goran Ericksson.

Eventually, buoyed up by Guinness, Shanny hoarsely agreed to loan his old friend ten grand until the film money came through. In addition he would look after the house and the noble hound while the Blacksters were away. No, no need to tell Mrs Shanny about the money. She'd only kick up.

The call from Professor Dalyell came out of the blue. He wanted Stan to go with him to see Julius Easterhouse. He'd pick him up. Something was wrong.

'Yes, he's really in rather a state, I'm afraid.'

Stan experienced a flush of satisfaction. 'I'm sorry to hear that.'

He sat in the back of the Jaguar with Dalyell while a young chap introduced as Tate did the driving. 'He hasn't been quite himself for a while, as a matter of fact. You wouldn't know. You two fell out years ago. I sometimes think that wasn't a good thing for him, you know. Julius has no friends.'

James Dalyell was a large, imposing man, always immaculately turned out, dressing the part in professorial waistcoats and bow-ties, with fastidiously trimmed white hair and beard, pipe never far away. His fondness for good living had for some years tested all waistcoats to their limits, and he had come to rely on the rather eyecatching stick propped at his side. This was, Stan knew, a length of mangrove wood from Tsaramaso Atoll presented to the Prof by, of all people, Roland, with whom Dalyell had struck up an unlikely relationship. He glanced at it now, feeling both a faint repulsion and an urge to reach out and touch the smooth, dark wood. The Professor himself had added the silver tip and silver goat's head handle.

'I haven't kept in touch, Prof. I'd no idea. What about the faithful Alice though? She'd keep him on the straight and narrow.'

'Ah. Dear Alice. Another blow, I think. In fact probably the main one. Easterhouse was never as self-sufficient as he liked us all to think. Alice left him, some time ago. Haven't heard from her at all, as a matter of fact.' He sounded wistful, almost disappointed. 'Good lord, he must have taken some putting up with - well, I don't have to convince you of that. Tate and I have been looking in from time to time. I'd bring Alice, if I could, but he has started asking for you. Seems quite urgent. His thoughts aren't very ordered, so there may be no sense in it. I do hope I'm not wasting your time. It's very good of you to come. I'm hoping it might help.'

There were nostalgic moments as the Jaguar rolled past the old Winchester pubs where they'd got plastered times many in the old days, his imperially-bearded self and a young Barracuda, sometimes straitlaced Ray – although he didn't like Easterhouse much, and came mainly to admire the lovely Alice - and reckless, impulsive Jules Easterhouse, who liked to play jazz piano when he'd had a few and needed an eye keeping on him. The young Julius. Impossible to picture him remotely out of control now, despite what Dalyell was saying.

Although absent for extended periods in various parts of Africa, particularly the east and south, the Easterhouse clan had for generations inhabited Easter House, an ivy-covered Georgian red-brick pile with gravel drive, extensive grounds and screening woodland. It was quite invisible from the road, on the outskirts of the customary leafy Hampshire village near Winchester: peaceful, privileged Gilbert White country, not yet engulfed by rising traffic tides. Stan had been here several times in the distant past, taking every opportunity to sneer at the Easter House lifestyle; now he was surprised to feel a whiff of envy. It was so peaceful, away from the concrete city. In those days Julius himself had ridiculed his exclusive, overbred family situation, with its inflexible codes and expectations; now he lived here alone.

Lithe, silver-grey forms rippled over the leaf-litter as the car rolled up the gloomy drive. The grounds were no longer immaculate. He'd forgotten about the squirrels though, how Alice and the young Barracuda used to get them to take nuts from their fingers while he worked the camera. How harmless it all seemed now. They passed the lake where Jules had proudly described his fish parasite study, the icy science which would soon take him over. The lake itself looked cold and lifeless now, with a blustery wind shivering its surface. Here Jules had systematically shot every heron which had the temerity to threaten his study fish. Stan had stayed up most of one night with him waiting for another, more elusive, four-footed piscivore to show itself - a particularly wily cat, they had assumed, since there were no otters around here. Jules would cheerfully have shot a dozen otters, had they appeared, but whatever its identity this particular miscreant had managed to evade the Easterhouse traps and weaponry. Stan could still recall the look on the white Easterhouse face when next day they discovered the remains of one of his tagged carp, tucked away inside a hollow tree. He could see now that everything you needed to know about Julius had been there in his face at that instant, if only he'd known how to look. The Jaguar rolled to a halt.

Dalyell knocked, but opened the door without waiting and went in. Immediately Stan saw, there among the coats and scarves, Julius's old African hat, a crumply pill-box affair made from strips of gaily-coloured and patterned cloth painstakingly stitched together. Easily spotted in a crowded pub; in a distant group of shimmering figures in the burning heat-haze of Tsaramaso, Julius was the one with the flat-topped head. On the wall were sombre portraits of dead Easterhouses, including Julius's forbidding father, Sir Archibald, whose rumoured habits might provide one or two ingredients for the Badass, now he thought about it. There was still space up there on the wall for Julius. Dalyell seemed to know he would find the great house's sole occupant sitting in the study, now apparently Julius's workroom, in front of a blank computer screen.

'Good afternoon, Julius.'

The face was as white as ever: older and uncharacteristically weary-looking, it was gratifying to see, but stamped still with that chilly, well-bred reserve he had learned long ago to despise. There was also a quite incongruous and shocking air of unkemptness, of distraction.

'Mmm. Blackster. Stanley. Stan. Yes.'

He spoke as he always had, with almost no movement of the jaws. A long pause then, as though to be polite.

'Thank you for coming.' A smile of sorts, as though he found it difficult to remember how. 'So. The fish-romantic. Have the sharks forgiven you?'

Stan started to reply, but Easterhouse held up a white hand.

'No matter. Professor. I'm most grateful. Would you excuse us for a few moments? Stan and I have something to discuss.'

Dalyell hesitated, leaning heavily on his stick, unlit pipe gripped firmly in his dentures. 'Very well. With your permission, Tate and I will withdraw to the kitchen for a cup of tea.'

The door closed behind him, and they were alone in a silent room much like Stan's own, albeit bigger, better equipped, and dedicated unequivocally to science. No loose ends or whimsicality here. No source of music. No shot glass. No hound. A cold room.

'Please sit down, Stan.'

Julius was again in charge, which had always been one of the problems: those cool, clear grey eyes like a British sky, the prim, permanently lifted eyebrows encouraging rapid review of your most recent utterance, the pale, thin-lipped mouth which spoke without moving, that frozen white face ... there had always been something slightly feline about Julius, an edge of cruelty, even in the wild old days of youth. It was more apparent now. Or maybe Stan was just older and less innocent, on the lookout for it. The grey eyes appraised him, measuring the years and their effect, searching. Judging. Which had always been another of the problems.

'You should never have masqueraded as a scientist, but of course you know that as well as I do.' He cut Stan off with a gesture. 'You like fish, Stanley - full stop. And you lacked the proper rigour to apply yourself even there. You are a sentimentalist.'

'Yeah yeah.' He'd heard all this before. Julius understood one person, himself. His opinion of anyone else was worthless. Why had Dalyell brought him here? There was nothing wrong with the desiccated old bastard. Same old Easterhouse. He wished he hadn't stopped himself hitting him last time. He could imagine him snapping, like a bone.

Julius was looking at the door, and appeared to be listening. 'Come. We'll talk next door.'

The adjoining room was smaller, furnished with items relevant to the owner's academic pursuits: books, natural objects, photographs; a clock ticked loudly. Something existed in this room which was absent next door, a trace of something alive. Julius hastened across to draw closed the door of a further small room, but not before Stan glimpsed a whirl of colour, incongruous in this austere house, where ranked garments of green and yellow, purple, blue, black and white hung in a recess by a full-length mirror. A feminine scene, and one he remembered.

'An old room of father's,' muttered Easterhouse, shielding the door as he turned a key in its lock with a quiet click. 'It has to be aired.'

Yes, Stan remembered. Young Jules and his mother had been forbidden entry to this part of the house, on pain of punishment vague but dreadful. He remembered sneaking in here once with Jules when Sir Archibald was away, and Jules pointing out the trapdoor from which a set of steps led down to 'father's dungeon, where he keeps people he doesn't like'. At the time he'd treated it as one of Jules's rare jokes. Looking back on it … people he didn't like, or people he liked quite a lot? A carpet covered the trapdoor now, and a heavy chest of drawers.

Those grey eyes were watching him. Julius was sitting, and indicated a second uncushioned, high-backed wooden chair. 'You know, of course, that she's gone.' A flat statement.

There was something disturbing about this room, and the faintest smell of … what?

'Alice? Yes, Dalyell told me. How did she tear herself away?'

The Easterhouse lips trembled. It might have been a smile. On the wall a set of shark jaws gaped spiky teeth, mounted in a glass-fronted box. *Negaprion acutidens.* Lemon shark, a big one. A half-familiar set of battered and bulging hardback books, labelled with aspects of shark research. Mementoes of the atoll.

'Alice. Yes.' An incongruous bark of laughter escaped, just one, then the icy calm returned. 'I'm talking about the adaptative gene, Stan.'

'Oh really. What's that when it's at home then?' Easterhouse brought out Stan's inner idiot, always had.

'Come on. We've all seen your television drama. You and Ray didn't do too bad a job, considering your limited resources, but the idea was mine. The mimic-adaptative gene complex is my name for it - plastic gene, if you prefer. Endlessly resourceful. Something the Human Genome Project is unlikely to encounter, and Tsaramaso is its source. You haven't been back to the atoll, I know that, but I should estimate that it occupies your thoughts a great deal, even now. It must.'

The atoll was in his head all the time, to a larger or lesser degree. Often at night he was in there too. Back on Tsaramaso. Trapped on the atoll. He felt a pulse of heat inside.

'Never crosses my mind.'

The idea for *Insidiator* was his? What desperate bollocks. And now he could see, there on a shelf alongside reference books, bound reports and studies, a neat stack of video cassettes. They were all, as far as he could see, labelled *Insidiator – raw footage*, and numbered. Bastard! What was the creep up to? Julius had shown a sort of interest in the early days, true, but this was when he'd started his metamorphosis into what he was now, and he'd soon risen above such childishness. But all this time he'd been following it, in characteristically geeky fashion, taping the whole thing … actually, this was better than he could have imagined. Wait till *Boscanion – The Movie* hit the screens. He almost licked his lips. Revenge was sweet, right enough. Strange, sometimes, and late. But sweet.

Easterhouse was amused again. 'You're a poor liar. Well. Perhaps it wasn't your happiest time. Very well, I shall explain. You will recall your final field-trip, just before you left Tsaramaso.' Julius had always pronounced the name with a particular flourish, in the Linois manner, Zara-*masso*. 'We were searching for juvenile sharks, in a remote part of the mangrove creek system. Bras Demzel, as they called it. No?'

'Yes, wait a minute. Wasn't that where we slogged all the way there, you got what you wanted, then we slogged all the way back?'

Easterhouse actually chuckled now, a mirthless dog-like noise. The big old house was silent in a pressing, unpleasant way, cloaked in its own small wood, no human sounds, not even traffic; just the clock ticking off time, the sighing of the wind, now and then the rasping call of a rook in the tall trees. A sound inextricably bound up with the sinister idiot-world of *Worzel Gummidge*.

'Yes. I got what I wanted. Are you still having problems with your memory? Then let me remind you. You were leaving the atoll, and your departure on the supply boat was imminent. There were problems between yourself and the staff - specifically over your ill-advised relations with the cleaning woman. You had become very unpopular and your work had deteriorated.'

Stan gave a loud sigh. This was like being back at school.

'Whereas you didn't let being Mr Popularity stand between you and a good dissection, yes we know. Jesus. Is there a point to this, Julius? Please do get there.' But he was feeling suddenly warm. Getting there was becoming less and less appealing.

Easterhouse was definitely smirking now, no question, a too-familiar expression. Nor did he seem to have lost his predilection for long, uncomfortable silences. Eventually he continued. 'On that trip we trespassed in a sacred place. We didn't know, how could we? We disturbed something. We saw something we weren't supposed to see. Or at least, you did.'

Stan looked at him and felt numb. Here came the heat again, and his guts were on the move. 'What bollocks Julius. Pardon me, didn't mean to be rude. What? What did I see? Hang on, it's coming back now, you're right. I saw sharks, turtles, mud and mangrove. I saw fish and rice, and rice and fish. I saw mosquitoes. And ... nope, that was it.'

'Yes. You also saw something else, which fortunately you described to me at the time.'

'Oh, did I? What?'

'You described to me a creature you were unable to classify, an amphibious quadruped.'

'Turtle.'

'Not a turtle. Legs, not flippers.'

'Cat taking a swim.'

'Not a cat.'

'There isn't anything else.'

'That's right.'

'Why can't I remember it then?'

'Because your ability to remember was interfered with.'

'Interfered with? How?'

Easterhouse leaned forward. 'You will certainly remember Roland.'

Roland. Stan nodded, biting into a forefinger.

'Roland prepared all our meals while we were in the field, and he practised the local version of voodoo, as you know, or as you used to know. Quite apart from that, at the time he considered the cleaning woman his wife. I could not believe you were so foolish.'

Roland. 'Hang on. You're saying the old bastard poisoned me?'

Easterhouse was still smirking. 'Not precisely, or not in the normal way – but I don't claim to fully understand. We tended to disparage their so-called voodoo, didn't we? I might tell you that to them we were the fools. However, I encouraged one of the old rogue's cousins to become drunk one night - no great challenge – and learned that you had been caused to forget. You underestimated Roland quite badly, you know. Perhaps, had his measures failed to induce a forgetting, you would not have completed the voyage back to

Margaritifer. Who can say? I expect you were quizzed on the voyage, and your answers were satisfactory – that is to say, a fragment of your memory had been satisfactorily suppressed.'

Bloody hell. The rooks sounded less like birds now.

'After you left Tsaramaso your description intrigued me. While you were not reliable as a co-worker, I did not doubt your description, and I shared your puzzlement.'

Roland! Bat-faced old bastard. OK, Julius was drivelling, but it was true, he never had felt right since then, his guts, his vision. His mind. All these bloody years!

'I began to pay more attention to the activities of the locals, and of Roland in particular. Bras Demzel was the key. I realized that research access to the area was being systematically prevented, in such a way that the Director, for what he was worth, never suspected. You know the Linois way as well as I - no guide available, tides unfavourable, accidents en-route, deliberate mis-identification of creeks. But why? Again, alcohol proved useful.'

A clear tumbler half full of Wild Turkey glinted, catching the light. Stan did not like this room at all. It was moving in on him.

'I learned Bras Demzel was – is – a sacred place. The Linois always did hold ambivalent feelings towards sharks - or so it appeared to us. I learned differently. And this was the site with most sharks, named for a very particular shark, *Galeocerdo cuvier*, and near to an oceanic channel. What was it you saw there? I went back.'

From being mildly amused, in total control, the old Easterhouse, he abruptly dropped the mocking tone. 'Stan, what you saw was Proteus. It - she – no, *it* - was their totem, the Linois. Their Deity, I suppose. I took it, of course. It was small then. What I found … an adaptable biology Stan, quite astounding, far beyond the precepts of mimicry. Capable of evolution towards a target. A target form.'

He looked up and locked eyes, and for Stan it was a disquieting sight. The clock's ticking was louder.

'And I had the full record, Stan. Everything. The past four years have been a totally unanticipated disappointment, a conundrum, after the staggering development which accompanied daily exposure to a human working environment. During the past four years the trend had become one of accelerating regression. But I began to wonder … regression, or a new direction? A better target?' He pointed back towards his workroom and its machines. 'There. Growth rates, developmental stages, diet, behaviour, learning response, physiology ...

video, audio, tissue and blood, full computer record, comprehensively backed up ... The fact that its commercial value ran into millions is a trifling consideration beside the value to science. And all of it is gone – removed, wiped clean or destroyed, all of it. Everything, Stan. Can you even begin to imagine? No, of course not. I can see it in your eyes. All I have left are those - ' he waved towards the cassette boxes marked *Insidiator – raw footage,* and gave another dry bark. 'And for her, irony was always just out of reach. How she tried. Ironic in itself.'

Stan was dazed, hot and supremely uncomfortable, still fuming about Roland, the bat-faced old bugger, the only bit he could make sense of. All the drivel about what he'd seen, what he had to forget – it was much simpler than that. Roland had poisoned him because of that bloody Talma woman, with her hips and her come-on. Bastard! All these years. What had he used? Wind gusted in the trees, setting off the rooks again. The world was outside, he must remind himself, and he'd be back in it soon, out of this unpleasantness. Dalyell's harumphing was audible through two closed doors. Easterhouse was scrutinising him again, back under control, intense.

'Sorry Julius. Thanks for telling me about bat-face. Nice thought, but I don't think so. As you can see, there's nowt wrong wi' me. And as to our last little trip together, I think I'll stick with my version, thanks all the same. The one I remember, that is.'

'You mean you do not permit yourself to understand what it is that you know already. A situation typical of you.'

He'd had enough. 'Look, Julius – you're not in love with me and I think you're a creep. We called the wedding off. Sad, but that's life. Tell me why I'm here and then I'm off.'

'She will come to you first. Has she come? For reasons of her own she became attached to you.'

'Alice preferred me to you? Surely not.' Jealousy? Easterhouse? The thin, icy smile.

'Something of Alice, yes. But not Alice.' The smile disappeared. 'We had an arrangement, which she adjusted to her own advantage. I relaxed my vigilance. She is cunning. Clever even, despite the regression.' There again, a flicker of some sort of emotion. 'In fact, I am forced to consider that aspects of the programme were in some essential way directed by her, for her own ends.'

Dalyell was right. Easterhouse was in big trouble, way out in the swamps. Stan was having to pay attention to his own breathing, which had stopped. This was getting creepy. He gulped. 'Righto Julius.'

Julius leaned slowly forward, head bowed. His breathing was audible, but he made no reply.

The Easterhouse cranium was starting to go bald. Now he really did need a hat. The shirt collar was visibly grubby, unthinkable for the old Julius in whatever far-flung circumstances. There was a small, purple-red mark there on the white neck. Jesus, drugs. That explained it. Jools had always been the wildest of them, the biggest drinker, the biggest drugger. He'd had some dodgy ideas about sex, too. Could he have been on drugs on Tsara? He'd kept it well under wraps if he had. They'd have kicked him off the atoll smartish if they'd found out. But in the neck? Jesus.

Should he slip discreetly away, round up Dalyell and clear off? His gaze wandered around the study. The books sat in perfectly ordered ranks, as though never intended for use as books, in keeping with the room's oppressive feel. Beside a preserved pufferfish and the bleached skulls of turtle and frigatebird stood a framed photograph: Julius, unsmiling beneath his hat, holding a steel tape measure while Alain and Bernard, the station guides, held down a lemon shark with a sack. Alain was beaming, Bernard's handsome black face looked hungover, uncomfortable against a background glare of palm trees and sand.

Dalyell was loudly signalling his imminent re-entry to the workroom, thankfully. Julius roused himself and gave the door a peevish glance. He leaned forward. 'I have money. You need money, I've no doubt. Just bring her back to Easter House.' There was an intensity in the clear grey eyes which was almost hypnotic. 'And better not to discuss this with Dalyell. He is not independent.'

Stan was out and into the workroom, where breathing was easier. Julius followed as the door swung open to admit Dalyell and a pungent waft of tobacco smoke.

'I'm sorry, Julius. I have to attend an extremely important meeting. We really will have to be off.'

Julius gave a tight smile. 'Of course, Professor. We've quite finished.' He must have inherited these old-fashioned suits, which he had started wearing once his juvenile aberrations were behind him. His father, the customary remote and terrifying figure, had been of the same spindly build. Now, side by side, even Dalyell looked more contemporary. In the corner, propped against the wall, Stan recognized the old tranquilliser dart gun they had used on Tsaramaso's goats. The ecology of the atoll's feral goat population had been Dalyell's particular interest, and Julius and Stan had helped from time to time with the field work, using the gun to dart suitable animals and fit them with radio transmitters. These goats had to be the highly sociable females, which when released would lead the researchers to the main groups. These females were known as judas goats.

At the door Julius became agitated, and appeared almost to shrink back.

Dalyell seemed to expect this. 'Come, Julius. You can see your guests to the car, surely.'

With a slow, deliberate shake of the head, Easterhouse declined. 'If you don't mind, I'll say goodbye here.'

This did not disappoint Stan, who was absurdly elated just to be back outside, back in the cool, living air. Normality had snapped back into place. He'd emerged from a place where things were not right.

'No worries, Julius. Good to know you're still lurking about. Do look after yourself. I'll give your best to Liza, shall I?'

'Yes, by all means.' Julius gave him an unfathomable look. 'If you're sure.'

Sure?

'Well, you see the situation, Stan. I thought it worth a try.' Dalyell sounded discouraged. Tate was edging the Jaguar forward through the heavy rush-hour traffic Dalyell had been keen to avoid.

'How long has he been like that Prof?'

'Hard to say. There has been a steady decline which has accelerated recently - you're probably aware it's several years since he last had anything published. For a long while after your ways parted – you may or may not be interested – he became extremely focused in his work, as only Julius can. Excited by it. Cytogenetics … ' Dalyell looked at Stan, who nodded. 'The topography of the genome. Mapping, fluorescent tagging of some sort – '

'FISH,' said Tate, with a glance at the rear view mirror.

Stan tensed.

'The technique,' Tate added. 'Fluorescent mapping. An acronym.'

Of course.

'Yes, Tate's more *au courant* than I. Not my field, but I did try to keep up, and he was making real advances, I'm sure of it. But he would never publish, or even discuss it much, which was perplexing. He was always so keen to publish, to establish propriety.' He sighed.

'However, Julius is not a collaborator, and teamwork is essential these days. He exasperated and excluded people he really needed. And he began neglecting his work, most uncharacteristically. His appearances became less and less predictable and finally stopped altogether. Well, as we see, he was applying himself at Easter House.' Another glance. 'Not a healthy environment, is it? Again, I tried to keep in touch, but my efforts were not reciprocated. Then, rather appallingly, he seemed to lose that magnificent focus, seemed to ... well, you've seen for yourself.'

Stan grunted. The Prof nodded in agreement.

'Do you know Stan, I believe he's convinced himself there's a force of some kind preventing him from leaving the house? That's very recent, isn't it Tate? Yes. And in a very sad, strange way, I suppose there is. He once gave me to understand, when he was particularly distressed, that I was one of several tormentors, or jailers, even. Yes, I see you're startled. He actually wasn't at all bad just now.'

'He was bad enough. He's gone, Prof, way out there. All this missing data and plastic gene stuff? Is it as wacky as it sounds?'

'Ah ... yes.' Dalyell heaved himself into a more comfortable position on the car's back seat. 'Do excuse me. Bit of a dicky hip these days. Damned nuisance. Witch doctor tells me I have to give up all the usual things. Won't consider a replacement unless I shed a considerable portion of this.' He patted the straining waistcoat, and Stan thought to detect a discreet whiff of scotch. Dalyell bared his dentures. 'Well, we all have our burdens, do we not? Easterhouse seems to have convinced himself that he'd identified a factor which enables an organism to adjust its morphology quite dramatically over time. Protective resemblance and mimicry, as you know from experience of reef fish, are not unusual in nature, generally for reasons of camouflage or, where a vulnerable species has evolved to resemble another with defensive capabilities, protection from predators. This was always an interest of his, along with his infernal parasites of course, even before your days together at Tsaramaso, but it grew into the obsession which has unbalanced him.'

This rang a tiny bell. Now Stan thought about it, Julius may have made some vague suggestion along these lines during the early days of *Insidiator*. Hardly worth an acknowledgement though. His idea? Bollocks! He said nothing, and Dalyell continued.

'I've pieced this together from various ramblings when he was feeling particularly low, and even then he seemed to be addressing himself not to me, but to some imaginary confidant, or even colleague, within that wretched study - I know, you will say this is a classic symptom, and I'm sure you're right. He was always unwilling or unable to show me anything, any evidence, because of course there never was any. It had its existence only in his mind, I'm afraid. And he had a brilliant mind, if not the greatest magnanimity – I'm thinking of yourself, and even more of poor Alice. I asked Tate here to search the computer record and so on. He's very good at that sort of thing. Nothing there, was there Tate?'

Tate kept his eyes on the traffic ahead. 'Nothing intelligible. Traces of odd, disjointed bits and pieces, nothing coherent. Definitely hadn't all been wiped recently anyway, the way he said.' This was the first time Tate had spoken; his voice carried the clipped, confident tones of white South Africa.

'His mind created the event in order to preserve an illusion,' muttered Dalyell. 'Such a waste. Although one has to say there were indicators. He was always too intense. An odd family, just between the three of us. Did you ever meet old Sir Archibald? Yes, I see. He was rumoured to have some rather peculiar interests, and there was some sort of scandal in South Africa, which the family hushed up.' Tate was nodding. 'Poor Easterhouse.'

'The family curse then. He wasn't always like that,' Stan began, struggling to remember. 'We used to have a good time, he was a great one for the pub ... drinking, jazz, the odd girl ...' He stopped there. 'We called him Jules, can you imagine that? He called himself Jules. He was a really good pianist, jazz ... ' Surely he was making this up. 'Big fan of McCoy Tyner, you know?' Possibly not. Leave it there. 'He seemed to mature overnight, if that's the right word for it, on Tsara.'

Dalyell nodded. 'Yes. There is this tremendous sensation of raw power at the atoll, as we both know. I miss it, to be perfectly honest, but although our motives for going were, by and large, worthy ones, I came to believe in the end that our presence there was ill-advised. Science ... we had no real understanding of what we were involved with, above and beyond our necessarily selfish research interests. We never looked up.'

On his ignominious return from the atoll, and fearing the worst, Stan had been surprised by the Prof's sympathetic reception, and by the interest he had shown in all that had happened, especially his falling foul of Roland. The Prof was a big man, more to him than met the eye.

The car crept forward in low gear, a few yards at a time, hemmed in by a press of other cars doing the same. Dalyell looked to be nodding off, then pulled himself erect. 'Did he wish to speak to you about anything in particular, Stan? He was quite insistent I bring you to him. Perhaps the re-showing of your TV series triggered something? I must say again by the way how much pleasure it's giving one aged field biologist and chastened romantic. Your unhappiness on Tsaramaso now seems to me perfectly understandable – I think now yours may have been the one true voice in our chorus of ignorance.' He patted Stan's arm in a quite uncharacteristic gesture, and bared his dentures. 'I can see I'm causing you embarrassment. Still, you of all of us brought something of real value from the experience, and I believe found your vocation.' A harrumph, then, 'I've been attempting to cultivate an appreciation of your work in Tate here, without notable success. We await *Episode Three*, and the ruined city of Dar, eh Tate?'

Tate's head nodded, limiting himself to 'The girl's extraordinary. Where'd you find her?'

'Yes,' murmured Dalyell. 'The remarkable Kim.' He stared sightlessly at the traffic, then resumed with a loud throat-clearing. 'I have digressed. My point is that I'm certain this will have had an effect on Easterhouse - you saw the video cassette tapes on his shelf? *Insidiator – raw footage*? There are indications of an obsession here, and the Easterhouse character is nothing if not obsessive.'

Stan chewed a forefinger. Was he saying Julius had lost his marbles and become obsessed with *Insidiator*? Or he'd become obsessed and then lost them? There was something in here, some sort of symmetry. Or cosmic justice. Things were blurring, sliding over one another. He could think of nothing useful to say.

'You know Stan, I do wonder, really … he sometimes seems to be confusing aspects of your fiction with his own reality. This occurred to me the other day - as I watched your Anakim staring at the mangrove roots, trying to recall her past life, as a matter of fact. A poignant moment. I challenged him with this thought, in so many words, but he gave me to understand I was being absurd – he has a facility for this, as you will know. Takes after Sir Archibald there. However, Stan, you seem reluctant to tell us what Julius had to say for himself.'

He'd do his best. 'Oh, it didn't make any sense Prof, you were right. At first he made some sense, talking about the old days on Tsara, but then he was off, rambling, incoherent, all this genetic stuff, his missing records, implying he's been robbed somehow. I thought he was going to cry at one point, which would have been one for the record books. Maybe he has got *Insidiator* a bit tangled up with his life, as you say. Very concerned about Alice, wants me to talk her into going back, I think. But he's in no state of mind for that, even if it was on the cards. You wouldn't want to put anyone where he can get at them, not the way he is. He thinks she's fond of me, thinks she'll contact me. I don't know why. Liza was her buddy, not me. Maybe that's what he meant.'

'Ah.' Dalyell's pipe wagged up and down. 'Part of the obsession, perhaps.'

'I know Liza hasn't seen Alice for years, and even if she knew where she was, which she doesn't, she wouldn't help. Liza could never stand the way Julius treated her, couldn't understand why she put up with it.'

He didn't go into detail over the atoll part of the conversation, Roland and Bras Demzel and so on. Dalyell had rather strangely been something of a fan of old bat-face. Which reminded him: what did *Dalyell is not independent* mean? No more than any of the rest of it, presumably.

'It's rather late for Alice, I should have thought. She left years ago. Alice? And poor Easterhouse still pining for her? I'd no idea. Of course, that is where it all went wrong for him. He needed Alice but would never admit it, especially to himself. Now he has, and it's too late.'

Stan too was tired now. 'Years ago? Jesus.' He looked out at the twilight, the rolling lines of car-lights, white over there, red up in front, in a whirl at a roundabout up ahead, saw the hulking youth mumbling to his wife the Black Star, who just now he found he was missing very much. He was impatient to get out of this. 'Well, no-one else is going to put up with him, money or not.' Sanity or not.

'Hardly,' murmured the Professor. 'But there was a girl, or so I heard, for a short while anyway, isn't that so, Tate? Did you meet her? He never brought her to me. She looked quite like Alice, apparently. I suppose it makes a grim sort of sense.'

'He's lost all sense of time.' He lived in a house outside time.

'He needs help, Prof.'

It took a moment for Dalyell to answer, and in the failing light Stan could see how weariness had settled firmly over the stern old face.

'I've made all the arrangements, Stan, but he won't hear of it. I'm seeing the consultant again, keeping him up to date. In the meantime, Tate and I pop in with things he needs, generally keep an eye on him. All he seems to do is work through his records, over and over, consulting endless blank pages and screens. It can't go on much longer.'

Stan knew he should offer to help. But he didn't.

'The station here will do for me, Prof.'

The newspaper billboard screamed more foot and mouth headlines: the Army was being sent in as the mass killing, burning and burying spiralled.

'Grim, eh Prof? What a state this bloody country's in.'

'True, and not just this one, sadly.' Dalyell was barely audible. 'And those few ordained to hold back the tide, what hope do they have?' He roused and patted Stan's shoulder. 'Goodbye Stan, and thank you again for coming. Please give my best wishes to Liza.'

One of the Barracuda's Gram Parsons tapes was gently playing, *The Old Soft Shoe*. He tried to like Gram Parsons, for her sake, but no. Perhaps some Zappa: *Hot Rats* - sprightly, aspirational sounds, more in tune with circumstances. And necessarily loud.

His black-bearded face, framed in turquoise, fishes in the background, considered itself. It frowned, arching a black eyebrow in the Boscanion manner appropriated so profitably by Roger Moore, and took a pull at the Wild Turkey. With some of the large-scale, less refined brews of beer – he was thinking here of Greene King IPA, John Smith's, Worthington's and so forth, the first mouthful was sometimes refreshing, but the illusion soon evaporated. How could the same apply to a spirit? But the Wild Turkey's bite, or peck, had surely faded, and wasn't the flavour rather basic and uncomplex? Did a flavour need to be complex to appeal? Foggily, he considered devising a table to record his investigations, as he had once been trained to do. Which mark would have aggregated most points so far? The Balvenie, or perhaps Old Pulteney with its trawler, or Laphroaig, or the one he couldn't spell or pronounce? Wild Turkey would not trouble the upper echelon, although it would score well for label appeal. A lifelong survey stretched ahead.

Easter House was a malignant place. Had generations of the clan made it that way, or had it worked on them? It had destroyed Julius. He could feel it, especially in that room. If he'd stayed there any longer he'd have caught something. He closed his eyes. Never far off now there was the shush of surf, soothing, the sleepy clattering of palm leaves. And the closer it came the more he welcomed it. Soon he would be among fishes once more, real ones – inexplicable that he had put it off for so long. Tranquillity over the seagrass beds, slowly waving to the rhythm of the rollers overhead ... cool, cool sand ... dead ahead the coral formations of the fringing reef ... fishes scattering, blues and yellows and silvers ... so cool, water sliding over him ... massed brown mangrove roots curving into the shallows ... His eyes snapped open. That final trip, his last atoll shark trip with Julius, had forced its way into his head ...

They had set off at dawn as usual, to catch the top of the spring high tide at the lagoon's far end, twenty miles or more away. This would allow them to travel by small boat up into the flooded creeks, into the mangrove forest, to search for juvenile sharks. Crammed into the small boat were Julius, himself - always in that order, even now - Alain and, at the back, hand on the tiller, pale eyes slitted against wind and glare, Roland ...

The fifteen foot canary-yellow fibreglass open boat bumped and banged through lagoon waves whipped up across twenty miles by the incessant southeasterly trade wind. They might as well be out on the open sea. Roland, the boatman, squinted ahead into the new sun in the east, dark face and beard glistening with salt spray. Alain, the young guide still learning the ways of the atoll, sat at the back with him, there to provide lighted cigarettes and change fuel tanks - always an alarming combination with the boat pitching about, but *here in Papa this is the way*. Julius and Stan sat forward, using feet and arms to pinion the flapping tarpaulin which covered their gear and supplies. All four of them wore hooded yellow oilskins which shone in the day's first light and glistened with salt spray. The outboard's whirling prop cleared the coral heads, seagrass beds and sandbars by a couple of feet at best, sending turtles and stingrays whipping off like shadows through the shallows. Here at the eastward end of the lagoon the tide had already been ebbing for over an hour. Bone-white boobies skimmed the waves in rippling lines of up to a dozen birds, on their way out to the ocean and its teeming squid and flying fish; occasionally the fin of a night-feeding shark passed them, moving steadily towards the channel and the open sea. Around the tiny yellow boat stretched the vastness of the lagoon, dark and distant mangrove lines to the south and north marking the nearest points of the atoll's rim. Behind them waves quickly destroyed their wake.

The outset of a trip was always exhilarating, if uncomfortable. Conversation was impossible over the roar of wind and outboard.

Roland adjusted course southward to take advantage of the blocking effect of the fossilised coral rim of the atoll, but for most of its long length the rim stood only ten feet or so above sea-level and the waves remained inconveniently large, slowing their progress. Wooden plank seats hammered at the base of their spines as the boat smashed its way through. The sunglasses worn by Stan and Julius were soon filmed with salt, but they gave protection from the stinging spray.

After an hour and a half, wet wherever the spray had found its way in and stiff all over, they entered the eerie serenity of a mangrove-lined creek: this was Bras Caret, the Creek of the Hawksbill Turtle, marked at its mouth by a sun-bleached orange fishing buoy tied to a tree. They could hear again. Already the sun was pouring heat into the creek for it to be trapped here by the dense mangrove forest which shut out all wind. Roland, morose and unspeaking at the stern, stood now with the outboard tilted up on shallow drive setting, peering ahead to guide the boat around rocks submerged by the twelve-foot tide; Roland claimed to know every rock, hidden or visible. From the glossy, forest-green thicket on either side, dazzling white boobies, their spade-like red feet wrapped firmly around mangrove branches, looked down on the yellow boat's passage; in the shallow, turbid waters lemon sharks, green and hawksbill turtles cruised and drifted. This was the power of the place, the purpose of their visit: the mangrove, with its tidal shallows rendered for the most part impenetrable by the latticework of curving prop-roots, provided a nursery for thousands of juvenile fish, including sharks; also attracted were predators, chiefly trevallies and larger sharks, which cruised the open channels.

Presently they reached the rough coral limestone slab used as a landing stage. Julius and Stan clambered out and set off at once with heavy backpacks and gear, while Alain helped Roland move the boat back to a deeper stretch and secure it. In a few hours the landing stage would stand high and dry in a sea of crab-infested mud. The two Linois would also catch small snappers and emperors for the day's meals, which Alain would help Roland to prepare and cook. A short walk over difficult terrain in blistering heat added a layer of sweat to the dried salt spray and brought the two researchers to the crude field-station where, crucially, rainwater was collected from a corrugated roof in an old plastic tank retrieved from the tideline. For the next four days, this was home.

The work proceeded, using the tides to get back out into the lagoon and catch sharks on hook and line from specified sites, measuring, marking and releasing blacktip reefs, fewer lemons, and just one grey reef shark, a species which tended to stick to the outer reef or oceanic channels such as Passe Cabris, visible to the north, a break in the atoll's rim marked either side by dark stands of casuarina trees. Along with data from sharks caught on the atoll's outer reef, this work would give an insight into growth rates, movement, breeding cycles, diet and population sizes. So far so good, and when he was able to ignore the baleful stare of Roland and the frostiness of Julius, Stan was even able to quietly exult in the vast, unspoiled peace of the place. He'd be leaving soon, and would never know it again.

Within reach of the camp the map showed Bras Demzel, or Creek of the Lady as the Linois called it, but as Demzel was also the local name for tiger shark, it was a source of interest to both researchers, for slightly different reasons. This caused difficulties: Roland insisted that the tides were wrong, that there was no passage cut through the mangrove roots because no-one ever went there, and that despite the name it was not good for sharks. This wasn't convincing, and Stan told him no problem, they'd like to meet the Lady. Nobody thought it was funny. The round pale eyes had fixed him momentarily, uncomprehending. Roland's English was rudimentary, and they relied on the other Linois to help. They could never be sure they got an accurate version.

Julius was as usual prepared to be bloody-minded, knowing that in the end, in the Linois way, Roland would comply then retreat to the moral high ground, a region of no interest to Julius. And so it was. Roland dropped the three of them with their gear outside the creek, and they had to wade in from there. On a coral limestone outcrop at the entrance Stan came upon a crude symbol, weathered almost to obscurity: twin curving torpedo-shapes set side by side to make a circle. The hot air smelled of lagoon mud and organic decay.

Since the decision to leave Tsaramaso had been made Stan had felt better in himself, and this must have had something to do with the lifting of the strange air of oppression from his house: voodoo, so-called, only worked if you believed in it. So they said. He'd decided to carry out the work to the best of his ability, squeeze what satisfaction he could from his final trip, get back to the station and be off in a few days without a backward glance. After all, on this trip there would be no cutting up or killing, and it was absorbing watching the activities of the young sharks in these mangrove creeks. It was always possible too that he would see a tiger, although they rarely entered the lagoon in daylight.

Their work had established that blacktips were around twenty inches long when born, lemons two to four inches larger: here in Bras Demzel there were plenty of sharks less than three feet long, and as they had come to expect in this habitat the lemons outnumbered the blacktips, which was the opposite of the situation in the open lagoon. They saw no smaller pups, which were presumably safe among the mangrove roots, and no tigers.

Catching young sharks was a messy affair. It soon became obvious that, even with a strong current, the movements of six feet agitated the soft, white mud of the bottom too much, obscuring rocks, roots and sharks, and causing abrupt headlong submersions which shook up both Stan and Alain, who was for some reason already out of sorts - surprising, as usually he could be guaranteed to cheer up away from Roland's brooding presence. But down there, trapped in warm brown soupy water, visibility nil, hands scrabbling in soft mud, surrounded by an unknown number of agitated and similarly blind sharks, even though most of them were small ... it got the adrenaline going. More significantly these mishaps, coupled with the threshing of captured sharks, attracted others, increasing the general consternation, and somehow the infallible Roland seemed to have misjudged the tide, so that the creek was slowly emptying of both water and sharks. Clearly displeased, Julius, who had as usual avoided falling over, had to agree to call it off. Alain immediately became more himself, smiling broadly, resuming eye-contact, eager to please.

Now that they had stopped though, Stan found it hard to shake off the feeling they were being watched; almost as though the mangrove forest itself was studying them.

They had one remaining short length of net to take up. Stan waded carefully towards it, aware of a small shark just beyond, swimming slowly in his direction. It was little more than a blurred shadow in the muddy water, but there was something odd in the way it moved ...

A soft, bird-like whistle came from high in the mangroves, and the next thing he knew he was on his knees in the creek with mud and water flying everywhere as Alain barged him aside. Terrified for an instant, he scrabbled convulsively back to his feet to find Alain apologising, he'd tripped on a big rock, very sorry, you OK Stan-lee? Stan, chest heaving, spat out water and mud, coughed and spat again. Yes, he was OK.

They packed up all the gear and slogged their way back along the channel then out into the lagoon shallows, where Roland waited for them in the yellow boat. They piled in the gear, pushed the boat out into deeper water and climbed in. Julius commented on Roland's fabled knowledge of Tsaramaso's complicated tides; Alain grinned half-heartedly but didn't translate. Stone-faced and silent, Roland fired up the outboard and they were off. And so they left Bras Demzel, the Creek of the Tiger Shark ...

Blue walls and hovering fish swam back into focus along with Stan's sweating face. The faintest of hums came from the cassette player. He could remember it all, in surprising detail and intensity as a matter of fact. Certainly the meeting with Julius had helped, jogged his memory, as it were - but there was nothing whatsoever wrong with it. His memory. It was just as he'd said - sharks, turtles, mud, the usual. Nothing special. Nothing sacred. No, it was the Easterhouse memory bank which had blown a fuse. Poor, deluded Julius. And this so-called poisoning – all right, he had the odd bad night, the occasional bad dream, hot flushes every now and then, an attack of bad guts. And he needed glasses. Big deal. Join the queue. Stress! Bloody hell. As Shanny said, these days every bugger's got it. Stress and age. That's all it was. Poisoned by Roland? Wishful-thinking bollocks! OK, Roland had been a malicious old bastard, with possibly some cause for grievance. Maybe something or other had been tossed into his meal one day, a few crushed-up berries or a bit of bat's brain. Maybe Roland had pissed in it. Be surprising if he hadn't. For an instant he saw quite clearly Roland's brown, wooden face, as he saw it sometimes at night, squinting through mangrove leaves, sheened with sweat. Music!

He changed the tape and pressed play: *Duke of Prunes*, a boisterous favourite which could be reliably expected to expunge all unsavoury thoughts, sensations and imaginings. He felt a pang of sympathy for Julius, which soon passed. And gormless, grinning Alain. Ray Collins declaimed boldly over Zappa's twanging rhythm guitar, *and you'll be my Doochess, my Doochess of Prunes*. He sang along, buoyant now. Pelagic.

He'd no reason to remember Alain fondly, but at least he used to smile a lot, have a bit of a laugh and joke - when he was out of sight of the others, anyway. Alain had just been too easily talked into things, particularly when the traditional Linois respect for elders was a factor. A factor not exactly widespread here in Southampton, or even noticeable. And what was that further nonsense Julius had come out with, about Stan being tested somehow on his way back to Margaritifer from the atoll? He had travelled back with Bernard - but Bernard had once saved him when he was hopelessly lost and about to die of dehydration. He'd taken some aggro on Bernard's behalf in return, and Bernard in particular had no time for Roland's old ways. No, none of it added up. Bernard had been a resolute outsider, who despite his youth had carried an only occasionally comical air of authority. And, maybe one day Bernard would become the thing he most hated - Roland. Maybe, far away in the enchanted islands of the Papalinas, he already had. Far away, but getting nearer by the day. He would be seeing Bernard again, he felt sure of it.

In the mirror his head shook. Julius. Who would have thought he'd go so spectacularly off the rails? There was a glint of satisfaction there, why pretend? That's life. But they'd had some good times, once. Maybe he should have a go at tracking down Alice. He couldn't even recall her surname now, but the Barracuda would know.

My Duchess of Prunes. He reached over, as he often did, to give the fierce, silvery Barracuda on the wall an affectionate pat. Yes, he felt better. And he'd given her something to look forward to, hadn't he, for a change? A surge of pride, the last of the Wild Turkey to toast his reflection. The meeting with Julius had disturbed him. But he was over it now, and Julius might never recover. Lost inside his mind, inside that house. He again felt a rush of pity, watched the blossoming of compassion in the mirror. A small tear.

Enough. He must look ahead, to where the immediate future glittered in equatorial sunlight. He would soon be down among the fishes, with his son. Genes? Wise Blacksters had mingled with defiantly unplastic Barracudas to inform every chromosome of every last cell in Gram's young body. Invincible. These would set him on his path. Stan's heart swelled. He'd promised to have a heart-to-heart with Gram, and so he would. He'd let things slide.

'Islands of the Papalinas,' he told the mirror: 'Margaritifer. Dragonet. Anchois. Pichelim.' He raised his glass. 'Make ready for the Blacksters.'

9. Gram

The Barracuda held him in a boxer's embrace, smacked him with a gin kiss, glass in hand, glossy brochure falling to the floor. A stiff tea-time G & T had become a necessity of late, and this evening there'd been two or three. A crucial part of the cycle. Stan held one too - not that he liked the stuff, just a small way of showing solidarity.

'Brilliant, Stanley! Brilliant, brilliant, brilliant! Mmm. I think you might just deserve me after all.' Releasing him with a whoop she put down her glass, snatched the brochure back up and found the page. Kato's tail thumped the floor. 'God, a whole month in this place - what's it called? - the Espadon Margaritifer. That's our style, Stan. And right there on the beach, that'll do me.' She held up a hand theatrically. 'No! Don't tell me how much it's costing. Whatever it is I'm worth it!' One of her playful thumps.

Inarguably. Stan had anticipated a little, allowing her to believe there had been some progress with *Boscanion – The Movie*, mumblings about going into production possibly next year, have to line up pre-pro meetings and so forth. In fact he'd still heard nothing from The Office Of Louis Vanderhorst. Yet. She was right again though – she was worth it. He loved to see her like this. Vibrant. Vibrating with life force. It was almost infectious.

She had tossed the brochure onto a chair and was kneeling, breathing gin over the noble hound. 'We can breeze through work now, can't we Kato? Float our way through it. Set the controls for the heart of the sun.'

'So no further developments on the defection front then Barra?' Meaning transfer from the National Union of Teachers to Management Inc., with an appropriate signing on fee. 'You've told that Arvind creep to get stuffed, right?' That was the gin. Tricky stuff.

Liza looked momentarily peeved. 'Well, I've had to consider it, haven't I? Even though it makes me cringe? And what makes you think Arvind's a creep? He's not bad, Arvind. You sound jealous.' She gurgled. 'If you'd been pulling your weight, making us some money … but now, thanks to all the gods of artistic people, it looks as though our luck has changed at last, touch wood – ' she slapped heavily at the table and Kato jumped ' – and with this movie thing I'll be able to ditch my fine, fine, superfine career altogether and paint, the way I was meant to.

That's the new plan.'

He loved it when she was in this mood, give or take the odd negative comment. Fine, fine, superfine career - that was from *Later that night*.

Her hands waved impatiently as she searched for her drink. 'But you read all sorts of horror stories, about things going wrong in Hollywood, all the double-crossing and law suits and bankruptcies and nervous breakdowns. Not to mention the adulteries and drug addictions and vendettas. Look at what happened to David Puttnam, bloody hell! We're not wide-eyed young sprigs any more Stanley, we'll not count too many of our chickens just yet.' Which is what she'd been doing. She looked at him, and her great eyes were soft, even pleading. 'Let's leave it for now Stanley, let's not spoil the moment. I need the healing rays first, then the world will be a different place. Let's leave it till then, eh? Deal?'

'Deal.' Stupid thing to bring up. It was Arvind, more than anything. Smarmy little bugger. 'Further intoxicant, Barra?' Another stupid thing to say. Only happened with gin. He'd noticed before, there was something sneaky about it.

The Barracuda flashed a grimace and gave him her glass. 'Why not? I'm in the mood. And make sure there's a fresh slice of lemon this time. You're always cutting corners.' She strode off. 'I've to give Sharma a call now.'

She had recently taken to working late, then going out with Sharma and the gang, and when she talked about work now even Stan had noticed it wasn't about the kids any more. Stan had mixed feelings about this – although he couldn't deny he had felt the odd prickle of resentment whenever she got too involved in their personal dramas, despite her insistence that she maintained her distance, at the same time he admired her for it. And he only had to go along to one of the college shows for any and all misgivings to be banished. She was a born teacher, like it or not. And fiercely alive in a way he could only marvel at. Hungry for life. And what course might their lives take after Gram left home, and they were finally, truly alone again, face to face? Not easy to predict. She might just turn on him. She might. Gram was so important. He had to talk to Gram.

The noble hound clumped up the stairs behind him. He knocked at Gram's bedroom door, paused for the OK and went in, Kato flopping heavily down to wait and maintain vigilance. Gram was working at his computer at the table set up under the window, amidst a litter of paper, discs and files.

'Won't be a minute.'

From the colours on the screen, Stan could see his son was out somewhere on the internet, but that was as much as he wanted to know and he looked away. He hadn't been in here for a while. The small room was stacked with books, mainly natural history, biology and ecology reference works, most of it paid for by Stan, plus state-of-the-planet-looking volumes he didn't recognize. He felt a pang: Gram always used to show him new books straight away - seen this one, dad? There was a stack of paperbacks and graphic novels, fantasy and SF in the main, plus magazines and CDs - the usual, or so he imagined. Alongside a poster version of the official *Insidiator* Bookmark – two white sharks circling on a strip of red - and a huge Save the Whales wall-chart, a sharks of the world and two commercial fisheries identification charts were probably not especially typical of a sixteen-year old British male's bedroom, but otherwise the place was a reassuring mess. No girls though, no pop stars. The fish charts had also been provided by Stan, and he hoped they weren't just on the wall to keep him happy. He wasn't that kind of father. He'd always been prepared to make space for his son to come to his own conclusions about the world. Maybe it wasn't too late to get him his own Fish of the Month calendar.

He stood there and made a conscious, ginny effort to capture and preserve the image of this youthful, vital figure at his work desk, long hair swinging, fingers flying over the keyboard. Soon this room would be empty.

Whatever it was seemed to be taking him forever, and Stan was beginning to wonder whether he'd been forgotten, when at last Gram swung round in his chair.

'Hi. Sorry about that, something I had to get done.'

Stan sat on the edge of the bed, feeling awkward. This was Gram's domain: parents didn't come in here much these days. Unless something was wrong.

'What's to do then, dad?'

Gram's upper middle two incisors were very slightly splayed, so he'd been Goofy at school, among other things. Stan and the Barracuda had been fairly sure at one time that Gram was being bullied, but he wouldn't admit it. The Barracuda had gone on a mission anyway, and it seemed to stop. As he grew older he could have passed himself off as the long-haired younger brother of the ace Brazilian

Ronaldo, especially when he smiled. Not so heavily built though. Anyway, football was gone and Gram was booked in for an honours degree course in Environmental Science at Sheffield University, assuming he got the A-levels.

'All OK Gram. And you?'

'Sure.' Gram nodded, his half-frown saying sure, what's the problem, why're you in here?

What was that on his chin? He was trying to grow one of those daft little beards they all had these days. For once he bit his tongue. 'Did you see NASA are trying to perfect brewing in space?'

'No, didn't see that.'

'Yeah, had to happen. Seems the yeast distributes itself more evenly, fermentation is more efficient, and you wind up with more alcoholic beer. In theory. Bound to be this sorry American BudMillerSchlitz pseudo-beer though.' Hopback Entire Stout; Young's Ordinary Bitter (food of the gods); Exmoor Gold; Archer's Best; Fuller's ESB; Cheriton's Pots Ale; Orkney Skullsplitter; Bateman's Triple X - it wasn't as if there was a shortage of worthy contenders, and these were just a few off the top of his head. How about Butts' Barbus barbus bitter, named for the river-fighting ex-Fish of the Month? Stan was momentarily distracted from the job in hand by a vision of crumpled beer cans orbiting up there forever in a Saturn's ring of plastic-wrapped turds, frozen urine and American millionaires.

'Yeah. Did *you* see they're slaughtering 800,000 animals and the chief vet has had to go up to Cumbria to explain to the farmers why their healthy cattle and sheep and pigs have to be shot and burned and buried?' He had the look of his mother.

'Yeah. Grim.'

'Grim. It'll never be the same after this. The meat industry's finally had it.'

'Don't be too sure.'

'Who's going to eat meat after this?' He sat straighter in his chair. 'Mountains of burning cows, on the TV screen every night?'

'Hope you're right Gram, really I do. But it's a global industry, it's too important, too powerful. People forget.'

'Don't you even care? You don't seem to. Why don't you get worked up about it?'

Because this is what it's like. 'Because I've seen it all before. Couple of years, they'll all have forgotten, until it happens again.'

'You should care. You should be writing stuff. If it was a heap of sharks burning out there, you'd care then.' Gram had swivelled slightly away, and was staring out of the window.

This wasn't going to plan, not that there'd been one. Gram was in for a lifetime's grief at this rate, once he got out there in the world.

'Have you had any more thoughts about university Gram? Your mother still thinks you're going, doesn't know there are any second thoughts.'

Gram was sulking now and looked like any other volatile young kid. He swivelled back and forth on the chair. 'I don't want to go.' He looked up at Stan. 'I've just had enough of being taught, you know?'

Yes, Stan knew. He also knew the proper response. 'Yep. I know just how you feel, Gram. But come on, this is a worthwhile subject, isn't it? It's not as if it's Media Studies, or Business Studies, or Surfing or whatever, is it? It's important Gram. And it's what you're interested in, after all.' In his way. The copyright off-centre Blackster approach.

Gram's unlined brown face worked. The silver shark glinted as it swung at his ear.

'Yeah, I suppose. But ... I don't like what they teach. I don't agree with it. They just teach you better ways to measure the damage, you know? And I'll get sucked into it, and I'll be a part of it.'

Stan knew he was wearing the noble hound's grin, but he couldn't help it. 'Like me, you mean?'

Gram spun around on the chair, scowling. 'Yes. No. Not really. You're not really a part of it, no. You got your degree and all, but you backed out, didn't you? I've read the atoll shark paper, I know it was standard life-history methodology of the time, and you did the right thing, of course. You're not part of all that. I expect you had a hard time over it too.'

Stan grunted.

'And you did Boscanion. I think, my dad made that, thought the whole thing up. Boscanion is my dad! Cool! That's the way you used to be. You used to be ... I don't know, engaged. I used to think you cared about what was going on, but now I think it wasn't that.'

'Used to be?' Not engaged? Didn't care? He should show Gram the pupfish article.

'Look.' Gram pushed himself across to a pile of papers, riffled through and came back with one. 'I bet you know this anyway, it's not even recent.' He read carefully: 'One trip by 32 Japanese vessels using drift nets caught 3 million squid. Casualties were over 1,000 dolphins, 52 fur seals, 22 turtles … and over 50,000 sharks. Damage measured. And by the time it gets in the literature it's ancient history, and while you're reading it things have moved on, five years down the line, and there's a whole backlog of other things, much worse things, and you won't read about them for another five years. And these are just the things that we find out about. No way can you keep up, and it's a distraction anyway. They don't want you to keep up. You're just fed bits and pieces to keep you occupied.'

'Yeah.' This wasn't what he was here to talk about, but he wanted to know. 'What do you mean, used to be? What's changed?'

Gram was looking straight at him now. 'You have. You've changed. I don't know, you seem to have stopped being interested in what's going on all around you, every day. Maybe I've changed too. Maybe I see it differently. But even mum, you hardly seem to notice her most of the time – '

This was going too far. Not notice the Barracuda?

'Gram, I think you're exaggerating. Besides, when you're not at school you're up here in your room all the time.'

'Why shouldn't I be?' Gram swivelled to stare out of the window. 'You're in the bathroom, how weird is that? It's as if you live in there and you don't like coming out. You used to go out, you used to be involved with all sorts of things, you used to meet people, you used to write good stuff, passionate stuff – '

'What makes you think I stopped?' The pupfish piece, he'd go now and print it out … 'Just let me get you my latest – '

But Gram was shaking his head, hair swinging. 'Let me guess: it 's about fish, right?'

'In a way. A very special fish, though. Do you know – '

'No dad, it's OK, I can look at it later.'

He couldn't let it go. 'I'm not sure what you're saying, Gram.'

More frustrated swivelling. 'I don't know myself. I remember thinking Boscanion is my dad. My dad is Boscanion. I remember that. Stupid. I know that's stupid, but, oh, something's gone. Maybe we've just all got old. Maybe this is just what happens. But you should be doing something, writing things, telling people what's going on … '

This wasn't what he'd expected. He felt empty. 'I've accepted that man is a poisonous species.'

'Yeah. Which means you don't have to do anything about it.'

He must try to understand. This was his son. His own genes

were speaking to him.

'Perhaps I've been a bit wrapped up lately.'

'In what, exactly? And it's not just lately.'

He didn't know. He was losing track. His mind had blurred.

'Dad? Dad? It's OK dad, it's OK. I'm not making much sense, take no notice. Dad? The movie news, that's great.'

The movie news. 'It should be good, yeah.' Shouldn't it? 'Look, we all need a break Gram, get away, get ourselves back on track. Your mother's frazzled too. The Synchronous Blackster Frazzle. We all get it at once.'

'What about Kato?' A small smile.

'The noble hound is immune.' Equanimity was returning. He got to his feet. 'I'll just print off that article anyway ... ' He was half way out of the door and the noble hound was struggling to his feet when he remembered his mission. Damn! 'Ah, one other thing Gram.' The mattress squeaked as he sat back down.

'What? About the Papalinas?'

'No. About animal rights.'

'What rights?'

'Well, yes, absolutely. What do you think about direct action?'

The faint Gram smile faded. 'What, you mean demos and stuff? Waste of time. They don't do any good, do they? They just make people feel better, stops them doing anything else, anything useful.'

Stan felt uncomfortable again. The Barracuda had got him into this. But he had to press on. 'OK, as far as I know you've never been on a demo, and I had wondered why. Now I know. But you do have strong feelings. What about these people who beat up lab workers, put bombs in the post, the Animal Liberation Front and the Justice Department? And this You Build It We Burn It brigade?'

Gram was nodding. 'The E.L.F. Earth Liberation Front. In the States. Is that what you think? Hey ... you've been looking on my computer, right?' He made a dry, whistling noise. 'I didn't think you'd do that. Oh ... it was mum, right?' He spun to face out of the window, muttering, a word that sounded like bitch.

'Gram.' She was too, sometimes. But it was disturbing to hear this. Stan followed his son's gaze: orange-grey evening city sky, the lights of a small plane banking towards the airport at Eastleigh; the wet grey tiles of a rooftop where one bleary night long ago someone or something or nothing had crouched, looking in at Gram.

'She's a mother Gram. She worries. You can't blame her.'

'Why not? This is my room. How would she like me going through her things? I'm not one of her students. Go on, tell her. Tell her I'm a fully paid-up member, been to the training camps, leader of the local cell, all that.'

'Come on.'

'She's sent you in to find out.'

'She hasn't sent me.' This was … disrespectful. 'I want to know, for myself. And I don't want her coming in here again, I've told her.'

'Yeah. I bet.'

Stan felt panicky. His heart was pounding.

'Look, dad. I try to keep up on the net, that's all. I agree completely with what they're trying to do, and so should you, if you had any guts. They get things done. The law is like a big game, isn't it? Designed to channel legal protest up a dead end. All the spokespersons on TV, wondering at the end of their lives how they could be so stupid, so easily taken in, if they still really care at all by then.' Gram sighed. 'Nah.' He shook his head. 'I'm with them in spirit, but I guess I don't have the guts either, take after you.'

'You've got it wrong. When you see this article - '

Gram was still staring out of the window, or appearing to. 'Yeah. Look. It's a trade-off, right? You've seen the modern mass extinction stuff, from the National Academy of Sciences?'

The pupfish. 'Yes of course. This is - '

'Like it says, some species go extinct, like about six billion of them, while others, the rats and crows and the roaches, do well. But the best trade-off is if we go extinct, and things get back to normal, right?' He spun slowly round. 'You think the same dad, I know you do. Or you used to. Isn't that what *Insidiator's* all about? You saw it coming, the wrecked climate, the rising sea levels. All this money and effort applied to one side of the equation, protect this, save that, conserve this, while the other side – us – never even gets discussed. And we've swamped all the environments here and now we're going to spread out into space - who'll be the pests and weeds then?' He spun round again, facing away.

'There are still a few special places Gram, that haven't been wrecked.'

'A few. It's only a matter of time though. You can't hide them, and making them World Heritage Sites is like putting up an advert.'

A sixteen year-old saw already the remorselessness of human nature. 'True.' Which was strangely depressing. He'd thought Gram was still a believer, an innocent on the verge of being pummelled by life. Youngsters should still believe though. 'We're the Guardians of the Biosphere. There are billions of us, each life sacrosanct. What do you think to that?'

He snorted, again like his mother. 'Billions? There's billions of billions of other lives out there. Not just us.' Spinning back he looked directly again at his father. 'Anyway, that's why I don't want to go to university. I don't want to learn how to think I'm making some sort of difference. I just want to get away from it, get outside it, I don't know.'

'I understand that Gram. I think you need a year out. Your mother though – '

Another snort. 'Yeah. The Stasi.'

'Come on Gram, try seeing it from her side, you've been distant lately – '

'Look who's talking!'

'And stop bloody interrupting! She's worried, she's frazzled, she's got things out of proportion I agree, and she's stepped out of line. But only because she's worried about you.'

'Kim being on TV again didn't help.'

'No. No, I suppose it didn't.'

'Look, dad. Is she a bit ... mad?'

'Mad? Your mother?' Fierce. 'Fierce. She can be fierce.'

'Sometimes I do, I think she's crazy, the things she does.'

'She burns brighter than most, now and then. Artists are meant to be crazy, aren't they?'

'Is it in me though? Somewhere?'

'No Gram. You take after Kato.'

A semblance of the Gram grin returned. 'Yeah, right.'

'I'll tell her it's just harmless research. No baseball bats.'

Gram's mouth twisted. A grunt.

'OK? And we keep the university thing for later, eh?'

Gram sighed. 'I can see she's close to losing it again.' He waved at the rooftop behind him. 'I don't want to see it, I never want to see her like that again.' Rain was beating once more against the window, this time as if it meant it. 'We will though, won't we?'

The call of the Barracuda came from below, impatient to learn what was what before she went out.

Gram grimaced. 'Things in this country are lousy aren't they? Sick. Completely screwed. We'll get away, we'll see it from the outside, yeah? See what it could be like? Get some perspective, some balance.'

Were teenagers supposed to talk about balance? He suddenly sounded so mature, like a different person. 'Absolutely. We'll have a fantastic time Gram. Just like the good old days. Better.' Who was directing the conversation, him or his son?

Gram nodded, the clouds gone. 'A place that hasn't been totally trashed yet. I've been reading up. I know the crocs and dugongs have gone, and most of the sharks, but the reptiles and amphibians, these massive palms, all the seabirds, the fantastic sooty tern colonies, the turtles – the hawksbills come ashore to lay in the daytime, and nobody knows why.'

This was Gram. 'And the fishes, Gram, the best of all. I've told you about this chap I know out there, Bernard, remember? Brilliant fisherman. I'll track him down. You can ask him about the turtles. You'll like Bernard.'

The Barracuda called again. She would depart in five minutes.

'She shouldn't have searched your computer Gram. She won't do it again, take it from me.'

Gram spun away again. 'Yeah, well. She's fierce, right?' There was a short silence then he spun back. 'Did you hear Saints are after Keegan?'

'Keegan? What's happened to Glenda?'

'Off to Spurs, now they've sacked George Graham.'

'Keegan.' Stan smiled, gave his wise nod and got to his feet, moving casually, mission accomplished. He'd done his fatherly duty. On the whole more unsettling than anticipated, but he'd managed it well, and an hour's peace and meditation in the bathroom with a golden glass was called for. The noble hound's tail thumped as he opened the door. Gram turned back to his computer.

The rain eventually relented Gram took Kato for his evening constitutional in Riverside Park. Stan was now quite alone in the silent house, but he'd locked the bathroom door out of habit. He was with a bottle of Lagavulin malt, pondering Gram's words, contemplating a return to the imperial moustache and chin-beard of his dashing youth. He toasted them in turn: the festive parrotfish; the plump and placid powder-blue; the emperor with its curiously haughty demeanour; the barracuda of course; the inoffensive, herbivorous rabbitfish whose venomous dorsal spines could cause pain and over-vivid dreams; the dashing blue trevally; the giant sleepy shark; and, finally, the mirror.

'The confraternity of the seas!'

He drank Lagavulin. So superior to gin – a thin and uncomforting distillation with an oily aroma which crept into the nasal passages like formaldehyde – and fit to rank alongside The Balvenie, Old Pulteney, and the unspellable one.

He and the Barracuda eyed one another. Still nothing from Vanderhorst, and he was beginning to wonder: his brain had not been performing reliably of late, due no doubt to insufficient unspooling opportunities, or shortcomings in the oxygen delivery system. Was it possible he'd somehow imagined the whole damn thing? Created it, as it were? That tinny kid's voice up in the clouds? That jet-paced lunchtime performance at the Hilton? The puckering Vanderhorst lips? Milt? Nonsense. He hadn't dreamed it up, and someone had sent the tape of the whole show to Vanderhorst. Was it in any way, shape or form, in any foggy phase of reality, possible that it had been AB? His head was spinning, albeit in a slow and rather deliberate manner. He must take the initiative - his son would expect no less. What would Boscanion do at this point? Boscanion would apply himself fully and obliquely to the situation. He must get hold of Ray.

Ray was uncharacteristically evasive on the phone, and didn't want to talk. He suggested they meet up in London, at the *Marquess of Anglesey* in Covent Garden, a long-favoured venue which served a beautifully-nurtured example of the beer they both esteemed above all others: Young's. Initially reluctant, Stan had to remind himself he was to cultivate a more outgoing, more adventurous phase. It was a couple of hours' journey, after all, and the *Marquess* had been the scene of some epic evenings during the *Insidiator* days with Ray, Charlie Chin, Harak and the rest. Ray generally started off here if he had something to celebrate.

Stan found him comfortably ensconced with two pints.

'Stanley.' He swallowed beer with theatrical gusto and smacked fleshy pink lips. Holding up the pale, barley-coloured pint, he allowed it to catch shafts of late afternoon sunlight filtering into the long, near-empty bar, and sighed. Solemnly he tapped the table beside Stan's pint, set properly on its ram-headed Young's beer mat.

'*Mandroso.*'

A Sunday, unmistakeably, with that devotional aura of peace.

Stan sat, hoisted the glass and swallowed, savouring the hush of this cathedral moment. Young's Ordinary Bitter could be reliably found at only one outlet in Southampton and environs, and did not travel well.

'To your Art,' announced Ray loudly to the barmen, who all knew him. 'Gentlemen!' Another loud swallow. Ray was in good form - Stan recognized the signs. Something had tweaked the bounding Cornish biorhythms.

The barmen polished glasses, chatting quietly. There was no juke box. Occasional traffic sounds could be heard, none of them close. The long room existed in a pool of tranquillity.

Ray took down more beer, Adam's apple bobbing unhurriedly, breathed another long, contented sigh and set down the glass.

'Well Stanley,' he said at last, 'she's finally got what she wanted.'

Ah. 'Your job.' It had been a long time coming.

'Correct. Dear Delyth's in, and to all intents and purposes I'm out. For now, anyway.' Ray's eyes were bright behind the Clark Kent specs.

Stan thought about putting on a bit of a show - mystification, outrage, solidarity - but decided no. Ray had made too many enemies, and was associated with more than one perceived failure. He didn't act like a TV producer. He didn't convince. While Delyth's streamlined executive pike cruised the prey-rich upper waters, Ray gave every impression - even to Stan, his oldest friend - of rooting enthusiastically around in the mud at the bottom of the tank. What was there to say? There was the sense that various strands had come together, demanding an evening dedicated to beer. Well, so be it. He felt he was on a quest, he was in the mood for adventure, and he felt he deserved a treat.

Besides, Ray didn't look particularly distraught, waving a chubby hand dismissively. 'It's all right. I saw this particular little ploy coming a while back and took suitable precautions.' He did the boyish chuckle, linked his fingers and cracked a few knuckles. 'When word came, I was not unprepared.'

Stan didn't want to know. That wasn't why he was here. He had problems of his own; or if not problems exactly, then puzzles. He would have to ask Ray if he'd heard anything about plans for a possible movie, but that should be done at the slant. You don't just charge in.

'Heavily mined scorched earth, Stan. You don't want to know.' Ray drained his glass, licked his lips hungrily and set off for the bar. He'd always favoured highly polished black shoes of the sort which made important clacking noises, which they did now on the uncarpeted bar-room floor. Ray was a fast walker, especially to the bar.

The second pint was at least as praiseworthy as the first, as was the third. They discussed the astounding TV spectacle of stupendous 1,600 year-old buddha rock carvings in the Hindu Kush disintegrating as the Taliban detonated explosives. The cameras weren't allowed to film the faces of the destroyers but voices could be heard praising God, or so the BBC man said. Stan brought over pint number four.

'Jacques Tourneur,' said Ray, shaking his head. '*Night of the Demon.*'

'Classic.'

'Due a remake Stan.'

'Do you think? The Satanist, what was his name?'

'Niall MacGinnis.'

'You're not going to improve on him Ray.' Badass material.

'We'd manage. And we'd make a better job of the Demon. Good for its time, but they should never have shown it at the beginning, bloody ridiculous. That wasn't Tourneur. The producer did that. And Dana Andrews, the obligatory Hollywood star ... '

Hmm. Genteel, middle-aged mother's boy, plump, every now and then just the merest suggestion of wings and smoke. Vanderhorst's cronies could handle that. And teeth. Maybe some Walton: *I am, Sir, a Brother of the Angle!* Maybe the lisp. Ray was burbling on.

Foot and mouth cases had gone through the 400 barrier. It had reached Holland and the Republic of Ireland. Mad Cow disease in people, five cases in a place called Queniborough in Leicestershire, had been caused through a process graphically illustrated with TV footage and computer graphics. Gram had actually called Stan in to watch: calves had been removed from their mothers after six days (mothers' milk required by the Guardians) and fed on a slush of cow and sheep leftover bits, then killed by captive bolt while being prevented from kicking inconveniently by a wire pushed into the spine: pithing, known to all schoolboys of Stan and Ray's vintage through frogs in biology classes. Sheffield Wednesday had won and Plymouth Argyle had lost. Then they got down to it. Audience response to *Insidiator* and reviews had not been considered by Ray's colleagues to be sufficiently positive. There would be no new series.

'It's so bloody good though Stan!' chortled Ray. 'Isn't it? I just don't understand why they can't see it! It must be some sort of mental dwindling brought about by over-exposure to the industry. They're so obsessed with re-designing everything that they can't see straight any more. Amazing I haven't contracted it myself.' Another chortle. 'They're not balanced, these people - I mean, look at Delyth. Change the sign on the door to ICI, or Tesco, or New Labour, and she wouldn't notice. Nor would anybody else. When you consider the budget, how fast we did it ... you'll see. One day. It believes in itself! And how much TV drama does that nowadays? We should feel proud, Stanley!'

'We do!' Stan was ready to be caught up in this futile enthusiasm. Hadn't Gram said much the same thing? And even Prof Dalyell, of all people? Two perceptive, intelligent human beings. Rounded people, people he admired. Plus himself. Old Charlie Chin and the Kims, not that the Kims were rounded exactly. Easterhouse too, in a way, although it would be fair to say he was mad. That made half a roomful, maybe more. They should all be here now – well, not the Kims. And Harak. What was old Harak up to these days? Hadn't seen him on TV for ages, not since that part in *Coronation Street* where he'd played a bouncer with bad feet. The mighty Harak. Most of all, what had become of Kim?

Ray hadn't finished. 'And Charlie pulls out all the stops, doesn't he, the old ham? Spot on. Never recovered from it of course, but there we are. And Kim, well ... extraordinary!'

They all said that: extraordinary. The Prof had said it, or was it his driver, Tate?

'Remind me now Stan - where did Alice find her? No-one seemed to have seen her before. Or since, of course, but that's another story.'

That's right, Alice had brought her along, to start with. The daughter of a relative, adopted. And afterwards, it had been Alice who had phoned to say Kim was going away, going abroad. He hadn't seen either of them since, Kim or Alice. Very nearly he told Ray about Easterhouse's sad situation – Ray would be chuffed too – but decided to keep it in reserve for later, in case an abrupt change of subject was required. Instead he described the chance collision with old Charlie, which led to fond recollections of major boozing sessions in the not so bad old days, in these very seats. Charlie would hold court, still in Boscanion's get-up, utterly in his element, a handsome terminal phase male parrotfish, colours temporarily exaggerated by the lunar cycle, presiding over the saloon bar reef. Heroic hangovers, Charlie had.

The poor old boy had actually telephoned Stan the night before, although where he'd got the number was a mystery since it wasn't in the book and he'd deliberately avoided giving it to him in the park. He'd sounded suspiciously full-throttle, demanding to know of any further developments with *the project*, pronounced in the grand, rolling manner – always a giveaway. He'd had to fend off a fairly determined attempt to arrange a meeting to discuss what Charlie termed *our strategy*. Sorry Charlie. Going away for a long break. The Papalinas. Yes, Indian Ocean. Be in touch when I get back, count on it. Hadn't he just done to Charlie what Vanderhorst had done to him? Which reminded him …

But Ray had returned to the inquest-come-eulogy. 'Let's face it, Stan. We over-estimated the viewers. It was too much for them back then, and it's still too much for them now. I did wonder. Poor old Kim especially didn't fit their bill, did she? Bit too real for them. Bit too raw. It's no wonder she attracted the fanatics. She did get better though, definitely. Less, I don't know, less awkward.'

She had. 'Have the Kims risen from the dead then, wailing and beseeching?'

'Well, yes and no. There were some calls and e-mails, more than you might think as a matter of fact. Mostly pleased to see it on screen again, naturally, some saying it made a fitting memorial to her, as if she's dead or something and they've found out. And they're disbanding.'

'What?' Here was a surprise. 'I thought it would have got them going all over again.'

'Me too. No mad accusations that we controlled her with drugs, or that we've got her locked away in some secret nursing home. No talk of us bumping her off. Who needs critics when you've got fans like the Kims?' Ray could chortle and drink simultaneously. 'Bloody amazing.'

Here was his chance. If he didn't ask now … then, when he knew, he could relax and enjoy the rest of the evening. 'Ray, I've been meaning to ask. Have you made any progress at all towards film rights, you know … '

Ray gave him a sharp glance. 'I keep in touch with all the worthwhile independents, as you know, and I've had a nibble or two. The new team over at Holdfast has been making adventurous noises. I'm seeing them next week, as it happens, so I'll let you know.'

'Ah. What about abroad? Anything?'

'I'm in contact with a couple, France and Spain actually. You're right, now's the time to go for it, and I am. All part of the plan Stan.

Don't worry – when there's anything to tell you, I will. You know that.'

'Yeah, of course. Just curious. How do you do it - I suppose you send off the tapes?'

Ray looked uncomfortable, or maybe peeved. 'I've got to be careful there, you know that.'

'Yeah, of course. There's been no American interest then?'

Ray stared at him, then slowly shook his head. The motion highlighted the tiny lumps on one cheek. 'No Stan. There's been no American interest, and there isn't likely to be. It's not for them. Anyway I'd have told you, wouldn't I? Why ask?'

Stan felt numb. Numb and very warm. 'Oh, I heard a big producer-director was after it, sent in the lawyers.' That was the Young's.

'Hoo! Hollywood? Someone's been pulling your leg Stanley.' Ray was again fully relaxed, tie askew. His pebbly cheek caught the light again as his face worked. 'The Welsh Wonder was it? No, she'd never be able to keep a straight face. No Stan, take it from me, there's been nothing. Thank God. Just imagine, they'd Spielberg it. Hair, teeth, muscles, Americans saving the world. Kids, cuddly critters, moralising. Johnny Depp as Boscanion. '

Stan swallowed beer to avoid responding. Depp would be OK. Ray had always favoured Oliver Reed as the big-screen Boscanion, and he had a point, but it was too late for that now. He was dead. They'd argued about this - Reed was just too bullish for the part, not oblique or vulnerable enough. But Ray saw qualities overlooked by others. He would have resurrected Reed's career. There followed a monologue on how he, Ray, would have used certain of the great wasted actors, such as Burton and McGoohan, Denholm Elliot, while Stan nodded, stared into his glass and drifted. He would continue to work up a Badass.

Ray made his way back to the point. 'No Stan, I see why you're worried, but I wouldn't let that happen. Something like *Insidiator* lives forever. We'll get the film made, and when we do, it'll be by the right people.'

Stan felt a flare of impatience. Ray's way would never work. 'Come on Ray. There are some decent American directors, even in Hollywood - '

'Firstly they're not American. And secondly, if they stick it out there for any length of time, they don't stay good.'

'It's not all crap … let me think, yes, what about *Legend of Xutha*? Good characterisation, layers of meaning … ' He tailed off and took a drink, avoiding Ray's appalled stare.

Wait a minute though. Ray wasn't totally convincing here, and he wasn't in charge any more, was he? Delyth was. He'd get on better with Delyth now that Ray was history. Lovely and vindictive Delyth. She would have the definitive answer, not Ray. With this straw to clutch at, he pulled out the cigars.

'Raymond. Further intoxicant?'

'Keep 'em coming.' Ray was in the groove, puffing away at his cigar. Not a smoker normally, he was always berating Delyth about it. Her pack and lighter would be on his desk now.

When Stan returned with more Young's there was a package on the table.

'You mentioned tapes. This is a presentation set, Stanley, for you. Limited edition, with out-takes and background.'

Stan picked it up, hefted it, inspected the slumbering red face on the cover. A strange feeling. He thought of that intimidating room in Easter House, of the tapes on the shelf, *Insidiator – raw footage.*

'It's the whole thing.' Ray waved his cigar expansively. 'I sort of worked out you'd lost your tapes, and you should have it. You should feel proud. I feel proud.' He raised his glass too quickly, spattering beer onto the table.

'To Boscanion!'

Stan hoisted his pint. Wasn't that a gorgeous colour? Gram should be here now, to hear this. 'To Boscanion!'

Newly-arrived drinkers glanced across.

'Har!' Ray hunkered forward in his seat. 'You know what they'd rather do? This'll show you what I've been up against. A bloody expensive serial about a football team of glossy pop-star types with attitude. Halfway through the season and they aren't doing well. New, shadowy owners start replacing them with glossy pop-star types with no attitude at all, but they can play football. Up the table they go. They're in Europe. Global merchandising, international power. Flash cars. A cohort of demonic vixens as wives and girlfriends, you get the picture? Supernatural forces. That's right! Looks as though you've guessed the rest.'

'Stepford United.'

'Stepford United. They're going to hold high-profile auditions, pop-star-style. And oh yes, they'll be looking for a wise old gramps-type who's secretly a white magician, so we'd better let Charlie know. And, the thing of it is, not one of those buggers knows a damned thing about football! Not a thing. They go along to the odd Chelsea game and that's it.'

Ray, as a lifelong supporter of Plymouth Argyle, could afford to be sniffy. Stan could see where this was leading.

'It's bloody Buffy we've got to thank for this!' Ray was prodding at spilled beer on the table-top with his Young's beer mat.

Stan nodded and drank. He wasn't sure Ray had actually ever seen Buffy, but he didn't want to pursue it. Even he knew Buffy was generally highly thought of, considered innovative and ironic. Gram liked it. It wasn't very hard to see why Ray had been overhauled by Delyth. More to the point, how had he lasted so long? He gave the conversation a timely nudge away from Buffy, and there followed an engaging review of all the old favourites, particularly *Worzel Gummidge*: the time was drawing nigh when the world would be ready for *Worzel – the Dark Side*, play up the rooks and the Crowman, focus on the basically primitive and sinister natures of the whole crew – Aunt Sally, Saucy Nancy, Worzel himself. Not that Pertwee, Una Stubbs and Barbara Windsor hadn't had a decent stab at it, but they'd been up against the insurmountable obstacle of scheduling for kids. Una especially, you could see her straining at the bit. Ray would sweep these restrictions away. To play Worzel? The Great Gambon. The Crowman? Charlie Chin, possibly, if he could stay on his bike. AB Defduf would rise from the grave to write some eerie tales – with full credit to Barbara Euphan Todd as original author of course, they both nodded in solemn agreement on this – and the hunt would be on for the new Aunt Sally. Maybe they'd be able to unearth a talent for the sinister in one of these TV weather girls.

It had all the makings of another cult failure.

Another pint and they moved on to fond reminiscences of *Doctor Who*. Ray had several axes to grind here though, since he'd been involved, and the conversation became one-sided and turgid.

Stan re-focused. 'Ray. Stop there. You just reminded me of something. A laugh. A quiet, dusty laugh. More of a chuckle in fact, but sinister. *Doctor Who* - The Master. Roger Delgado.'

Ray nodded, hair flopping on his shiny forehead. 'Roger Delgado. Killed in a car crash, Turkey was it? Not noted for laughing though. Glowering, that was his thing. You mean Anthony Ainlie.'

'Ah, the Master after Delgado.' Masters, like Doctors, could of course re-generate as a new actor whenever necessary. The Master, overall, was a decent Badass.

A. A. Jameson

'Anthony Ainley.' Ray sounded respectful. 'One of the classic evil laughs. Quiet, but he meant it.' He had a try himself, but had to settle for a coughing fit. Stan swayed out of the firing line. 'Quiet ... ' gasped Ray, ' ... but sinister.'

Stan nodded absently. Quiet, suave, only occasionally sinister – the George Sanders type of villain. Plus a quality laugh. In fact Louis Vanderhorst himself had such a laugh, an Anthony Ainley laugh. A quality Badass laugh. Curious. But the thought drifted away.

Other drinkers half-filled the long room now and the early evening serenity had long since passed. Ray insisted they get a cab to Bloomsbury, to another comfortable Young's pub on the old *Insidiator* circuit, the *Lamb* in Lamb's Conduit Street. In the lounge they managed a sandwich between more exalted pints of Ordinary, admiring as they always did the unchanging green upholstery, the snob screens, the snug, the gratifying murmur of erudite drinking. Stan pressed on Ray and a couple of nodding strangers the untold story of the charco pupfish, but was uncertain the major points had registered, even with Ray, despite a few supportive noises. The two of them then fell to reminiscing about university days and, inevitably, Easterhouse.

'He always was a weird bugger. Remember his room? All those bits of animals in jars? All those glass tanks full of lizards and snakes and fish? Feeding time, the cockroaches and live mice? And he was always trying to set them up in colonies out in the wild, remember? The scorpions? Alice told me he used to infect his little pets with parasites too. You could never tell. I expect we all thought it was a laugh, did we? Christ. And Alice, smiling along with it, thinking one day he'd grow out of it.'

'Julius co-authored a book on fish parasites when he was sixteen, Ray. Sixteen. Did you know that?' In fact it had been this book which first brought Julius and Stan together, for better or worse.

'No, I never knew that. Fascinating.' Ray fanned his open mouth in a stage yawn. 'Now I can see what Alice saw in him.'

'Well, he did have something about him back then, give him that. He had charisma, he was pretty good on the pub piano Ray, even you thought so - and he was always ready to go one step further than the rest of us with recreational chemicals ... '

'His Aleister Crowley phase, sacrificing his pets ... '

Stan laughed. 'Come on Ray, he never did that.' He did though, in the name of science.

'And his clothes. Christ! That was charisma, was it? Like

202

something off the cover of *Sergeant Pepper*. He was an embarrassment to be with, sometimes.'

Of course Ray and Julius were polar opposites.

'Seriously, I never understood why Alice went for him Stan, did you? He was a real bastard to her. And he wasn't that good on the piano either, not really, not when you subtract the alcohol and the drugs and the noise and the hormones in those places. He was just playing a part. You know what, I bet he hasn't touched the piano for years.'

Playing a part. Stan had once wandered into the forbidden part of Easter House while Sir Archibald was away, found a door open and come upon a figure he quickly realized was Julius painted blue, head to foot, wearing only his hat, gazing into a full-length mirror. White symbols were daubed on his blue chest and his blue face. He should have burst out laughing, but it was a shock, one of those freezing moments. He had backed out quietly, never sure afterwards whether the grey eyes in the blue mirror-face had been watching. He'd kept this to himself, hadn't even told the Barracuda – he wasn't sure why, she'd have hooted - and he wasn't about to mention it now. It had happened though, hadn't it? Assuredly. But in reality? A fine distinction, of little significance.

'His juvenile phase, Ray. He called it that himself, afterwards. It didn't last long.'

'Juvenile? Infant, I should say. My round, I believe.'

Worn tartan carpet in the *Lamb* silenced Ray's clacking shoes. It was evident he was brooding about Alice and his one-way feelings for her. The longevity of people in the mind should never be under-estimated: some appeared only to depart, almost certainly to reappear sporadically in dreams – did the dreaming brain, in its quiet and vital unspooling, recognize faces which the waking brain was no longer able to? Others, many others, were with you forever. Look at Niall MacGinnis. All around him now, in this bar, a thousand people he would never even see, let alone meet, were carried securely in fifty drinking skulls. Near the centre of his own mind he sometimes thought he sensed, as now, an almost invisible smudge, around which everything else slowly revolved. Somehow it defeated all attempts to bring it into focus, always drifting slightly to the side, like one of those planets they detected from time to time not by seeing the thing but by observing eccentricities in the behaviour of its neighbours. If there really was something there, what could it be? It would be helpful to know if other people had one, but who could he ask? Not Ray.

Across the room Ray was upbraiding some harmless bar-propper about something or other, watched warily by the pint-pulling barman. In his own way, Ray would give Julius a run for his money when it came to being difficult to get on with. No, that was unfair to Ray. Julius had once trapped all the squirrels in the grounds of Easter House and spray-painted them with individual colour combinations, then released them to study their interactions. On Tsaramaso, in the absence of paint, he'd been keen to perform identifying mutilations on the atoll's giant tortoises, but had been stopped by the Director before a mutiny broke out among the Linois. When those grey eyes measured you, you were being registered and entered in the appropriate column of the internal Easterhouse database. Ray was normal.

Ray sat down heavily. He seemed to have pulled out of his brooding over Alice, but you could never be sure. 'And old Charlie, eh?' He was rubbing at his pebbly cheek where the glass pellets from his chemistry mishap had gone in and, eventually, come out. 'I'm sorry the old boy's gone through a rough patch, give me some credit. I've helped him out more than once, between you and me, and I don't expect I'll see any of it again. But I know he was feeding the Kims all sorts of tripe about how we were treating her, telling them whatever they wanted to hear. And now I hear he's making pantomime appearances for them. OK, it's sad. But that's the power of it. It sucked him in, didn't it, the part? You could see that at the time. That's why he was so good. Boscanion took Chinchard over, and when it was all finished he couldn't cope.'

Ray took a long pull at his drink. He was quite unbuttoned now and finally launched himself on the expanded diatribe against Delyth and other colleagues which had been threatening for some time. Stan let him go.

Soon he would be back out there, back in the glare and burning heat, this time in comfort and on his own terms, killing off memories. They wouldn't be going to the atoll itself, which was far too remote and difficult to get to, and was hardly a holiday destination anyway, but the mere thought sent a little shiver racing through him, which he tried to ignore. Back in Papa on his own terms. He'd look up Bernard and his wife - what was she called, Atherina? There were bound to be some of the old ex-pats still hanging around out there. One or two hadn't been too bad. Forgive and forget. He'd had his own juvenile phase, let's face it. Above and beyond everything would be the diving: he'd do the full training course alongside Gram. Then they'd go out on dives with the local operators, of which there must be several these days. They'd buddy for one another. It would mark a changing point in their lives. It would be great.

He hadn't entirely believed Gram about his lack of involvement with the direct action brigade, despite his subsequent depressingly realistic outburst. No, he was too wrapped up in it all, the fight for the planet. And he was sixteen. Restraint and judgement were not prominent considerations in the lives of sixteen year olds, or at least they shouldn't be. Gram was looking for a way to do the right thing. But he didn't see human life as sacred, or perhaps even anything special.

Where had he come across the zoomorphs? These were intelligent and educated people in the prime of life who paid for cerebral surgery so they could roam the countryside in packs, freed from the tedium of everyday responsibilities and expectations, just living for the moment. Yesterday's gone, forget it; tomorrow - what's that? One of Eugene Wolfe's novels. This was Easterhouse territory: as thousands of schoolkids had learned at first hand, when the cerebrum of a frog is destroyed it remains outwardly a frog, hopping when prodded, swimming when dropped in water. Julius would trap the zoomorphs, give each a differently coloured head - blue, green, orange, red - with a contrasting colour for the naked body and, in anticipation of successful breeding and an increase in the zoomorph population, a more intricate arrangement of colours for the limbs. Then he would release them and watch. Maybe he would infect some with parasites first. Paint would wear off, and people live longer than squirrels. An implant would be better. Or a brand, distinguishable through a telescope. This was deeply demersal thinking, which he must shake off: it was clear that zoomorphs were not the answer. Fishes were better. An image formed, of *Lutjanus argentimaculatus,* the mangrove jack, finning quietly in the rich waters of the flooded mangrove forest, patiently waiting for an unwary young school-fish to drift outside the safety of the submerged root-system. This was more like it. Nothing half-hearted about the mangrove jack, a bold, red, snapping pirate of a fish. He and Bernard had found a place in the lagoon, long ago ...

A sound must have brought Stan back to the room, which he quickly recognized as the lounge of the *Lamb*. Ray was over at the bar, and had clearly started making a nuisance of himself. Time to find a cab.

'An agreeable evening,' summarised Ray from the back seat. He was attempting to re-order his hair, his doughy face set in a fixed, slightly alarming smile. Behind the Clark Kents his eyes sparkled, and his pockmarked cheek showed a smudge of red. His tie was out of sight over his back.

'Good luck then Ray. I hope things work out.'

Ray waved this away. 'Don't worry about it, Stan. I can take care of myself. I've made some arrangements. She won't last long, hasn't got the chops. Anyone with a short skirt and an accent's in with a chance at the moment.' Ray's own twang hadn't exactly vanished over the years. 'The knives are out already.' He aimed a meaningful look at Stan. 'Until the next time, then.' To the south the night sky flared intermittently, overcoming the chemical orange glow of London after dark. There was no sound, no thunder, just the loud ticking of the diesel engine. They watched for a while with the cab-driver.

'OK driver.'

The driver nodded glumly and put the cab into gear.

'Ray. Who is Diodary, really?'

But the cab was already pulling away.

On Waterloo Station Stan clutched his package of tape cassettes, swaying, among scattered would-be travellers peering up at the departure boards. Why did they put the boards so far away? Why did they make the writing so small and blurred? The perversity of human nature. You could make a living here hiring out binoculars. In all probability he had eight minutes before the last train to Southampton. At 11pm on a Sunday night the concourse wasn't busy, although you had to remember there were always extra folk about when you were drunk, some of them folk who normally stayed put in your head where they could be more or less ignored, there just to provide background. They were on his side anyway, for the most part, and the stupefying effect of a gallon plus of Young's enabled him to treat the vaguely threatening station ambience with amusement. He found himself eyeing people who quickly looked away, several of them swaying noticeably, and he experienced a companionable glow: non-zoomorphs like himself, haunted by their own folk.

Had he told Ray about Easterhouse's sad decline? He'd meant to. Ray needed cheering up. Delyth was prominent in his mind. Delyth would help him. They had a lot in common, mutual admiration on the quiet. He'd ring her, first thing. Delyth was the key. She would have missed nothing. Ray was deluded. There would be no triumphant comeback. But Ray was not a man to cross. A slim blonde girl in a black business suit went up on tiptoe, squinting at the lists of destinations and times. Young and vulnerable, in need of protection. He directed a wry smile of understanding at her. She grabbed her bag and moved off.

He should ring the Barracuda, let her know where he'd got to. She'd be worried; or if not worried, interested. No, still not right – she would just want to know. Well, she would have to get used to it. He was his own man. And he'd need a lift. He made his way across to the call boxes in a series of lurches, correcting course after each one.

Making the call was not straightforward, and there was no reply. He tried again, and Gram came on. His son Gram. Gram didn't know where his mother was, she'd just said she'd be late. He'd tell her Stan the Man would be at Southampton Central at twelve twenty-five. His tongue was uncooperative, wilfully uncooperative, but some Prof-style harrumphing helped. He ended with a hiccup. Bye.

Halfway to the platform he was tilting, starting to veer, missing ballast on one side. Back at the call-box a predatory character in black leather jacket and jeans was eyeing the potential bomb inside. Stan pushed his way past and grabbed it.

He grinned at the man, some sort of undercover type. 'Almost forgot.' Another damned hiccup, then he was heading back as carefully as he could, using people to disguise course corrections. There was the train. Where could the Barracuda be at this time of night? If she didn't turn up he'd have to find a cab, not so easy after midnight. Mustn't miss his stop this time. He would stay alert.

'Aaarh!'

He was sitting up, sweating, head pounding. It was dark. He'd been in the sea, trapped, rolling and turning, helpless, carried by the current, dark shapes whirling by in a green mist, distorted by glass. It was dark. He was still on the train. No, the snoring lump was his wife. He was in bed. He must stop drinking. Tomorrow.

The Blackster expedition shop was providing stimulation. Southampton's city centre streets heaved with girls of all shapes and sizes braving the cold in tight tops and trousers, clumping competently along on stack-soled boots, swinging giant plastic bags advertising the big stores, many of the pinched, marching faces sporting studs, clips or rings: West Quay shopping mall, consumerism on the march, and in there somewhere was the Barracuda, hunting tropical beachwear while Stan remained dutifully at hand by the entrance. Gram had already peeled off to a sale of one million CDs in the Civic Hall, aiming for tropical music. Snorkels, masks and fins had been acquired, wetsuits and jackets they could hire out there. *The Phantom Menace* was in your face, sold remorselessly wherever you looked and Ray's voice was booming smugly in his head - Stanley, I rest my case. Buskers were banging out hillbilly music, a placard urged *Look again at your neighbour,* folk rattled cans for this charity or that and a lad with a dog was selling *The Big Issue.* Shanny was grudgingly not unhappy about Sheffield Wednesday, now starting to pick up points under Peter Shreeves, and Kevin Keegan had in fact taken over - at Manchester City. Stuart Gray had been promoted to Hoddle's vacant executive chair at Southampton. The still abundant and unshowy roach *Rutilus rutilus,* usually overshadowed by more exotic species, was a very worthy Fish of the Month. Out there in the countryside the mass slaughter of livestock unlucky enough to have cloven hooves rolled on, but here in the city the fumy air carried a whiff of spring. It wasn't raining, and the river of bag-swinging girls looked set to flow on forever.

She appeared beside him with a bang, looking furious. 'Stan! I'm fat! How could you have let me get like this? You've got absolutely no thought for anybody but your bloody self! You should have said! How could you let me make such a fool of myself!'

'You're not fat.' He pointed at the flowing girls. 'They're fat, most of them. Fat girls. You're a big girl. Big boned. You're powerful, not fat. Slim wouldn't suit.'

'You'll have to come in with me.'

This was part of his role. You wouldn't believe it.

'I forgot to say,' she called, riffling through swimming outfits, 'I phoned Alice's mum.'

'Oh yes?' From the side, in a long mirror, and considering his essentially sedentary way of life, Stan had to accept that the bathroom mirror had been telling only half the story: he didn't look too bad at all. His straw panama, slightly angled, cried out for shades, a juicy havana and a long glass of Mauritius Green Island rum. He might get away with swimming trunks after all. Folk here in Britain weren't used to being seen out in the daylight without a disguise, and by and large this was sensible. The Barracuda though looked magnificent and had nothing at all to worry about. She just liked to be told. 'You look fabulous Barra. You must have picked a duff mirror. What did she have to say for herself then, Ally's mum?'

'Hasn't seen Ally for years. They never did get on, I know. Ally used to say she thought they never really wanted a daughter. What an awful thing to grow up with. I'm glad my folks never made me feel that way.'

Stan thought guiltily of Old Vera Blackster, watching her snooker in solitude up in Sheffield. He would go up there as soon as they got back and show off his tan, bring her back a knick-knack of some sort. Instantly he recoiled from the thought. He didn't want to think about getting back. 'Yeah. Poor Ally.' Something major will have happened before they got back though, he could feel it.

'Oh, she never let it bother her. Or so she made out. Ally had her hands full with you-know-who anyway, your animal-torturing friend. They got a letter, telling them she was going abroad, South Africa, couldn't say when she'd be back, if ever, and that was that.'

'South Africa, mmm. When was this?' In the mirror he cocked an eyebrow, Boscanion-style. No doubt about it, he should definitely get rid of the beard, resurrect the old imperial. He would look more dynamic, more focused, and with a tan even prosperous. A touch of Hollywood glamour. Liza couldn't argue with that, surely? Gram would go for it.

'Around five years ago, she thought. It shows how time zips on by, doesn't it Stan? I could've sworn I'd seen her since then, maybe a couple of years ago, but when I think about it, the last time I actually *saw* her must have been before she rang to say you-know-who with the face had cleared off abroad to look for her real family. In some swamp somewhere.'

Her real family. He'd forgotten that. She'd never mentioned any family. Had she found them?

'Everyone's gone abroad Stan. So, it must have been, what, five years ago? Now I'm old and fat and it's your fault.'

'You're not fat. You're statuesque.' Liza and Alice. Tropical Barracuda and thyme-scented, chalk-stream grayling. Big, black and boisterous versus Home Counties refined with a sometimes-glimpsed core of wildness. Both of them arty, in different ways. It had worked, and it was a shame they'd lost touch.

'Magnifico.' He meant it.

A filmy dress of turquoise, a dazzling, eye-flashing smile and dark velvet skin glowed in the under-lit boutique. 'It'll do, until you take me into the flash shops.' She twirled, swinging her long, black banner of hair, under the scrutiny of both shop assistants. 'There was always more to Ally than you thought, Stan. She wasn't a complete doormat, you know. Obviously she finally came to her senses, saw Easterhouse for the slug he was - is - dropped everything and decided to get as far away as she could. She's not exactly hard up, after all. It comes as no surprise to me. She poured a lot of her life into that anaemic, inbred ... yes, slug.'

'And she never sent you a card? Maybe she and Kim went off together - '

He shouldn't have said that, used the name. She swivelled.

'Well, you never know, Barra. They must have been pals of some sort. And Julius has strong family connections in South Africa. Just thinking. Anyway, maybe you'd be a bit kinder to Julius if you could see what it's done to him. It hit him so hard he's fallen apart.' Although there had to be more to it than that – losing himself in his work, in the worst way; the pressure of that awful house. Inbred. Timid genes, lacking the wherewithal to avoid the pre-ordained descent, incapable of adventure. Maybe Liza was right, as she so often was. 'He still seems to think she'll go back to him.'

She shot him a glare, strode off with the dress and queued impatiently for five minutes to have a row with the woman at the checkout. They moved on to a giant sports shop where she selected smart but inexpensive polo shirts for Gram, all in bright pastel shades on the basis that there was no such colour as black in the Papalinas. Gram would tell her thanks but he preferred to choose his own stuff, she would threaten to take them back to the shop, the shirts would be packed and Gram would end up wearing them.

The vast, overheated space was milling with unathletic Brits, by no means all of them young, desperate to throw money at the team of identically-dressed teenaged girls and lads darting about behind the long counter. There was also a band of eastern Europeans of some type, more smartly turned out than the overweight locals and far more purposeful in movement, like a shoal of pickhandle barracudas. *Bekin* was the Linois name for *Sphyraena forsteri*, an impressive schooling species not to be confused with the mighty and solitary great barracuda *S. barracuda*, known to the Linois as *tazard*. Even shopping had its points of interest, if you knew where to look.

At last Stan fought his way back outside and stood with bags clumped around his feet, watching the river of girls on their platform soles, trying to picture the Barracuda dressed up in the same style. A quartet passed close, swinging bags of booty, immaculately dressed and made-up, talking animatedly. He strained to tune in, but the language was unintelligible: Lithuanian? Polish? Serbian? Ukrainian?

At Waterstone's he bought a new copy of Lieske and Myers' *Coral Reef Fishes, Indo-Pacific and Caribbean,* smiling fondly at the cover, and a photo guide to the fishes of the Papalinas - this was new, and an indication of the increase in tourism and diving. He folded easily into a relatively quiet corner of the bookshop, out of the flow, turning pages slowly. Here were the groupers: the splendid and delicious saddleback coralgrouper *Plectropomus laevis*, white with bold black stripes, yellow fins and snout, which the Linois called *babon sesil* and rated so highly they had it pictured on a bank-note; the mighty potato grouper *Epinephelus tukula*, one of which used to follow him like a wary dog when he was snorkelling at Tsaramaso, but all wiped out long ago in the northern tourist islands the Blacksters were to visit. He turned pages: this was the way to shop. The black marlin, fish among fishes, *Makaira indica.* At times, when internal systems were performing flawlessly, he felt he shared certain qualities with the marlin's supremely pelagic tribe. And wasn't *makaira* the local Linois name also? Wait until Gram saw with his own eyes, maybe not a marlin, but a squadron of eagle rays floating past at eye-level, long whip-tails trailing, or an orange shimmer of goldies over the coral, or a big old moray watching from a hole in the reef like Sharma's granny with her dentures out. Then he would understand. He sensed the Barracuda, and there she was, framed in the West Quay doorway, in search mode.

At some point he'd agreed to be taken off to the City art gallery. He could kill two birds with one stone: where the steps led up to the art gallery a left turn took you into Southampton library. Perhaps, in the spirit of research, he would call in and seek out Hermann Hesse.

This was the show she'd taken her students to, an exhibition of paintings, photographs and constructions drawn from Southampton's seafaring past and present. Gram had not re-materialised, but Stan enjoyed being shown round, having the works contextualised for him by his own art teacher; and, crucially, her focus was entirely on the art. He spent most of the next hour, as usual in these situations, sliding sidelong glances at her as she talked, revelling in the luxury of being fully in her presence and not under scrutiny. And, a bonus, the stuff was interesting, especially the old shipping and dockland photos and accompanying text. In the old Papalinas days, unlikely as it seemed now, deliveries of special supplies, equipment, and occasionally personnel, had actually been made to Tsaramaso Atoll from Southampton docks, via Durban or Mombassa on the East African coast. The Prof told colourful tales of some of his own epic journeys - when he'd cadged lifts, as he put it - to be put ashore at the research station with his pipe, tobacco and bottle of scotch. He recommended it, so long as you weren't in a hurry, as more instructive and stimulating than travelling by plane to Margaritifer then sailing down on the supply boat. It was the only way to appreciate just how far away the atoll really is from everything else.

By the time the Barracuda strode off to hunt down Gram in the music fair, Stan's mind was flagging. Nodding amiably to an attendant he arranged himself on a comfortable seat in front of a long, restful oil painting of waves on a beach with the sun going down, folded his arms and nodded off. His mind was drowsing, as it must ... images from the *Phantom Menace,* a film he would never see ... crass, overblown ... successful ... drown them out ... fishes triumphant ... chuckling Badass ... rooks in the trees ... birds in the Forest ... man on the roof ... smoke on the ceiling ... circle in the sea ...

He awoke refreshed, sun still going down beyond the waves, to the distant but approaching sound of the Barracuda. Well, he was rested and ready after a satisfactory and intermittently rewarding day, in which he'd played his full part. He would gather his family, or allow himself to be gathered, and they would return to those familiar walls, where a robust tumbler of Tullamore Dew glistened and glinted.

The short drive home was unnecessarily frosty following the discovery that Stan had neglected his chief task for the day - feeding the meter - and they'd been fined thirty quid for a four hour stay.

'Stan, or do you prefer AB? Hello. How ambitious of you to get in touch.'

As though he hadn't tried a dozen times; but Delyth always seemed to be involved in meetings, and she was very important nowadays. Perhaps he imagined it, but her voice was crisper, more decisive, with not so much of the old, fondly-remembered sing-song. Still lovely though.

'You'll have heard that we lost Ray, I'm sure. Of course. He's history now, sadly. Still, it does open things up for the rest of us. He'd been there a little too long, to be honest. Like Ceausescu. I'm sure we'll be able to keep him involved, every now and then. Yes, it's a highly competitive world, and we can't necessarily afford to toss assets away just because events have rendered them obsolete. It was an amicable parting, fairly. We're all grown up here.'

This was one of Delyth's longer speeches. He could picture her tapping at a keyboard and authorising directives as she spoke. And she'd be smoking, naturally, firing smoke from her Welsh nostrils, laying claim to Ray's conquered kingdom.

'Well, my congratulations Del.' She didn't like Del. 'If anyone deserves it, you do. You've worked so hard for it.' No, he had to stop the snidey stuff, he wanted Delyth on his side. She didn't respond. 'I hear you're going for the demonic soccer-glam kids' market.'

The shortest of pauses, then one of her machine-like smoker's chuckles. 'My, how abreast you are, Stan. Has Ray been crying in your beer? Well, yes. You'd love it, I feel sure, but it's not really your area of expertise. This is topical, sexy, intelligible, mass-appeal.'

'No. You're right. Not my line at all. Am I to suppose that from now on it's don't call us, we'll call you?'

Delyth seemed to lose interest. 'As far as I'm concerned, that's the way it always was. Look Stan, I shan't pretend I'm the generous type. If you can point to anything even halfway successful that you've produced in the past, I'm prepared to call you a has-been. I can't say fairer than that. And I try to help struggling has-beens when I can, you know that.'

'Yes, known for it you are Del.' Bitch.

'Was there anything else? I do have things to be getting on with.'

This didn't look at all promising, but he had no choice.

'Yes, Delyth, there is. I know how damned busy you are, but it's about *Insidiator* - '

'Yes. Part three of four tonight. After that you'll have to look for it on the History Channel.'

'Yes, yes. Tell me though, have you had any enquiries - let's say a tentative approach, American - about film rights?' He stopped breathing.

There was a short silence. 'Are you serious?'

'Mmmm.'

'This is pretty feeble stuff, Stan. Have you considered the possibility that you're losing your mind? It happens, you know.'

His heart was thumping. He couldn't speak.

'Well. It's all very sad. I suggest you and Ray go off to some dingy corner of some grotty little *pub* and console one another over a tankard of Old Wallop. *Ciao* Stan.'

10. Dar

Boscanion and his companion Anakim stood near the top of the tallest sand-dune on the coast, shaded from the merciless sun by a tight-knit thicket of aromatic shrubbery. Boscanion's craggy face was burned brown and patchily crusted with sea-salt, his extravagant black moustache and neat beard now bushy and blurred by new growth; a crude hat woven of palm leaves rested on long, black hair, a length of dried creeper holding it in place. Beside him, in her habitual half-crouch, Anakim wore the old red, broad-brimmed hat, once the property of Boscanion, tailored now to accommodate her crested hairstyle. Small lizards and other reptiles moved jerkily in the warm shadows, hunting insects and one another.

Boscanion surveyed the scene before them: 'At last, Anakim. A pivotal point in our journey. Behold, the terrible and ancient city of Dar.'

Beyond his theatrically out-thrust arm stretched a vista of humankind's triumphant past, gone to ruin: miles of decayed grandeur, the tallest of a multitude of tall structures trembling hazily at the far edge of vision, denoting the distant heart of the city; smoke, much of it heavy and black, rose from a number of points; broad-winged scavenging birds wheeled in the turbid upper air.

'An awesome prospect, is it not?' Boscanion spoke as though to himself.

Anakim's great-jawed face, possibly lacking flexibility to contort in quite the normal manner, nevertheless detected disagreeable odours. 'The scent is of death, Boscanion. And more ... '

'Yes, yes. I share your apprehension. However, despite the sad ruin and decay, knowledge will persist. There will be charts to show us the location of Lemperyal, and there will be a vessel to transport us. But the situation requires us to remain together at all times, Anakim. The great city is clearly now a place of danger, as perhaps it always was. We must remain alert and guard one another constantly, deploying our various abilities to utmost effect.'

'I shall watch for your safety, Boscanion,' promised Anakim fiercely. 'This is my purpose.'

A warm feeling engulfed Boscanion as he considered the wide-eyed, intent face beside him. He gripped her sinewy shoulder. 'And likewise can you rely on me, Anakim. As you know.'

The sun's glaring disc continued on its slow journey to the western horizon and presently the travellers left the sheltering scrub to approach the outskirts of Dar. On the baked streets nothing moved but for large, droning yellow insects which, though purposeful, were clumsy and easily avoided. Vulturine scavenging birds hung in the glare, pacing them easily without the flicker of a wingbeat, casting ominous, fleeting shadows. The smell of blood and death grew stronger, and soon the first body lay propped against a wall, head missing, upper body-clothing stiff and red-brown. Yellow insects clustered in torpor at the neck-stump.

The two exchanged a quick glance but said nothing, moving carefully on, from building to building, from shadow to narrow shadow. And so it was, for mile after mile: more headless bodies and other remains, some attended by the great vulturine scavengers which regarded them warily but did not give way.

As the light faded, Boscanion and Anakim peered out from concealment on a carefully selected rooftop. A handful of figures presently appeared in an alleyway between buildings opposite, and muffled voices only accentuated the brooding stillness.

'They hunt,' hissed Anakim. She had at last learned the trick of modulating the volume of her voice.

'And they are mere men, if such still exist in this strange world.' Boscanion ducked below the pitted stone parapet as the band emerged furtively from the alleyway. Men, yes. Four in all, and carrying weapons. They neared a sunken pit-trap on the ancient pathway with sounds of suppressed excitement. Something had evidently crashed through, and a man in serious distress was soon dragged forth. The four clustered around, performed a series of thrusting and hacking actions, and a new headless corpse lay against the wall. The group then re-arranged the pit's disguise and moved off with an air of purpose. One lagged behind and was snatched into the shadows by a pair of lurking, man-sized figures.

'Knifejaws,' hissed Anakim.

'Nature's smile,' muttered Boscanion, 'is a faded dream. The placidly grazing herbivore, the butterfly dancing in a shaft of sunlight, the songbird hosts - expunged from the world. Or have they retreated to some remote Shangri-la, there to await Man's own final extinction?' He recited the warning of the Malbar, Mugil: 'In Dar it is the custom for men to kill men.' He could read no expression on his companion's face.

They watched on but saw nothing beyond small, scampering movements in the shadows until Anakim pointed off across the rooftops, where half a dozen vast, winged black shapes sailed in the near-dark, tacking and gliding towards the city's distant centre; one curved away and dropped silently from view between buildings.

'Jactators.'

Boscanion nodded grimly. This was one brute he could identify without assistance. 'Come, I shall put up our defences.' Small, dark shapes were moving around the body below. Rats of some sort, he supposed. Rats will prosper in Dar.

'Anakim, we must now review our situation here at Dar.' They sat on another rooftop, now in the heart of the crumbling city. All around them baked brown masonry, freckled here and there with faded remnants of whitewash, had been brought low by uncounted generations of neglect, erosion and strife: balusters and balconies, crenellations and spires, domes and towers - all now mutilated and degenerate.

Boscanion frowned. They had made best use of their time and the various abandoned facilities they had chanced upon, and his small, square black beard and drooping moustache were again neatly trimmed, to his great satisfaction: he firmly believed that uncontrolled growth - a beard - tended to suffocate nuance in his well-practised range of facial mannerisms, for example his thoughtful frown.

'Allow me to summarise. We have seen a pitiful, crepuscular remnant of humankind tearing at itself with unremitting savagery amidst the ruins of a once glorious city. We have seen a host of lesser creatures whose existence rotates about and is maintained by this havoc. Were we to step out at night we would undoubtedly be slaughtered and beheaded within a few strides and our remains wolfed down with immediate relish by a variety of scavengers. Humanity is here beyond the brink of the pit.'

Anakim waited. She had taken to gnawing at a stubby forefinger.

'One question, which I will not ask, concerns the fate of Man. Nowhere else have we seen this mindless ferocity, so some other agent is at work here in Dar.' He studied Anakim. 'The other question you may be able to answer. We have now witnessed several killings of the local type. Are you able to distinguish between the groups, or between individuals within those groups? What is it that sets one man against another? They wear no uniforms, no coloured signals or tribal marks. Is there some tribal signifier I fail to detect? Or is each small band set against all others?'

'I see two tribes, Boscanion.'

'Ah. Then I am blind. Tell me the sign.'

But Anakim looked troubled, confused. For the first time. 'I … cannot say. It is just so.'

His frown reformed. 'Is it some element of behaviour, or comportment? Or is it something you sense but cannot see?'

Anakim shook her black-crested head. 'It is as you say. I cannot find the words. Still, it is clear to me.'

That evening they found themselves outside an imposingly vast and intriguing building, which had somehow failed to succumb to the surrounding ruination. They had earlier sought out the harbour, only to find it half-underwater, deserted and bereft of seaworthy craft; a search of several promising-looking buildings had failed to produce intoxicants. Despite his best intentions, Boscanion had become despondent, and was by this stage less than fully alert. It was already dusk, and they found themselves confronted by a gang of four men carrying well-used weapons.

'I am a wizard!' tried Boscanion, who had rehearsed his lines against just such an event. 'Beware!' He flung a glittering swirl through the air which caused them to step back.

A garbled, barely human exchange of sounds ensued before their assailants once more inched forward. Their focus was Boscanion, and to his astonishment and dismay Anakim, far from leaping to his defence, abruptly stepped through their line and turned to watch with a strange expression. The Dar-men, for their part, ignored her.

'Anakim! What is this?' Another magic pass, tinged with desperation, produced only a scarcely noticeable pallid ripple, which vanished on the instant. 'We are companions! Blood brothers, to be sure! Do you now desert me?'

Anakim's face worked, a tumult of unfamiliar emotions wrestling there. The Dar-men advanced, sure of themselves now. A detached part of the Boscanion brain noted two of the blue-black, Ruahari type, a third with the olive skin and sharper features of the Malbars; the fourth, tall and powerful, bore the brutal red face of the south. All shared the same blank, staring expression. Curious.

'Very well! So be it! Report to the world that Boscanion died as he lived!' Brandishing his shaving blade he backed slowly up the wide, stone steps. 'Though quite why I am selected as victim, while my ex-companion is not, is a question which hangs heavy in the air.' He took a swipe at a Ruahari. Four pairs of eyes followed the ineffectual move.

Suddenly, as though released from a spell, Anakim sprang forward, blade flashing at knee height, once, twice, three times, and three attackers slumped to the ground with cries of pain and astonishment. The fourth whirled about, staring in perplexity at Anakim and mouthing inarticulations. One of the fallen lunged at her and she skipped aside, so avoiding the rush of the survivor, cutlass flailing, who carried on, off into the gathering gloom.

'A cunning ploy!' chortled Boscanion unsteadily. 'Ahem. You note also my clever reference to 'ex-companion'?'

They considered the three fallen assailants, each crawling off awkwardly now through thrusts of the remaining good leg, each casting back an occasional meaningful look.

'And this is the mark of a true man, that you should learn!' shouted Boscanion after them. 'We show you the mercy you would have denied us. Or at least, myself.' He waved his blade then sheathed it, not a straightforward procedure, turning to Anakim whose countenance showed, insofar as it registered emotion at all, signs of confusion and unease.

A series of massive flapping sounds signalled the arrival of a Jactator, which fastidiously arranged the capacious folds of its black wings before striding deliberately towards one of the crawling figures.

'Come, Anakim. We are on the steps of our fortress. And do you sense a resonance in the air?'

They sat by a window, disinclined to light a fire, and dozed fitfully, roused at intervals by sounds of conflict in the streets below, or of Jactators quarreling in the night skies above. At one point Boscanion awoke to find the black night fitfully ablaze with crooked red lightning. Perhaps he still dreamed.

The airy, vaulted rooms held row upon row upon row of books, seemingly untouched for aeons, evidently protected by some force from the city's descent into barbarity. Boscanion tingled to the heady pulse of time's long process; his senses brimmed with the savour of exalted cogitation, patterns of logic, high-minded debate and philosophical transaction, of solitary and silent meditation. And its very essence, its vitality and crucial detail, surrounded him now, set down in a universe of painstakingly inscribed and illustrated hide and vellum-bound volumes arranged in endless ranks upon all walls. How many such treasure houses remained upon the Earth, he wondered aloud to his companion, and what ultimate fate awaited these distillations of the aeons of Man? Dust, he was forced to assume. And then, less than dust. He felt at ease here, in his rightful place, for the first time since ... well, that was unclear, but it was at a time and, he was certain, a place, beyond the impenetrable grey curtain in his mind. The tendency to magniloquence, rodomontade and futile vapouring which he felt sure had plagued him all his life, thwarting his fullest flowering, were here utterly banished. He drew in the deepest breath, released it slowly with a sigh. Boscanion strolled the walkways, pausing at whim to select and leaf through a volume. He must locate the geographical section, wherein to make a search for the mysterious, oceanic Lemperyal described to him by the Ruahari.

Regrettably, he soon discovered that he was quite unable to decipher even a single line in any book. He studied the meticulous portrayal of a sinister and quite unnatural gleaming, wheeled box: within sat a man, tight-lipped in his imprisonment. Boscanion shuddered. Had it meaning for him? This was somehow worse than the Jactators.

Anakim had attended his initially excited search, but after the first hour had grown disinterested and wandered off. She now re-appeared, to stand quietly at his back.

'There are many rooms. All have these books,' she reported. He had told her about books, and of his feelings for them.

'Ah. And, notice.' Boscanion's long finger left the coloured plate to gesture significantly. 'No insects, or other crawling and destructive pests. All windows are screened against the sun's onslaught, and there is no evidence of barbarian penetration, despite our own easy entry.'

'There is protection,' agreed Anakim huskily.

'Indeed. There must, somewhere, be a Custodian of some sort, a Guardian. A Librarian.'

'We will search.'

'I think not.' He considered the dull, lacquered gleam of the table for a moment, then glanced down at his boots and rose. 'No, I rather think not. I am here, where I was intended to be. All will be made clear ...' Turning slowly, he found before him a tall, ghostly white figure, wearing a loose, priestly robe of purple and a purple, square-topped cap.

'Aha! Speak of the Devil. No offence, my dear sir. A figure of speech. You are a great traveller.' Here stood the camp-fire visitor, without a doubt, or at the very least a pallid colleague. 'Forgive our intrusion, but last night we were under threat and in urgent need of shelter. I am Boscanion, and may I introduce my travelling companion Anakim?'

The Librarian's features were seigneurial, featuring a precisely trimmed tuft of beard beneath an unsmiling mouth which was thinly pink-lipped. The pallor of the face suggested several lifetimes' avoidance of the sun; the eyes were pale and conceivably mocking.

'Welcome, Boscanion. I had not expected to see you here, but welcome. You have done well, all things considered. You may address me as Argulus.'

Boscanion detected a certain condescension in these words, or the manner of their delivery. 'Ahem. From my researches I had anticipated the name Jaff. No? Very well. Greetings then, Argulus. As I say, this is my estimable travelling companion, the fearless hunter Anakim.'

Argulus approached her on feet invisible beneath the robe, seeming to glide over the floor. 'Yes. The Aspidont. You travel with a marvel, Boscanion, although you do not realize it.' He was smirking as he looked down at the slight figure of Anakim, poised in her usual half-crouch of readiness, his head tilting this way and that as he carried out an inspection of her singular skull.

Boscanion was aware of a brittle, electric atmosphere between the two, and looked from one to the other. Anakim was an Aspidont - he had almost forgotten. 'I must dispute that! Naturally I recognize Anakim to be unique, a Nonpareil. She has saved my poor life, not once, but twice!'

'Once was in order,' purred Argulus, as though for Anakim's ears only, 'twice was … unexpected. Still, we must all follow our natures. He chuckled, a dry and dusty sound in that vast room, and to Boscanion curiously familiar. The Librarian continued: 'It would not fit were the great predators to graze the meadows, or fishes take to the air. Or not until I direct it.'

Boscanion saw his chance to dissipate the charge now gathering disturbing strength. 'Ah yes. Quite. Am I to take you for a fellow wizard? Of course I am myself an adept, able to wield over the physical world a full range of manipulatory skills - '

'These are now withdrawn.' Without taking his eyes from Anakim, the Librarian made a clutching motion.

Boscanion's eyes went wide; his mouth sagged. Something was draining from him, leaving him, gone. Crestfallen, he attempted one or two exploratory flourishes: nothing. At the same time, images welled up. 'You directed my course to this place, from the forest clearing.'

'Of course. I wished you to bring this one. They are very rare. Perhaps one will appear in a human generation. It is thought the sea brings them in immature form, but even I am not certain.'

Anakim's wide-spaced black eyes stared up into the disdainful white face with ferocious concentration.

Argulus held her gaze. 'But from this one, I shall learn.'

Boscanion moved to stand behind Anakim, placing his hands firmly on her solid shoulders. 'Certainly we agree Anakim is unique, or nearly so. She is, moreover, my companion. And what of myself? You may see one Boscanion every ten generations, but even this is not to be relied upon. Grandfathers will tell – '

'You are merely removed from your customary setting. Here, you are an alien introduction, exotic flotsam, adrift. But in fullness there are many Boscanions.' Argulus had lifted his attention and now exerted the full force of his person. Boscanion winced, took a half pace back. 'You are counterfeit, Boscanion, in wizardry as in much besides. And I have pricked your foolish and overblown self-regard. No matter. This will not trouble you for long.'

'Anakim,' croaked Boscanion. 'What is your wish? To travel onward with me, or remain here to assist the Librarian in his researches?'

Anakim's voice was possibly huskier than usual. Her shoulders beneath his hands were taut. She spoke not to him but to Argulus. 'I will remain here, if Boscanion may continue to his destination.'

The Librarian clapped white hands, once. 'Excellent! This confirms my earlier observations. In an Aspidont such behaviour is most interesting. Very well, since I am at heart a merciful being, and anyway intended no lasting harm, so be it. You may both remain under my protection for the night, then in the morning you will bid farewell to Boscanion. Until then, needless to say, the barriers to exit as well as entry are set to maximum.'

Argulus withdrew.

An irritable muttering issued from the bookshelves. These books, or some of them, bore faces on their covers, and it was these which conversed.

'Hello?' enquired Boscanion. 'And good-day.'

'Good day,' replied a book peevishly. 'I am just now engaged in discussion with an over-praised colleague. If you will excuse me.'

Boscanion drew closer. 'Ah yes, forgive me.' He saw how it was. These were learned books. 'My name is Boscanion, and this is - '

'We know who you are. Naturally we know. Do you think we allow in any passing vagabond?' The face was blue, plump, with pursed lips and an incongruously benign expression.

'Do you mean to say that comings and goings in this admirable place of learning are controlled by you and your colleagues? It is as I thought. And the purple-robed functionary recently departed?'

'Hoo!' A scoffing tone. 'He nowadays styles himself Argulus, the binomial specific of a tiny and unremarkable ectoparasite of the *Cyprinidae* family of fishes, although he believes otherwise. Argulus is our entertainment at the present time. It is not wise to devote all one's hours to cerebration.'

'Yes, my own maxim precisely. And why was I - were we - ' He looked around. No Anakim. ' - permitted entry?'

The blue face blew out its cheeks. 'You seek knowledge. We are knowledge. To accumulate, protect and appropriately disseminate knowledge is our purpose.'

'I see. Of course. A foolish question.' Boscanion became thoughtful. 'And is this how our friend Argulus comes to be here?'

'Argulus thirsts for knowledge, certainly.'

'It is most amusing,' added the blue book's colleague, this one a rich ochre, glossy and sad-faced despite its mirth. 'We encourage him.'

'Understandable. He is an entertaining fellow. And would I be correct in my guess that Argulus is unable to leave the repository?'

'In physical form, essentially yes.' The blue face spoke precisely now. 'He has learned the trick of projection from a colleague. In this way he may travel, within certain limits.'

'Hmm.' What might Boscanion himself learn in such a place as this? 'And what does Argulus intend with my companion?'

'He learned of Aspidonts from another colleague. We permit him a small space for his researches and experiments. He believes he can isolate the creature's defining principle, which is reckoned to reside in the head, and that by manipulating this element with knowledge gained from us he will be able to usurp our authority, which he is coming to recognize and resent. He will then be free to do as he wishes in the world.'

'Your aim is to thwart him, naturally.'

The two books gurgled merrily at this, and were joined by several more which were listening in.

'He is our entertainment,' repeated Blue patiently. 'For the moment.'

Boscanion bulged with questions, but the books felt they had spared him enough of their valuable time, and besides, they were weary: eyelids drooped, lips pursed in, out, the great room was again silent but for the whisperings of slumber.

Exasperating, thought Boscanion as he paced the floor. For him sleep was impossible. Questions! He was unimpressed with the attitude of the books. They were here to serve - they said as much themselves!

Anakim appeared. 'Boscanion. We must go.'

'What? And where have you been? No, my dear. I have decided to stay on here for a while with you, and pursue certain long-term avenues of research which I have been neglecting. It transpires I am after all able to translate and understand the meaning of the books. All of them. A simple slantwise application of the intellect. Think! All my questions answered! And more. Questions which have yet to occur to me!'

Anakim was very restless. 'And the wizard? What of his plans ... ?'

... *for me*, she had been about to add. He gripped her arms. She tried to pull away, but he held her. 'The Books, Anakim. The Books themselves rule here. This Librarian is their plaything. I shall learn of my destiny, my origin ... you also.'

He could not recall seeing sadness in her peculiar face before, but thought to see it now.

'Boscanion. Do not listen to the Books. They will keep you here. Both of us. Like the wizard. They are ... ' she struggled for the word '... they are sick. Sick with the ages. They crave only amusement.'

He stared at her. 'And how do you know this? You have learned something. Who has been instructing you?' A Book? No, not a Book.

'The Ruahari told you of Lemperyal, and of Mappa, who is its protector. Mappa has visited me. The Books ... this place ... it draws in men from the world, and this is why men kill men at Dar.'

She was right. He saw this clearly now, just as though the voice of this Mappa spoke in his own mind.

Up and up they went, climbing wide and endless spiralling

stone steps, floor upon floor, Anakim pausing whenever Boscanion needed rest, to finally emerge in the dim pre-dawn onto a pristine white roof, terraced and tiered. Spread out below and all around lay the ravaged magnificence of the city of Dar. To seaward the pale strip of beach stretched away north and south into darkness, while beyond it the ocean was a misty grey, featureless but for the black bulk of a single large island to the north. The onshore wind generally lessened at night, but at this elevation was still strong and laden with salt. Black smoke drifted inland from the ruins below.

Boscanion saw that Anakim held a small tablet, but his attention became distracted: a large, transparent and glistening sphere settled silently before them; a threadlike filament stretched beyond, bowed and taut in the sea-wind, leading off to seaward.

He looked at Anakim, back at the sphere. An opening appeared and they entered. The sphere lifted and they were floating above the desolation of Dar, passing over the ancient harbour half-swallowed by the waves. At the sea's horizon the sky was lightening: sunrise. A pair of Jactators, beating heavily homewards, swooped to investigate but could not come to grips with the material of the sphere and resumed their course, calling guttural comments to one another.

Riding easily on the waves below was a glittering, glass-like version of the strange vessel they had found beached many miles to the south, a near-transparent, shark-shaped capsule, low in the water, the basal parts of lateral, oar-like appendages intermittently visible with the gently rolling motion. A single black pirate-bird circled above the vessel, but no occupants were visible.

Boscanion looked down in awe. 'Our vessel,' he whispered. 'All is as it should be, Anakim, although there are one or two aspects requiring clarification at a convenient later time. Our destination, I take it, is not in doubt? Lemperyal.' Then, more loudly. 'And where is our Captain?' It was good to see that fleeting smile. He felt he had somehow neglected her. 'Anakim, you are becoming increasingly accomplished at this arcane craft of smiling. Am I an adequate instructor? More practice!'

Relentlessly the filament reeled them in, and presently the sphere settled gracefully to the deck and slowly evaporated, leaving a tingling, moist sensation in the air. Instantly a quiver ran along the deck, the limbs tensed, began to work, and the vessel surged forwards.

So Boscanion and Anakim left the once proud city of Dar.

11. **Kato**

The eve of departure: Shanny had arrived to guard the fort and stood with Stan, Liza and the noble hound looking out at veils of half-hearted rain sifting down from a blank, orange-grey evening sky. These proto-early-spring evenings were pulling out, grudgingly, but days were still generally short, dreary and underpowered. The Barracuda was energetically endorsing the well-known theory that this sort of thing shaped the national character and imagination. She hated - *hated* - dragging herself off in the morning dark, along with the bulk of the toiling population, then back again, exhausted, in the darkness of evening. It didn't help that she no longer enjoyed the job which had for years inspired her. On top of this the fact that she no longer produced artwork of her own had left a simmering guilt and frustration, which could make her a difficult companion. Not this evening though.

'God, is this place really going to kill me, the way it kills everybody else? Have you noticed that, the way everybody round here dies sooner or later? Without ever being more than half-alive? No wonder everyone's such a washed-out grey colour. I'm going the same way, I can feel it. I'm ready for a top-up. Just think, the sun's belting down out there right this minute and I'm stuck here.'

'It's the middle of the night Barra, they're three hours ahead out there.' Or was it four?

She snorted and thumped his arm. 'Don't be pedantic! All right, but it's bloody hot, isn't it, right now, even at night?'

Shanny looked on admiringly. 'Not a bad time to be getting out of it, anyhow,' he muttered, motioning with his drink at the dismal scene outside. The streetlights had come on early, blocks of dull orange in the gloom above files of swishing car headlights. Blackster Towers stood in a once-quiet suburb slowly succumbing to the rising tide of people and traffic.

'That's right!' Liza did a twirl. She wore the turquoise dress. With her shining black hair tied up, and wearing tacky, palm-tree ear-rings, she looked luminous. The noble hound gave an excited yelp. 'Perfect timing, just before I shrivel up and die! Anyone between me and the beach, watch out!' Shanny had bought her the ear-rings, as a thank you for her help with Kevin. He seemed to understand her style.

Stan handed his drink to Shanny, crouching down to grip the

noble hound by the jowls. 'Right our Kato. I want you to take good care of your uncle Shanny. Take it easy with him while we're away. Not too many walks, and not too far. And not too fast. And no hills. And don't get him fetching sticks out of the Itchen, he's no good at it.' The noble hound stared into his face, grinning and slavering. 'You're just like bloody Gram, hound. Did he teach you that expression, or did you teach him?' He let go, then cuffed him around the ears, one cuff for each word, first one ear then the other: 'You've. Got. Only. One. Expression. Haven't. You?' Not strictly true - there was his perplexed frown. The retriever gave a yelp and a clumsy little jump, sensing action.

'Daft dog.' Shanny was smiling. Another P & O trainee had moved in with Kevin and Shanny had his fingers crossed that this would work out, that things were slowly heading in the right direction, thanks largely to Liza. He could pop round from here to check, and Kevin's formidable mother - 'our lass' - would be down soon for a couple of weeks to help out. 'Always grinning though, your Kato. I mean, how can you tell when he's got munk on?'

A munk was a bad mood. The Barracuda normally took care of munks.

'Don't worry, he'll let you know. Won't you flash?' A final cuff, and Kato half-rose - 'And I'm not taking you out in the rain, so you can forget it matey' - then reluctantly subsided.

The Barracuda was singing along in the kitchen to Bob Marley. Stan would normally object, but in the circumstances he was prepared to be tolerant. Once in Papa there would be no way to avoid Bob, the voice of a thousand blasters, and anyway it was a real charge hearing her sing again. She slow-danced in with the oysters, handed Stan the Verve Cliquot for opening, and they smiled into one another's eyes as the heavy, chilled bottle changed hands.

'*I'm not satisfied*,' croaked Stan, easing out the cork.

'*Everything I try*' she replied, rolling her eyes. '*I don't like the way.*'

Pop!

Shanny joined in: '*Life has been abusing me.*'

Stan poured.

In unison, '*Na na na naaa na,*' clink glasses, and again, '*Na na na naaa na.*'

At that *Ruben* moment he had no qualms about the loan from Shanny, or any of the other minor events and developments he'd kept from or misrepresented to her - she looked radiant as hell, and that was enough. Bob had finished, for now, and Stan put on *Ruben*, as planned.

Shanny was soon nodding and muttering along, '*Darling, darling, please hear my plea, God only knows what your loving does to me ...* Bloody good times eh?' he blurted suddenly, looking at Liza. His eyes were glistening. He would even drink champagne for her.

'Bloody good!' she agreed, and they clinked glasses. 'Here's to cheap thrills!'

They drank, Stan re-filled, finding an extra glass for Gram. 'To the ocean, the ultimate solution!'

'And to the sun!' declared Liza.

'To Sheffield Wednesday back in First Division.' Shanny. 'Time for a bloody miracle.'

They turned to Gram, who looked uncomfortable. 'What, me? OK ... how about, to a countryside free of cattle and sheep?'

'What?' Shanny looked bewildered. 'But they'll all grow back Gram, won't take 'em long. They'll soon be back.'

'They shouldn't be there in the first place though. It's like a giant concentration camp, the way they're treated.'

'All right Gram,' sighed his mother. 'Just lighten up, let's have a break. We're celebrating. Try again.'

'Yeah, right.' He hadn't forgotten her intrusion. 'OK.' He raised his glass, looking uncertain, not normally a drinker, and the only southern voice in the room - if you discounted the noble hound. 'Here's to the first shark. How about that?'

'Impeccable!' The Blackster genes, working away unseen. Stan felt almost tearful.

'Yes, good one Gram,' hooted Liza, giving him a hug. 'Long as I'm on the beach.'

They clinked glasses. 'Nobody'll be eating meat after this anyway,' Gram mumbled into his champagne, with a glance at his father.

Shanny was kneeling in front of the noble hound. 'Aye, they're buggering off Kato, have they told you? We'll be all right though, won't we Kato, you and me?' In the old days Shanny's tough little Jack Russell, Swanny, used to come to the pub with them and curl up under Shanny's chair. Named for an old Sheffield Wednesday hero. Partial to a drop of Guinness, was Swanny. Used to travel around the country with Shanny in the cab of his lorry. Swanny was long gone and badly missed.

When she was in the mood the Barracuda could push the boat out further than anyone, and tonight she was in the mood, dishing up parcels of scallops, tiger prawns and smoked halibut, with aubergine with yoghurt and other bits and pieces for Gram, a tray of roasted root vegetables, another of steamed green beans and black Lincolnshire cabbage. They got through bottles of sancerre, saumur, shiraz, malbec and Guinness. Then goat's cheese to follow, a favourite of hers, with black cherries. The noble hound's eyes followed every vanishing mouthful.

Stan found himself talking about the Papalinas, reluctantly at first, then actually enjoying it. Even today, when Sunday colour supplements vied to discover the most exotic, the most expensive, the most ecologically reckless destinations for the jaded traveller, these islands somehow retained a dreamily remote and unattainable aura when compared to places like the Maldives, Mauritius, the Caribbean. And Liza never took her eyes from him, silently urging him on, soaking it all up: the white, near-empty beaches lined with coconut palms and casuarina trees, the steaming, forest-covered hills, Bob Marley belting out from every other house, the impossibly blue seas full of fishes and corals, fruit bats the size of New Forest buzzards and frigatebirds three times the size of fruit bats, beach barbecues with grilled red snappers and wahoo, the famous octopus and coconut curry, rocket-fuel export Guinness if you were in the mood, six-inch giant centipedes which moved like trains and punched venom into your big toe through specially sharpened forelegs if you went out at night without shoes - Liza drawing her long brown legs up off the floor with a pantomime grimace – and back again to those impossibly blue seas, warm and placid, safe - the sharks which used to swarm around the inhabited main islands had long since been killed off, leaving just a few of the more-or-less harmless reef species for divers to admire. For the Barracuda this was pre-requisite number three for a beach holiday, after a blazing sun and an empty white beach, and Gram, champagne-pink now, was bursting to speak.

'Well we will see sharks, I know we will, and the more the better. They wouldn't attack you anyway, unless they were provoked. They're harmless, unless you go pestering them.' He looked to his father. 'They've got more right to be here than we have. They've been around millions more years.'

'Folk have right of way though,' said Liza. 'Folk and sharks don't go together.'

Regrettable, but by and large inarguable. 'There are still a few, we'll see some, don't worry, white-tip reefs, nurse sharks, maybe grey reef. The only remotely dangerous ones are the bulls, not that there's many, and they hang around the tuna canning factory. Never been a shark attack recorded in the Papalinas.' This was true, if impossible to believe. 'No shark of any description will come within a mile of where your mother's paddling about.' Not if they were sensible sharks. Gram was looking away, mouth set. Damn, had he been too flippant? Bloody champagne. And wine.

'They're digging a massive pit,' muttered Gram, 'up near Carlisle. Big enough to take half a million dead cattle and sheep, they reckon.'

'Bloody hell,' growled Shanny. 'He's back on that.'

Gram looked pink and angry. 'But foot and mouth wouldn't even kill the animals. It just makes them worth less. Less profit.'

'Not now Gram,' snapped Liza. 'Be told. We're leaving all that behind tomorrow, and good bloody riddance. Come on Stan, tell us more.'

Stan tried to catch his son's eye, but he was staring at the wall.

'Come on Gram, your mother's right.'

'She's always right.'

'Listen to your father. Come on Stan, let's hear some more, just keep it coming eh?'

He did his best.

They'd be taking a boat trip to see hundreds of thousands of screaming seabirds on the nature reserve island of Anchois, couldn't afford to miss that. There'd be turtles and dolphins and flying fishes; guitars and fiddles would play the gentle music of Papa and the Linois would have Bob Marley belting out at top whack. When the sun was sinking, which happened too rapidly for there to be much of a dusk, crickets would chirp and mosquitoes would be whipping out their tiny dentists' drills.

'Mozzies! I'd forgotten.' Even the few strays on summer evenings over here were too many for Liza. 'Put spray on the list.'

'Yeah, better do that. They're not bad though, not on the coast, where you get a breeze. In the forests, that's different.'

'I'll not be going in any forests. I'm off forests.'

'Crickets are good value.' They were. And Gram was listening now. He'd love the crickets. Even after all these years Stan could recall the different cricket sounds: an electric, machine-like buzzing, like one of those executive toys where suspended steel balls clicked together, only speeded up; another had a short, much drier buzz of about five seconds; while a third - his favourite - sounded exactly like glasses clinking together twice, *clink-clink, clink-clink,* which started just as the light was going, when clinking glasses was the best thing to be doing. He would miss proper beer, no question, but he was willing to make sacrifices for his family. Cold beer, meaning cold, fizzy lager, would have to do. He'd cope.

Liza was hooked, a believer. He'd never talked like this for her or Gram. He'd shied away from it, which just now he found hard to understand. Well, its time had come.

'After all these years,' she sighed, wine-glass cupped in both hands, supremely alive in the candlelight. 'We're finally going. One day on the sunbed – OK two – then I'll be out there making drawings again, painting. I'll take the digi camera for when I get lazy, work them up when I get back. If I come back.'

'Aye. But you'll soon get fed up of all that,' predicted Shanny flatly, reaching for the cherries, his face markedly redder. 'Odds on. They'll want to be back, won't they Kato? All that sun? We're not meant for it. It's not in us.'

Admirably, Gram was making an effort to join in again. He slapped the noble hound on the head and the heavy tail thumped. 'Kato!'

'You speak for yourself,' purred Liza. 'It's where I belong. It's my heritage, matey. I expect I'll grow right into the ground out there, turn into a big old tree.'

He could see the headline in *Papa Nation*: killer fish re-incarnated as mangrove tree. Locals would nod wisely. Life would become easier and less eventful.

'I'll see if I can track down my old friend Bernard. He'll take Gram and me out fishing.'

'No dad. You go. I wouldn't enjoy it, killing things.'

'But you'll learn something about fishes there Gram, better than any book. This is how people like Bernard make their living. It's … well, it's not industrial, and it's not for sport.' He'd almost used the word sustainable, but Gram scoffed at it, and besides, if it was true, where had all the fishes gone? There'd been concerns even in his time out there, and it must be worse now. The introduction of outboard engines in the sixties had changed everything, and the glossy new hotels had to be fed. Good news for people like Bernard, bad news for the fishes.

Gram managed a grin. 'Thanks, but no thanks.'

The Barracuda looked thoughtful. 'Bernard. Yes. I'd like to meet this Bernard myself, find out what you used to be like, what you really used to get up to. Discover all your dark little secrets.' She showed him her teeth. 'Will we get to meet some of your old Creole lady-friends?'

He hoped not.

Coffee and Lagavulin came out while Gram put on one of his holiday compilations before disappearing upstairs: the Beach Boys' *Warmth of the Sun,* hopefully a no hard feelings selection for his mother. Music from well before the thrashing in the New Forest which had resulted in Gram. Stan had requested one or two of Durutti Column's less doleful efforts, some early Frank, some old blues and some cry-in-your beer country stuff, and the Barracuda wanted the Band, Gram Parsons, Neil Young, Steely Dan, that kind of stuff. No Bob. Gram was supposed to be padding out these wrinkly ingredients with music of his own, outcome unpredictable. It was also Gram's job to get their luggage to scrape in under Air Papa's 22kg per person limit.

Shanny and the Barracuda were on the settee discussing Kevin:

'I mean, Liza, he's not a lad any more, he's a *bloke*. Well, he's not a bloke, but he's not a lad neither. All he's after is drink, girls, smoke, drugs, you know, and aggro. That's it. And clothes, yeah. All costs money, which means thieving. Not even interested in the football. Oh, and cars.'

'Just like half of mine at work, the lads that is. They're all the same. Well, nearly all.'

'We were never like that though Liza.' Shanny sincerely believed this. 'A few pints on a Saturday after the match, that was us.'

The phone cut in. Stan took it out into the hall.

'Hello Stan, James Dalyell here. Yes. I hope you're well? I thought you should know that Easterhouse has disappeared.'

'Blimey.'

'He hasn't come to you, clearly. I was rather hoping he might.'

Stan set down his drink on the stairs. The Barracuda was hooting at something next door while Gram Parsons sang *Return of the Grievous Angel.*

'Sorry Prof. Haven't heard from him since our visit.' God knows he hadn't been able to shake him out of his mind though. 'How do you mean, disappeared?'

Dalyell sounded tired. 'House empty. No sign of him. And I know he hasn't been able to step outside the house for many weeks - well, you saw that for yourself. Tate spent last night round there and will do the same tonight. Perhaps he'll return. Otherwise I think I shall have to inform the police. I don't think he's in any condition to look after himself, do you?'

'He didn't seem too on the ball, no.'

'Tell me, when do you travel out to Papa?'

'Tomorrow morning, as a matter of fact.'

'I see. Well, not much chance of his contacting you now, I suppose. Still, you never know. You have my number, anyway. And Stan, you must give my regards to anyone over there on Margaritifer who still remembers me. Tell them I often think of them and hope to manage one more visit, to the atoll as well if I can. I'm so pleased you're going - this must have been a last-minute decision for you. I expect you're taking young Gram along with you?'

'Yep. Probably the last time he'll be able to put up with us two old duffers.'

'Jolly good. He'll have the time of his young life. I've had a thought. If it were still possible to locate any of the old main island fish transects, it would be rather useful to have repeat counts. Might you be prepared to mix a small amount of work with your well-deserved pleasure? Perhaps I shouldn't put you on the spot like this – I certainly wouldn't wish to spoil your holiday. Something of a sentimental return, I should think.'

'Something like that. I've put it off too long. Liza's been on at me for years, but the place had its effect on me, as you know. Not all my memories are happy ones. And the counts would be a pleasure, Prof. Gram can help. We'll be doing a dive course out there.'

'Excellent.'

'What about maps, methodology and so on?'

'I know - let me have the name of your hotel on Margaritifer. I can then fax the details through to you. It's very simple - those were pioneering days, no computers and GPS then. And please don't worry too much about it. It will be a welcome bonus if it happens.'

'I'll do my best, Prof, cheers now.' He should say something sympathetic about Julius, but what was there to say? 'I'll send you a card.'

After the others had turned in Stan sat up alone for a while, on the pretext of wrapping up some work before the great adventure. His thought-provoking article on people reincarnated as sharks, those who returned to help out their families by looking after business on the reef, had been rejected. Entirely tangential to the subject of shark attack, they'd said, once again completely missing the point. Maddening.

He picked up the ferret skull from his desk, rubbing it slowly with a thumb. Except it was no longer the skull of a ferret: Gram, as keen a frequenter of second-hand bookshops as his father had once been, had found a cheap copy of the Collins Field Guide, *Mammals of Britain and Europe*, and had re-identified it: it had not after all once belonged to *Mustela furo*, but to *Mustela vison*. An American mink, an exotic animal not naturally part of the national fauna, had apparently been making its fish-eating way in the wilds of Hampshire. It or its forebears must have been freed by well-meaning troops of the animal rights brigades - he vaguely recalled some liberations in the New Forest. He was fond of the skull, the only reminder of Kim he could touch, and wasn't a bloodthirsty mink a more genuine creature than a poor, half-blind, mixed-up ferret kept solely to deter rats and catch rabbits for the pot? A memory came to him: the invisible fish-eater of Easter House pool, back in the old days, the one with the temerity to kill Julius's prize study carp, leaving a trail of scales – *M.vison* fitted the bill perfectly. A mystery of almost twenty years solved.

He smiled to himself, stroking the white bone. Dear Kim. He felt sentimental and increasingly warm, possibly the drink. How brave she had been as Anakim in the ruined city of Dar, how resolute, following her moment of doubt on the steps of the great library. The firmness of that jaw, those round black, black eyes; which somehow seemed less and less distracting with each episode – improved acting skills, no doubt. The fourth episode, the epic and final journey of Boscanion and Anakim, he itched to see it now, but he would watch it in Papa with Gram, which was fitting. Now he should concentrate on not forgetting anything crucial, like money and credit cards. The Barracuda was guarding his passport, which he hadn't looked at for a long time. And the youthful, gormless face looked more like a missing Marx Brother, or even a tramp, than an undiscovered Mother of Invention, let alone Boscanion the dashing romancer.

He'd packed his laptop to go. If the Barracuda could anticipate inspiration, so could he – how often did you come across an article about Papa, apart from the very occasional glossy travel feature? There were a thousand untold stories in Papa.

The powder-blue surgeonfish floated restfully on his screen.

Roland floated briefly in his head, staring with round, sandy eyes. Sweaty ant-trickles inched down his back. There were other pictures of Papa he could have painted this evening, but the Blacksters would see only the deluxe, sun and surf-soaked Papalinas proper, not that farthest-flung atoll outpost hundreds of miles to the south. They were going on holiday.

The noble hound, stretched out on the floor at his side, gave a heavy, shuddering sigh followed immediately by a jaw-stretching yawn. He'd inherited and demolished a rich pile of leftovers.

'Yep, know how you feel Flash.' Stan yawned too. His big diving watch, not properly tested for years, told him it was approaching 4am. How long had he been sitting here, staring at the contented blue fish? He was thick-headed, bloated, bone-tired and too hot. In a few short hours Shanny would be driving them to Gatwick airport. He and the noble hound both yawned together.

It would be fun to track down and record Dalyell's fish transects with Gram. There was nothing to beat counting fishes, and he began to drift off at the mere thought. Old Prof - had he mentioned this Papa trip to him at Easter House? He couldn't remember, but he must have. It seemed a long time ago, a cold and grey place, not a pleasant memory.

The Barracuda stood impatiently in the queue at airport check-in along with Gram and two baggage trolleys. Queues weren't her thing, and a combination of hangover and airport stress had burned off her sunny mood. Stan was feeling grimly demersal due purely to alcohol, having delegated the stress. Sustained concentration would steady him, and he was applying his analytical powers to a simple question: were the gritty bits which made his eyes hurt the same as the little black specks floating about? They should be visible in a mirror, drifting over his eyeballs on a sliding film of lachrymal fluid. He was also trying to blank out the look on the noble hound's face when the truth finally sank in.

The sight of an arrow alongside the words *Gatwick Hilton* had earlier caused him to steer his trolley into a pillar. He could have taken Liza and Gram to the restaurant, shown them the very table, pointed to where the Vanderhorst lips had puckered. He could have demanded a menu, pointed to his lemon sole. Asked to see the register, found Vanderhorst's name. Not that either of them had expressed any doubt. He had done none of these things, but would need to apply himself to the whole affair at some point, when he was functioning more competently.

The electronically-controlled perpetual motion around him was making itself oppressive. He pulled open most of the buttons on his festive going-away shirt, selected by the Barracuda. No matter what he put on he always overheated sooner or later. He picked up a discarded film magazine and hid behind it, staring through a slow swirl of specks. Over at check-in a heated exchange gathered volume - the Barracuda had reached the desk. Gram was beckoning. He donned his shades and made his way over. They wanted to check Stan in against his passport, and he managed a smile for the harassed Air Papa check-in girl before returning to his seat, leaving Liza negotiating for some sort of special treatment.

Back in his seat he gripped the magazine firmly. Soon they'd be at thirty thousand feet and he'd kick off with a bloody mary, follow it with a cold lager or two until the food and wine turned up, and from then on it would be painless. But he'd rather not wait that long. The nearest bar looked more like a clinic, but it wasn't as if he wanted to live in it.

A self-important gaggle strutted by, trailing some movie or pop queen in artfully wild sort-of blonde hair, tight white dress and shades, and Stan's eyes turned with all the rest. When he looked back at the page he was confronted by a familiar doughy-white, all-American face: top Hollywood producer-director Louis Vanderhorst, the wonderboy in black. His innards flip-flopped. He made out words through the speckles: Louis was teasing the film-going world with titbits from his new venture.

'No. You probably know this,' he told the interviewer, 'I work on a major studio project, then the profits, they go into something a little more personal.'

Boscanion - The Movie. Go on, say it. Say it Louis. Say it.

There was Louis pointing skywards in rock-star black, wearing a searching expression. The boy-genius warble rang in Stan's head. He read on, sweating and numb.

'Hey. I'm not going to say too much about my next one … fantastic project … on location next year … '

'Go on Louis, say it.' Get the words out, onto this page that I'm holding in my sweaty paws, you little freak.

Louis went on to reveal that this fantastic project would be a sensational but serious affair, looking at … the genetic manipulation of human beings. More profound than even *Legend of Xutha* and *Religion of the Trees* and even more pertinent to our times.

Which didn't sound right at all.

'Something like *Gattaca* then?' asked the interviewer.

'No!' Louis assured her. 'Good film, but no. More scary than *Gattaca*. More scary, and more real. I can tell you that. Hey. This is the issue of the day! Our own genetics have already been modified, yours too, sitting there with your mike. Your buddy there with the camera. You've both been modified. Scary. No! Not by some guy in a white coat hiding out in a lab someplace. Bacteria! Bugs! Anyone can check this out. It's right there in the scientific record. Bugs changed our DNA. That's all I'm saying.'

Stan's heart was in his boots. He could hear the dusty chuckle of the Master. No sign of Milt, but otherwise the whole performance was eerily familiar. And Vanderhorst was talking about science faction, dry dry stuff, not a setting in which Boscanion would flourish, or even survive, or even appear in the first place. The Barracuda had been right: another pipe-dream. He could never tell her, never. Bastards! He slumped deeper into his seat.

It didn't take a boy-genius to work out that this misguided genetic manipulation project would take up the next year at least, then it would be time for Vanderhorst's next blockbuster ... all right, maybe this was marketing flim-flam of some sort, and it would never happen. Maybe Vanderhorst ran two projects at a time; or three, or four. He was the boy wonder. Yes. And these things took ages, years. That must be it. *Boscanion* would be the next personal project in the pipeline, after bugs messing with DNA. He pressed on with the article.

'... state of the art ... cutting edge of science ... Depp's keen ... '

'Bastards!'

'What is it Stan?' The Barracuda towered over him, frowning fearsomely in her holiday hat, fresh from the heat of battle.

'Nothing. Just more *Star Wars* bollocks.' He closed the magazine carelessly and forced a smile. Then he tightened his grip on his soggy brain. 'Am I to assume the formalities have been satisfactorily negotiated? I thought to detect agitation.'

'I need leg-room, Stan, you know that. I've got long legs. I showed them. We're only in economy. Longer legs are more prone to economy class thrombosis - I would have thought that was obvious. Anyway, yes, we're all sorted. You look dreadful. Who's first in the duty-free then? Come on, Miz Blackster wants her holiday bottle.'

Reassuring to hear her call herself that. It meant she didn't know how useless he was. Yet.

'Come on then Stan, shake a leg. Gram's wandered off somewhere, but we've still got plenty of time.'

'You go. Bring me a cold lager too, please Barra, *rapidamento*. No, make it two, eh? Time to light the touchpaper.' Lager was OK for this sort of thing, scouring out the tubes, cleansing the palate, dissolving speckles. Easing back in.

The Barracuda strode off through the bodies and he dropped the film magazine into a bin, took it out again, tore it in half, then again, tossed it back in the bin. Vandertwat. Feed him to the slingjaws, a limb at a time. And the man didn't even understand his own films! It was beginning to look as though his writers were the real creative force behind his successes; Louis just found the money, did a bit of pointing and took the credit. The old, old story. Just like Ray. Heat and confusion was spreading through him like a virus. He had to ask himself: had he read this article before somewhere, when he was drunk - on the train, maybe? - then allowed his strange brain to fashion it into a real event? The similarities were too obvious, and he wouldn't put it past him – Christ, it was just the kind of thing AB might get up to. Jesus. *His mind created the event in order to preserve the illusion*. The Prof had said that, about Julius, Jesus. It was all getting away from him.

The Barracuda marched up with the lagers and a litre of Plymouth gin. Nothing was going to stop her enjoying herself. There'd been some kind of dust-up at Hardwicke's College, in which it seemed she'd interacted physically with one of her colleagues, who had asked for it. She was refusing to apologise.

Stan knocked back the first puny bottle of Beck's, belched a sound like *wee-eep*, then finished the second en-route to select an appropriate bottle of duty-free, pushing off from the muddy bottom where he'd spent the morning, moving slowly up into clearer upper waters, gaining momentum and rhythm, settling into cruising mode. He'd had a brainwave - cognac. A whole field unexplored.

When he returned with a bottle of Hine Gram was sitting there.

'Fit then Gram?'

Gram looked thoughtful, then nodded and smiled. 'Fit.'

The weight was lifting from all three of them, you could see it.

'You don't look so good though.'

'Didn't get much sleep. Quality time with the noble hound.' Guilt.

'Poor Kato. It's not fair.'

'He'll be OK Gram, he's a big lad now. He'd be no good on a ten hour flight, and the heat would kill him.'

'Yeah. Uncle Shanny'll be dead soft with him, you can tell. And it's not as if he's in some strange house, is it? It'll soon pass anyway.'

'Let's hope not.' He couldn't see that far, it wasn't even a blank. 'We'll bring him back something, a coconut maybe, or a fruit bat. He'd like that.' No, a fruit bat would terrify the noble hound. As might a coconut.

'Yeah.' Gram giggled.

'OK Gram, here she is.'

'Hey you two, you gone deaf? They're calling our flight. Let's go.' She looked really pumped-up.

The blue and gold Air Papa 747 bore on its nose a long-winged black frigatebird, king of fliers, alongside the name *Roi de Fregats*. The Barracuda turned as they were about to board. 'So long Grey Britain. And good luck.'

People were piling up behind them. In they went.

12. The Papalinas

Stan slapped his cheeks, shooting a mouthful of warm, wonderfully salty Indian Ocean towards Gram. They both laughed, treading water a few feet apart. Here they were, hard to believe it, on day one of their diving course, and wasn't everything just exactly as he'd promised? Like fast-forwarding into a favourite fantasy. Right now they had to show their instructor they could tread water for ten minutes. Here in the brilliant light of a big, fat tropical sun sinking lazily towards a dreamy skyline of misty green hills, to the muted background sounds of surf and carefree, deluxe western tourism, here in a calm blue sea buoyant with salt and warmth – well yes, they could manage to tread water for ten minutes. The smooth white strip of beach, with its strolling tourists and forested backdrop, was fifty metres away.

'Ah! Something touched my leg!' Gram's face was comically agitated as he swivelled frantically round, searching clear sea over sand.

Stan had his own spurt of terror, which lasted one tenth of a millisecond before he realized. 'Just pompanos Gram, little silvery fishes. Small-spotted pompano. *Trachinotus bailloni*. They like the sandy areas. Flattened, silvery, quite small, lovely long caudals. They reflect their surroundings, makes them hard to see.' A small roller surged in and they lifted with it. 'Duck your head under, you'll see them, even without a mask.'

Gram complied, still treading, and came back up grinning, his long, dark hair streaming.

'There's nothing to worry about here Gram, ask your mother. Even if there was anything, a shark or whatever - which there isn't, unfortunately - you'd see it coming a mile off. Clear water over sand. Don't worry, if a two foot nurse shark turned up here it'd be like *Jaws* during the false alarm, you remember? The kiddie with the fin strapped to his back? Don't get trampled in the rush. Sharks are a novelty round here these days, a tourist attraction. As I keep telling your mother, a shark might as well try to sneak up on you in the bath.'

'Even if there's any left, they won't come in here. Too many boats and people.' Gram had recovered, still grinning, feeling foolish, just slightly embarrassed in front of his father.

'On the other hand, you can always hope. Jaws came in didn't he? And there's always a chance of the odd barracuda slipping in. They're silvery too, damned fast when they want to be, and they can be quite sneaky.'

They burst out laughing again. Why the hell hadn't they done this years ago? Liza's occasional snappishness about his failings as a father, which he'd been batting away for some time now, were justified – he hadn't felt this close to Gram for years. He'd taken his eye off the ball. Five years wasted, absolutely thrown away. Five years asleep. This was just the kick up the arse he needed, the bloody shock she'd been on about.

'Look at the Brits, Gram. Like runty weeds blossoming in the sun.' No need to point out the few home-grown lumps among the sleeker Europeans, Russians and South Africans. Fat would be better than runty, but weeds couldn't really be fat. He pointed to a small, pure white seabird winging in, a tiny fish held cross-wise in its long, black bill.

'Fairy tern, Gram. Taking the fish to a chick, up there in the forest somewhere. They're the ones that breed in trees but just lay their egg on a branch, no nest.' It was all coming back.

The steep, densely wooded slopes began to climb immediately inland of the narrow coastal strip of beaches, road and hotels. There had been an all-too evident expansion of the tourist industry since Stan's day, as expected, but just now he wasn't complaining. Gram had already got the commoner bird names off pat. These islands, set as they were in the Indian Ocean hundreds of miles from the African and Indian mainlands, were too small and remote to support many species, but this remoteness had allowed most of the landbirds to evolve sufficiently for the scientific world to consider them distinct forms. The commonest bird though was the indian mynah, a raucous strutter around the hotels, a version of the starling really, introduced to the islands from India. A fully paid-up member of the pests 'n' weeds brigade, the mynah flourished in the tank-tracks of the Guardians of the Biosphere.

Gram checked his new present, a black-faced diving watch with an alarm which the Barracuda thought might be useful for early-morning university lectures. 'Time's up.'

Another roller lifted them as they waved to Rainer, the dive centre's trainer, who watched from the beach while chatting with two of the tanned and svelte bikini women.

'Italians,' Stan advised. 'You can always tell.'

Gram peered at them. 'How?'

Rainer waved back, indicating they should now swim one hundred metres parallel to the beach and then the same distance back.

Peace spread through Stan like a slow shot of one of his top five scotches as they moved languidly through the warm shallows to a soundtrack of gentle, watery plops and swirls, the periodic hiss of surf, and, just occasionally, a distant voice. How he hoped the Barracuda was basking in the glory of it all too. Of course she was. A rhythmic breaststroke pulled him easily along, keeping pace with Gram's steady crawl. His son cut a fine figure on the beach: his physique he had inherited from both parents, but he moved with the power and grace of his mother. Stan had made his full fatherly contribution though. And Gram's obvious shyness made for an appealing contrast with the daily parade of tanned narcissists. Whatever lay in wait for Gram further down the line – for all of them - this was here and this was now and this was a pinnacle.

They reached the marker together and turned back. Stan studied the beach-strolling tourists as he swam, a few of them frolicking self-consciously in the mini-waves. The women had been through rigorous selection procedures to weed out those afflicted by plain features, age or bulk. They'd been left behind, like the noble hound. Not that he was complaining. A scientific sampling here would suggest the adult male human is over fifty, overweight and rich. Make that the adult white male: a gang of Linois lads playing beach football provided the entertainment, an extremely self-aware spectacle of dark muscle, brilliant white teeth and flying dreadlocks, not to mention some very nifty ball control. A few small boats were moored offshore, rolling on the slow swell. All in all pretty laid-back and fabulous, as advertised.

'Dad. This is just brilliant.'

It was going well. Today they had been taken through the first two modules of the diving course, watching demonstration videos at the dive centre then trying it out in the pool. *Time to gett vett*, as Rainer put it. Rainer was a big, blond German midfielder-type - a potential Harak the headman in fact - and now they had only to tow him, as a casualty, a short distance through the water, and they would be finished for the day. They could manage that.

Soon enough they were sitting with their cold drinks at the

beach bar, watching waves slop onto the sand, watching the hotel chefs in their whites deftly flipping fish and meat on the barbecue, watching the aromatic smoke curling up into a black night sky blazing with stars. Gram was still telling his rather gorgeous mother about the day. If Shanny could only see his cheap and tacky palm-tree ear-rings now. All in all this seemed an eminently sensible way to spend money. What else is the stuff for? Stan silently thanked uncle Shanny. He must take him back a bottle of the local version of Guinness. No, don't think about going back.

A party of half a dozen Italians burst into loud laughter, and he was aware of both Liza and Gram peeking across as they sipped at their drinks. He took a look himself: two couples, plus teenage boy and girl, all immaculately tanned, immaculately dressed, relaxed and confident, loudly at ease with their place in the world. Whatever it was they did for a living, they certainly got paid. Stan was feeling reasonably accomplished and successful himself, after a generous shot of Hine champagne cognac and three fizzy beers, with no time for the usual petty prickles of envy and resentment. He signalled for another round of drinks, failing to catch the eye of the waiter who was hurrying - or at least sauntering purposefully - towards the Italian bacchanal. No worries. Stan slid the Italians another glance. Why were they always gesticulating like that? No wonder they had the waiters dancing round. One of the men, a silver-haired drugs baron, met his gaze and offered a ducal nod and half-smile before turning back to his companions.

Another waiter brought the drinks: cold local beer, Western Cape pinotage, and fresh mango juice. The large adjacent dining area was filling up now with tourists in quiet couples – the Brits - and large, noisy groups. Among the confident French, Italian and German voices the only loud English to be heard was the heavily-modified South African version. Stan had calculated that if he got another round of drinks now, while the Barracuda secured a table, it would save time later. No point waiting for a waiter, he'd go to the bar.

He lingered at the counter to watch the Barracuda and Gram making their way side by side across the sand, handsome mother and handsome son. There was no one here to touch her among all these glossy magazine women, not even the Italians; and he'd yet to see another black tourist.

On tables laden with fruits, salads, flavoured rices, breads, vegetables, sauces and meats, and decorated with bougainvillea flowers and banana leaves, four great whole fish took pride of place:

this was the famous red snapper, or *bourzwa* to the Linois who prized the head for their soups. Stan had seen fights at Tsaramaso in the old days over the head of a *bourzwa*. *Lutjanus sebae* was a strong, high-backed, pink-red fish with bold stripes of darker red when younger and a mouth crammed with sharp snapper teeth at all ages. As the Blackster plates were piled high the staff wished them *Bon appetit* and Liza flashed them an easy, top-of-the-range smile which said *This is me, here I am.*

They knocked back pinotage as a bonfire blazed and cracked on the beach and local musicians pumped out gentle dance rhythms or, every now and then, western middle of the road stuff, plus the odd blast of Bob Marley – you could see they couldn't help themselves - while the hotel's dreadlocked entertainments co-ordinator coaxed guests without much trouble out onto the sand for a dance. A grey day in the frozen New Forest it was not. Odd how some things faded from the mind, became unreal, while others just didn't ... but the Barracuda was trying to get him out there onto the dance beach and he had to fight her off, hadn't taken on enough wine yet, maybe later ... instead she managed to tow Gram out onto the sand.

Stan sat back to enjoy watching. The Barracuda was, he knew, a natural, an athlete with rhythm, and Gram had her long limbs and natural poise. On the back of his *Insidiator* T-shirt the gaping white tiger shark jaws stood out, seeming to move, flexing in the firelight. The Italians were watching too, and the eyes of the drugs baron particularly were glued to Liza and Gram. Presumably Liza. Who could blame him? Eat your heart out, Luigi. You might have the clothes and the money, but you'll never have anything like her. She's mine. The Barracuda waved, laughing and clapping at the end of the number. Perfection. He clapped too, annoyed that most of the tourists were too engrossed in themselves and their blather to even notice the hard-working musicians. Well, perhaps not hard-working, but they were doing a good job and deserved some encouragement.

The cocktail of sun, travel and alcohol gradually brought Stan and Liza to a level of agreeable stupefaction. Gram leaned over and murmured: 'Further intoxicant dad?'

That was nice. The T-shirt was nice too. The Barracuda was easing up on it all. Things were working out. His head lolled towards her. 'You had enough yet Barra?'

Her generous pink mouth still remembered how to smile, but her eyelids were drooping, giving her a slightly sinister look. 'I've never had enough Stanley, you know that.'

He peered at her. Were his own eyelids drooping like that? Did he look slightly sinister?

'You are flown with insolence and wine.' Milton? Maybe one for his lisping Badass to declaim during the Queen of the South Yorkshire Impi's cannibal feast following the annihilation of a sparsely populated Bramall Lane. But he had to think bigger than that. Available evidence might suggest that a certain amount of immediacy had gone out of the Badass situation, but he would not be deterred.

The Barracuda gave a hiccupping hoot. 'Right. But this is *me*, Stanley, right here. This is where I belong. I'm in my element, watch me. Hey, let's forget about the room, wherever it is. Let's just lie down on the sand. We're bound to wake up in bed in the morning.'

'Yep, usually works.'

She was nodding. 'You always wake up in bed. Let's not … let's just stay right here, eh? Whaddaya say?'

In Stan's mind the noble hound was staring beseechingly at him, one eyebrow cocked. 'I'm getting the noble hound's what about me? look.'

'Oh yeah. The eyebrow thing. He'd be OK here too, he would. He'd like it. We should have brought him. We should have. Noble hounds need a break as well.'

'Yep. I'll ring Shanny tomorrow. He can take him down to the docks, put him on the boat to Durban, or Mombassa. He can swim over from there. He likes a swim.' He would ring, just to check.

The Italians were still going strong at the next table, applauding their two teenagers who were out there dancing on the sand. Gram seemed, through the number of furtive sidelong inspections he was carrying out, to have taken a shine to the pretty Italian girl. He'd dropped out of the conversation, such as it was, some time ago. The Barracuda noticed too and winked heavily at Stan, her other eye trying to follow suit.

'Come on then Barra. When you wink with both eyes, it's time to go. Up. We'll get another shot at it all tomorrow.' He rose and picked up the bottle of wine, swinging it easily by the neck to make a casual, stylish exit, but the Italians were far too engrossed with themselves and their offspring to notice. Gram wasn't tired and would stay on for a while, maybe go for a stroll along the beach, and see them in the morning.

As Stan helped the thankfully genial, half-leathered Barracuda across the grass towards their room, he found he was thinking of that moonlit beach walk of his own, long ago, on that distant island so very different to this one, when he had met Roland's woman, and someone had been watching. Down there someone was always watching.

Next morning Liza, apparently fully restored and then some, lithely stretching a new turquoise bikini into shape beneath wide-brimmed straw hat and shades, came down to wave them off on their first dive. Stan felt hungover, clumsy and self-conscious as they waded out to the boat carrying weight-belts and day-glo fins, towing air bottles clamped to buoyancy jackets. Gram though looked quite at ease. Stan had been taken aback at just how rusty he was, and Rainer had made loud judgements on his *finning teknik*. They passed up the gear and climbed aboard while morning beach strollers looked on.

There were ten other divers, a representative mix of Italians, Germans and South Africans with just two other Brits, a quiet couple sporting angry pink sunburns who kept to themselves. The rest gave a solid impression of confident, thrustingly successful businessmen suddenly unleashed, wives and girlfriends for the most part left round the pool. After an introductory talk in English, with French and German sub-titles, the skipper fired up the twin Mercury outboards and off they roared out to sea.

The years fell away, and despite the headache Stan just could not keep the smile off his face, half-drunk on exhilaration and the forgotten taste of salt spray. Green hills, marked here and there with a spot of whitewash, an orange-tiled roof, or a wisp of smoke from some remote dwelling, slid past and fell behind. One of the Linois divemasters, a tall, slim young man with long black hair fastened in a ponytail, was in charge of pointing things out over the engine roar. The islands' history of slavery and colonialism, both British and French, had resulted in some eye-catching faces: this one showed sharp features, high cheekbones, a smooth, caramel skin and flashing Banderas eyes. Dashing, with something of the brassy trevally *Caranx papuensis*, or was it *sexfasciatus*? He'd check later. In heavily-accented Linois English the divemaster indicated a line of twenty or so small silver fish bouncing in and out of the water in bizarre synchronisation. It was like a dance, and Stan smiled to himself. The first time he'd seen this he'd thought for a long moment that someone on shore had them on a line, and was making some kind of surreal local joke or entertainment. He should have known better. Fishes were constantly surprising, capable of almost anything. Gram was laughing, scarcely able to believe his eyes, and the Italians were applauding enthusiastically, *Bravo! Bravo!*, all part of the show.

A small, forested island ringed with rock outcrops grew steadily larger, on its near side a thin white strip of beach with tall coconut palms and casuarinas; rollers reared up milky blue-green before crashing onto the white sand. Stan shook Gram's shoulder and pointed. This was the famous protected seabird island of Anchois, pronounced *Ansh-wa*, the skies above and the ocean around it dotted with screaming birdlife. Between the two of them they picked out the dark, tern-like noddies, the white fairy terns they'd already seen, the huge black frigatebirds hanging overhead and, rolling on the blue swell - heavier now, beyond the protective bulk of Margaritifer - a dense raft of black and white birds which they thought must be shearwaters. The two other Brits were also pointing, whispering discreetly to one other, but the rest were busy shouting and laughing and took no notice.

'It's just awesome!' Gram was overcome. 'This is how it all should be! We've got to bring mum out here. Let's book on the boat trip to Anchois.' He leaned closer. 'No one else is interested, are they? Amazing. How can they do all this to watch fish, and not be interested in all these birds?'

'Well, I don't think they're here to watch fishes exactly. They just want to dive, more of a sporty, macho thing. You'll see.'

They reached the dive site. While the other divers tumbled backwards over the side in approved flamboyant fashion then worked their way down to the waiting divemaster, Rainer took the two trainees methodically through the safety checks, then:

'OK. Time to gett vett.'

Seawater hit and engulfed them in a welter of thrashing limbs, fins and bubbles. The initial shock passed instantly, and Stan felt peace fold around him as he surfaced. Even breathing would spoil it. The slap of the waves, the sense of a vast harmony. A first shaky, amplified breath, taken through the mouthpiece, filled his ears. Rainer and Gram bobbed in the sea beside him. Rainer made the 'O' sign with thumb and forefinger: OK? Gram and Stan responded: OK. Clinging to the anchor rope, they released air from their jackets and descended.

Stan's ears hurt, and he was the last to the sandy bottom. Here they adjusted their jackets for neutral buoyancy, so that merely by breathing in and filling their lungs they could lift clear of the corals, the touching of which was of course *verboten*. Rainer patiently tended to

Gram, whose movements were jerky and unsure, helping him adjust his jacket pressure, indicating he should clear water from his mask, generally reassuring him and giving him confidence.

Brave lad, thought Stan, distractedly: he was utterly transported. Around him coral towers and gardens swarmed with all his colleagues of the turquoise walls, and more - parrotfish and angels, butterflies and wrasse, trevallies and snappers, a soundless, slow-motion rainbow whirl in a dreamy blue universe. Welcome home. He became aware that Gram was already moving more confidently, and how he had ached to see this, to watch his son underwater among the fishes, and he'd put it off so many times, for such puny little reasons.

Four big, black shadowy diamond-shapes condensed into eagle rays, flying in silent slow-motion out of the blue haze, metre-long tails trailing dead astern, white undersides showing with each wingbeat as they ignored these multicoloured invaders and their bubble-streams, passing once more into the blue shadows. A pack of divers set off in eager pursuit but were soon left behind. Gram looked across at his father, who nodded. Divers. If only they'd been on their own, just the two of them.

He wanted to do some pointing out of his own – over there a cloud of paddletail snappers, over there a lone slenderspine grouper, very wary, and there, perching like a hawk on that coral head, a big freckled hawkfish. Well, big as in six inches …

But Stan's beard, holiday-trimmed though it was, kept interfering with the seal of his mask. Time and again the mask filled with water, and he repeatedly had to clear it with a blast of air from his nostrils. That settled it - time to get rid of the damned thing. Time for a new image; or rather the return of an old one.

Rainer tapped the dial on his air-hose, indicating they should check their own: pressure was down to 50 bar, signalling the end of the dive, and they began to ascend slowly. Stan's ears cringed with the pressure change. At the surface the sea was choppy as Rainer gave them practice in use of the compass, then they were unstrapping at the side of the boat and handing up their gear to the crew as waves slopped against the hull.

Back at the dive centre Stan helped Gram fill out his log-book with details of depth, time, current and visibility. They'd do their fish ID in comfort back at the hotel, an activity almost as pleasurable as being down there with them. Giving them their names. How had he ever allowed himself to become reduced to evenings in the bathroom back in Southampton? Reduced, that's what he had been. But now he was back. The dive log-book was quite incapable of incorporating all the fishes they'd seen but he'd brought extra notebooks for the two of them. Rainer stamped and signed, and Gram's first dive was officially on record. Not such a bad chap, Rainer. Stan shook the German's hand.

'Bedder. The finning teknik. Bedder.'

On the hotel verandah Stan and Gram worked through the books, recognizing fishes, pondering the finer points distinguishing the different bannerfish and batfish, separating threadfin, chevron and vagabond butterflyfish, trying to decide why the emperor angelfish *Acanthurus imperator* made those alarming blipping sounds. Bliss. The Barracuda, impatient to get started on the fantastic forests and granite outcrops, had marched off with her straw hat, sketchbook and oilsticks. Already there was a detectable diminishing in the heat as evening beckoned.

In fact, although he didn't say anything, Stan was feeling decidedly odd. It was as though a balloon full of cotton wool had been squeezed into his head, where it had expanded to a size slightly greater than the space available. No amount of snorting or jaw-grinding would clear it. He was maddeningly detached from everything going on around him. Similar sensations years ago in the aftermath of dives were tingling in his memory, but none as severe as this. Age. Stanley Blackster was no longer quite the unstoppable young quester after knowledge and experience of fifteen years ago, out in the field from dawn or earlier until late morning, then again from mid-afternoon until dark, then spending the evenings reading and writing up under a mosquito net. And he was so tired. As a snorer he was hardly in the same class as the Barracuda, but he was improving steadily. By the time the fierce heat began to drain from the day, and the sun sank quickly from view, he was bushed, and the routine was crash, drink, shower, drink, buffet and drink, drink then oblivion. Black oblivion, no dreams he could remember.

The laptop sat in the corner of the room, unused apart from an unobtrusive daily check of the e-mail in-tray. Stan was willing a message from the boy wonder to appear on the screen, some sort of response to the polite requests he'd fired off in the direction of California. It had occurred to him that he hadn't checked the date on that film magazine back at Gatwick. It could easily have been an old one, couldn't it, discarded by a slow reader with a deep bag. His new outlook was unremittingly positive, had to be. This thing would happen. He would make it happen.

Day three of the course brought more videos and tests, more practice in the pool, and a dive of 11 metres. Stan was looking the other way when a six foot guitarfish, an impressive but rather awkward-looking combination of shark and ray, cruised over the sand between them, trailing sharksuckers. Gram tapped him – a shock - and he turned with a convulsive kick which caught Rainer in the head. OK? mimed Stan. OK. You couldn't hit anyone really hard down here, and the old chestnut about punching a troublesome shark on the nose was a non-starter, although the Barracuda was counting on it. For a while they followed a hawksbill turtle, at a distance, then Rainer took them through more training. Stan tried to ignore the fluffy wasteland between his ears for the time being, but it was getting worse and he'd have to get it checked out. Gram loved it down here, and that was all that mattered. He was only sixteen, just the right age for your life to change. Rainer was signalling, time to go up. He could now relish the first drink of the day, and more fish ID with Gram.

The Barracuda had been waylaid by brilliant green geckos on sunlit green palm fronds, and was keen to show off her sketches. Stan concentrated, then had a doze. They had a drink on the verandah. Gram had evidently paid attention to the routine of the Italians and had taken to loitering around the beach when diving was finished for the day. They watched through binoculars as he played beach football with the Linois boys, matching their effortless athleticism, while the two Italian teenagers watched quietly from the shade of nearby coconut palms. The Barracuda was buoyant: 'Look at our Grammy! This is all working out Stan. Didn't I say? It's like a dream. Better.'

So far so good. Perhaps it was time to go on a little expedition.

Bernard wasn't hard to find, sitting with the other fishermen on the tumbledown wall by the local fish merchant's with its big, foul-smelling ice-room. This wall had always been the gathering place, the place for boasting, schemes and gossip. And drinking. At their backs small fibreglass fishing boats were moored a few yards out in a raft of yellows and blues and reds, and beyond them the long curve of the bay, a placid sea, and a big, sinking sun.

'Bernard. My old friend. *Bon soir.*'

He saw an instant of wariness, even hostility, then a broad

smile and an extended hand. There was no evident surprise: like most Linois, Bernard lived in the moment, and he might last have spoken to Stan yesterday rather than fifteen years ago. Catching up wouldn't take long.

'Stan-lee. Hello my friend. You have returned to the Papalinas. Your face, it is not the same, I could not see.' His hands sketched on his own face a drooping moustache and a small chin beard.

Stan gave a rueful smile. He'd lost his individuality when he got rid of the imperial, should never have let the Barracuda persuade him. Now he was just another middle-aged bloke with a beard. Their hands stayed clasped for a long moment as they weighed one another up, while unseen signals put Bernard's cronies at their ease.

Bernard. The arrogance and impetuosity of youth, which had made him a loner - almost an outcast under the overbearing authority of Roland - were clearly buried now, but how far down? Bernard had his abrasive side, especially when drunk or hungover, and it was difficult to read his thoughts, but he was always resourceful and sharp, and occasionally reckless. Had been, Stan reminded himself, had been: that was back then, but he wouldn't have changed that much, would he? Almost alone among the local workers, Bernard hadn't given him a hard time when things went sour on the atoll. They had made the long journey back to Margaritifer on the supply boat together, a time of many long conversations, mainly about fishes and fishing, and had met up several times in Tarataka, the capital, while he hung around awaiting a flight back to the UK. When Bernard was on leave there were always fishes to be caught, beer to be drunk and gossip to be spread – gossip was currency to the *Leen-wa*.

The narrow, haughty black face was weathered and more cautious now; the narrow moustache showed flecks of grey, the strong white teeth were tobacco-stained. Bernard's eyes held a familiar fierce glitter, and empty beer bottles and caps were strewn about the ground. His cronies were eyeing the shocking pink plastic carrier bag which Stan now hefted, clinking, onto the wall. There were nods and smiles. Bottles of super-strong export Guinness were opened in flamboyant local fashion, one cap against another, and handed round. Without a word from Bernard the others re-distributed themselves to make room on the wall for Stan. Conversation around them resumed in Creole.

'Cheers.' The everyday word sounded odd from Bernard, as though he hadn't used English for some time. To Stan, with a large, rustling space between his ears, everything sounded odd, to greater or lesser degree.

'Cheers, Bernard. I see you're still fishing.'

'Of course. What else are Linois to do? Fish and tourists. This is our life.'

The heads of three vanquished sailfish lay nearby, magnificent bills gone, long meaty spines trailing in dirt and bottle caps. Scruffy-looking cattle egrets stalked warily, looking for a chance to dive in and make a grab. Flies buzzed.

'Stan-lee. The fish have gone from many of the good places. To live, you must go far. For me it is OK. I know the good places, all of them.' The hot-blooded young man of feuds and fights had become the respected elder. The younger men must listen when he spoke. He had after all become a sort of Roland.

'And your wife, Bernard. How is Atherina?'

A dismissive wave. 'He - she is OK.'

Battered cars cruised by on the coast road. Occasionally one would screech to a halt in a tumult of dust, thumping music and beer bottles to pick up or drop off. Always men, of various ages. This was not a place for women, which was one reason for leaving the Barracuda at the hotel; another was her forthrightness, which would go down here no better than it had in the *Dolphin* and several other situations back home. Ten bottles of 7.5% Guinness had been emptied in minutes. Stan waved a one hundred rupee Papa banknote, with its picture of *babon sesil*, the saddleback coralgrouper. Bernard nodded to a youth who had dreads crammed into a big red, gold, green and black woolly rasta hat, sending him on his way with a volley of rapid-fire Creole.

For a while they talked about fishing and fishes, easy and unforced chat in the old way. The karang - trevallies - were running, and Bernard had the perfect squid bait, the fish could never resist it; its use was restricted to the best fishermen and even then it was rationed. He pointed out his small boat with its Yamaha 40 outboard, which he now owned outright. If he could be believed, fishing was giving him a comfortable living, thanks to his unrivalled skill and knowledge and the insatiable demands of the hotels for fresh fish. Beer and respect were the only rewards Linois like Bernard valued. As he had hoped, Bernard invited Stan to go out with him, but he somehow had the strong impression that the offer was a result of formal courtesy and drink, and that perhaps it shouldn't be put to the test. The carefree days of drinking and fishing together as friends were, he now saw, past. Possibly it had never really been like that. It was hard to be sure.

Another clinking pink bag arrived, and a big cassette player was cranked into action. Bob Marley, of course, *Jammin'*. Two fruit bats lurched out of a casuarina, twin silhouettes moving jerkily across the fading grey-blue and pink sky, while on the densely forested inland side of the narrow coast road hundreds of mynahs had set up a terrific, chortling din as they jostled for roosting places in an immense stand of glossy-leaved takamaka trees.

Stan swallowed Guinness, wondering how Shanny would get on with this rocket-fuel version of his favourite drink: treacly black, frothing a chestnut-brown, it had an intriguing dry fruitiness to it, far superior to the so-called draught stuff Shanny pumped into himself. And an agreeable jolt. Just the thing for the stands at Hillsborough. He would definitely take the old soldier one back, just a single bottle, then stand back and watch, wait for the red Shanny head to detonate in a final apotheosis. He sighed and looked up into the majestic takamakas. Roland still knew how to make the heavy, traditional pirogue-style boats out of takamaka wood, or so they used to say. Much stronger and less easily damaged on rocks and coral than modern fibreglass but much, much heavier. In the old days it took planning and plenty of manpower to even get a boat into the water and out beyond the surf. Nowadays, thanks to fibreglass and outboards, a fisherman could decide to go after his tenth Guinness and be out there in minutes. Traditional boat-building was a vanishing art. Roland, the old bugger, had certainly been skilled in carving the dense, dark wood of the red mangrove, producing curiously powerful little figurines, totems and charms whose meaning was not discussed with the research staff. Roland wasn't merely an old bugger, let's do him justice - he was an eerie, malevolent creature belonging to another world. Stan was just drunk enough now not to feel the usual prickle of - what? Anxiety? Hatred? Fear? None of these words was right. It was more a sensation of being somehow at a permanent disadvantage with him, a feeling of ... guilt. How stupid. After all, here he was, in T-shirt and shorts, bottle in hand - empty in fact, and it clunked to the floor with the rest - having a good time in this fabulous place. He pictured Roland pegged out amidst the smoking ruins of Dar, awaiting the arrival of the jactators, the first rats already sniffing at spindly brown legs, the skinny chest, the necklaces; that dark face, initially impassive, those round pale eyes – a delicacy – staring skywards, anticipating the beat of vast, leathery wings. Great stuff.

He was handed a bottle of the local lager-type beer and took a long, fizzy swallow. A refreshing follow-up to the Guinness. He belched, rocking slightly on the crumbling brickwork.

'The atoll, Bernard. Tsara. Did you go back there?' He had to ask.

Bernard rolled bloodshot eyes, shouting now over the thumping music. 'Tsaramaso. I go back, yes, I stay one year only. This guy Roland ... you know? A crazy guy, this guy. We call him Lookdown. Always he think the other guys, they want his woman, you know? Always he is watching.'

Stan thought to see a sly look, but he was pretty far gone now and settled for a nod. Yes, he knew.

'Roland, he try many, many women. But he have no son, he have only the little girls. For a guy like Roland, this is very bad. Now, he is too old.'

The music stopped abruptly, disconcertingly. No traffic noise disturbed the night. Mynahs roused in a ragged chorus, a few crickets creaked, his favourite *clink-clink, clink-clink*. Men shouted. Sound blasted out once more, thuds and crashes accompanying some overbearing, finger-pointing rapper.

Bernard continued, eyes glistening. 'Alain. You remember this guy? We call him Sleeper. You remember?'

His voice seemed to be coming from a long way off. Stan nodded, concentrating on the green bottle in his hand, not sure what his voice would sound like if he tried to speak. Maybe there would be no sound at all. The Linois had nicknames for everyone. What had his own nickname been?

'*Oui*, Alain. Sleeper. This guy, he is dead.' Bernard caught his eye, held it.

'Dead? How?' he croaked. Alain was younger than him. Had been.

'They say, his heart. He was taking his breakfast. You know this guy Roland, he would prepare the meal for the guys.'

Yes, he knew.

Bernard was handed an open bottle of Guinness and a lighted cigarette, and inched closer on the wall. 'Roland, this guy, he think Sleeper take his woman. He is *Gran Ke*, this Roland, you remember this word?'

Stan nodded, a nodding dog. *Gran Ke*, pronounced *Gron Kay*. Within certain families, old men still practised voodoo, using natural ingredients - parts of forest plants, pilfered toenails, bits of hair. Blood.

Bones. Tsaramaso had a reputation as a place of power, where many of the strong plants grew, second only to Madagascar itself. It had been a running joke among the research workers at the time - when they were together, that is, and acting tough. Sometimes things had happened which hadn't been so funny, and it was obvious that several of them were desperately counting the days and envied his early departure. Julius had not been one of them, and Julius had not joined in the jokes and the scoffing.

'Come on Bernard. You don't believe in voodoo.'

There, he could get a whole, coherent sentence out, as long as it was short. He took a heavy-handed swipe at a mosquito and nearly fell off the wall.

'*Non*. This is for old people. I have an education. I believe in the great God. But I have a cousin, he has seen things, very strange things.' He whistled through his teeth. 'At night. He has seen the *Gran Ke* fly around his house. Land on the roof. *Oui!* He has seen his own wife pass by, he run to her, it is not his wife, it is not a woman even. *Oui!* It is true! My cousin, he would not lie to me!'

Stan must have looked more sceptical than he was capable of feeling. The beers kept on coming.

'*Oui*, Stan!' He was quite worked up now, more like the Bernard of old who had only ever dropped the formal *Stan-lee* when drunk. 'For myself, I do not believe in voodoo. But, if my eyes, they see a thing, then I believe this thing!' His pink and shining eyes bulged vehemently in the handsome dark face. The old Bernard, submerged and arisen. 'Roland. This guy, still he is on Tsaramaso. He will never leave. *Oui*. Always his family has been there. Now, even Linois will not go there. Only the family of this guy. Definitely this is so. Roland, he say he send the scientist away, he say Tsaramaso it does not want them to be there. *Oui*. This guy, if he want, he fly through the air. *Fregat*, this is his bird. You think he is there, he is not there, he is here.' He peered into the surrounding darkness.

Again the music had stopped, and the gathering had dwindled. A pack of furious dogs had started up down the road. They both slapped at mosquitoes. Even dulled by alcohol, the smarting, itching sensation that hit you just after the little swines departed was excruciating.

Bernard leaned over. 'I heard this Sleeper, this Alain, a guy see him on Dragonet. He is fieldworker there.'

'You said he was dead.'

Bernard winced. Stan must keep his voice down. Dragonet, a large but sparsely-populated neighbouring island, also had a rather sinister reputation.

'*Oui*. He is dead, but, maybe not dead, you know? You say zombie, *non*? Roland, he can do this, this guy. Maybe he sell Sleeper to a guy on Dragonet, he work in the field, he eat only *bouillon*, some rice, there is no pay. He die, they put him in the ground, his family they do not know. Is possible, Stan. The scientist, they do not know all things.'

Stan stood abruptly, swaying, scratching at legs and arms.

'Stan-lee.' Back to the loud voice of authority. 'Saba will take you to your hotel.'

One of the youths busied himself with a decrepit Toyota while Bernard drained his Guinness and accepted another glowing cigarette. It was quiet now, waves slapping sluggishly, a distant car winding up into the hills.

Bernard blew smoke, pursed his lips. 'Stan-lee. This guy Easter-house.'

This took him by surprise, for some reason. 'Julius? What about him?'

'He lives?'

Stan snorted. 'Of course he lives. Why shouldn't he live?'

Bernard was shaking his head in what looked like disappointment. 'Easter-house,' he sighed. None of the Linois staff had liked old Julius much, or at all. Hardly surprising.

Saba was at last revving the engine. As usual it was not possible to tell from Bernard's narrow, pink-eyed face what was going through his mind, but he seemed to come to a decision.

'Saba will take you. We speak again.'

The dogs had started up once more. On the winding coast road there were no lights and Saba drove at full throttle. It was like watching a film: the car, the dark forest, the occasional wandering figure caught in the single headlight, sudden snapshots of shining sea and stark black rock, none of it real. Stan's attention came to rest on the back of the driver's shaven brown head, watching the play of hidden muscles, the flexing of the small blue shark tattooed at the base of the skull.

A Cuban doctor diagnosed an ear infection and prescribed boric acid, but he'd be OK to dive – crucially, this being the last day of the course. The small hospital pharmacy had no boric acid - *No, we do not have* - and after an interminable phone consultation comprised almost entirely of long silences the prescription was changed, to acetic acid - vinegar. *Vin-ee-gar? We have.*

Outside, blinking in the streaming sunlight, Stan looked round for a taxi. He was determined to complete this course, resolved to overcome all obstacles, be they fungi, bacteria, ears or toxic black Guinness fumes. No way would he let Gram down. A genial old cove in a cloth cap took him back to the tourist area for a fee. It soon became clear this wasn't in fact a taxi, but the drive was enjoyable in a soporific, distant sort of way. Stan sank into the shabby back seat, banging up and down in time with the potholes while the driver sat at the core of a beery fug yodelling along with Hank Williams, which made a soothing change. The world rattled by in a tropical glare of sunlight and greenery. He badly needed a drink, but alcohol and diving were not supposed to mix. Not too hard to picture Rainer ordering him humiliatingly from the boat – *alkohol ist verboten!* – and the look on Gram's face. One wouldn't hurt though.

Two dives were planned for this final day. As the dive boat roared out, dolphins and frigates gave exuberant chase to flying fish alongside. The dive site this time was further offshore, near a bare rocky lump known as Francais Mort, the dead Frenchman. Stan thought about asking the skipper how come, but decided to wait and ask Bernard. Bernard was bound to have a more interesting answer. As they prepared their gear the swell sent seawater surging repeatedly up Francais Mort's smooth pink slopes, filling its cracks and hollows, then sucked it back again. A ragged line of red and green shore crabs danced to the rhythm, forward and back, forward and back, advance and retreat.

The descent was again an agony for Stan, but Rainer showed no signs of impatience, and he finally made it down to 15 metres. Rainer then watched as he and Gram removed and replaced their gear piece by piece, jackets and cylinders, masks and belts; then they each had to tow him a short distance. The German found a mean-looking giant moray, half-emerged from a hole in the coral; while they watched, Gram spotted an octopus which had crammed itself into the hole next door. The tidal surge was more pronounced today, and whenever it lifted Stan even a couple of feet pain shot through his head and he had to gingerly regain his position to ease it. Pressure. Back aboard the dive boat he wondered how he would ever manage the afternoon's final dive.

At the dive centre they completed the fifty question test fairly confidently, then had a short breather. Stan walked the beach, shaking his head, wondering where he could find a pair of forceps to start teasing the vinegar-soaked cotton wool - more likely a football-sized globe of mucus - out through an ear, or maybe a nostril.

In no time they were wading back out to the dive boat with their gear. Off Francais Mort a lone Linois stared at them from a yellow fibreglass boat as they roared by. A dark head surfaced nearby and an arm raised a small trident. Octopus fishermen, supplying tourist demand for Papa's famous coconut curry. The man in the boat turned his head to watch them pass. His face seemed vaguely familiar. Probably he'd been drinking on the wall alongside Bernard, and would be doing the same tonight.

On the descent, inching his way down along the anchor rope, grinding his jaws more or less continuously, eyes watering with pain, Stan was on the point of calling it off three times. But below him he could see Gram, hanging just above the reef, looking up, watching him, and he kept going. Slowly slowly. When 15 metres registered on his depth gauge his ears cleared and the coral forest, shimmering with fishes, swam into blue focus. But he knew that wasn't the end of it. Rainer made an OK? the two Blacksters made an OK, and they prepared for the controlled emergency ascent. Meaning they had to go back up. Meaning they had to come back down. They had to get back to the surface as quickly as possible, but not so fast as to cause medical problems, giving a kind of drawn-out groan to release expanding air from the lungs. *Aaaaaaaaaaaaaaaaah*

They both got that right, thank Christ, bursting out into a world of sound and sunlight. But coming up was the easy part.

Then back down, slowly slowly slowly. He was destroying his ears, wrecking the eustachian tubes, turning them into a mangled spaghetti junction. He would never hear properly again; he could feel irreversible damage accumulating with each metre. And balance, his balance would be shot. But still his body inched its way downwards, crazy, as if it had a mind of its own. Call it off Rainer, please, for Christ's sake, make the decision! The man was reckless, all that emphasis on care and safety and now he was allowing this! Then his fins were nearing the corals, he was surrounded by fishes, Gram was hovering alongside, OK? and Rainer, OK? Stan managed a strained smile, OK. And there, a few feet in front of him, yellow pectoral fins flicking like tiny wings, the most perfect powder-blue surgeonfish, monumentally calm, smug and reassuring. Peace spread through him.

Could there ever be a sensation to beat the simple release from pain? He closed his eyes for a moment, taking pleasure in the calm workings of his body. Steady chap, Rainer. Belay that order to peg him out for the jactators.

The estimable Rainer led them on over a vast tract of stagshorn coral, through an exotic cloud of moorish idols soaring like black and yellow birds over a forest. Gram found a trumpetfish, a bizarre and predatory yellow truncheon patrolling the reef margins like a surreal joke, then Rainer waved them over: an ominous dark bulk rested in sandy shadows beneath a coral overhang, the brown-grey hide showing the characteristic denticular roughness of a shark. Stan's heart bumped as they finned closer, but he already knew what to expect - tiny eyes, blunt snout with small barbel protruding from the nasal opening either side of a small mouth, two large dorsal fins set well back: a big nurse shark, *Nebrius ferrugineus*, around twelve feet long. An imposing animal, harmless unless foolishly provoked, a scavenger and devourer of shellfish, sea-urchins, crabs and, if it could catch them, small fishes as well, but particularly fond of octopus. At Tsaramaso they often used to see a long, single-lobed tail waving above the surface as one of these sleepy sharks - a better name - rooted vertically to extricate an octopus from its refuge in the reef. So many memories.

Gram watched the big shark with obvious reverence, and Stan watched him watching. The giant sleepy shark was naturally not the most dynamic or pelagic example of its kind, but it had the power, the purpose, and – when it moved – that universal, sinuous shark rhythm and style. Dolphins? Well, yes, hats off to dolphins of course, racing along on the bow wave and so forth, but when seen underwater their up and down contortions were really quite clumsy, like men trying to get out of sleeping bags. They should never have left the sea in the first place of course, but at least they'd had the sense to go back in. This shark was perfectly content to remain at rest, and they left it in peace. Rainer gestured for them to check tank gauges: their air-tanks were emptying and Gram was beginning to rise in the water as his buoyancy increased. Rainer grabbed him, slipped an extra kilo of lead inside his jacket, then when he had steadied, beckoned Stan closer.

There, as the three of them rested on a sandy patch among the corals and fishes, Rainer solemnly shook their hands. *Gut.* You have passed. Now you are divers. OK? OK.

That night they celebrated, Stan especially. He felt he had

achieved something genuinely worthwhile, against not inconsiderable odds. In fact they did nothing they weren't doing every night, just more of it, particularly the Hine in Stan's case, and he retired early with a rare feeling of job well done, leaving Liza and Gram to their own devices. One minor blemish niggled through the glow: the Italians had apparently remarked on his determination to applaud every track on a music tape long after the band had packed up and gone home. English politeness, they thought. The Barracuda had hooted.

Over the following days the Blacksters did the things tourists do. They island-hopped at 6,500 feet in Twin Otters painted the blue and gold of Air Papa, bumping down with giddying abruptness onto grass strips cleared in coconut jungle. They strolled through plantations of tea, vanilla and cinnamon, inspected old colonial retreats high in the hills, visited craft centres and art galleries. In the cool shade of coconut leaf thatching they ate marlin and smoked sailfish salads, washed down with viciously overpriced South African wines, while looking out over near-deserted bays of white sand and a glittering blue sea, the scene framed by ever-present palms and casuarinas. They swam, they sunbathed, they snorkelled and dived. On Anchois, the seabird island, they hit the beach in a zodiac driven at full tilt to clear the breakers, then spent the day with two Linois guides and thousands of screaming terns, noddies and tropicbirds; after a sweaty climb to its peak they looked down on circling frigates and tropicbirds while dolphins and turtles broke the surface over the reef far below. They ambled around Dragonet, famed for its soporific atmosphere and zombies. Stan discreetly checked passers-by for glazed expressions and trance-like walks. Would he still recognize Alain after his transformation? The Linois had called him Sleeper and now here he was, a zombie. And Alain had always been extremely nervous of Roland. Stan had the creepy feeling he was getting one or two odd looks himself - a figure in a shop doorway, a group drinking under a tree. Faces from the old days, perhaps, but he didn't recognize anyone.

The Blacksters swam, snorkelled and dived; they sunbathed, they took photographs and read books; they bought drinks, they gave tips; Liza sketched, photographed and painted; they dozed and they slept and they snored. It remained perfect.

And Gram was slowly but surely getting together with the pretty Italian girl, Gina. Her parents and their friends were staying at the Belonary, Margaritifer's most exclusive hotel, tucked carefully away a little distance up the coast from their own Espadon in the midst of an immaculately tended and water-hungry forest of imposing non-native trees. Both Italian men were dedicated divers and had chartered an ocean-going catamaran with skipper and crew to visit some of the outer islands. They also seemed to like Gram - why wouldn't they? - and had welcomed him both at their hotel and on the boat. An invitation had been extended to his parents, who would be most welcome at any time, and Liza was predictably keen. Stan's cotton-wool head was still cushioning events, and he felt foolish sitting around with an earful of vinegar. They were sleeping like stupefied logs, but the dreams had returned and he would wake up wrapped in a sweaty sheet while the muscular lump next to him snored on.

His holiday bottle of Hine had proved most acceptable, if in the final analysis very slightly sugary and short on staying power, and he'd moved on to something called Hankey Bannister, an absurdly expensive whiskey he'd spotted among tins of syrupy preserved fruit and boxes of brillo pads on the shelf of a chaotic Indian shop in Tarataka. Outrageous price, but priorities had to be flexible.

He'd managed a couple of good dives with Gram, although these had necessarily been with a local operator and a boatful of other adventurers. They'd seen a second shark too, a five-foot white-tip reef cruising the coral banks, and they'd watched their fellow divers chase after it despite the best efforts of the Linois divemaster. The Prof had faxed through, almost before they'd arrived, details of the fish transects established around the coast of Margaritifer twenty years earlier, and they'd so far located three. Identifying and counting fishes in three rough size groups had been great fun for them both, and it seemed that at long last the scales might be falling from his son's eyes. They were keen to know how their counts compared with those made fifteen years ago. The corals had clearly been hit by the bleaching of 1997/8 for a start, which must have had some effect. Naturally Stan's underwater memories were the rosiest he had of Papa, and they featured more and bigger fishes of more species, even here around Margaritifer. Especially sharks. Well, tourism was up to 100,000 a year now, more than the Linois population. What would you expect fishes to do, increase?

Gram came bounding in one morning, bursting with the news that the Italians had heard a party of whale sharks had been seen. Each year a number of these colossal creatures spent a period feeding in the waters around Papa's main islands, and this year they were early. A specially-arranged boat was going out to find them, and the Italians would be aboard. It was expensive, yes, but there were places left and there was really no choice. Come on dad! So off they went.

Outside the designated hotel the sight of welts and rashes on the faces of the returning boat-load of tourists calmed everyone down: these huge, slow-moving sharks, devourers of plankton, squid and small fishes, were feeding in a soup of such stuff, much of it barely visible and some of it - small, virtually transparent jellyfish - equipped for defence. Liza started to have second thoughts, but this was what Stan had promised her that day in the bloody pub, after the birds in the Forest, a hundred years ago and a million miles away. He paid over the banknotes and they went aboard.

A microlight aircraft high overhead guided their skipper by two-way radio and within half an hour they had homed in on a big blunt dorsal and, ten feet behind it, the upper lobe of a majestically sweeping tail. They were told to get their snorkelling gear on and minutes later they were tumbling overboard in a melee of fins, arms, bubbles, and Italian whooping, to find themselves gawping at an immensity of white-spotted, sea-grey shark hide sliding by like a slow-moving train.

Stan was overcome. His heart slowed, his breathing, everything slowed to the timeless sweep of that great tail, driving the biggest shark there is through the seas of the world. *Rhincodon typus.* The sheer, imperious bulk of the thing! The Italians were still whooping, some having set out in hot pursuit then given up. Beside him in the water Liza looked half-terrified, half-inspired, coughing and spluttering, eyes bulging madly in her mask, pink lips swollen around the snorkel mouthpiece. She managed a muffled whoop of her own as Gram finned over to hug his brave mother. Stan ducked his head under to gaze again at the filmy broth of tiny organisms which had brought about this collision of tourists and leviathans. All around him the upper waters were blurred, shivering and shimmering with restless life. This was all so right. The exuberance of life! The glorious confraternity of the seas!

The boat motored over and they clambered back aboard. The microlight overhead had been doing its stuff and at least five sharks had been spotted, the largest around thirty feet long. So they really had seen a shark bigger than Jaws, just as he had promised – not just seen it either, but practically touched the damned thing.

Twice more the band of snorkellers was put into the water

alongside a massive, slow-moving whale shark, with strict instructions from the divemasters not to harass them. On the last occasion Stan and Liza stayed aboard to watch and take photographs. Aurora, an elegant and reserved Italian wife who had not entered the water, wielded a video recorder. She was thus able to capture on film the infuriating sight of the rest of the Italians grabbing excitedly hold of the wing-like pectoral fins for a ride, exactly as they'd been told not to.

'You harass him!' shouted a Linois divemaster. 'You must not harass him!'

The great fish submerged, leaving a wake of triumphant Italians shouting and waving.

That evening, back at the Hotel Espadon and agreeably numbed by drink, the surf sounds in his head more distant, Stan went to hotel reception to hand over a couple of postcards. Cards were far more enjoyable than electronics, and anyway it was no use pretending that Shanny would ever get the hang of e-mail or even fax. One card was addressed to the noble hound and Shanny, the other to James Dalyell. Both featured the image of a powder-blue surgeonfish, used very sensibly on all kinds of merchandising here in Papa to project the required laid-back ambience. He re-read what he had said to the Prof:

'All well here. More hotels now, plus one of your pet hates - a golf course. Coral still in bad shape after sea-warming, three transects found and recorded. Most enjoyable, but I'm sure number and size of most species will be down. Good to be back – gave your regards to Bernard. Do you remember him?' He would. The Prof remembered them all. He felt compelled to add: 'Hope Julius has shown up.'

By this time he'd got to know the girl at the desk well enough for a smile and a chat. Marinette. A tiny girl, with a perky little brown face which almost vanished when she smiled, which she did a lot.

'There is a message for you, Stan.'

He'd stopped the *sirs* and *Mister Blacksters* straight away. Puzzled, he unfolded the scrap of paper.

STANLEY. MY FRIEND. TOMORROW WE GO TO THE GOOD FISHING PLACE 9AM YOUR SON ALSO. YOUR FRIEND BERNARD.

This was a pleasant surprise. He'd been wrong then, when he

thought Bernard didn't really mean it, that he'd regret it when the Guinness had worn off. Gram was pushing for them to go aboard the catamaran the Italians had chartered, but this would do him far more good - if he could be persuaded to go. He'd loosened up a lot since their arrival, which was a profound relief to Stan, but he mustn't push it. And on no account must he make any smart-arse remarks at Gram's expense. A day afloat with the Linois would completely revise Gram's views on fishing. He yawned, feeling or hearing his ears crinkle, he wasn't sure which, maybe both, and turned the yawn into a smile for little Marinette.

'Life here is very tiring, Marinette.'

The enormous smile enveloped her face. *'Non!'*

'Oh yes. We have been to see the whale sharks today.'

She looked puzzled.

'The big shark, *gro gro requin.*' With a Boscanion frown he indicated colossal size.

'Ah! This is s*agren*, we call him s*agren.*'

Pronounced s*a-gran.*

'Yes.' He had run out of sensible things to say. 'Very tiring.' Another yawn, in combination with his affable nod.

A good night's slumber was called for, in due course. Perhaps he'd stick to wine and Hankey Bannister from now on, cut out the fizzy beer. Here in Papa a day in an open boat could be something of a test.

13. Bernard

Bernard stood upright, swaying with the roll of the sea, shielding his eyes from the mid-morning glare. He was sighting his secret landmarks, lining up a distant island peak to the northwest, a particular coco palm on a tiny sand cay off to the east, until he was finally satisfied they had reached the fishing mark. Leaning over the side he searched clear blue depths for patches of light and shade - find the coral, find the fish. A few gestures to Saba, working the outboard, then the engine was switched off. They would allow the current to carry them and their baited hooks over the reef, then motor back to repeat the exercise.

Bernard and Saba wore old T-shirts wound elaborately around their heads and looked piratical. Already, and despite the sea breeze, it was hot. The bottom of the boat was a mess of fishing lines, fish-clubs, fish scales, beer bottle caps, oilskins, rusty machetes, rusty chain, anchor, broken oars, ropes and fuel-tanks. There was no spare outboard as usual, Stan noted, and no VHF radio. Pride of place went to a large and grubby plastic tub covered with palm leaves and filled with smashed ice and bottles of beer, on which the two Linois had already made a start.

Out here there were no other boats, and apart from the rustles and grunts of their own preparations the watery slap of the waves was the only sound. Saba and Bernard were busy now unravelling fishing lines, crimping on squares of lead sheet, tying hooks and preparing the squid bait. Gram was absorbed, Stan was pleased to see, holding the reef fishes guide on his lap with the water bottle. There'd been resistance, but he'd agreed to come along, just as an observer, in the spirit of gathering new experiences. Also, he'd made friends with several of the Linois beach boys, and clearly found something in their company, their attitude to life, that he felt comfortable with. As Stan had hoped.

Saba held a hook, drawing the line tight around it with strong white teeth, lips curving in a smile for Gram.

'Can you do that dad?'

'Not as well as them.' In fact they used to laugh at his efforts. 'It's easier if you can find a hook with an eye in it, then you can just thread the line through and tie it off.'

Stan and Gram were provided with heavy nylon lines wound around lengths of wood, baited with strips of squid. All four lines went over the side, and the small boat drifted. Gram was fishing! Stan bit his tongue, not that he could have managed more than an incoherent gurgle. Gram was fishing. All the way from the hotel he'd been insisting he was just coming along for the ride, on condition he wasn't expected to fish himself, but he'd spent most of the outward journey in deep discussion with Bernard, and now here he was, wetting a line. Gram was fishing!

The first fish was pulled up by Bernard, which was only right. He and Saba laughed and chattered excitedly as he hauled.

'Varvara!' exclaimed Bernard, lips tight around a cigarette, and a big, angry-looking snapper with gleaming, coppery-red scales flopped heavily around the deck until Bernard hit it twice with the club.

'Varvara!' agreed Saba, hopping with delight as he hoisted a near-identical fish aboard.

Stan's line was plucked, but he pulled and missed. Gram hauled eagerly, then swung in a detached lump of coral.

'How can you strike properly without a rod?'

It wasn't easy, but the Linois managed well enough. They grinned at one another. 'Linois, they do not use the rod,' said Bernard. 'This rod is for tourist.'

More fishes came in, then they'd been carried beyond the reef and the bites stopped. Saba passed round the beers, although Gram stuck to water, then after a couple of pulls he got the engine started and they surged back through the waves to their starting point.

Fishes came in steadily again as they drifted over the coral, with a couple for Stan and Gram's first, a small pale emperor which the Linois called *baksou*; Saba hit it for him, and it was some time before Gram rebaited and put his line back over the side. Empty beer bottles rolled and clinked around the deck. They discussed fishing and football - both Linois knew the Premiership teams and a lot of the players. Both knew of di Canio, but were vague about Sheffield Wednesday, and Stan's mime of an owl was no help. The small boat now smelled pleasingly of fresh fish. Gram admired Saba's shark tattoo, Saba admired Gram's silver shark earring. Every so often a seabird winged by heading for the islands, and Gram rehearsed their Creole names, going to sit by Saba for tuition.

Bernard moved next to Stan, looping his line around a scarred brown finger.

'Stan-lee. You remember, the time before. We come back to Marga on the supply boat. You wait for your 707 to UK. We go fishing, we drink beer.'

'Of course. Today we catch more fishes than we did back then. You have learned a lot, Bernard.' Stan was feeling expansive. The local beer, so-called, had its place and time.

'*Oui*. This is true. I have learned many things.' He paused to tug the line, testing for a fish, then let it fall. 'This guy, this Easter-house. When he go, he take the boat. All the way to UK. You know this?'

Saba had got Gram drinking beer from the bottle now, and they were both laughing.

'You know why he take the boat, Stan-lee?'

Stan wondered where on earth this was going. 'That was years ago, Bernard. No, I didn't know he'd gone by boat. So? Flights weren't so easy back then, were they? A lot has changed in your country, over the past fifteen years or so. OK, if you say so, he went by boat. Maybe he wanted to stop off in Africa on the way, I don't know. He's got family in Africa.'

Bernard's pink eyes held his. 'All Linois know, this guy, he take a thing he should not take.'

'What? What did he take?'

Bernard leaned closer. 'You work with this guy, *non*? And you do not know?'

'No. I don't know. I worked with him then, yes, but not after ... I left. You know this. You came back with me on the supply boat, for your leave.' He couldn't quite grasp this.

Bernard's hand twitched. He straightened and stood to haul in a fish, something bigger this time. Saba and Gram searched the water for the first silvery flash.

'*Bourzwa*' muttered Bernard with satisfaction. This was the fish to bring a big price from the hotels, to be barbecued for the international elite. The tourists loved *bourzwa*, and the hotel workers loved the head. Bernard had set himself for the contest, a couple of pulls then let it struggle, another couple of fast pulls. Saba was babbling excitedly in Creole and Gram let out a giggle.

'*Bourzwa, bourzwa*,' chanted Saba, the small boat tilting as they all peered over the side.

Suddenly the line sprang from Bernard's hands and hissed

through the water, the crude wooden reel bouncing and clattering along the deck as he grabbed for it. Both Linois were cursing vociferously as Bernard hauled in the line to hoist over the side a large, open-mouthed pink head which he let drop to the deck. It was easy to see where the shark had taken it, crosswise, removing the entire body.

'Wow!' croaked Gram. 'What was it? What did that? A shark?'

'Shark,' murmured Stan. 'Probably silvertip, do you think Bernard?'

Bernard didn't answer.

Minutes later the performance was repeated, this time Saba eventually pulling up the severed head of a *varvara*.

Bernard looked stern. 'Who has sent this here? We must move. We will catch no more.'

'But,' tried Gram, 'if he's just taken two big fish, he won't want any more, will he? The shark will be full.'

Bernard looked at Gram, motioned with his head that they should exchange places. 'Gram. The shark it is never full. Always it will eat. And you will learn, all sharks they are not sharks, as all men they are not men.' He glanced at Stan. 'All Papalinois know this.' The formal, exclusive *Papalinois*.

Saba nodded in sombre agreement.

Near a small sand cay they stopped to fill up with a shoaling trevally called *karang disab*, a favourite among Marga's fishermen and usually found over sand. The mood soon lightened and they shared dry local biscuits with cheese and fruit from the hotel, washed down with more beer. Above them the sun blazed, but the sea-breeze brought relief. By this stage Gram was making noises about a shark tattoo of his own. He and Stan worked through the fish, using the book when necessary, making a note of Creole, English and scientific names. Gram practised the Creole names with Saba - *varvara, kwarson, zob, bourzwa, kaptenn rouz*.

All the ice had long since melted. Saba rinsed out the tub in the sea and filled it with fishes, making a half-hearted attempt to gather up the rolling beer empties. A young booby beat in the air just above the boat like a brown gannet, goggle eyes inspecting them around the heavy, pointed bill. Gram was, as always, fascinated.

After one failed attempt Stan postponed thoughts of picking up his conversation with Bernard, who had closed up after the mishap with the shark. Would Julius steal? Certainly, if it was the only way to get what he wanted. Finally, to his secret relief, Bernard decided it was time to go, to catch the fish market. The glare and continuous rocking were beginning to take their toll: he was feeling queasy, with the beginnings of a headache.

Saba pulled off the outboard. Nothing. And again. Nothing. Several pulls later, and after a bit of tinkering, still nothing. Saba's smile had gone and he was muttering darkly as he removed the engine's hood for more tinkering. It came as no surprise to Stan that the spark plugs were sculptures in rust.

Gram grinned at Stan, whose stomach was rolling along with the boat, then returned his attention to the circling booby.

'No spare engine then, Bernard,' observed Stan eventually.

Bernard shook his head. 'You must have faith in your engine,' he said testily. 'If you do not have faith in your engine, then the engine it will break.' He located a rusty screwdriver rolling about underfoot and went to help Saba.

No other boats were to be seen, and wind and current had already carried them far from the little sand cay, its reassuring coconut palms no longer easy to pick out in the shimmering haze. The bird was staying with them though.

'Next stop Somalia then,' called Stan with a tight grin. The more pleasurable aspects of the beer had really worn off now.

Saba was watching the booby, flapping again just feet above Gram's head. He muttered to Bernard, who turned around.

'Oui. Gram. You must stand to your feet. Up! Up!'

After looking at Stan, who shrugged, Gram got unsteadily to his feet, staggering slightly as he fought to keep his balance. The big, silky brown bird dropped, rose again, dropped, then reached out grey, spadelike webbed feet, touched Gram's hair and settled, wings half-closed, jockeying along with Gram to maintain its position.

'Allez!' Bernard clapped Saba's shoulder and he pulled at the starter. The engine spluttered, died. 'Encore!'

The engine fired. Bernard made an urgent motion for Gram to sit as Saba revved and blue-white smoke billowed from the engine. Gram sat heavily, the booby lifted back into the air, executing an all-over shudder as it did so, and Saba instantly slammed the gear-lever forward and twisted the throttle. The bows tilted upwards as white water flew.

With no let-up they made it safely back to the little sheltered bay at Tarataka and came ashore. Stan and Gram agreed there was no point in telling the Barracuda about the near miss part of their little adventure. Gram didn't want to go back just yet and went off to the fish market with the two Linois. Stan watched them go with mixed emotions – good to see the lad was getting on with his old friend, but he'd been looking forward to chatting over the day on the way back to the hotel. Still, no matter. He'd been fishing with his son!

Stan returned alone to Hotel Espadon to wash off blood and scales, down a jolt of Hankey Bannister with a couple of paracetamols, and crash out beside the snoring Barracuda.

Gram got back drunk with his head shaved.

'All the guys were doing it.' The Gram gap-toothed grin was lop-sided. 'Like a brotherhood thing. Looks cool, no?'

This was the way the Linois spoke.

The grin sagged further. 'Feels cool too. Papa style, eh dad?'

Actually, when he got over the shock, Stan agreed. It did look rather cool, even natural somehow. No longer Ronaldo's little hippy brother, but Ronaldo himself, or his less chubby younger self. Gram was flourishing, and he was all in favour.

The Barracuda had a shouting fit which alarmed other guests. She didn't like surprises, especially this one. Gram disappeared to the beach while Stan tried to pacify her.

'It suits him Barra. He's expressing himself. He's happy, for Christ's sake.'

'His lovely hair.'

'I expect it'll grow back.'

'Yes, that's just like you, your own son and you don't give a damn!'

'But it looks good.'

'All right, you have one then, go on, ask him where he got it done, go on, let's see what's bloody under there!'

'Just Yorkie bone, same as you. Wouldn't suit.'

'You really couldn't care less, could you?' She sniffled. 'His lovely hair.'

'Wonder what his little Italian friend will make of it.'

'Gina? If she really likes him it shouldn't make any difference.'

'That's right. It's only hair.' Only hair in normal places, he remembered uneasily.

At a suitable point later on Gram pulled up the sleeve of his shirt to show his father the big plaster on his bicep. 'Shark tattoo. It's cool, just like Saba's. Or it will be, when it clears up. Don't tell her. It's a bit of a mess at the moment. I'll tell her myself, later on, when it looks a bit better.' He was learning.

When the Blacksters strolled into the buffet that evening Gram's gleaming skull brought some admiring looks. Clearly though, little Gina's was the attention Gram was after, and he went off to sit with the Italians for a while. He'd taken to wearing the pastel-coloured polo shirts his mother had packed for him, in the manner of the Italian males. The sun had enhanced his naturally bronze face and arms, at the end of one of which was a drink, and it wasn't mango juice.

'Quite the young man now,' observed Stan; Gram's shirt sleeves were just long enough, thankfully. The Barracuda was acting as though the haircut had been her idea now, and the drinking obviously didn't concern her – why should it? – but surprises were best spread out.

She nodded proudly. 'So much more stylish Stan, you see? Makes an impression. You should try it, or try something, smarten yourself up.'

'Mmm.' The imperial. The noble hound would have a couple of shocks to handle. He could see the furrowed face turning quizzically this way and that. 'I've been thinking. Time the old imperial – ' but she wasn't listening, she was talking.

'This trip is doing him the world of good, just as I expected. It'll give him the confidence to grab the upper hand at university.'

'The upper hand over whom, exactly?'

She snorted and waved an arm. 'The upper hand over everyone! He's going to have to push for it, it's the only way to get on. They don't just hand things to you Stan, you should know that.'

'Yeah. Maybe we should have sent him to a public school.'

Her eyes flashed. 'Don't patronise me Stan! I just want the best for him, trying to learn something from the past thirty-odd years. I'm his mother. That's my job.'

'Right.'

'Anyhow.' She picked up her glass and took a gulp. 'He's growing up here. And he was actually fishing? Pulling the little things in? To be killed? It's about time.'

'He's a natural. Bernard seems to have taken to him, and vice versa.'

'And when do I get to meet the famous Bernard?'

'No worries, I'm sure we'll be seeing him before long.' He tried to flag down a cruising so-called waiter.

'And what about this Italian girl? He says this boy's not really her boyfriend, just a friend, you know? That's what he says. What do you reckon?'

She had fixed him with one of her sharp looks: he'd been nibbling a finger when a response was called for. He cleared his throat.

'Mmmm.' She would have to be told about Gram's university intentions soon, although things were changing fast out here. If Gram could bring himself to go fishing, and enjoy it, he could certainly change his mind about university. Best to leave it, for the time being. 'Gina? She seems harmless enough. Not so sure about her parents though.'

'Too rich, eh Stan?'

Gram was waving to them from the Italians' table.

'You're right. Probably very nice people. Very family-orientated, Italians are. Known for it.' There went the waiter, obviously something on his mind.

'It's going to broaden his outlook. Give him a bit of polish.'

'And what about you, Barra? How's your own outlook coming along? Broadening? I believe mine is you know. I can feel it.'

'Bollocks.' She was smiling.

'No really.'

'Bollocks again.' One of her affectionate punches to the arm.

'It'll be odd when he's gone though Barra, when there's just the two of us.'

'It will. Uncharted waters Stanley.' She stretched and yawned. 'Where are those bloody waiters? A girl needs a drink here.' She yawned again. 'OK, who's going over to get the drinks?'

When Stan got back Liza was on her feet. 'I'll take mine over to join Gram and his friends. You coming?'

'In a bit.'

Free to stare, Stan did so. The sea was calm, glittering with reflected tourist light. The noble hound loved the sea, as did all Blacksters. Of what order of magnitude had been the noble hound's contribution over the past ten years, grinningly piddled in at Keyhaven or Lymington, or in the River Itchen itself for that matter? It all wound up in the sea. If he took this empty wine glass down to the beach now and filled it up, how many molecules of noble hound urine would be galumphing around in there, tiny tails flagging, along with God knows what else? The ultimate solution. How were things going in the old bathroom without him, five thousand miles away? Quietly. In the mirror, Shanny's scarlet face. A hotel bathroom was hardly the same thing. Anyway, all that was history. A phase. An overloud burst of laughter erupted on the Italian table. These Italians represented success. Somehow he would make himself a success, make it happen.

'Come on Stanley, everyone thinks you're being anti-social.'

The Barracuda, looming over him.

'I've been sent to get you. Come on, it won't hurt - they're only rich, handsome and successful, after all. It's not a crime.'

Perhaps it should be. She was wearing that long, black hair tied up all the time out here because of the heat, which only served to emphasize her warrior-like face. The Barracuda was still easily the most striking woman in the place. Although there were several who might be termed more elegant, or more svelte, they were like glossy, farm-fed trout in comparison. Look at the way she strode through the evening revellers, parting them. Almost a super-Liza, a reinforcement of herself. Impressive. He marvelled again at his ability to cope, and shivered inwardly at the prospect of those uncharted waters.

Stan realized he was still staring in the manner he found all too easy, and got up to follow his glorious and slightly alarming wife.

La Belone rolled gently at anchor fifty yards offshore beyond the breakers; its orange rubber dinghy was pulled up on a small beach, secured to a casuarina stump. Trampled sand showed where the crew had patiently ferried gear across to set up table, chairs and barbecue, and now a large wahoo was roasting. The beach was deserted, as was the rest of the tiny island of Pichelim, and the setting was idyllic - or more accurately it had been until their arrival, Stan reflected, and would be again when they had left. Gram was splashing about with Gina in the shallows, healing tattoo safely covered by his shark-jawed T-shirt; the young bodies were slim and brown against the almost fluorescent colours of their swimwear. Little Gina was really quite attractive. A handful of frigatebirds circled high overhead, while on the beach numbers of small crabs had appeared and were edging closer in search of scraps. The first beers had been lifted from the ice-box.

Gianni was in charge. Comfortably in his fifties, silver-haired, urbane, at ease with English, deeply tanned, wealthy, he was accustomed to the role. Stan had immediately spotted the trinket nestling on a gold chain amidst curling white chest-hair at the neck of the Italian's yellow-peach silk shirt: the distinctively curved, notched and serrated tooth of a large tiger shark, set in a gold base. Gianni exuded the heady aroma of the rich and successful predator.

'Stan. Your son tells us, you have the knowledge of fishes, of sharks.' Film-star voice, film-star smile.

'I know a bit, yes.'

Eyebrows were politely raised, the smile encouraging.

'It was the subject of a study at university. A long time ago now. My youth.' Stan tried a smile of his own, aiming for the disarming version. 'I've forgotten a lot.'

'But Gram, he tells us you are very good.'

'Gram is my son.'

'Ah yes. We have all forgotten many things, no? But the fishes, the diving. Now, it is my passion. The sharks, I must see the sharks. The great whale sharks, they were *magnifico*, no? But they are eaters of plankton. For me, they lack the excitement of the real sharks, do you understand my meaning?'

The heavily accented English was rolled out with an assurance Stan could only admire.

'Yes. You mean Jaws.'

Another easy smile as the Italian removed expensive sunglasses rimmed with tortoiseshell – all too easy to believe this was genuine, made from the shell of a hawksbill. '*Si, si*. This is a great movie, certainly, but this shark, the great white, it is not a shark of the tropics, I understand this. Here, there should be the hammerhead, the bull shark, no? And, of course, the greatest of them, the tiger shark.'

'They were here once, Gianni. Now they're quite rare.'

'Rare, yes. I have visited these islands many times over the years, and I agree with you. Once I could find bull sharks here at Marga, big bull sharks, and they are very dangerous, very exciting. Now they are gone, they have all been killed. And never have I seen the tiger shark.'

'You have a souvenir though.' Stan nodded at the gold-set tooth.

'Ah yes, you recognize this tooth, of course. Like the teeth on your son's shirt. This was removed from the leg - you say the femur? - of a friend of mine. It is, as you say, a souvenir, a reminder to me of a real shark.'

'Did your friend survive?' Any friend of Gianni's had probably been asking for trouble.

The Italian slipped the sunglasses back into place and looked off towards the catamaran. 'My friend did not survive. But let us talk of other matters. Perhaps, Stan, you would accompany us on a dive. Not now, of course' - he waved his beer bottle - 'we have been drinking a little. But it would please me, and Gram I know is very keen. And *La Belone* is fully equipped, with her own air-compressor. It is a great pity that Roberto has had to return to Rome.' The Italian party had been halved overnight by illness.

'That's very kind of you, Gianni. I would of course be glad to join you.'

As well as his passion for diving and sharks, Gianni was a football fan, and so the conversation proceeded: Roma, the increasing number of Italians playing in England - how to get the best out of di Canio - the difficulty of bringing to mind any Englishman playing in Italy. In fact Gianni now preferred to watch the English Premiership, flying whenever he could to London to watch Chelsea's home games. Sheffield Wednesday should never have parted with di Canio or Carbone, he insisted good-naturedly.

Liza arrived back with Gianni's wife Aurora, the supremely poised lady with the video recorder from the whale shark trip. With them came Fabien, the French skipper of *La Belone*, and one of the Linois crew, Timucu.

'Phew!' She dropped into a chair. 'God, Stan, what a place! You should have come. Not a soul! The fantastic shapes of the leaves, the rocks … the whole place has such an incredibly primitive feel to it, you know? Prehistoric. And the colours!' She picked up a fan of woven palm leaves and wafted air across her face. 'I've taken plenty of photos. So many birds, lizards. And the most enormous black things, millipedes, like that hosepipe you get with the steel bands round it, God! I'll be dreaming about those things tonight.' Strangely the Barracuda had a horror of creepy-crawlies, even the economy-size versions back home. Stan was in charge of spiders in the bath.

Timucu brought drinks: cold beers, mango juice with ice.

'Thanks Timu. You're a lifesaver.' They smiled at one another, already friends. She saluted him with her fruit juice and swallowed.

Raja, the other Linois crewman, went down to bring Gram and Gina. The wahoo was ready.

Stan had been noting the numbers of small crabs, large insects and lizards, and of course the seabirds, most of which were nesting on the ground. That usually meant no rats. Boats brought rats.

'Who owns Pichelim, Gianni? Who gives permission to land on the island?'

'Ah yes. Ownership, permission - these are things of the world in which you and I have to make our living, Stan, no? Here, it is different. It is … more relaxed. Here, people are reasonable. Here, you can always talk to people.'

'I'll go along with that Gianni,' agreed Liza. She had moved on to wine now and raised her glass. 'Here's to reasonable people. Where we come from they're thin on the ground. In fact I can't think of any, and I can't think of one good reason to go back. They say welcome to Paradise, and I'm not arguing.'

'Paradise, *si*. We salute Paradise, and the beautiful people such as yourself who belong here, Liza.' Gianni turned his smile to Stan. 'And Stan, we must salute also Roma, Chelsea and of course Sheffield Wednesday. The beautiful game.'

Shanny should hear that one. 'Cheers.'

Timu and Raja laid the charred, marinated wahoo carefully on an enormous banana leaf then arranged the salads, fruits and rice to Aurora's quiet satisfaction. Now he'd seen more of her, Stan realized she was very good-looking, in a pert, Audrey Hepburn, elegantly middle-aged sort of way. A slim, near-translucent dace, perhaps. And Gianni had paid full and noticeable attention to the extrovert Barracuda in her bikini, an arresting sight, although Aurora seemed not to have noticed.

After they'd eaten, Stan stood with Gianni and Fabien knee-deep in the sun-warmed shallows, each holding a cigar, going up on their toes with each gentle, incoming wave. Local dive sites were under discussion.

'The diving around here, it is OK. But the outer islands … ' Fabien kissed his fingers. '*Fantastique!*' Fabien had washed up in the Papalinas years ago and had never left. Another with excellent English.

'Ah yes.' Gianni nodded reverently. 'The outer islands. This is our aim. Next week, we go. Without Roberto I had thought, we will not go. But no! We must go there.'

Exuberant bird-calls drew Stan's attention to a party of long-winged, black and white terns passing *La Belone* with extravagantly deep wing-beats: sooty terns, making for the huge colony they had seen on Anchois a few days earlier. He thought about pointing them out, but had already come to realize that the interests of his companions were not boundless. Besides, he thought he could see where the conversation was heading.

'Yes,' continued Fabien, who wore long shorts with deep

pockets, blond stubble and a pony tail. 'The island of Prodigalson is near to the drop-off, where the water is very deep, and they catch there the marlin and the other game-fish. And in the lagoon there they have the fly-fishing, for these fish, these bonefish. The hotel there at Prodigalson is always full. And at Batrikan there are the turtles, more than anywhere, and the coral wall it is *fantastique*. But the best of all, they say, the best it is the great atoll of Tsaramaso.'

Even though he'd been expecting it, Stan's heart lurched at the name. His toes flexed in the gritty white coral sand. Surf sounded from the reef and echoed in his head.

'Tsaramaso,' repeated Gianni slowly, a syllable at a time. 'The great atoll. Yes. It is far. But it is the best, all are agreed. A long journey, no Fabien?'

Fabien pulled a French face and waved his cigar. 'It is far, yes, certainly it is far. But for *La Belone*, this is not a problem. Four days, perhaps. *La Belone* knows these islands well.'

'*Si*.' Gianni was thoughtful. 'But she has not taken you to this far atoll before?'

Dismissive cigar-waving. '*Non*. This is true, but I have spoken to many skippers. It is not a problem.'

'What of your crewmen, Fabien? Do they know the atoll?'

'*Non*, sir.'

Gianni turned smoothly to Stan, still silently wriggling his toes. 'Stan. Gram has told us, you worked here in the islands many years ago. At Tsaramaso Atoll itself, in fact ... ?'

They were both looking at him now, Fabien rather moodily.

'Yes Gianni, that's correct. Many years ago. No doubt a lot has changed. In those days it was difficult ... you needed the permission of the government - '

'Ha!' Gianni turned back to the glittering blue sea, adjusting his sunglasses. 'I know many people in this government, very well. This is not a problem. And you have dived at the atoll, Stan?'

'Yes, again many years ago. It is not a place to be under-estimated, Gianni. It can be dangerous. The tides and currents are powerful, complicated ... '

'I have spoken to divers,' snorted Fabien. 'It is *formidable!* You fly with the fishes there.'

'And there are sharks,' murmured the Italian. 'Many sharks.'

'Many sharks,' agreed Fabien vehemently. 'Many, many sharks.'

'Stan? You have seen this?'

Certainly he had seen this. 'Yes, there are many sharks. At least, there were when I was there. There is no tourism at Tsaramaso.' The word, so long in his mind, felt strange on his tongue. 'And only a tiny population of Linois. No tourism, no hotels, no fishery – which is why the sharks hopefully haven't been wiped out yet. They're always the first to go. There are sharks, yes, and also sharp rocks and strong currents. Help is a long way off if there's a problem, Gianni.'

Fabien stabbed with his cigar stump. 'There is another island, with an airstrip. Fiantsifer. It is not so far.'

Stan nodded. 'True, but hours away in your vessel, no good in an emergency. Also, if anyone gets decompression sickness, I don't think there's a decompression chamber in the country, let alone on the atoll.'

'But,' smiled Gianni, 'we are careful divers, very experienced, is this not so Fabien? And there is always the satellite phone. This will be our great adventure. In a great adventure, there is always risk.'

There was a short silence, then the Italian turned again to Stan. 'Stan. I have decided. You must accompany us on our diving adventure to the atoll.' He held up a gold rolex-weighted hand. 'Yes, Stan. I insist. It is the perfect solution. Poor Roberto and I, we have dreamed of this many times. Now, Roberto cannot go, so you must go in his place, with Gram of course, and your fine wife. *Si*. You have the - what do you say? - the local knowledge. It is fate.'

Stan was just drunk enough for a tingle of excitement to have risen to the surface of his confused emotions; a yearning even. He was feeling the tug of the current. Liza and Gram were lying full length in the shallows with Gina, rocking on the easy roll of waves already broken out there on the reef where the surf showed gleaming white. Just beyond rode *La Belone*, graceful and also flawlessly white.

'So Stan. What do you say? Perhaps you wish first to discuss with your wife?'

'Well, Gianni. This is very generous of you.' He could see instantly from a subtle tightening in the Italian's tanned and smiling face that he hadn't chosen quite the right word. A cash adjustment would be involved, then. Well, that would give him a certain independence, which his pride demanded: he wasn't about to go as part of the crew, as hired help. And after all, he had no choice, did he? Somehow, deep inside, he'd known this would happen. Fate, as Gianni said. He had to go. In for a penny, in for the whole bloody national debt. After all, what would Boscanion do? Boscanion would lead the way, obviously. And he had a score to settle down there. The decision was made.

'It's certainly very tempting. I've always wanted Gram and Liza to see it, but it's so damned difficult to get to. Which is why it's still going strong – hopefully. It is one of the wonders of the planet, after all, a UNESCO World Heritage Site. I'll have to work out one or two business details, you understand … '

'Of course.' Geniality was resumed. 'We can come to a good understanding, you and I. We are reasonable people.'

They looked off out to sea once more. Beyond *La Belone* stood another small island, a low, misty-blue, palm-fringed hump beneath a white puff of fair-weather cumulus. Its small beach faced into the trade wind, and even at this range rollers showed tall and green just before they hit the sand. A colossal cruise-ship had appeared there and dropped anchor. Sheer and antiseptically white with orange lifeboat splashes near the top, its alien mass eliminated all sense of scale from the scene.

Gianni pointed with his cigar. 'Fabien, this island. It is open to tourists?'

'*Oui*. Yes, sir. This is Chozame. The cruise-ship, it is *Xiphias*, an American vessel, she is here often. But the landing at Chozame, it is for the moment very difficult. The waves, they are very big.'

'*Si*.' The Italian tossed his cigar butt into the water, where silvery shapes rose almost invisibly to inspect it. 'Stan. These small fish … ?'

'Small-spotted pompano, Gianni. They like the sandy, surfy areas.'

'You see, Fabien?' Laughing his deep, rich laugh, eyes hidden behind the designer sunglasses, Gianni clapped Stan on the shoulder. '*Voila!*'

The Frenchman was watching the cruise-ship, now slowly turning end-on as it readied for departure.

'These tourists,' he pointed out, 'the waves are too big, they could not land.'

Liza needed some convincing: on the one hand, yes, this would be the trip of a lifetime, with their son, to a key place in her husband's past which he had never shared with her; and the artist within her hankered after the exotic inaccessibility of it all; on the other hand were piled the tedious concerns of their grey half-life back in Britain.

'Stan, should you not have heard something more definite from this Vanderhorst by now, some sort of timetable?'

'These things take time Barra, you know that. It's a pain, but that's what these directors are like. It'll come through. I'm sketching it out, that was the agreement. The lawyers are the next step, and that'll have to be done in writing, through the post. Kato's probably guarding a fat package right now.'

'Yeah.' She was sitting in a bamboo chair, fingers working at the handle of her fan, twirling it slowly back and forth. 'It will happen, won't it Stan?' Her eyes were almost pleading. 'We need it. Not just now, for this, but ... when we get back ... '

Back to those uncharted waters, she meant. 'I know Barra. It will happen, don't worry. I'll make it happen.'

She stopped her twirling and took a deep breath. 'Yeah. I'm not even going to think about all that. This is here, this is now. You'll do it. I know you'll do it, I can feel it. You're coming back to yourself, aren't you? God I hope so Stan, you've got to. I want to believe Stan, you know? I do, I need to believe, otherwise ... well, you'll not want to be finding your best sharkskin suit thrown out on the lawn, on top of some dog waste, will you?' Her laugh, as she gave him a thump on the leg, was one of her throaty aggressive ones.

Later that night. The Mothers, and who could say the Barracuda lacked a sense of humour? Fierce, perhaps, and fitful, but it was there. 'We'll be OK Barra. We will.' He couldn't think of anything else to say. Was he near tears?

'Of course we will. Come on Stan, don't look so worried, let's forget all that. This is us now.' She leaned up to give him a resounding kiss. 'We go to Tsaramaso. We go and we have a damned good time.'

'Absolutely.' The name still provoked a pulse of something like excitement. It was like a long, low wave far out at sea, slowly getting bigger. He felt better. Even so, the words 'Tsaramaso' and 'damned good time' sat awkwardly together.

Gram could see no obstacles. 'We have to go! This is once in a lifetime. Bernard's told me all about it. There are manta rays down there! And whales! Humpback whales go there from the Antarctic to breed, like the ones on the telly, the ones that leap out of the water and wave their tails in the air and throw themselves all over. It's a place of power, Bernard says, full of bizarre animals and birds, miles from all the people ... he says the animals are protected by the power.'

Stan experienced an unsettling flurry of dismay and irritation at being by-passed like this. He'd never really spoken to Gram much about Tsaramaso, to his sudden regret, and now here was the famously taciturn Bernard doing it instead. Odd. When had Bernard had time to tell him all this stuff?

'Yes Gram, it's quite a place, one of the last. And yes, there are humpbacks. They used to arrive a bit later than this I think, but who knows, what with climate change and all ... the whale sharks were early, after all. Cycles change.'

'El Nino,' nodded Gram. 'Global warming. Lots of places in the Indian Ocean will get swamped, first the Maldives ... Tsaramaso is pretty low-lying as well. Bernard says all Linois know it has been submerged before, and that one day it will vanish again. The whole atoll, everything on it, all drowned, just like the end of *Insidiator*, but it really happened. We've got to go and see it now! Dad, I want to pay my way, if you can just give me a loan.'

Stan smiled. What was left of Shanny's money might not cover everything, but he had his credit cards. He'd actually been doodling away at research for an article on the Papalinas, focusing on its internationally-recognized, environmentally invaluable sites, its progressive conservation laws, and the corrosive effects of man, both in the global sense and, more immediately, through the desperate need here for foreign currency which fuelled ever-increasing tourism. He was keen to involve Gram and had made a point of asking his opinion now and then, assuring him it would make them some money. Therefore, in the way of these things, Gram was a consultant and should be paid. The Barracuda, as a talented wielder of digital and orthodox cameras, had taught photography courses, and would provide illustration. A family effort. To be able to include a first-hand report from Tsaramaso would multiply the piece's interest – and value - immeasurably.

Gram had been aboard *La Belone* again and was enthusing about Gianni's expensive and sophisticated underwater video gear: he was sure the Italian would let them have some shots for the article too. Perhaps, thought Stan. Underwater shots of representative fishes and corals would be a big plus, certainly, although there would be a price.

But there was a new attraction on board: *Il Padrone* had bought his daughter a fruit bat in a cage, because she thought it looked cute, and Gram had had his first little row with her about it. Rather than feeding mangos and bits of banana through the steel mesh, then cooing as hooked wing-claws manipulated them expertly towards the poor creature's foxy snout as it hung upside-down in its cramped quarters, he wanted her to set it free. The worked up, animated look suited him even more with a shaven head. Gina had responded by going into a sulk and Gram had left her to it, but he was obviously disturbed by it all.

'Don't worry Gram,' advised his mother. 'She'll come out of it. I expect she's used to having things all her own way.'

'But the thing's never going to fly.' He shook his head. 'Keeping it in a cage, just because she thinks it's cute.'

'She's only treating it like a pet.'

'It's not a pet though. It's a wild animal, it's not like Kato. It should be out there, flying around with all the other fruit bats.'

'I bet it is soon, too,' said Stan. 'Gina looks like someone who gets bored easily.' Did that sound bad? 'I don't mean with you.'

'I know that.' Gram flashed a nervy smile. 'One thing though. You remember Raja, the crewman? Gina says he won't go on this trip to the atoll. He says he has a family problem here on Marga.' He looked at his parents in turn. A fuzz of new hair had appeared on his scalp. 'Gina reckons it's really because he's scared. He told her Tsaramaso's a bad place.'

Stan and Liza were alone on the verandah, sitting in local-style deck-chairs, drinking beer and tossing back handfuls of tough, dry salted peanuts from a can, an addictive salty crunch when combined with the chilled golden lager which Stan was coming to quite like. Every time he brought his jaws together the sound resonated mushily in his head. No signs of improvement there, despite the vinegar. Gram had gone off to meet up with Gina at the swish Hotel Belonary further along the coastal strip, then they were off to a local disco, once more the best of friends.

'Well Stanley, come on then. We're definitely on, aren't we? I mean, it's too late for second thoughts, isn't it? Gram's so charged up for this he'd go stowaway on the bloody boat if we backed out now. I'll leave the money side of it to you. We should be OK with the film money to fall back on, shouldn't we?'

Stan had already seized the moment with his customary flair, over several Johnnie Walker Blacks, to make an initial credit card payment to Gianni. He would deal with part two later - the large balance, to be paid on their return when the bill was complete, in case of unforeseen extras. Somewhere in the foggy future waited *Part Three - The Aftermath (Picking up the Pieces)*.

He clinked her glass. 'Worry not, my little warrior. It was meant to be. The decision is made, all is in order, and our adventure lies before us. We travel to another, better world.'

She took off her sunglasses and a slow smile grew, one of her best. Clink. 'To another and better world. Really? I don't see how it can be much better than this one.' She nodded at their comfortable surroundings, the sensational vista of ocean and islands.

She had something there. The trip down should be unspoilable, assuming normal weather conditions, but Tsaramaso was by no means a tourist destination. Gram would be overwhelmed; he wasn't so sure about the Barracuda. 'All right, let's say different then. Unique and awesome.' Which almost covered it.

A local fishing boat was setting out, plodding doggedly through fair-sized waves on a sea which had grown choppy and patchily dark beneath an advancing bank of purple-grey stratus. A breeze had sprung up, refreshing here on the verandah, the first to cause the heavy curtain across the door to flap since they'd arrived. Stan knew all about the sudden, swamping downpours on which life in these islands depended. He reached for the binoculars: this wasn't one of the high-tech Japanese or Spanish tuna vessels which could be seen most days in port at Tarataka and which pursued their doomed quarry through the seas of the world using satellite guidance, until one day they would haul up the last one and sell it for a fortune. Four Linois clustered at the wheelhouse of the wooden thirty footer, two of them busy climbing into bright yellow oilskins. Black dots streamed past the boat - noddies heading back to dry land for the night. Stan lowered the binoculars and lifted his beer.

Two fruit bats flapped erratically out over the sea, a hundred feet up, heading for one of the offshore islands. Liza took the binoculars from him to watch their uncertain progress but they soon thought better of it and turned back, passing above them, tawny fox-heads and black leather wings, returning to the forest.

Stan brought the fishing boat back into focus, less distinct now on a sea dark and drained of colour. He wondered idly if Bernard was aboard, having run out of beer and money, going off for a few days to fish more distant waters. The trip to the atoll loomed inside him, this return after so long to the place which had pushed him out. Every now and then – when he was sober - he experienced a surge of apprehension: this time he, Stan, would be the one with 'the local knowledge'; he would be the guide. Responsibility for the safety of them all would be down to him. And it wasn't quite like other places, down there. There were so many ways of making a mistake and he'd seen them made. Made them himself. Liza here beside him, Gram at his disco, little Gina, the Italians ... he saw them all looking at him. *What do we do now, Stan?* Also, he imagined Gianni could be rather unforgiving when things came off the rails. And then there was Roland, old Lookdown, and his crazy round fruit bat eyes - getting even with Roland didn't seem so important any more, even if there was any reason to, and he should forget what Julius had said about him tampering with the food. Julius was off his head. Also, with Roland it had never been easy to predict how things would go. What if he pulled one of his unpleasant little tricks? For the briefest instant he felt again the ghastly crushing sensation which had settled on his little house on Tsaramaso. It was sensible to feel uneasy.

Bernard. His jaw tightened. Of course. He must have Bernard at his side. At once it felt right, and he relaxed. This was why Raja had dropped out, surely. It was meant to be. He must find Bernard.

Out on the sea there was no sign of the fishing boat, but he found three long-winged black specks: frigatebirds - he had his eye in now - which circled effortlessly higher, higher, climbing before the advancing rain.

Yes, Stan assured Gianni, he had just the man to take the place of his absent crewman, a mature and reliable boatman and guide who had actually worked at Tsaramaso and had extensive knowledge of tides and currents. After an initial hint of suspicion - which Stan may have imagined, and the fuzziness in his head did make it seem that events were occurring at long range, as though he were watching TV - Gianni agreed. It was established, in so many words, that this new recruit would be responsible to the skipper Fabien while at sea, but that of course Gianni himself would have final authority - not Stan, in other words. Bernard would be paid the going rate, with a bonus on satisfactory completion of the trip, as was the local custom. And it would be appreciated if Bernard could put in an appearance forthwith at the harbour to help Fabien and Timucu with provisioning.

Gianni was arranging to re-fuel at Fiantsifer, the island nearest to Tsaramaso, through the good offices of some acquaintance in Papalinas officialdom. The journey down would take a minimum of a week, almost certainly longer, depending on the weather and the quality of the diving at islands en-route; there would then be a week at the atoll, after which Gianni had arranged for a very expensive flight back from Fiantsifer to Marga while *La Belone* made her way back into the wind, which would ensure an uncomfortable journey for skipper and crew. The flight alone would knock a hole in Shanny's money.

The Barracuda would be late back to work. He wouldn't mention it yet, no use in her fretting; besides, he didn't think she'd object.

Now to find Bernard.

Atherina, Bernard's wife, was every bit as small, slender, pretty and shy as Stan remembered when she appeared at the doorway surrounded by children - four or five, perfectly quiet and well-behaved, if watchful - and cats of various sizes. He remembered the family house too, white-washed and immaculately clean, way up in the hills, with an attractive, multicoloured patio of tile fragments set in cement. A miniature hammerhead shark, carved in dark wood, was fixed to the door. Around them the forest was clamorous with the calls of mynahs and bulbuls; mango and banana trees cast welcome shadows. Yes, of course Atherina remembered Stan-lee, but his most engaging smile and a series of brief reminiscences failed to get him invited in. Neighbours – not that any were visible – would spread gossip, no doubt. No, she didn't know where Bernard was, he should ask at the fish merchant's. Stan got the impression she hadn't seen her husband for some time, but she was extremely shy and had only broken English. Atherina had hated life on the atoll, although Bernard had treated her well enough compared to some of the others. They had both been outsiders, not part of Roland's sullen gang of family and friends, and Atherina had been miserable so far from her own family on Margaritifer.

Well, he told himself as he climbed back into the open hire-car, at least she didn't tell me he's gone off on a three-week fishing trip. That would have been ticklish. The fish merchant's had been his first stop, naturally, but in broad daylight, and without Bernard himself there to smooth the way, his reception had been decidedly cool. Saba had scarcely responded to his hello and wouldn't meet his eye. Where was Bernard? He could not say. Presumably Saba was hungover.

Soft white cumulus rode high in the burning blue as he steered the car down the narrow, winding hill road. The hot, dry weather was back with a vengeance and sweat travelled down his back and sides.

Cars and driving were not his favourite things, but needs must and at least the traffic out here, although vastly increased, was still well below saturation point. With a wrench on the wheel he took himself smartly out of the path of one of the local ashok buses which roared gigantically past, engine straining, wheels within inches of the edge of the tarmac and concrete as it swung round a hairpin bend on this tiny road deep in the forest. Dark faces looked down incuriously.

Back down on the coast road there was no breeze to relieve the sweltering heat. Passing the local disco where the Linois beach boys congregated to play music, pose, and admire the tourist girls, he spotted the only Sheffield Wednesday away shirt in Papa reclining alongside Gina. They were sitting on the grass with some of the local lads watching the kickaround, and he glimpsed a big cigarette doing the rounds. The fellowship of youth. Stan smiled, but out here use of cannabis could mean big trouble - meaning no-frills prison on one of the tiny islands - for local and tourist alike. He'd have to have a word. Gram spotted him and waved, a sudden gesture which alerted the others.

Back in the shadows of the coconut grove stood a wiry figure, a man, watching. Something about the stance, knees slightly bent as though on the point of motion, small black body almost unnaturally still ... he'd glimpsed someone similar around the hotel once or twice, just on the edge of vision, standing under the trees. There was something of Roland about the slight figure and he shivered, despite the heat. No, Roland was much older. Ancient. Possibly even dead by now, which would make things easier. He had Roland on the brain. With a wave to Gram he drove on.

Stan was searching as he drove, but there was little chance of the nowadays rather austere Bernard allowing himself to be seen in a tourist area like this, and there was no sign of him. At length he pulled into the hotel driveway, itching for a shower, a Hankey Bannister and a beer, then an hour or two's oblivion. Later on the Barracuda was taking him out to an art gallery she'd found.

She was soundly asleep, snoring loudly; sawing wood, as they called it back home, with a vengeance. As carefully as he could he lay on his own bed, shower postponed, and watched the sleeping figure: her breaths were so slow and deep, untroubled; the fine, unflinching face, usually as familiar as his own, at times unrecognizable, sagged very slightly towards the pillow, as though under a mild excess of gravity. Could he really see there the faintest beginnings of creases and folds? Was she after all just as vulnerable as everyone else? Did even this fearless fighter need to grab a break between rounds? He sometimes – no, nearly always - forgot she was just another struggling human among billions of struggling humans. Doing her best. She needed his protection.

Stan felt the tears welling up. If he could break through this mush in his head, put out his hand, hold her, tell her it would be OK, they would be OK ... He lay down next to her, working his arms around her, kissing her soft brown earlobe. The snoring hitched for a moment, then resumed.

The coast road running south out of Tarataka, the island-nation's capital, was roaring with the local version of rush-hour traffic: overloaded and straining buses churning out fumes, cars and government landcruisers, taxis with reggae belting out, pick-ups full of locals and imported Indian labourers, plenty of horn-blaring and absurdly ambitious attempts at over-taking. The Barracuda piloted the little hire-car expertly through it all. She was an enthusiastic and aggressive driver, a natural. On either side of them the walkways too were packed.

At a little waterfront bar they pulled off the road until traffic eased a little. Liza was still bubbling about the paintings they'd just seen: after a long conversation with the gallery owner and the artist Mendo, whose work she particularly liked, she'd taken lots of photos and set up a further meeting for when they returned from Tsaramaso. Stan hadn't much cared for Mendo, a very pale Linois with tobacco-coloured dreadlocks and green eyes, but his subjects, especially Tarataka's fish and vegetable markets and local fishermen, were handled in an engagingly affectionate manner. Liza wanted to bring Mendo over to the UK, and discussed whether they could put him up in Southampton. Stan mumbled something, but just now he found it impossible to see beyond Tsaramaso into this supposed real world, this soon to be Gram-less real world where they had a spare bedroom.

While she talked on, Stan, with an ear cocked for ominous pauses, studied the ranked yachts, motor-cruisers and canopied tourist runabouts, and beyond them the big foreign tuna vessels packed with merciless electronics, the luxury power-boats of the wealthy and influential, and the humbler local fishing boats. *La Belone* could be seen further along the dock, Fabien and Timu out on deck having a smoke. He still hadn't found Bernard, and time was running out.

Liza set down her beer bottle with a clunk and ran a hand across frothy lips. She'd stopped bothering with a glass. 'I nearly forgot, Stan. I spoke to Shanny earlier on. Finally got the time difference right.' The first time she'd phoned she'd got him out of bed at 5am thinking there was an emergency.

She belched. 'Pardon. He's fine anyway, Kevin is off on his P & O course, so no worries there for a while, and Mrs Shanny is going down to help out. Sounds as though he's enjoying himself, as much as he ever does. Says Kato's moping around a bit, thinks he's pining for us, not eating as much as he should.'

Stan could picture it, easily. He might never be forgiven. You couldn't afford to take noble hounds for granted. He'd make it up to the old dab. At this time of early evening, with work and sightseeing dealt with and gone and the sun low, the scenery took on a languid glow, including the women. Languid wasn't a word he would normally associate with the Barracuda, but how different she looked now from the striding warrior of the college art department. A new version of Liza: hair up, sunglasses, gentle half-smile, placid. Placid was wishful thinking: unexcited, relaxed. Recharging.

'Shanny says to tell you Wednesday are still doing OK.'

'For now. He won't let himself get used to it.'

On a small island in the harbour white egrets were gathering to roost in a scrawny stand of casuarinas, all part of the pleasant winding-down of the day. His attention was diverted to the other side of the road where a beaten-up minibus pumping out Bob Marley had pulled up outside the local video shop. Several Linois spilled out and went inside. The one in the lead was Bernard.

'Barra. I'll be back in a tick. I think I see my man.'

Bob continued to pound out from the abandoned minibus parked slantwise with open doors at the kerb. *No Woman No Cry*. Saba, head newly-shaved, squatted in the video shop doorway sucking on a bottle and watching Stan's approach.

'Saba.' Stan nodded, squeezing by when it became apparent the man was not going to move. Moody bugger. The small shop was full of Linois, and the noise of loud Creole conversation overlay the blast from a video playing at full volume behind the counter.

'Bernard, hello.'

Again, he thought to see that instant of something very like hostility, then they shook hands. The over-bright, bulging eyes, the pink-tinged whites and the directness of the stare indicated that

Bernard was drunk again, or still. Stan could feel the others watching.

'I've been looking for you, Bernard. I went up to see Atherina. She looks very well. Still very pretty, eh?'

Bernard nodded. 'He - she - is OK.' He gestured dismissively. 'I have some little business. Now it is finished. We celebrate. You will join us, *non?*'

'Thank you, Bernard.' Perhaps not, in fact, but this was the customary formal exchange. Both had turned their attention to the rows of lurid cassette covers. Stan's eyes roved automatically, ready to lock onto anything familiar, or at least recognizable. There was *Gattaca*. He thought fleetingly of Louis Vanderhorst, and opened his mouth to speak, but *Gattaca* was not a film Bernard and his cronies would get much out of. Down to business.

'Bernard. You are a busy man, I know this. I have an important opportunity for you, which I would like you to consider. I have decided to visit the atoll again, with an Italian businessman - '

'*Oui*. Mister Conti,' Bernard nodded. He said it *Meester*. 'I know this guy. All Linois know this guy. I heard that *La Belone* is taking on supplies.'

'Ah. You are very well-informed.'

'Timucu, she – he - is my cousin.'

'Oh, I see. Bernard, I have made a strong recommendation to Mr Conti that you should go as boatman and guide.'

As always, it was difficult - or impossible - to know what was going on in that dark, narrow skull. Another consequence of the colonial past, of the fact that Papalinois came in all shades, from pallid Mendo-types through to the near-black of Bernard and most of his cronies, was a sort of racism. Stan recalled drink-fuelled and heated arguments about this years ago, which hadn't always turned out too happily - Bernard's fierce pride could look very like arrogance, and he was proud to be black. In fact he often appeared to despise those who weren't. Stan had got involved in one bad fight himself, on Bernard's side, which hadn't gone down well with the Director, or with the other researchers. Typically, Bernard had never subsequently referred to the event in any way whatsoever.

'Well, for me ... You go to dive? This guy, he want sharks, *non?*'

At least the idea hadn't been dismissed out of hand, to Stan's relief, but that wasn't the Linois way. Loud action continued on the TV behind the counter, where a painfully thin young black girl stared at the screen and sucked sweets.

'That's right. Diving, and yes, I assume the sharks are still there.'

'You always like the sharks.' A simple statement, an accusation almost. Bernard was studying him. 'You went to them, at night. To the sharks. We saw. We think, perhaps you are not scientist, you are *Gran Ke.*'

He had to laugh. 'A *Gran Ke*? If I'd been a *Gran Ke* I'd have done something about that old bugger Roland, wouldn't I? He'd be out on Dragonet right now, working in the fields for a bowl of soup.'

Bernard smiled a thin smile. Stan shouldn't have mentioned this. 'Easter-house. He kill sharks, this guy. You like sharks, but you help him kill sharks.' *Keel*, it came out.

'Well, we killed a few, yes. It was research, Bernard. To find out what they'd been eating, when they were breeding ... ' No one had wanted to eat the carcases. 'How else could we learn these things? There was no better way.' He felt queasy and uncomfortably warm. Soon he'd be telling him it was for their own good. 'And if we know these things, we can protect them better if we need to.' There. All the things Gram hated about science, but it was meant to be true and at the time he'd been prepared to believe it. To start with, anyway.

'This guy, Mister Conti.' *Meester*. 'He kill sharks.' *Keel.*

Immediately Stan saw the tiger shark tooth in its gold setting, the expensive silk shirt. 'Not as far as I know, Bernard.'

'Fishermen say, the shark, the ray, they are like Papalinois. Like a ... cousin. Some, they are good cousin, some very bad. We do not kill.' *Keel.*

'Yes, I understand Bernard. It was all a long time ago, the work with Julius - you know how I felt about it. I refused to do it in the end. There will be no killing of sharks while I'm around, you can be certain of that. Just diving, sightseeing.' He waited. 'Are you able to come, Bernard?'

Bernard had returned his pink-eyed scrutiny to the video cases. He picked one up and appeared to examine it. Hollywood action. 'Well,' he said at last. 'I cannot say. This place. Many Linois will not go there. It is not a good place for the tourist. But I have a family. I must bring them food, clothes.'

'I understand. You will be well-paid, of course. Double the normal rate. Plus bonus, at the end. I would be very pleased for you to come. We had some good times there, in the old days.'

They discussed money, in the elliptical manner Stan knew of old. He had at the outset considered Gianni's proposed bonus inadequate, and now found himself doubling that too. Somehow, he knew, it would all come out right with Bernard at his side.

Bernard picked up another video. He seemed to have relaxed.

'You see this one, Stan-lee?' He indicated exaggerated shark jaws and quoted carefully: '*Deep Blue Sea.*'

Two of his cronies were now at his side, grimacing their approval. They had a pink plastic bagful of videos and were waiting to go, and these days Bernard was the one they waited for.

'This one, we have seen this one. This one, the scientist, they make the shark very big, very fast.'

He produced a whooshing noise and made to punch the air. His cronies cackled, pink eyes glistening like their leader's.

'They make the shark, the mako shark, too big, too fast. They,' he pointed at Stan's head, 'they do something here, to his head, inside, his brain.' Bernard waggled the box. 'The shark, he eat all those scientist guy.'

Was that a sly grin? Hard to say.

'You have video at your hotel? Take it.' He pressed the box into Stan's hand and shouted over his shoulder: 'This one, my account,' to the thin girl, who gave no indication of having heard. Then, in a lower voice, 'And this guy Roland. You have seen this guy, *non?*'

'Roland? No. He's down on the atoll, isn't he? You said he would never leave. That's what you told me.' The sudden prospect of Roland here on Margaritifer had set his head pulsing. 'Is he back on Marga?' That figure, skulking among the palms near the disco?

Bernard seemed to lose interest, and gave a fatalistic shrug. 'This guy, he is there, he is here … I cannot say.' He too was now ready to go. There was no further mention of a celebration.

'Listen, Bernard. My wife Liza is just across the road. She's been looking forward to meeting you … '

'But she will be on *La Belone, non?*' Bernard smiled, extended his hand. They shook, the doorbell clanked, and he was alone in the shop.

He had been left in a situation he recognized, where the strong impression was that Bernard had agreed to his proposition, but there remained a maddening element of doubt. The Linois had run rings round the researchers in the old days, including the Director, and this sort of thing had tested even Julius's upper-class *sang-froid*. He could hear the quiet, precise voice now: *Matters have once again been left unresolved. We must resolve them.*

Despite her apparent obliviousness, the girl had the *Deep Blue Sea* cassette ready for him, its cover a poor, smudged, black and white photocopy of the garish original, and he could see now that behind her all the videos waiting to go out were the same - all bootlegs, and it was odds-on the picture and sound quality would match the cover.

'It's OK. Thank you. I'll come for it tomorrow, maybe. Not now.' He and the girl smiled at one another. He'd seen the film already, when it first came out, and it did neither sharks nor humans any favours. They enlarged a shark's brain in order to increase the yield of a chemical needed to improve human life - a repulsive and entirely plausible thought, and almost the reverse of the zoomorph situation, except the shark hadn't been given a choice. Was there a reason Bernard had given him it? Was it some sort of test?

He heard doors slam outside, then the receding roar of engine and music.

Dusk was over so fast out here. Now it was almost dark, and the traffic had tailed right off. The Barracuda was waiting in the car.

'Secret meeting over then, Stan? Picking up some of your old loose ends?'

He sensed she'd been over there, watching through the window. She just hated being left out. Without the sunglasses she looked fully the Barracuda, back on the alert.

'Just Bernard.' He leaned over to kiss her and a bag fell lumpily to the floor.

She laughed. 'I know. Look, Stan, look at all this beautiful fruit - mangos, bananas, a lovely paw-paw. Young lad with a hairdo like Gram's brought them over. Said they were a present - *pti cadeau* - from Bernard. Isn't that sweet?'

A surprise. 'Our Bernard's a charmer, right enough.'

'Is he coming with us then, on the boat, instead of Raja?'

'He's coming.'

'Great. At last I'll be able to hear about the old days, you and Julius, the Prof, all your deeds and misdeeds. I expect the Prof was chief tearaway in those days.'

'Well, don't hold your breath. Bernard's not the most talkative bloke in the world.'

'That's not what Gram says. Those two get on like a house on fire. Gram hasn't stopped, Bernard this, Bernard that.'

'Yep. Well, Gram's not a woman, you are.'

'Oh, like that is it? Well, we'll see about that. I take as I find Stan, you know that, and he's made a good start with this fruit.'

She liked a challenge. This instant bonding with Gram was a big surprise though. It had taken him months to form any sort of understanding with the younger, more talkative Bernard down on Tsaramaso, even though they were working together regularly. In time it had gone on, he liked to think, to become something stronger, but he was taken aback at the way things had clicked between his son and the stern Linois fisherman-elder. He felt a prickle of envy.

Liza moved the car out onto the road, where now only an odd taxi or hire-car rattled by, containing mostly tourists like themselves. Stan leaned back in the passenger seat. Yes, Bernard would go, he was sure of it. He'd found him in the nick of time. Fate. Within days he would be at the atoll again. A deep breath. One thing had to be done first though.

After the Barracuda had drunk up and turned in for the night, Stan quietly took out the *Insidiator* tape Ray had presented to him, brought Gram in from the beach where he sat with his Linois friends, and commandeered the hotel video machine. It was time for *Episode Four – Circle in the Sea*. During the long sea voyage in the living glass boat Gram would be reminded just how much more there was to Boscanion than the preening, pompous, adventurer: he was in his way brave and doubting, and would try to do the right thing whatever the forces against him. Boscanion was the better sort of human figure, worthy in the end of respect.

How bizarre the eerie, familiar music sounded here. Stan smothered a hiccup.

'Weird.' Gram looked up from an inspection of his tattoo. 'We're actually going there.'

A German couple stared at the opening sequence in audible perplexity, then departed when the Red Book spoke its words. The sunburned pair of Brit divers, the only others in the lounge, whispered excitedly to one another then settled back into their chairs. Fans.

14. Circle in the Sea

For long days following its departure from Dar the strange, glass-like vessel drove forward through the rollers, filmy screens deflecting spray, accompanied always by a lone black pirate-bird. But for the occasional ragged cloud of madly plunging seabirds, or a sudden flurry of flying fish, no other living thing troubled the endless sea-miles. The vessel's screens protected Boscanion and Anakim from the sun, and one of a complex assemblage of transparent pipes running the length of the interior delivered water with only the merest hint of salt. Filaments trailed astern, and every so often the array of limbs ceased its rhythm as a madly thrashing hunting fish was hauled in. Following an unequivocal response to an early attempt at a small fire, Boscanion ate his fish raw, albeit without his companion's gusto. Fishy bodies could clearly be seen passing along larger pipes among the tangle, proceeding via pulses in sequence with the methodically beating limbs towards a shadowy area near the front - or head - of the vessel, the only region where its remarkable transparency was reduced.

'We must maintain our best behaviour,' advised Boscanion solemnly. 'Our host is carnivorous.' As a further mark of respect he had removed his trusty boots at an early stage.

After initial hours spent squinting out over the featureless, rolling ocean, Boscanion passed large parts of each day prone on the deck, staring into the blue depths beneath them. Again, there was little to see - a sudden scatter of small but brilliant blue and yellow shoaling fish; larger, murky shapes which could not be identified - but the experience was restful, and led naturally to introspection.

'This is most pleasant,' he murmured at one point, enjoying the vessel's easy roll as he gazed down, down. 'Our needs are attended to, we are in all practicality safe. We rest, we cogitate.' His shaving routine was suspended through trepidation over use of a blade so near to the thin, transparent envelope around them, and an increasing black beard offered new opportunities for a range of piratical and prophetic poses and mannerisms; when he put on his best smile the effect was probably startling. The vessel, however, lacked a satisfactory reflective surface, and he felt increasingly disinclined.

'Almost, Anakim, one could wish this journey to be its own end. I have become apprehensive as to our arrival.' He looked sidelong at Anakim, who lay beside him. 'What of your own feelings? You rarely reveal them.'

'My mind is not clear, Boscanion. I feel ... I am returning. It is strange for me. Already I feel a pull ... ' She gazed down into the blue depths. 'The ocean. It pulls at me. I also am apprehensive.'

He had not seen her confused before - or perhaps once, outside the great Library of Dar. Always she was single-minded, acting to an exclusive, albeit mysterious purpose which happily matched his own needs, for the moment at least. He waited, saying nothing.

'I must resist. I must accompany you, Boscanion, and become better.'

'My dear. And how are you to become better than you are, when you are already in the fullest sense the unique and estimable Anakim?' He sighed. 'Your single-hearted courage gives me hope. But you may as well know, I have at last become disillusioned with humankind. I am depressed by what I have seen, and am forced to wonder whether it might indeed be better were the seas to rise and cleanse the Earth.' Holding up a hand to still Anakim's protest, he continued, 'I know, I know. Probably you are right. I am not quite myself.'

'You require intoxicant, Boscanion.'

Boscanion's fine white teeth showed through the matted blackness of his beard.

Two shadows loomed up from the deep, resolved into racing blue torpedo-shapes, a pair of hunting fish, pulsing with miniature lightning flashes as they struck at a shoal, fading back into nothingness.

'Meanwhile, in the here and now, and en-route to this legendary place of Lemperyal, we exist and have our being here in the open ocean. A world without men - I discount the two of us, for compelling and obvious reasons.' Boscanion stirred dreamily, his beard irritating the deck, which shivered. He reached out to hold her hand. 'This world, your world, is strange to me, Anakim. Where I must go will also be an unsatisfactory and disturbing place, since it will contain men. Far better for us both to stay dreaming aboard this wondrous craft, forever swimming on the world's seas. But this cannot be, can it? My dear Anakim, you have chosen to accompany me to journey's end, and I am honoured.'

One evening they came unexpectedly on a frenzy of life in the empty ocean: for as far as they could see the waters were opalescent with a host of tiny, floating creatures. Their vessel's transparent hull permitted them to view the mass in all its variety - strange, translucent animalcules with multiple limbs, swarming feathery fragments sporting outsize proto-eyes, ferocious-looking would-be scorpions and wall-lizards no bigger than a Boscanion thumb, pulsating, tentacled sacs, all jostling in a living soup alongside miniscule fish and a million other oddities in miniature.

'The great adventure,' murmured Boscanion. 'And what awaits these bizarre scraps of life at their journey's end, I wonder? What will they become, should they survive the voyage?'

For through this broth of proteinaceous vigour moved immense fish, titans, larger yet than their own vessel, tall-finned and driven by majestically sweeping tails, sea-grey hides dappled white, vast mouths open to draw in the precious life. Boscanion surveyed these giants sliding by in the milky haze, marvelling at their lack of interest in his presence, or in that of the vessel itself, which was ignored. 'Such is the savage and miraculous confraternity of the seas.'

He turned to address a thought to Anakim, who was nowhere to be seen. His heart jumped.

Seconds later she materialised as part of the epic scene outside, fading quickly into the dim blue distances with that effortless, swaying action of the body she had displayed to such effect in the swollen river at Ruahar.

Great silver hunting fish were there, following shoals of their smaller brethren which fed on the limitless soup and each other. Dramatic explosions of water at the surface showed where the hunters made their strikes. Moving up from the depths came yet mightier grey shadows, cousins surely of the terrible predator in the flooded pit at Kilwa, to take the hunters themselves. White seabirds plunged from the skies, pinpointing fish in a whirling surge of bubbles, while up above pirate-birds awaited their resurfacing.

Boscanion stood there on the pliant deck, surveying the scene and exulting. 'Here is the exuberance of life! A myriad lives winking out, that the greater mass moves onward, and in this there is no ending at all!' A frown. 'Is it life though, that I see now and admire? Or is it youth?' He searched the boiling waters for a sign of Anakim. 'Just so long as my good companion does not contribute herself to the grand scheme, and returns safely.' He had the growing apprehension that she had gone for good, and found himself fighting back despair. What would he do without her?

Alongside now rode a second vessel, a reduced version of their own, complete in all respects but no longer than Boscanion was tall. Some interaction appeared to be taking place between large and small, signalled by a trembling of the deck and a gentle waving of the limbs. Presently the lesser vessel moved off, to be replaced immediately by another of identical size. Again the floor quivered beneath his feet.

Now Boscanion was entertained by another curious sight: on the troubled surface, carried serenely by powerful currents past plunging birds and striking fish, travelled one of the large, armoured reptiles he recognized from his wanderings in the coastal regions to the south. Evidently the horny carapace retained air and was buoyant. The primitive, beady-eyed head peered around on its snaky neck at the passing scene. Atop its gleaming shell, and for the moment clear of the waves, rode a small, white-throated bird.

Boscanion felt moved to address these fellow travellers. 'In the name of the confraternity of the seas!' he shouted through cupped hands. 'May we all make a happy landfall!'

He turned, and Anakim stood before him, glistening in the evening light.

'We draw near, Boscanion.' Silvery scales glittered at her jaw. She pointed. Small birds, lost on the open ocean, fluttered from the skies to land about them on the deck, impossibly delicate and tiny things of green, white and yellow, with bright, white-ringed black eyes. The wet, curving length of a palm-tree drifted by on the current, carrying in its tangle of yellow-green fronds a restless freight of insects and small lizards.

'You are right, Anakim, without question. I feel a tension building within me. Do you share it?'

The new day dawned. At intervals during their journey the vessel had split off a bubble to send it far aloft for a time until the extending filament retrieved it. A larger sphere formed now to stand, trembling, before Boscanion, who eyed it warily. A break appeared, large enough for a man to enter.

'Well, we are invited for a viewing of our surroundings.' He forced a smile. 'I feel the end is near!' Carefully he stepped in. Instantly membranes coalesced, excluding Anakim who pushed and pulled, mouthing her distress. Inside, Boscanion made calming gestures.

A tug, and the sphere was out over the stern, hovering above the waves in the never-ending oceanic wind; as the filament lengthened, so the sphere and Boscanion ascended.

From a dizzying height the near-transparent vessel was almost invisible. The rumpled surface of the sea was overlain with dusky silver. A small group of scythe-winged black pirate-birds sailed below him, turning hook-billed heads, flexing deeply forked tails. As one they spiralled round, rapidly gaining height to circle Boscanion in his sphere, scrutinising the intruder.

'Well, this is all most interesting,' Boscanion told himself. 'An adventure. Although I see nothing below but trackless ocean.' So musing, he chanced to look between his large-toed feet, and there was the sight his eyes sought: far below, a hazy lacuna in the eternal rhythm of the waves, a pool of sunlight in the sea. Gradually he picked out a pattern to the patchy area of turbulence surrounding it: an enormous ellipse, broken in places. Here was the lost world of the Ruahari. Here was the broken ring set in the ocean. Here was Lemperyal.

The sphere trembled: the filament was contracting. As they descended, Boscanion was able to discern a shadowy greyness beneath the surface chop: coralline rock. The contrast in sea-colour within and without the near-submerged, ring-like land-mass was astonishing and beautiful: a pellucid and tranquil lens of dusky turquoise set in the shimmering midnight blue of the great deeps.

Once back aboard and freed from the sphere, Boscanion made his report with due solemnity. 'Anakim. We are indeed at journey's end. Here is the broken ring we seek. Here without doubt is the legend of the Ruahari. We have found Lemperyal, and it is enormous!'

Anakim drank in every word, upper body with that slight tilt, ready as always for instant action, pointed white teeth nibbling at a forefinger.

Boscanion likewise gnawed and sucked, contemplating the immediate future. 'However, you must prepare yourself for disappointment: this fabulous oceanic ring-world is under assault from the sea, and is in fact almost drowned. Lemperyal cannot be our final destination, or at least mine. I cannot begin to imagine what will happen next. Surely our vessel will not return us to the desolation of Dar?'

The troubled surface waters marking the rim of the sunken land-mass could now be seen and, upthrust in the turbulence, small prominences and the upper galleries of scattered trees. Birds were gathered there, clinging to branches, numbers of them setting off at intervals into the skies to seek new land or drown; reptiles clustered on dwindling rocky pinnacles; black pirate-birds hovered and swooped, plucking titbits from the waves.

The vessel drove forward, setting a curving course which brought it opposite a gap in the turbulence: a channel through the submerged reef. Beyond lay the transcendent green-blue glow of Lemperyal's flooded lagoon. What next indeed?

Anakim produced the small tablet which had been given her at Dar by her apparent benefactor, Mappa, the magician who supposedly guarded Lemperyal. Its lid bore the symbol of two torpedo-shapes chasing one another in a circle. From it Anakim took a pair of forest-green leaves which shone as though lacquered.

'Boscanion. I am to give you a leaf of the great tree.' The second she closed in a sturdy fist.

Driving into the channel, the vessel extruded screens which rose above and about them, more robust than those employed to ward off sun and spray. The two were completely enclosed. Around their vessel Lemperyal's disordered waters teemed with fish, shadowy, tall-finned predators amidst great hosts of their prey. As the limbs adjusted their angle of attack, and they began to submerge, Boscanion placed his arm around Anakim's shoulders.

15. Tsaramaso

La Belone rolled at anchor five hundred metres off the small and remote island of Fiantsifer. From his deck seat in the shade of the canopy Stan could see the orange dot of their dinghy drawn up on the distant white strip of beach. Fabien had gone ashore with Bernard and Timu, plus Gina with her new pig in her lap, to confirm arrangements for re-fuelling and the return flight to Margaritifer. They would also deliver the post and packages brought to Tarataka harbour on the morning they had sailed by friends and relatives of the dozen or so Fiantsifer residents; a third and pressing aim was to try to buy beer and cigarettes. Liza and Gram were snorkelling near the catamaran with Gianni, Aurora was as usual invisible, and Stan was ostensibly working on his Papalinas environmental article while leafing through his Lieske & Myers fish guide.

Things were going reasonably well. The trip down had outwardly been every bit as good as they could have hoped, a week of secluded coralline islands, swaying palms and easy swimming, then evening beach barbecues of yellowfin tuna and wahoo caught by trailing a lure at speed from the inflatable dinghy whenever feeding seabirds, dolphins or the surface explosions of the striking tuna showed the way. Aurora also supervised the preparation of raw tuna slices in soy sauce, with pickled ginger, seaweed and wasabi - a favourite dish of her husband's. There was always plenty to drink.

However nine people and one fruit bat in close confinement, with restricted facilities, had inevitably generated a certain degree of smouldering friction, which had once or twice been fanned into something livelier, generally by alcohol. One particularly convivial evening, their first at the millionaires' game-fishing island of Prodigalson, had seen them all dancing on deck to, most vividly, Durrutti Column's *Home* - even Stan, who later passed out. Next day Fabien's sunglasses only partly hid a black eye. The Frenchman had been getting on Stan's nerves ever since the moment they first shook hands, so it was entirely possible he was responsible, but this somehow bore the hallmarks of a lunge by the Barracuda. Misty images drifted around in his head, of the Frenchman being irritating, of raised voices and some sort of uproar, of the faces of the Linois looking on in silence. Liza said she couldn't remember either, and didn't want to talk about it. There'd also been an adjustment to the expedition's personnel. The wretched bat's persistent upside-down, round-eyed stare had been unsettling Stan, Gram had been agitating for its release, and its rotten-fruit body odour had been the cause of complaint all the way down. At Prodigalson, rather mysteriously, the unfortunate little captive was found dead, claws still wrapped tightly around its roosting bar. Bernard immediately volunteered to dispose of the carcase. Stan, with the help of his binoculars, subsequently observed a furtive meeting on the outskirts of Prodigalson's small Linois settlement, where Bernard had made some sort of deal with an elderly island resident. As fruit bats didn't occur on any of the Outer Islands – with the single exception of Tsaramaso – it seemed a fair bet that the meat, a valued ingredient for curries, had been traded; the Linois would also find a use for wings, bones and claws.

To placate his distraught daughter, who was indeed proving to be rather spoiled, Gianni had, the same day, purchased from the Prodigalson hotel manager a small, bustling, flesh-coloured pig, which Gina thought looked cute. 'Gazza' had soon been kitted out with collar and lead for excursions ashore, and had been annoying everyone ever since, especially the Linois who had to clean up behind him.

Tropical hangovers were an experience he'd forgotten about: where in the old days he'd had to get by on local beer and the occasional illicit cup of *bacca*, now he was knocking back an impressive selection of wines and spirits, using the local beer to wash it down. Gianni, Fabien and the Barracuda were keeping up. Gram and Gina stuck to beer and the occasional glass of wine, Aurora drank wine sparingly, and Gianni thought it best to restrict the Linois to beer. In addition to the upgrade in his intake, the youthful spring and resilience of Stan's inner workings had undeniably diminished over the years, such that mornings were, in general, observed at a distance. Matters were complicated by the shushing in his head, and sleep was erratic. He found the best treatment was spend a proportion of the daylight hours lying motionless in the shallows, observing the unobtrusive comings, goings and interactions of the humbler inshore fishes and crustaceans. The situation would doubtless resolve itself presently, as at this rate the drink supply wasn't going to last the trip.

Diving was Gianni's focus, and the dives had been spectacular, although everywhere the corals showed the same extensive bleaching they'd already seen around Margaritifer and the other main islands well to the north, the result of sea-warming a couple of years earlier.

They'd seen turtles and rays, many barracudas, moray eels and, despite the state of the coral, huge numbers of reef fishes. Beyond the diving though, Gianni craved sharks, which had been in short supply. They'd come across two or three sleepy sharks, a handful of white-tip reefs, and once, while they were fishing from the boat, a silvertip circled them just below the surface, on the lookout for easy pickings. This was presumed to be the species which had interrupted their fishing that day on the boat with Bernard and Saba, and Gram studied it closely. Gianni instructed Timu to tempt it closer with a piece of wahoo, but it faded back into the depths.

The Italian demanded to know, Stan, where are all the sharks? Fished out, was the answer, as Stan had predicted back on Pichelim. Some of the islands, especially Prodigalson, had expensive game-fishing operations targeting marlin, sailfish and tuna, but photos of themselves beside a large, bloody shark – necessarily dead – were still a popular trophy for a certain sort of sporting tourist, and the idea of tagging and returning them alive was only just becoming established. Worse, the never-ending demand from east Asia for shark fins had led to many sharks being thrown back in, still alive, with no fins – no longer sharks. A Chinese fishery operation to satisfy this and the demand for live groupers in Hong Kong restaurants had recently been established in the islands, as Stan had recorded in his notes for the article. There were also, Fabien had heard at Tarataka Yacht Club, reliable reports of cyanide fishing boats from southeast Asia which took the prized groupers back in tanks, alive, having killed lots of unwanted smaller species to get at them. So, plenty of good reasons for sharks to be hard to find.

However, Gianni rose above his disappointment to put in a polished performance as godfather, and proved adept with a smooth intervention whenever the tension needle crept up. Stan and the French skipper were usually involved, or Gazza and almost anyone. After the leisurely activities of the day, the lavish meal would be prepared by Timu, usually helped by Liza, under the close supervision of Aurora; Italian wines invariably accompanied the food, and brandy or scotch followed. They were more or less drunk every night, mainly more. Gianni was generous with beer for the crew - surprisingly so, it seemed to Stan, since it soon became evident that skipper and crew were drinking during the day too. The Barracuda found this less irritating than he did:

'Why shouldn't they enjoy themselves? They're doing all the

work, aren't they? You're just flopping around. Besides, the godfather's in charge, not you.'

Gram was transformed, wonderfully at ease, fit and relaxed in shorts and flip-flops, shades and white teeth, T-shirt wrapped around his scalp in the local style, helping the crew whenever they let him. He spent most of his time with them in fact, sharing beers and listening to their stories. A couple of days after leaving Margaritifer he'd decided to reveal the healing shark tattoo to his mother, choosing his moment carefully and getting it right. Certainly she had not been delighted, but this was her only son growing up in front of her eyes, becoming a man. Besides, she'd already guessed. What she thought she'd seen on Gram's computer was part of another world.

Stan had paced himself with the dives. The sensation that the sea had found its way into his head was now a part of daily life, but the thought of it getting worse brought him close to panic. Far more agreeable to simply float about on the surface in snorkel and mask, with or without fins, observing life on the reef at his own pace. He let Gram go down without him every so often, trusting Gianni and Fabien to keep an eye on him. Gram was by nature cautious, and was becoming increasingly assured underwater. Liza had thrown herself whole-heartedly into the lotus-eating lifestyle, a life's ambition, although her initial seasickness had briefly threatened to ruin everything. A combination of stugeron tablets and wrist pressure bands provided by the capable Aurora had saved the day, touch wood.

After a while the luxurious tourist operations on dreamy paradise islands had fallen behind, along with the sport fishing and dive boats, the small aircraft in blue and gold droning in and out of grassy strips in palm forests, and the VHF radio chatter between boats and islands which kept Fabien and the Linois entertained. As they sailed southwards they passed islands with no airstrip, just a cluster of simple whitewashed or corrugated homes among the coconut palms for the dozen or so residents, two or three small fishing boats, and with luck a working BSB radio to keep in touch with families on Marga or Dragonet. Every couple of months a schooner would appear, delivering post and supplies, perhaps a new worker, and taking off a cargo of copra and dried fish - neither much in demand following the advent of freezers and the petroleum industry - along with anyone with leave due or at the end of their contract. One island, where landing was not permitted, belonged according to Fabien and the Linois to an arab sheikh, another to a film star who was involved with the mafia. Yes, certainly this is true, all Papalinois know this.

There followed three days of empty seas, where they saw only the occasional distant tuna vessel. None of these responded to the playful VHF calls made by a half-drunken Fabien. Liza took her photographs: the image yesterday of a huge, blue, empty sea with a tiny red oil-tanker on the horizon would serve to illustrate the ever-present and universal threat of a spill.

And now here they were, anchored off Fiantsifer, last port of call before the atoll itself. Fiantsifer was a small island with a short concrete airstrip, emergency lifeline for the tiny relict populations maintained by Papa's government on these furthest flung outposts. The snorkellers showed no sign of returning to *La Belone*, so Stan drew down the brim of his straw hat and settled back for a doze. Nights had not been refreshing: usually he would tumble, stunned by alcohol, into deep pockets of disturbing visions and scramble quickly out if he could. Roland was there every night now, and sometimes in the day. Roland, watching without expression as Julius examined a dozen embryos removed from a seven-foot female lemon shark lying dead in the bottom of the boat, his round, sand-coloured eyes watching as the scientists collected, preserved, labelled. Although Roland had always given Stan the uncomfortable sensation of being judged and found wanting, Julius was impervious, regarding the attitudes of others as just another aspect of the trivial world, no more and no less significant than anything else unless it bore on his work. Getting rid of the shark bodies had been no problem, even when it became clear the staff would not eat them: other sharks were always on hand to do the job of tidying up, and, to start with at least, the spectacle of thrashing tails, lunging grey and white bodies, teeth and open wounds had attracted a small audience of research staff. In time the weight of Linois disapproval, stemming from Roland, had made disposal a furtive affair.

'Dad!' Gram's voice, far off, very excited.

Stan jumped up awkwardly, grabbing at the rail. Fifty yards away floated Gram, waving, with Gianni and Liza in the water beside him.

'Dad! Hammerhead!'

Immediately he saw it, the unmistakable, lazily undulating grey shape of a big shark moving closer, getting steadily closer and bigger, passing beneath *La Belone*, the broad hammer-head outspanning the pectoral fins, twelve feet at least from its weird snout to the tip of its slowly sweeping tail. Stan stared, absorbing what he saw, the rhythm of the tail's sweep fixed in his head, then he clambered across to the other side of the catamaran. Out it came. A great hammerhead, from the shape of the head. *Sphyrna mokarran*. A stingray-eater, and a formidable beast with a bad reputation, but not a confirmed man-attacker. Used as a charm in some cultures – wasn't there a skilfully carved wooden hammerhead on the door of Bernard's house in the hills of Marga? The shark was curving round, back towards *La Belone*. He had Liza's camera in his hands now, could see through its viewfinder the single sharksucker clinging to an iron-grey flank. Once again the shark passed beneath him. Again he scrambled to the other side. The wavering grey shape neared the surface, and the tall, grey dorsal appeared, raked back, heading for the snorkellers. Just stay calm he sent at them, stay calm and don't thresh about. Don't punch it Liza.

Aurora was beside him, anxious, shading her eyes. 'Shark.'

It was unusual to hear her speak English, but everybody knew this word. The tall grey fin cruised past the four stationary heads, which stayed calm and didn't thresh about, and presently slid beneath the surface. Stan resumed breathing.

When they climbed back aboard Gianni was cursing his luck, in reasonably cultured fashion, in not having his underwater camera with him - but at last he had seen a real shark! The Barracuda and Gram were matching one another in post-adrenalin excitement.

'Dad, you should have been in the water! Mum was terrified, but she did really well, she didn't splash about!'

'Inside I was splashing about.' She looked paler than usual, but it might have been sun cream, and her eyes were still bulging.

Stan kissed her wet and salty face. 'Well done Barra. You saw him off.'

'Yeah, I was quite proud of myself. I mean, in the middle of these two, I must have looked like the meat in the sandwich. Wait until they hear about this … Stan, its eyes were so strange, right on the end of those … those things on its head, the hammer? It looked right at me, with one eye.'

'Dad, did you see the size of its dorsal? And it moved just like the whale sharks. They all move the same, don't they? So deliberate. It's as if someone somewhere just puts them in the water and switches them on, and that's it, they just keep on going forever. It is so not like telly. Was it a great? I'm going to check the book. That's five species now.'

Later Stan sat on his bunk in the cramped cabin staring at the

red face on the *Insidiator* cassette box while Liza worked up the first
tentative snores a few feet away. It hadn't taken long to get fed up of
the few videos aboard - Red Sea dive sites, a couple of Hollywood
blockbusters, *Mr Bean* - and, one boozy night when the Barracuda had
retired, he'd put it on. There was a certain feeling, a sensation of
completeness. Only now did he recognize it, realize how badly he'd
been missing it. The ever-loyal Anakim. He was hooked all over again.

There had been a few good-natured smiles from the Italians at
first, and none at all from Fabien, but they soon lost interest. Bernard
and Timucu, however, seemed to find it fascinating, murmuring to one
another from time to time without taking their eyes from the screen.
Gram sat with them, muttering. On most days since then, at a point
when they had no work, the two Linois had watched an episode with
Gram. They seemed perplexed by Anakim, often looking away from
the screen and at one another, genuinely fearful whenever a jactator
appeared, or the wizard, and they found the antics of the Ruahari
especially entertaining. They watched the Dar episode with stony faces,
but were entranced by the final episode, which induced frequent
hushed comments from Bernard to his younger cousin. The two Linois
were the perfect audience.

Once or twice Stan thought Bernard had burning questions he
was about to ask, and was disappointed when he never did. If he asked
them at all, he preferred to ask Gram. Now, looking at the sleeping red
face, rubbing gently at it with the fingers of one hand, stroking it, his
own eyes started to close. A small buzzing became the sound of an
approaching outboard: Fabien and the crew were heading back from
the island of Fiantsifer.

Ten minutes later the orange dinghy was pulling alongside, the
skipper and the Linois obviously in good cheer, and an outburst of
squealing signalled the return of Gazza. Beer and cigarettes had been
secured and were brought aboard, along with a large palm heart, a gift
from the island manager. There had clearly been a bit of a party, and
Stan was gratified to see Gianni at last chastising his skipper, albeit
discreetly. Gina was offhand with Gram and it appeared she'd found
something new to sulk about.

When the dust settled they prepared to depart for their last
port of call, the most remote outpost of this island-nation of the
Papalinas, Tsaramaso Atoll. Gram and Timu brought up the anchor
and compared muscles, laughing and poking fun. With wind and tide
favourable, *La Belone* should reach the atoll before sunset. Stan watched

preparations, trying to ignore the blankness in his head and the low-level churning at the pit of his stomach, which was now more or less continuous. Useless to suppose they could avoid Roland, even on an atoll over twenty miles long - they would have to make a landing at the settlement first anyway, to notify them of *La Belone*'s arrival.

A week ago, just before they left harbour at Tarataka, while Stan was still pacing up and down the quay wondering whether Bernard was going to show up, a very elderly Linois man had silently handed him one of the ubiquitous pink plastic carrier bags, loosely tied up with fishing line. Protruding stems and leaves indicated some kind of plant, in a crude pot of clay or something similar. The man was so small and quiet Stan hadn't seen him - it was as though he'd just materialized there in front of him, in a way which was disturbingly reminiscent of so much that he'd tried to forget about Tsaramaso. He'd looked down into an ancient, leathery face marked on the cheeks with old scars, like the machete nicks on tree trunks which marked the secret way, looked into sightless white eyes which stared back, through and beyond him. The old man was unbelievably scrawny, his dark, mottled skin stretched so tight over a framework of wood, sinew and stringy muscle that the lot altogether couldn't have weighed much more than a well-fed cat. He wore only a loincloth and a crude necklace of several large, blood-coloured plant seeds or dried fruits, and was drawing sidelong looks even from Linois on the quayside. This was a creature from another world, a forest world of deep shadows and soft bird-calls, a world of monkey-men who perched high up in the canopy, peering down through leaves and sunlight and shadow.

Timucu had translated the few papery words with evident respect: would Stan please pass this small gift to the manager of Tsaramaso Atoll, from his brother, who had travelled from his home on Dragonet for this purpose. A daunting journey for a frail, blind old creature from the hill forests of Dragonet to the harbour at Tarataka, which must have involved days of walking, not to mention the crossing in an open boat, but there was no other way he could have got here. Maybe someone had carried him - it wouldn't be difficult - but he seemed to be alone. He might as well ask, although there could be no mistaking whose brother this was: what is the name of this manager of Tsaramaso Atoll? His name it is Roland Boniface.

The plant stood now beside his bunk as Stan again made a futile attempt to grasp the sequence - how could the old boy have known about *La Belone*'s trip to the atoll in time to set off on his trek to

Tarataka harbour? He gave up – this had always been the way things happened out here in Papa.

Bernard had recognized the plant. 'This, it is for *Malgache*. You say, Madagascar.' He had pronounced the word carefully, giving full weight to each syllable. 'We call this *Bwa Malgaz*. Very powerful, in voodoo, *oui*.' He clearly disapproved.

'Really.' No surprise. 'But why did the old boy give it to me? Why not you, or Timucu, or the skipper?'

Bernard shrugged. 'Well, I cannot say.

In the old days the standard policy had been that a non-native plant should not be introduced to a remote and biologically unique atoll, even in a pot. A sensible British policy, circumvented in all manner of ways by the Linois, who continually exchanged such items as a matter of course and courtesy between the islands. The Brits had gone, so now there were no rules, but it was still a sensible policy, and he didn't intend doing any favours for old bat-face. He would quietly drop it overboard when they were at sea. This is what he had told himself at the time. In the event either Timucu or Bernard always seemed to be watching, even at night, and whenever they weren't, he would forget, and the plant remained in its pot next to his bunk.

They were under way now, moving out of the shelter of Fiantsifer and into the swell, *La Belone* creaking, a few seabirds winging by. Fiantsifer had been exploited for its guano phosphate long ago, its vegetation wrecked, and its huge seabird colonies were not even a memory to the present Linois residents. A brown young booby, no doubt from a nest somewhere in the mangrove forests fringing Tsaramaso's lagoon, was trying to land on the mast but couldn't quite manage to match the catamaran's rolling. Liza took photographs while Fabien shouted drunken comments from the wheel.

Bernard came forward to sit beside Stan, a departure from the normal routine. His favoured place when not working was at the stern with Timucu and, often, Gram. He breathed beery fumes and gestured ahead with a slim black hand.

'Stan. We return at last to the atoll. You are happy, *non?*'

Not exactly. 'Of course Bernard. Very happy. And you also? Did you enjoy your visit on Fiantsifer?'

'Well, it was OK. This guy, this Bib, he the manager, he take down the coconut tree, he cut out its heart, he give it for us to eat, *pti cadeau*. You see? Palmiste, the heart of the palm. You remember this thing?' He was talkative.

'I remember, yes. Millionaire's salad. You must kill the palm. Take its heart.'

'*Oui*. This one, it is not the best palm. The best palm, it grow near my house, at Marga. But this one, this is OK. The wife of Mister Conti, she very happy. She make salad. Some, she give to the pig.' *Peeg*. This he obviously regarded as wasteful, not to say inexplicable. 'Soon, Timu, he will clean up the millionaire's *kaka*.' Dealing with Gazza's mess had devolved firmly onto Timu.

They both looked off across the heaving blue sea, now rising above them, now below, the deck tilting them this way then that. Here between the islands, beyond their encircling reefs, the blue changed, to the deep dark blue of the tropical night, as the sea-bed fell away over a thousand feet below *La Belone's* wallowing twin keels. Stan licked salt spray from his lips, exhilaration seeping through him, the sea-noise in his head finding equilibrium. They were on course for one of the world's largest atolls - and surely its most remarkable - and these profound deeps were its greatest protection. Tsaramaso was unique in the world, and not just for the reasons laid out in the wealth of scientific literature which had flowed from it in the twenty-odd years following the first expedition in the late sixties. Certainly no other island in the Papalinas could show even the ghostliest hint of its undisturbed magnificence.

'This Bib,' interrupted Bernard. *Beeb*. 'This guy, he say another boat go to the atoll. Since two days.' He was nodding, as though to himself. 'This boat. *Malgache*. From Madagascar.'

A tickling sensation ran across the back of Stan's neck, an ant or a fly, but his hand found nothing. *Malgache*. 'Who would it be, Bernard? Fishermen maybe?'

Bernard shrugged, a characteristic gesture, took out his cigarettes and lit one expertly behind a cupped hand, holding it turned in away from the wind and spray. 'This guy Bib, he say the crew *Malgaches*, but the skipper, no, he South African.' *Skeeper*. 'They take turtle maybe, tortoise maybe. Fish.' *Feesh*. 'In Malgache, there is much money for fish. The fish of Malgache, they have no fish, they have taken all the fish. Now, they take the fish of Papalinas.' He shrugged again. Only when drunk was he talkative, and then there were limits.

Stan let it go for a while. The news was disappointing. It hadn't occurred to him they wouldn't have the atoll to themselves, apart from the small population at the settlement, who could be expected to keep themselves to themselves. He was no different to any other tourist after all. And in his day it had not been permitted for foreign vessels to come direct from Madagascar, or anywhere else apart from Tarataka. In theory foreign vessels had to register at Tarataka to enter the country. In practice the Papalinas had no navy apart from the odd coastguard vessel, Tarataka was hundreds of miles away, and customs and immigration were simply words out here; and, as Gianni had observed, at these latitudes people tended to be reasonable. For bona fide visits to the atoll the government would, for a fee of several thousand dollars, fly down the relevant officials to do the paperwork on Fiantsifer. But they were not talking about a bona fide visit.

Bernard stood, screening his eyes with a hand to watch the booby still trying for the mast. Stan was staring down at the pink-soled feet of the Linois on the wooden deck, watching the long toes flex as *La Belone* rolled, dark brown toes gripping warm brown wood.

'*Malgaches*', hissed Bernard. 'Very bad.' He went off to re-join his cousin, Gram and the skipper at the wheel.

Beyond the halfway point the number of seabirds began to increase, until they came upon a great rolling maul of thousands feeding alongside a hundred or more dolphins, all brought together by myriads of shoaling fishes driven up from the depths by tuna. Dense crowds of brown-black noddies milled just clear of the boiling surface, swooping to snatch, as the larger, snow-white bodies of boobies crashed through them into the sea. Gleaming dolphin backs were arching everywhere and the sea exploded wherever yellowfin tuna struck. Bernard and Timucu were galvanized, scrambling to get the tuna lines overboard, but the wallowing progress of *La Belone* was surely too slow to make the lures convincing. Overhead, patiently, hung the now ever-present, sickle-winged black silhouettes of frigatebirds, most showing when they dropped lower the white chests of females or the white chests and white heads of younger birds.

Gianni and Liza wielded video and camera, taking in as much as they could. Stan could overhear Gram explaining to Gina that the birds depended on the tuna to do this, to herd the smaller shoaling fishes to the surface where they had them trapped – after all, these fishes couldn't fly. Not only sushi-lovers would suffer when the tuna were wiped out. Gina was cuddling Gazza, with his idiot blond eyelashes and his little collar, cooing to him in Italian.

After miles of emptiness, this frenzied concentration of life roused them all. Stan and Liza clung together at the rail to watch the spectacle of boobies hunting super-sized flying fish: the big, gannet-like white birds were dropping one at a time into abrupt dives, powered by purposeful, clipped beats of black-edged wings, down to within a couple of feet of the roller-coaster seas, where they would flatten out and career along in a breathtaking pursuit of the four-winged fish, swerving and dipping over the contours of the waves for a hundred yards or more, before the fish either found itself snatched and taken aloft in a towering ascent or plunged back into invisibility, to take its chances with the tuna down below.

'Don't you feel wild?' yelled Liza. 'I want to dive over and join in!' She threw back her head and laughed, an exultant bellow which would have silenced the *Stargazer* on a Saturday night, let alone a sixth-form college staff room. Gram had joined them, beaming, and the Barracuda pulled her handsome son to her for a kiss. 'This is fantastic, isn't it Grammy? Isn't it? My little grievous angel?' One hand squeezed Stan's arm till it hurt.

Finally the atoll appeared. Tsaramaso. All around *La Belone* seabirds were streaming in undulating lines and loose flocks towards it. This, for Stan, was a moment overloaded with doggedly suppressed emotion. He barely noticed that the others were disappointed: Tsaramaso was not a place to impress at first sight. It was too big. It was too low-lying, most of it barely the height of two men above the sea. Here were no mountainous forests, no gentle picture-postcard scenes of leaning palms and pristine white beaches. Here instead was a vast, elliptical reef of long-dead coral, built over the aeons around an extinct and deep-sunken volcano, a seamount thrusting up from the black sea-floor, showing to the surface world this shallow rim of weathered grey coral limestone clothed in low, arid scrub, encircling an immense central lagoon. The eye discerned only a narrow, dusty grey bar on the horizon; the mind that knew it - Stan's mind - saw something overpoweringly awesome, beyond full comprehension, an ominous and brooding place, a place, as Dalyell had acknowledged, of power. He remembered the nagging feeling that people, people like him, shouldn't be here, that there was no place here for them. People belonged outside. This feeling hit him again now. He'd forgotten. He found himself wondering what he was doing here, what were they all doing here?

For almost an hour they tracked west along the grim grey wall of Tsaramaso's south side. They saw dunes, tiny beaches and ripping black rock, endless lines of curling white breakers. It was late afternoon, and they were headed into the glare of the sinking sun.

Gianni inspected the forbidding sight with a frown, fingering the shark-tooth at his throat. This was obviously not what he had expected.

'Stan. This is indeed a remarkable island. It is not like the other islands, not at all … I have read of Tsaramaso in the books, I have spoken with the yachtsmen, but still … '

'Nowhere can we land here,' shouted Fabien, waving at the atoll, with Bernard at his side. Timu had the wheel. 'At the backside though, you will see, *non* Stan?'

Gianni took his skipper and Bernard back into the wheelhouse to confer, and shortly afterwards *La Belone* angled southwest, away from the atoll, steering until it was almost out of sight before turning north.

Stan watched with interest, wondering why he hadn't been included in the conference. Through binoculars, and only because he knew exactly where to look, he could just make out the cluster of buildings which had once been the centre of his world for the best part of a year. There too was the blue and yellow flag of Papa, tiny atop the white flagstaff. This was the landing place, where they should really check in and show their papers, and *La Belone* was avoiding it, sneaking by well offshore. He made his way astern.

'Gianni, we've just passed the settlement. We should anchor there and introduce ourselves.'

'Ah yes', agreed the Italian urbanely. He was smoking a havana, tanned stomach jutting comfortably from an open silk shirt of ice blue. 'Certainly we will do as you say. Of course. But it is late.' He smiled broadly. 'We will not trouble them now. I have been advised by experienced travellers at the Tarataka yacht club. You, Stan, will of course know the Passe Fregat. We will anchor there for the night, and tomorrow … ah, forgive me, Stan … ' the cigar waved vaguely as he drew a flat leather pack from a breast pocket and offered it.

The Director of the old days, a meticulous scientist-bureaucrat, would have fretted away at this blatant disregard for procedures, hailing them repeatedly on the radio and eventually despatching a boat at the first opportunity. But the old days were long-gone now, and there had been no Director for years. Now, presumably, members of Roland's family had responsibility for visitors, if any, under his direction.

At a point well past the settlement Fabien brought them in

again. The three Blacksters sat on deck, gazing in silence at the low, grey shelf of rock, its grey-green crown of scrub straggling off into the distance, the rollers rearing up blue-green and pounding white at its base.

Liza had calmed down. She gave him a hug. 'Well Stan. After all this time. Must be strange for you. I never really believed I would see it. Sometimes I even wondered if this place really existed, the way you wouldn't talk about it. If it hadn't been for the Prof ... OK, things didn't work out, thanks to that creep Easterhouse, but that's all history now. It can't have been that bad, can it? Now here you are.' She was staring uncertainly at the silent atoll.

Now here he was. He'd buried the memories for so long now that it wasn't easy to bring them back. Objectively, he felt she was right. It couldn't have been that bad. She looked uncharacteristically grave, with her hair up, shades on, big straw hat, her face in shadow. Now he thought about it, to Liza the atoll was nothing more than a series of images glimpsed years ago, now faded and distorted in the memory. He'd never told her much about it. She'd seen some of the Prof's photos, and possibly some of Julius's, although Julius had never been a great one for photos unless they involved his research: he had an exhaustive collection of shark pictures naturally, all taken on dry land but for a few of the bigger specimens which could only be measured approximately in the water alongside the boat. Julius had books filled with little sharks, medium-sized sharks, shark pups, shark embryos, sharks sliced open, shark organs, shark teeth, shark jaws, shark stomach contents. Stan had no photos. He'd lost them, probably left them all on Marga, or even Tsaramaso itself, all those years ago, during his hasty and unscheduled retreat. Not that the Barracuda believed this.

A Gazza squeal from the stern, abruptly choked off, was followed by an excited outburst from Gina and some Linois murmuring.

'I did warn you it wasn't much to look at, not from the sea. It's not like other places.' He could see what was going through her mind now: is this it? Is this what all the fuss was about? Big Deal. And, maybe, why didn't we stay at Prodigalson, where we were having such a ball? Well if they had, they'd be radioing for a new skipper by now. In its way Prodigalson was just another Fiantsifer, being exploited for profit, only nowadays the steamroller was tourism.

La Belone ploughed onwards, escorted now by a squadron of spinner dolphins. Gram and Gina were hanging over the side, shrieking to one another, exulting over the racing, twisting torpedo-shapes in the glassy green water below them. Once again Gianni was kept busy with his video while Liza, trying to position herself to capture both dolphins and teenagers, tripped over the skulking Gazza and almost went over the side in pursuit of the camera.

'I'll slotten that bloody pig!' She had the camera though. 'Sorry Gina, but he does like getting in the way doesn't he? He's a little scallywag, that one.'

In time the dolphins left, but they could still be seen in the distance, leaping and spinning, twirling in the air, crashing back in depth-charge detonations of white water.

Ahead of them emerged a long line of dark trees, a familiar stand of casuarinas used many times in the past as a landmark by expeditions from the research station. Here the sea had long ago broken through the atoll's rim to create the largest of the four channels through which the hidden, twenty-mile long lagoon filled and emptied twice daily. The sea continued its assault as they watched, pounding into the ancient grey limestone. In bygone eras the atoll had been submerged, not just once as Gram thought, but several times, always to rise again as the waters sank. But Gram was right - one day the waves would reclaim it.

Passe Fregat slowly appeared, flooding Stan's head with images from the past, of plunging boats and stuttering engines, of buckets of fish guts, of sharks thrashing about on slippery decks, shark blood and innards, notebook columns of figures stamped with bloody fingerprints, of black faces watching impassively, of the expressionless white face of Julius Easterhouse as he wielded the gutting knife, of heaving seas all around. Gianni and his absent friend Roberto had planned this visit to take advantage of the big spring tides around the full moon in a few days time, when the currents would be at their most powerful and, they hoped, flying with the fishes in the surging current of the channel would be at its most spectacular.

Fabien, using his screen profile of the seabed, directed the crew to settle *La Belone* at anchor off the entrance to Passe Fregat, out of the main current. It was low water, and they were on the sheltered side of the atoll, out of the wind and out of the swell.

Celebratory beers were distributed and a start was made on preparing food. Out on deck those not involved watched the seabirds streaming in. A young booby, quite possibly the same one that had joined them near Fiantsifer, had settled on the mast for the night.

Shark People: the urge to submerge

Through the channel, several hundred yards broad, could be glimpsed the other-worldly serenity of the lagoon, its flat, islet-dotted distances mirroring the steely blue, peach and pink of the evening sky. Fruit bats and small doves winged back and forth across the channel in search of fruit or roosting places for the night. Conversation was hushed, until the Barracuda surprised Gazza rooting in her bag of art materials and sent him off squealing with a hefty kick.

'Stan, that bloody pig!' she hissed. 'Why is it always me? He eats bloody anything.' She took out her pad and oil-sticks and, ignoring Gina's sulky stare, settled on the deck and began sketching the tranquil evening scene with sure, rapid strokes of colour.

Despite Stan's suggestion, no VHF radio call was put in to the settlement. This was no surprise. *Il Padrone* had made it amply clear he did not much care for the petty rules of other people. Well, Stan had to leave decision-making and responsibility to the Italian, at least for the time being, but he was surprised at how affronted he felt at this flouting of the old Station rules – rules he had considered silly at the time. It seemed disrespectful. On the other hand, if it meant they avoided a meeting with Roland, he was not about to go into a terminal decline. He took a swallow of cold beer from the green bottle, feeling it run down soothingly into his internals. Hard to see now why he had ever scoffed at the stuff. Delicious. Invigorating. He drank again, and soon felt bolder.

So. It had been ordained that he should return to this place to face down the past, meaning, above all, that malevolent old Boniface. He was accompanied by his divine partner in life and his brave and innocent young son, here to see this place from his past. Any initial sensation of unease, of trespass even – well, this was understandable, given the history, but it was unjustified. It was necessary for his personal development that he should be here. And when he sailed away, never to return, having straightened things out once and for all, life would be different. This was long overdue.

More cold beer travelled down as he craned his neck to bring Liza's drawing of the epic sunset into focus. In the west, towering altocumulus was a tumult of magenta and orange on a backdrop of silver-yellow and palest silver-blue - a dramatic and rather bloody scene, a setting fit for the valiant Boscanion's quest. The valiant Boscanion, who had disappeared beneath the waves at the end of the series, along with his faithful companion Anakim. Stan sat on with his thoughts, sitting on the wooden deck, arms wrapped around his knees,

315

oblivious to the human sounds around him.

Some time later, on his way below, Stan paused at the stern where the two Linois ate their fish and rice closely attended by Gazza. No matter how choice and plentiful the food prepared in *La Belone's* galley might be, he knew that Linois could go for only a couple of days without fish and rice before becoming tetchy and uncooperative.

'Bernard. No sign of the other vessel, here or at the settlement. Maybe they decided to go somewhere else.' Bernard said nothing. 'Maybe they never were coming here, maybe they told your friend Bib that just to cover their tracks. What do you think?'

Bernard looked up and grunted, white clots of rice rimming his mouth as a messy white bolus paused on his tongue. Stan followed his gaze to the swinging masthead, an inflexible, man-made thing in the starry night. The booby had gone. With one of his shrugs, Bernard pushed away the pig with his foot and returned to his meal.

'Well, I cannot say.'

Stan tried again. 'A boat like that wouldn't check in at the settlement anyway, would they? They'd hide.' Like us, but he didn't say it.

Another shrug. 'It is the same thing. If they come here, Lookdown will know.' Beside him his cousin Timucu, who had never before been to the atoll, nodded his grave agreement.

'Will he know we're here then?'

The two Linois exchanged an amused glance. Bernard shovelled rice. 'Roland? Sure he will know. You think he will not know, this guy? You cannot hide from this guy. Everything that happen here, this guy he know.'

'Hmm. Maybe the skipper should call him in the morning, on the VHF. Will the settlement still have a radio, do you think?'

'Roland, *non*. His brother, his cousin, perhaps. Roland does not understand these things. He is too old, this guy.'

16. Roland

Late next morning Bernard took them ashore in the zodiac at a small beach of coarse sand to one side of the broad channel of Passe Fregat. A deep-cut set of tractor tracks had been left on the beach by a turtle. Gram and Gina went running up to find it, but Bernard pointed out a second set of tracks further along, leading back into the water: the turtle had departed. He showed them - or rather he showed Gram - how the heavy animal had used first one front flipper then the other to drag itself up and down the beach, leaving a pattern of alternating marks characteristic of hawksbill turtle. The larger green turtles used both flippers at once to lift their greater bulk, leaving the imprints more or less opposite one another. Only female turtles ever came ashore, for egg-laying, but it was possible to see the even bigger males underwater, so Gram should keep his eyes open when he was out there - look for the longer tail, which contained the male sex organ. Gina found this amusing.

'Will we see baby turtles?' she asked. 'Like, real little ones?' She had spent time in America - *liddle, turdles* - and in the excitement had forgotten she was displeased because Stan had insisted she left Gazza on the catamaran. Old habits were reasserting themselves, rather surprisingly, and he didn't want to be responsible for introducing pig parasites to this uninhabited part of the atoll. Or any other part, for that matter. The Prof would be impressed.

Bernard did not answer, but Gina persisted. 'Well, Bernard. Will we or won't we?' The American Ber*nard*.

Bernard was not accustomed to direct questioning from womenfolk. 'Well,' he responded eventually, 'I cannot say.'

Stan took Liza to the edge of the near-impenetrable scrub, dry and tangled stuff somehow gripping grey rock which had been pitted and fluted over the ages into fanciful and aggressive formations wherever it broke through the thin soil. A harsh environment. He knew what she was thinking: on the tropical island paradise register, Prodigalson was up there in lights at the top, Tsaramaso off the scale at the bottom. She might invoke the Trades Descriptions Act at some later time, but they'd only just arrived. She would learn to see that there were plenty of places on the planet like Prodigalson, but there was nowhere else remotely like Tsaramaso. The vast enclosed lagoon was the atoll's great glorious heart, but even there you had to be vigilant.

Unexpected currents or a rapidly falling tide might leave you stranded, miles from cover, at the mercy of the blinding sun. And if you'd neglected to take extra water you were in big trouble. Your zodiac could hit a submerged rock outcrop at speed and rip open the belly even if it was reinforced. The outboard could fail while you were in one of the channels on an outgoing tide, and before you had the chance to repair or replace it - always assuming you were carrying a spare - you might be miles out at sea. And if you'd neglected to take a radio, or extra water ... all these things had happened in the old days, and more.

The atoll's saw-edged fossilised coral rock did not encourage sitting down, but he found a near-prostrate tree trunk for the two of them in the shade of the scrub. The others were wandering around but Stan knew they couldn't go far. Much of the atoll's scrub was toothed and clawed, and in this area there were no trails, or at least none that had been revealed by Roland. This had been one of the many frustrations in the days of the research programme - nothing had been written down. Local knowledge was stored only in the heads of the Linois guides, and was susceptible to individual interpretation. One guide - say the doomed Sleeper, Alain - might tell you that a two hour march on such and such a trail would bring you to a certain navigable creek, then another - Bernard, say - would flatly contradict this. Usually some ulterior motive came into play, the desire to visit a favourite fishing spot, avoidance of a tricky or little-known area (or, he had suspected once or twice, a place with bad associations of some sort), simple laziness or one-upmanship, or the frantic compulsion to get back to the settlement because of woman trouble, real or imagined. It had been a cherished dream of the Director's to get all this knowledge recorded and mapped, but it was obvious that Roland would never allow this to be completed. Roland himself had remained loftily above all the jostling and rivalry of the subordinate Linois, without appearing to discourage it. In his narrow brown skull resided all the local knowledge, passed down to him by earlier generations of Bonifaces, to be hoarded and paid out piecemeal to the favoured few. This was totally exasperating for the researchers, and especially the Director, who had to supervise the planning of the expeditions, but more importantly it meant that, whoever might nominally be in charge out in the bush, you offended the guide at your peril. It also meant that at least one Linois was always at your shoulder, watching.

Out in front of them now the sea poured inexorably through Passe Fregat into the lagoon as the current picked up, surging around outcrops on the shoreline, creeping visibly up their little beach. In mid-channel, where wind opposed tide, there was increasing turbulence. As he watched the lagoon breathing in its long, colossal breath of life, Stan passed his arm around Liza's waist and pulled her gently to him. The little beach was now heavily disfigured by their activities, and the turtle tracks had been obliterated.

'You were right about your friend Bernard. He's not too keen on women is he?'

'You mean our little *signorina*? He's not alone there. Anyway, it's not that he doesn't like them, he just thinks they should know their place, like most Linois men.'

'Yeah. You're going to say it's a cultural thing.'

'It is. Why, he's been OK with you hasn't he?' Something was nipping his right buttock, and he shifted his position.

'In a polite kind of way. I can't say I'd swap places with his wife. And I've seen more convincing smiles on the adverts. Did you two ever get really friendly Stan? I mean real friends, like back home?'

'Ah!' He jumped up, scratching frantically. Needles of pain shot down his leg. A curiously-shaped, brown, many-legged something slipped sideways into an eroded knothole on the tree trunk he'd just vacated. 'Bastard!'

'There's a big red lump.' Liza had pulled up his shorts. 'I'd say you've been bitten.'

'Bastard!'

'Yeah. The only place you can sit down and it bites you. Tourists will love it.'

'It's going off.' It was just a tingling now. In fact it was already beginning to itch. Bugger. A bite though, or a nip, not a sting. No venom. 'Wasn't a centipede anyway, or a scorpion.' Small stroppy crab? Large spider? Chances were he'd just been assaulted by a creature unknown to science.

She put a strong arm around him. 'My little adventurer. I know, let's stand.'

Fabien and Timucu had stayed aboard *La Belone* to fill the dive bottles with compressed air and prepare the gear. They were to time a drift-dive in the channel late enough to catch the strong current which would make them fly but not so late as to risk being caught when the tide turned, which would sweep them out into the open sea. Stan was apprehensive. His ears were slowly responding to treatment with aureomycin from Aurora's medicine cabinet, which was encouraging, but by this stage he had begun to feel uncomfortable with his fellow divers.

Earlier that morning they had made their first dive at Tsaramaso, near the catamaran, off the mouth of Passe Fregat, to see the big fish gathering to enter the channel with the tide. They had not been disappointed. All around them thousands of fish ranged over the coral steps like stars in the tropical night sky: a herd of big bumphead parrotfish, grazing on live coral like drab green sheep with white parrot-beaks; swarms of predatory trevallies flashing silver in their hundreds, twisting and turning as one; fleets of snappers and emperors; glittering clouds of blue and yellow fusiliers fading into the blue distances; a host of unicornfish, each with the face of a horse and a single rigid spine sprouting from its forehead. There were stingrays, at least three green turtles, and spinner dolphins which made plenty of eerie noise but kept their distance. Visibility had been reasonable, surge had not been a problem, and the dive had been straightforward. Again they had seen only one shark, and that just the swinging, black-edged tail of a grey reef vanishing into the haze. Gianni and Fabien had immediately set off after it but soon gave up.

The Frenchman had a bad habit of aggravating resting fish such as rays and morays as shark-substitute entertainment for his employer. He used his dive-knife to prise loose coral and shells as mementos for *Signora* Conti, was forever picking reef animals up to fool around with, and generally did all the things responsible divers weren't supposed to do. There had been some frank exchanges. Both Gianni and Fabien were clearly, as they claimed, experienced divers, which allowed them to routinely by-pass the standard safety checks so recently hammered home to Stan and Gram by Rainer on Marga. In short, they were reckless, and Stan decided not to let Gram go down without him any more. In the channel particularly, with a 5 or 6 knot current ripping along, things could get quickly out of hand. It was better not to trouble Liza with this. She'd only fret.

A group of tiny birds moved past them on the edge of the scrub, green and white and yellow, eyes ringed with white, calling softly, like restless items of exquisite jewellery amidst the grey and grey-green drabness.

Liza had become absorbed in watching the sea flood into the lagoon – a mesmerising sight. 'There's a strange feeling here,' she said at last. Her ebullience had gone. She sounded and looked uncertain.

'What do you mean, Barra?' He saw what she saw. What she was feeling, he felt too.

She shook her head slowly. 'I don't know. Nothing.'

Gram was calling them.

They had found a brown and olive bird with the size and demeanour of a small, scrawny chicken. Long in leg and bill, it was pecking vigorously at a fragment of chocolate biscuit which lay on the ground next to its wrapper, oblivious to its audience. How could Stan have forgotten about these little chaps? Here was a Tsaramaso flightless rail.

'Is that neat!' Gram squatted abruptly, sending the bird scurrying off, but he stayed where he was and it soon returned with halting, jerky movements to resume its meal. 'Just like in the book,' he breathed.

Liza leaned forward with her camera. 'Oh look Stan, look at his smart little white throat. Isn't he lovely? Come on little bird, look at the camera.'

Gianni's camcorder was aboard *La Belone* being recharged.

'It's a bird, and it can't fly?' Gina was sceptical. *Burrd*.

Gram explained. 'Out here, there's no need, Gina. He can run, he can climb, he can find his food. He's got nothing to worry about, no natural enemies here. He's called *tamboril* in Creole - Bernard's told me about him. There were flightless birds on lots of islands, not just here. You've heard of the dodo, Gina, that was on Mauritius, and there was another famous one, the solitaire, on another Indian Ocean island, Reunion I think, but there were loads more, in the Pacific too, all over. Only thing was, they couldn't handle it when we turned up, with all our dogs and cats and rats and pigs and stuff. Then they needed to fly. Bernard says the cats here are the worst, for a little guy like this.'

'Pigs are OK though,' insisted Gina, who had heard of the dodo. 'See how they like chocolate?'

A weird shrieking issued abruptly from deep in the scrub. Instantly the *tamboril* became alert, cocking its narrow head to listen. It then gave vent to a shrieking volley of its own and galloped off into its scrubby underworld.

Gram was quite taken with the flightless rail. 'Neat little bird!' he beamed. 'A star, isn't he mum? *Tamboril*. Did you see the way he ran off, those great big feet? He looked pretty bossy too, nobody here to push him around. Did you get your photos? He was so cool, didn't seem bothered by us at all, did he? That's the problem though, that's why these things get wiped out so easily.'

'He was close enough, yeah, but he seemed to keep himself in the shade all the time somehow.' She was examining the image on the back of her camera. 'Hmmm.' She showed it to Gram. 'Could be better, eh?'

'You'll get another chance,' said Stan.

'The only place on Earth,' muttered Gram. He bent down to scoop up the chocolate wrapper.

Gianni had lost interest some time earlier. 'And now,' he announced, consulting his rolex, 'now it is time for us to return to *La Belone*. And then we must fasten our safety belts for our adventure in Passe Fregat. Stan, do you think we will finally see some sharks this time, some real sharks?'

Far better to let Gianni go off and stay here with Gram and Liza. Stan restricted himself to a tight but optimistic grimace.

Half an hour later they had to hang on tight as Bernard bounced the zodiac through the chop to the shallow shelf at the eastern side of the entrance to Passe Fregat. Gianni and Fabien slid over the side immediately, followed more deliberately by Stan and Gram, who went through their safety checks together, knees on the sandy bottom, out of the current's grip. Even here though they could feel it tugging.

'We pick you up,' Bernard waved towards the lagoon, 'two kilometres.'

Timucu stood beside him, nodding and smiling, a picture of easy confidence, this newcomer to the atoll. Linois estimates of time, distance and dimension were generally little more than wild guesses, but Stan knew that Bernard was totally reliable and would be there to pick them up. The plan was to move out into the incoming current and be carried into the lagoon by it – flying with the fishes – then be retrieved by the zodiac.

Stan made the OK sign, but only Gram responded.

To begin with everything went all right. They half-crawled, half-swam out into the channel, finding it increasingly difficult to maintain position as the current tightened its grip, then they pushed off, out over a wall of corals which slid away below them into blue-green murk, out and down through teeming fish. Here they felt with a shock the immense power of the ocean. Stan's ears were an agony, but for once this was the least of his worries.

They were rushing - yes, flying - over a bare, rubble-strewn channel bed scoured clean by a million tides. Huge stingrays hugged the bottom, long stinging tails angled upwards. Turtle shapes flashed by. Very quickly visibility was down to a few feet, then less.

Stan was being whirled helplessly along in a thick green soup. Something hit him on the shoulder - a fin, an arm, a flipper? - in an instant of wild terror. He was out of control. Where was Gram? A dark shape loomed, bigger than a man, to be whipped away again almost before panic registered. He couldn't steer, and if he hit a rock at this speed ... he was blind, everything was green. This was crazy, they were all crazy. He tried to manoeuvre himself, desperately clumsy, towards the grainy yellowish light which must be the surface, fighting down the dangerous impulse to get up there as fast as he could, praying that the light really was increasing, slowly slowly, must control his breathing ...

Suddenly he burst out into brilliant sunshine and the slapping of waves. Snatches of distant birdsong. The shore's scrubline was visible only intermittently through the mid-channel chop and he was still being whirled along like a leaf, but he could see. He tore out his mouthpiece, coughing up salt water. A new sound grew, the whining roar of an outboard, then the dazzling orange inflatable was with him and he was grabbing desperately at the ropes.

Over the following twenty long minutes Timucu and Bernard retrieved Gianni and Fabien, more than a hundred yards apart and obviously shaken. But not Gram. No one had seen him after the first, dizzying moments when the current had grabbed them and the visibility had collapsed. Bernard took the zodiac in a long arc across the breadth of the channel's wide lagoon end, bumping and banging through the waves. They could see nothing.

Stan stood, balancing with difficulty, still trembling and weak, to scan what he could of the lagoon: an inland sea stretched away into the glare and heat-haze, dotted with black islets; miles away to the south a vague, grey-green shoreline shimmered. Thank Christ in Heaven Liza wasn't here. She'd be in a mindless frenzy, chewing up the boat. Bernard was unflappable, and had the near-supernatural sight of most Linois; and Bernard, not Stan, was the one with the local knowledge, given to him by Roland. He must stay calm and look to Bernard. This was precisely why Bernard was here.

As though accepting this, Bernard pointed. 'There, Passe Fregat it go into two channel. One it go this way' - he indicated the distant southerly shoreline - 'one it go this way' - the endless watery expanse to the east. 'In one hour the current, it will go outside. Perhaps less than one hour.'

In an hour it would be dark too, and it would get dark quickly, as it always did out here, but nobody said so. A tremendous *whoosh!* startled them all as a huge black frigatebird shot low overhead in pursuit of a desperately gurgling booby, then the sounds of wind and wave pressed in again.

Gianni patted Stan's leg. 'Stan. Gram has plenty of air. He is a good boy, a strong boy. He will not do anything foolish. He will find the shallow water. He will be safe.'

Stan grimaced, grateful for any encouragement. It was no use looking out for a flare or a balloon, or listening for a whistle - they didn't carry them, another stupidity. Timucu stood upright at the bow, gripping a short rope for balance, searching the glittering vastness for a tiny, waving figure.

They were at the point at which Passe Fregat split into two arms, Bernard maintaining the dinghy's position over the shallow area between, over six feet of perfectly clear water in which reef fishes swarmed among sculpted coral heads. Lines of white boobies swept by, heading for the mangrove breeding colonies; nearer the shore, black-tipped shark fins cruised.

'Gram!' bellowed Stan through cupped hands. 'Gram!'

As the sun crept down towards the western horizon, colours steadily intensified. The lagoon's dreamy turquoise was everywhere, hypnotic. Overhead, in a deepening blue sky, the bellies of slow-moving white clouds were flushed with turqoise.

'Gram!'

Bernard steered them along the larger, southern-flowing arm of the channel, standing as he drove, searching, the clear-cut deep blue of the channel becoming less defined as it emptied itself into the lagoon's shallows. Still they were a long way from the dark line of silent mangroves, but the current's force had dissipated. Gram would not be here. Bernard brought the orange zodiac around. They headed back the way they had come, the sun now low and glaring. The two Linois cousins were muttering to one another: the tide had turned.

Stan pictured his son, out in the open ocean, lost in massive, rolling seas, a thousand feet of nothing beneath his feebly waving fins, terrified, abandoned, calling for his father ... What if Liza had seen him from *La Belone*, watched her son being swept by and out to sea? Liza would dive in after him ... He heard Bernard's murmur, something about *canot* - a small boat.

'Timu, he see something,' repeated Bernard, easing off the throttle and bringing them round to face east, where the skies were already dark. 'Timu he see small boat, coming.'

Stan stood, teetering, straining his eyes. At first he could see nothing, but then he picked up the faint whine of an engine. There - a small, trembling white speck, a bow-wave, and poised above it, scarcely discernible, a darker spot. Was it a boat? He cursed his hazy vision. Bernard brought them around again and accelerated back down the deep channel, sending Stan heavily into the Italian's lap.

'A boat!' shouted Fabien, over the engine roar. 'It will help us search for Gram. We will find him, Stan.'

Bernard was concentrating on the approaching boat as he drove. 'Is Roland,' he finally announced calmly, with a glance at Stan. 'Is Roland boat.'

The two boats came together at the channel fork, a vivid orange zodiac full of tourists and diving gear, and a battered fifteen-foot fibreglass *canot* driven by Roland, with a second Linois standing at the up-tilted bow, gripping a rope for balance, as it smashed and bounced its way through the waves. And, seated in the middle, was Gram. Gram waved.

Thank Christ and all the little fishes!

'I'm OK!' he shouted. 'It's OK! I got carried away by the current. They found me, miles away over there. It's OK.'

They helped him climb across, and Stan hugged him. 'Gram! Bloody hell! Are you sure you're all right? Are you sure?' Never, never would he let this happen again. Over his son's shoulder he at last met the eyes of Roland, the eyes that haunted his nights, and how could he ever have predicted the circumstances?

Roland was old. Much older than he remembered. And much, much smaller. He'd dwindled somehow. Roland was a child-sized carving in dark, fretted wood. The impassive face had not changed, nor the round, unblinking eyes which were too close together and too pale for that dark face. Something malevolent lived in there, had always lived there. Left hand resting on the tiller, Roland returned Stan's gaze without expression.

'Roland.' There was no sign of recognition. 'It is good to see you.'

Roland said nothing.

'I must thank you for finding my son.'

Gram tapped him. 'Dad. I don't think they understand English.

I tried.'

Roland's English had always been rudimentary, and must have fallen into disuse. Stan recognized the other man now, one of Roland's many brothers and cousins. Sesil, was it? A surly young man back then, grey-haired now, still squat and immensely muscular. Like Roland, he wore only a loin cloth, with some sort of necklace.

'Sesil?'

No response, beyond a blank, slightly hostile stare.

'Bernard ... '

Bernard took over, and a four-way exchange in Creole sprang up.

Eventually Gianni intervened. 'Please, Bernard, tell Roland that I too am very grateful to him for finding our missing young man. And my apologies ... our radio, we have a battery problem. We have not been able to contact the settlement.'

Bernard gave the Italian a long look, then conferred with Roland. He was clearly aware of Fabien's close attention: Creole was descended from French, and the Frenchman was listening intently.

Again Gianni interjected. 'Bernard, please ... you must ask your friends to come to *La Belone*. We must repay them for their assistance.'

Bernard conferred again: the word *wheeskey*, repeated several times, was easy enough to translate.

Roland's small boat trailed at the end of a rope, twenty feet astern of *La Belone*. In it, in the dusk, Bernard sat talking with Roland and Sesil, a litre bottle of J & B passing from hand to hand.

All Gianni's invitations to come aboard had been declined, and Liza's tearful gratitude had been accepted in silence. Stan wondered just what they were discussing out there in the gloom. Did Roland really not recognize him? Unlikely. Feeling furtive, he took his bottle of beer to the back of the catamaran and, crouching behind the dive gear, focused binoculars on them. The scotch had brought animation to Roland's leathery old face, but not much. Even now, with his own kind, he was so damned, so damned ... self-contained, so unreliant. And so tiny. Like some wiry black primate from deep in the forest, a seeing version of his brother, the blind stick-man from the hills of Dragonet. He must have grown in Stan's mind over the years. A shiver passed through him. This man – this man who had just saved his son - was to him the malign essence of the atoll. This man was the atoll Badass.

How many generations of Bonifaces had lived out their lives here at Tsaramaso? Roland used to boast about it occasionally, when he was drunk. The ancient face was listening now, smoking a cigarette, attentive to Bernard who was gesticulating with the J & B bottle. Roland nodded. What the hell were they talking about? He thought he saw Bernard take something from the old man and tuck it away in his pocket, but it was darker now.

Finally Bernard stood and signalled, and Stan put down the glasses. Timucu pulled in the boat until it was close enough for Bernard to swing himself easily back aboard *La Belone*.

The blind stick-man. Stan suddenly remembered the plant, the plant from Madagascar, which he had neglected to dispose of. On a surge of emotion and alcohol he dashed in to get it.

The shiny pink plastic bag, with its fishing line and bits of leaf showing, looked pitiful.

'Roland. Your brother sent this for you from Marga.'

Roland nodded. He understood. Sesil reached up and took it from him without a word, stowing it carefully under a wooden plank seat amidst the fishing line, rope and other debris littering the deck. On the side of the *canot* was the badly faded painting of the black scything wings, forked tail and long, hooked bill of a frigatebird. Roland signalled curtly to Timucu, who cast them off.

The little fibreglass boat roared in a foaming half-circle, Sesil standing thick and black in the bows as before, then headed back into the lagoon, disappearing around a casuarina-topped jut of dark rock, its wake gleaming on for minutes afterwards.

Another tumultuous sunset had faded from the skies, and stars were appearing. Stan looked at his watch. The tide was still dropping as the lagoon exhaled water back out into the sea. 'Bernard. Will there still be enough water for them to get all the way back?'

Bernard nodded emphatically, eyes glistening. 'There is water, *oui*.'

Music started up, Poco's *Crazy Love*, one of Liza's. Voices were loud, especially Bernard's, in the drunken boastful mode Stan remembered well as a reliable precursor to some sort of trouble in the old days. These were the early stages of a Thank God We Got Away With It party. He'd seen a few of these in his time, but there'd never been the overwhelming, humbling sense of relief he felt now. He couldn't take his eyes off Gram, playing a noisy game with Gina which involved Gazza having to guess in which hand a chunk of coconut was concealed. After a while he decided to try to find out what Bernard and Roland had found to talk about.

'And how is your old friend Roland? I don't think he remembers me. Must be the beard.'

Bernard's face was sheened with sweat, his eyes were pink and glistening, but his expression became grim. 'Sure, he remember you, this guy.'

'Oh, good. Well, maybe I've said a few unkind things about him in the past, but just now he's my hero. We're very lucky they were out there, weren't we? What had they been up to, to be coming from that direction?'

There was nothing to take them so far east, as far as he could remember, so far from the settlement. This had been the route back from the scene of Stan's final field-trip on the atoll, with Julius and Alain and Roland himself. This was the remotest part of the atoll, a secret world of mangroves, muddy creeks, turtles and sharks, which he had earlier decided the shark-hungry Italian and his French sidekick must not be allowed to visit.

Someone changed the music and turned it up, something jaunty and French. Aurora brought them each another beer. 'I prepare the raw fish. Yellowfin tuna, the best. For Gram.' This was the most she had ever said to Stan all in one go.

'Is bad, what have happen,' murmured Bernard when she'd gone. 'This guy, he have power.' *Pow-air*. 'You must accept nothing from this guy. No *cadeau*. No gift.' *Geeft*.

'What are you saying, Bernard?'

'This guy, he give to your son his life. He give to you your son. He give to your wife his - her - son.'

Stan swallowed beer. True.

'And I'm forever grateful, Bernard. What should I have done, said no, take him back where you found him Roland, I don't want him?'

Bernard was muttering in Creole. Then. 'You give *Bwa Malgaz*.'

The bedraggled magic plant. 'That's right, but I was only delivering. And he got a bellyful of scotch from Gianni. We're even, sort of. What's the problem?'

More muttering, then the usual disclaimer: 'Well, I cannot say.'

Over their heads the vast night sky glittered with a million stars. The moon, nearing full, cold yellow with a milky halo, was just beginning its ascent over the dark and silent atoll.

Every so often a late booby would sweep in, flaring briefly white in the only man-made light to be found in a wilderness of black ocean. On the landward side of the gently rocking catamaran Gram and Gina played a powerful dive torch over a huge shoal of trevallies attracted to *La Belone* by the intermittent trickle of food scraps and human waste.

Soon they sat down to thin, purple-red slices of yellowfin, glistening with lime juice and soy sauce, alongside glasses of chilled verdicchio. Gram was teased about his adventure. He had a grazed arm to remind him of flying with the fishes. Liza wasn't saying much, which meant she was not pleased. If Gram had been lost, she would have ripped into Stan.

'And so,' announced Gianni presently, 'we really have had our first adventure at the famous atoll. We have all learned a lesson also, no?'

There was general murmuring and nodding. Stan hadn't quite admitted to being at fault, since he tended to blame Bernard, and expecting Bernard to offer anything contrite was futile.

But Gianni hadn't finished. 'At Tarataka yacht club, Fabien and I were told of the atoll's east channel. Here it is not so deep, the current not so strong. And the water, it will be more clear. Good visibility. You agree, our two veterans of the atoll?'

If there was sarcasm, it was exquisitely restrained. Stan cleared his throat. 'Well. Basically, yes. Passe Cabris. It's a lot smaller, safer. The moon is nearly full, so there'll be a strong current. Visibility ... Bernard?'

Bernard, at his accustomed place off to the side, spoke through a mouthful of rice. 'Well, I cannot say.'

'Very well,' continued the Italian, giving Bernard a long look. 'In the morning we move east to - how is it? - Passe Cabris.'

'More diving?' Liza looked thunderous. 'After what nearly happened? Tell me you're not serious, please.'

Gianni smiled indulgently. 'Ah yes. But Liza, we learn and we continue, no? For now, the tides are right for us, and we must dive. This is the purpose of our visit, you understand.' The gold chain with its single tiger tooth gleamed in the deck-light.

Liza turned her attention to Stan. 'Gram's not going diving again. Ever.'

Beside her, Gram looked uncomfortable.

'But no.' Gianni reached over to Gram and patted his arm. 'It is the best thing to go down again soon. This is well-known, is it not Stan? Otherwise ... perhaps Gram will not be able to dive again. He will have lost his nerve, you understand?'

Liza hadn't taken her burning gaze off Stan. Fabien was changing the music cassette. Bob Marley. *No Woman No Cry*. Again.

'Stan? Let me hear you say the right thing please.' Strong brown fingers were working at the base of a wine bottle, gripping it, turning it slowly, gripping again. 'Right now!'

Everyone was looking at him. It was a hot night. His mind was slipping. The tiny, shifting blur at its centre had expanded hugely. Everything else had gone. There was nothing left to grasp.

'I'll be OK.' Gram. He had a hand on his mother's arm, the one with the bottle. His voice was firm. 'I need it. I need to do it mum. Mr Conti's right. I have to go again soon.' His fingers were digging into her arm. The bottle was still. She turned to him. 'There's no need to worry, we'd never make the same mistake again. We just weren't careful enough today, that's all. We've all learned.'

Liza seemed half-hypnotized, then abruptly her body relaxed. She let go of the bottle, placed her hand over Gram's and squeezed. 'Everybody on this boat has gone crazy.' She wasn't shouting. She and Gram were looking into one another's eyes. 'Even me.'

'No mum. It's OK.'

'A tiring day,' smiled Gianni.

Stan came back. A spectacular explosion had somehow been averted. 'Liza. Passe Cabris is very different. It peters out after a few hundred yards, runs into shallows. We should have gone there first. It's like a fish-tank, absolutely no risk even if the vis is no good.'

She looked from son to husband, and now she was glaring, and the glare spoke. Stan tensed, but she turned back to Gram again. Which was unexpected, confusing even, not the normal bruising behavioural arc. What was she going to do? There would be something, some act of retribution. She blamed him fairly and squarely for the near miss, and she wasn't one to let things fester. Well, he could count on finding out in due course.

Conversation resumed. As Gianni poured more wine, the epitome of affability, a weird series of yodelling cries came from the dark casuarina stand. All was bathed in a silvery light as the brilliant disc of the moon stood high, now cold and white, clear of the Earth's atmospheric filter.

'Wow! Now that's real creepy. Sounds like red indians.' Gina sounded amused but looked unsettled. 'What is it?' She had Gazza on her lap, stroking the fuzzy pink head.

Fabien answered in a stage whisper. 'It is the spirits of all those who have died on the atoll. The ju-ju man has sent them to *La Belone*.'

The cries came again, a hair-raising sound. Gina was unhappy. She dropped the pig to the floor and stood up. 'Fab, stop it! What is it, really? It's louder now. Are they coming here?'

'*Fregats*,' said Bernard at length, addressing no-one in particular.

That was it. At night the frigatebirds, aloft all day, roosted in the casuarinas. A night-sound of the atoll.

'You see Gina,' persisted Fabien, 'the fregat. This is the bird of the ju-ju man, Bernard, *non?*'

A pause. 'Well, I cannot say.'

Gina scowled at the skipper. 'Well, it's creepy. I'm going in. Timu, you can look after Gazza now.'

Presently Gianni and Fabien began discussing the special excitements of night diving: 'Certainly we will do this,' declared the Italian. 'At night, the reef it is quite different. The lobster, the octopus, the reef fish which hide in the daytime, they come out. And the sharks - many of them feed at night. We must see some real sharks.'

Stan didn't have to look at Bernard to know what he was thinking. No Linois would go into the water at night. Or in daylight either, but it was at night that *demzel*, the tiger, the big shark with the unfussy eating habits, left the deeper offshore waters and came up over the outer reef, through the channels with the tide and into the lagoon to hunt turtles, stingrays, other sharks and anything else that crossed its path. It was clear now that this was what the Italian meant when he talked about real sharks. Gianni had been persistent in his probings about *Galeocerdo cuvier*, and of course Stan was an admirer himself. In the old days he'd twice managed to play a torch-beam along the wavering grey hide of a big tiger entering the lagoon. But the thought of being down there, near-blind in black silence with an overly-focused Italian, an excitable Frenchman and endless possibilities held little appeal just at the moment.

Sleep that night was elusive. The air was heavy, oppressive, and wherever he tried to send his mind the face of Roland reared up. Somehow this dried-up little twig of a man had again got the upper hand. Stan had accepted a *cadeau* from Roland - his own son. No, this was the wrong way to look at it. Roland had saved his son for him and into the bargain averted a bloody and almost certainly terminal collision with Liza. Like it or not, Roland was a hero. He'd got away with it, and it was unfortunate he had Roland to thank, but thank all the powers he'd got away with it, and Gram was safe.

Some time later he was able to usher in a procession of powder-blue surgeonfish, counting them as they finned placidly by, and the sounds of the atoll night receded.

17. Mangrove Jacks

La Belone travelled slowly eastwards along the atoll's barren north coast. As before, a long, low scrub-line of unvarying grey-green stretched before and behind them; as before, seabirds passed back and forth, dolphins and flying fish sprang from the blue rollers. No one remarked on it any more. It seemed that despite all the alcohol none of them had slept well, apart from the two Linois, and conversation was subdued.

Timucu spotted a distant vessel ahead which moved off, away from the atoll, heading east. Stan found it with the binoculars: a small fishing boat with a single white mast, a large yellow wheelhouse festooned with green, pink and orange fishing buoys, and a dark blue or black hull. Two black crewmen could be made out. He passed the binoculars to Bernard.

'*Malgaches*,' he confirmed. 'Two only. Also, you can see, they have no *canot*, no small boat.' He grimaced, still watching. 'They have AK 47s.'

The vessel passed from sight behind the atoll rim.

Off the mouth of Passe Cabris they found an anchorage. As before, casuarina stands stood tall and dark on either side of the channel, which opened onto the shining, islet-dotted expanse of the lagoon. A series of shallow bays at the margins of the channel held small beaches of white sand.

Their two dives, first on the outer reef close to the catamaran, then in the strong channel current, were uneventful. That is to say, there were no unpleasant surprises, both Stan and Gram recovered their equanimity, and even Liza, although looking uncharacteristically edgy, seemed to relax a little. A big male green turtle shadowed Gram for a while before melting back into the shadows, there were several large and attentive barracuda, and the mass of fishes seething around the stupendous walls and fields of corals included four or five solemn, Kato-sized potato groupers queuing to be cleaned by tiny bluestreak cleaner wrasse. An ancient-looking but quite shy giant grouper, even bigger than the turtle, kept an eye on them from a distance. Visibility was reasonable, and the four of them duly flew along Passe Cabris, Stan staying tight on the shoulder of his son. Afterwards Gram was jubilant, partly from relief. Even Gianni was impressed and Fabien wanted to repeat the performance immediately. Again though the only shark was a grey reef, passing close to inspect them with a round black eye before merging back into the blue haze.

At low tide Bernard took the zodiac into the channel, easing carefully through awkward breakers on the reef at the entrance, and they were able to wade about in the lagoon shallows for almost an hour - long enough in the burning heat. In the crystalline waters they could watch corals and fish, fat sea cucumbers as long as a forearm, young turtles foraging and shallow-water morays wriggling from pool to pool in search of prey, while around them stalked fishing egrets of dazzling white or dark slatey grey. And, for as far as they could see, shark fins patrolled the shallows, dozens and dozens of them in water less than knee deep.

Gianni wanted to know more about the sharks, and Stan was able to oblige: those showing a single tall, black-tipped dorsal, with a sandy-coloured body, creamy-white flank stripe and white underside, generally of five feet or less in length, were *Carcarhinus melanopterus*, the blacktip reef shark, easily the commonest shark species here, a hunter of small fishes and a species more likely than others to wind up in a seaside aquarium for tourists to gawp at. In Tsaramaso lagoon at high tide there were thousands. Less numerous, but still common, were lemon sharks, *Negaprion acutidens*, which showed two large, unmarked dorsals and large, wing-like pectoral fins. Several lemons approached quite closely, an overall brown-grey, paler beneath, bottom-feeders looking for reef fishes and smaller rays. This shallow-water species occasionally lived up to its name in the mangrove creeks, where the hide could be a striking yellow. These were bigger than the blacktips. One around seven feet long cruised to within a couple of yards of the Italian's bronzed legs, close enough for them to see the tiny eye, count the five gill slits, see the pink bite marks made by larger jaws across its head. Gianni became animated, recognizing clearly the bite of a big tiger. The fact that females have developed measurably thicker hides because biting by males is a regular feature of shark mating behaviour did not impress him. No, this was a tiger Stan. His eager expression relaxed when the inquisitive lemon shark at last identified him as something to avoid and surged dramatically away. Gianni fingered the tooth trophy at his neck.

'Here around us are many sharks, as you promised, *si*.' He waved at the slowly cruising fins. 'The black-tip, the lemon. But they are quite harmless, no?' White teeth flashed beneath his shades, in the shadow of a sleek straw hat.

They were near the zodiac, which Bernard had secured with a small anchor. Bernard had stayed aboard, to watch and smoke, despite the skipper's ban on lighted cigarettes near the zodiac's wafer-thin inflatable tubes.

Gianni shouted across: 'Bernard! Please, Fabien has said before, no smoking.'

Without a word or change of expression, Bernard flipped the cigarette into the current.

'*Grazi*. And Bernard, tell me, how many shark attacks have there been here in Papa?'

'Well,' offered Bernard grudgingly, 'I cannot say. But you must give to the shark your respect. All Papalinois know this.'

'There are no recorded shark attacks in Papa, Gianni,' added Stan. 'Not one.'

The Italian shook his head with a smile. 'This is what they say, yes, I am aware of this, but it is not true. They do not wish to damage tourism. There have been attacks here, you must take my word for this.'

Stan pointed to another sizeable lemon shark moving past them to the deeper waters of the channel. 'I have no trouble believing you, Gianni. The locals aren't great ones for reporting and recording, you know? A shark takes someone out here one night, a tiger ... it must have happened. Notice how the Linois stay out of the water. A lot of them can't even swim. And, if you see a big shark, with only one big dorsal, a long upper-tail and a square snout, it might be better to get out and use your camcorder from the deck.'

'Ah yes. I know. And, it will have the dark marks on the side also, for this one is the tiger shark. A real shark, this one, but I am not afraid. We must find a tiger shark Stan, and I think we will not see him in the daytime.'

When they got back aboard the catamaran, Fabien and Timucu were fishing. Catching fish here, using a small piece of tuna from the freezer as bait, was easy. The two already had a pile of small groupers, emperors and a couple of trevallies, more than they needed, and Timu wound in his line, but the Frenchman, drunk again, carried on fishing noisily for fun while Gianni pointed the camcorder. Fabien hit something bigger.

After ten minutes of excited hauling, a pale, flickering shape could be seen, then one of the big potato groupers, roughly the size of the gawping Gina, was dragged aboard. Its belly was grotesquely distended by the swim bladder, inflated by the sudden pressure change. Fabien whooped, dancing around the great fish as it flapped sluggishly on the deck.

Bernard squatted, looking into the great cod-head, at its bristle-toothed jaws opening and closing. 'This one is not good. *Tukula*. Is too big. Good for saltfish only, for old men.'

Gianni filmed the *tukula* being manhandled back over the side and into the water with a heavy splash, then he tracked it floating away, carried by the current, swollen belly aloft, unable to right itself, unable to submerge. As well as the customary anti-pirate shotgun, Fabien had a .22 rifle on board and decided on some target practice, but the grouper was out at sea long before he got organized.

'Fabien, for Christ's sake, you're going to shoot one of us if you're not careful, you drunken cretin. Give me that bloody thing - '

As Stan tried to wrestle the rifle away from the Frenchman, Gianni stepped in.

'Stop this! You two, you are like children! I have not made this great journey, with all of this expense, to waste my time like this.'

Stan and Fabien glared at one another.

'This is a serious expedition. Fabien, you will stow the rifle. It is for serious matters.'

The Frenchman reluctantly moved to obey.

'And Fabien. From now on, there will be no drinking before lunch.'

Stocks were getting low.

After a somewhat taciturn lunch they all retired for a doze. Liza hadn't even appeared at the table, and lay on the bed facing the wall.

'Everything all right Barra?'

No reply.

'Not hungry?'

Nothing.

'Got a munk on then?'

'Are you going diving?'

'No, we're going for a little cruise into the lagoon. It's fantastic at this end, you should come Barra. This is what the atoll's all about, makes Prodigalson look like the Isle of Wight.'

A grunt.

'Look, this diving thing, it's all right, honestly.'

'Yeah.' *La Belone* lifted gently on a swell and sunlight glimmered on the smooth brown muscles of her shoulder.

At high tide they went back into the lagoon in the inflatable, cruising quietly beneath the booby colonies with engine set to shallow drive, staring up at goggle-eyed birds staring down, able at this range to admire pink and blue faces and brilliant crimson paddle-feet wrapped securely around mangrove branches mottled and splashed white with guano. With each French or Italian shout or gesticulation birds struggled into the air and flapped heavily away. Small white feathers drifted slowly in their wake.

Gianni aimed the camcorder up above, where frigatebirds hung almost motionless. 'The birds, they put on a show for us,' he muttered. 'Bravo!'

Gina clapped. 'Bravo!'

'They're waiting up there to steal nesting material,' said Stan.

'Why?' asked Gina. 'There's plenty of sticks around. The whole place is sticks. Sticks and rocks.'

'They can't land in the water themselves, or even walk around. All they can do is fly.'

At that moment a frigate swooped and snatched a billful of twigs from an unguarded nest, and a booby egg tumbled into the water. The frigate, losing its grip on all the twigs but one, flapped away with extravagantly deep wingbeats.

They clambered with some difficulty up onto one of the small, heavily undercut coral limestone islets, where fabulous white tropicbirds crouched in the scrub shade, protecting eggs and chicks, rearing up and bellowing defiance when the camcorder came too close. Gina wanted two of the foot-long, red central tail-feathers, one for herself and one for her mother. After a bit of hunting around Gram was able to find a couple of cast-offs in the grass near one of the nests before Fabien tried taking them from live birds. Stan had to stop him tormenting a shrieking bird with a stick for the camcorder. These birds would stand their ground and fight, which was why there were none left on most of the islands.

Well, he'd urged the Barracuda to come along, and now he was damned glad she hadn't. She was in a weird state, for her, sort of turned inwards. In the past such interludes had been rare, brief and the prelude to uproar. We shouldn't be here we shouldn't be here was crawling like a mantra through his thick head. A mantra from the old days, now he thought about it. Somehow he'd forgotten, or he hadn't thought about it, or he'd assumed it would be different, coming here like this, as a visitor. A tourist, face it. They should have jumped ship at Prodigalson, pick us up on the way back if you feel like it, if not don't bother. But the thought of the Italians and Fabien having the run of the atoll without anyone to say no was appalling, even though that's exactly what would have happened had Roberto not been stricken. Stan was here and the responsibility was his.

Gram was looking increasingly ill at ease too. He watched him pick up a discarded blue cigarette pack, one of Fabien's, and push it into the pocket of his shorts. Gram wasn't saying much, at least not to him. In fact to his increasing annoyance, Gram was spending all his time with the two Linois. Bernard didn't seem to have much time for him now either. Bernard and Timucu did the work, ate and slept out on deck, spoke when spoken to, and watched.

Every now and then, while keeping a careful eye on the Italians and the idiotic Frenchman, Stan's attention was drawn inexorably to the distant southeast corner of the lagoon, to those shimmering green smudges in the heat haze which he knew marked the densest area of mangrove forest. Beyond lay the arid grey wilderness which comprised the southeastern landmass of Tsaramaso; a vast, near-trackless expanse where the vast majority of the atoll's top terrestrial animal, the giant tortoise, lived. Tsaramaso was a relic, a lone persisting echo of lost eras when reptiles ruled the land. And a nagging thought crystallized: why hadn't they seen any giant tortoises? In the old days there had been over 100,000 of the ponderous brutes, far more than on Galapagos. The places they'd landed at so far had never supported dense populations, but they should have seen some, or found tracks. No droppings either, and they were difficult to miss. Perhaps he would ask Bernard if anything had happened. Then again, they were bound to come across one soon. Gazza would find one, Gina would whoop, and Gianni would expend camcorder battery time on a prehistoric spectacle.

Stan studied the far-off, trembling patchwork of dull green smudges. The air was so milky, so vibrant. Looking through it hurt the eyes. The distant mangrove forest concealed the winding entrance to Bras Caret. Hawksbill Creek, site of his last field trip in the old days. And, next to Bras Caret, Bras Demzel. He had the strong feeling Bernard was watching him. Only when the battery pack on Gianni's camcorder ran down again were they able to return to *La Belone* and leave the lagoon in peace.

In the evening they all went ashore for a barbecue, including Liza. Bernard manouevred the zodiac in with care along a narrow passage through the reef flats. The skies were a clear, dark steely blue, and there would be stronger light later on as the near-full moon rose. On the small beach above high water mark they were startled to find a muddle of human footprints around a blurred central groove where a small boat had been drawn up. A gruesome reek led them to the butchered remains of a green turtle nearby.

'This other boat,' said Fabien. 'These *Malgaches*. You notice, when we arrive, it went away straight to hide. And it did not have its *canot*, Bernard, *non*?' He nodded to himself. 'Here is why they come to the atoll. To take turtle.'

Bernard said nothing.

Stan could see that Liza and Gram found the sight of this magnificent turtle reduced to bloody flippers, head and shell upsetting, as did the Italians, but this had not been an uncommon sight down here in the old days – in Papa the meat of the green turtle was a traditional food. The atoll's remoteness, and the lack of freshwater, which discouraged long-term visits by poachers, had always combined to protect the teeming wildlife; Papa's environmental legislation defined penalties, but – the occasional special effort by the government apart - it was absurd to expect any meaningful enforcement out here. They had talked about this many times before, he and Julius, the Director and the other researchers, the Prof - just how influential in the conservation equation was the atoll's sinister reputation? Many Linois, like Raja back on Margaritifer, were genuinely too frightened even to pay a harmless visit. Dalyell particularly had set great store by this reputation, advising the beleaguered Director to overlook various transgressions by the Linois staff, and adopting at times an almost deferential attitude towards Roland.

Gina was clearly upset, and complaining to her father in Italian; then she turned to Gram:

'Gram. It's disgusting! How can these people eat turtles? How can they do that?' *Turdles.*

Gram shrugged, looking uncomfortable.

Stan roused from his semi-stupor. He had by and large managed to retain his patience with Gina so far, for Gram's sake. 'It's a traditional food in Papa, Gina. You know, like ham back in Italy.' He was watching Gazza, rooting about at the edge of the scrub. The pig had been brought ashore by Gianni in the second zodiac-load without a word to Stan. Bloody Godfather's expedition, wasn't it?'

Gina pulled a face. 'But it's so gross! Did you smell that? How could anyone … Bernard, you don't eat turtles, do you?'

Bernard pretended he hadn't heard.

Gina didn't like this. 'Bernard.' Ber*nard*. 'I'm talking to you. Do you eat turtles or not?'

Gram stepped in. 'No Gina, of course Bernard doesn't eat turtles. It's against the law.'

Bernard was staring at the Italian girl through slitted eyes.

Stan listened as though from a great distance. All the diving had left him flat and lethargic, and there was no let-up from the sea-sound; it was a part of daily life now. This was no longer a happy group. It never had been a happy group. A classic holiday relationship, stemming from a teenage romance. It had grown complications and now it was getting messy. Gianni's urbanity, and his wife's endless unassuming patience, had to be admired.

Bernard fired up the outboard and set off with Timu back to the catamaran to bring ashore the ingredients required for another convivial evening.

A little way into the scrub Gianni, Gina and Gazza came upon another of the atoll's distinctive inhabitants: a purple-blue robber crab, the size of a football. Twin sets of antennae twitched, tasting piggy exhalations, one set moving up and down, the other from side to side, while fearsome knobbly-toothed pincers were held in readiness for nutritional opportunities: coconut, animal carcase, turtle hatchling, or perhaps on this occasion barbecue scraps. Stan, the hired guide, was summoned to tell them that this giant, naturally-armoured hermit crab had for decades been largely restricted in Papa to Tsaramaso. Although in theory able to re-colonise the other islands because its larval stage formed part of the planktonic soup, it was also unfortunately a popular ingredient in curries, which is why it had been wiped out in the first place and why it would never regain a clawhold anywhere else.

Bernard had returned, and Stan could hear him talking in a low voice to Gram and Timu, telling them about *cipaille*, the robber crab. He felt a surge of resentment. Gram should be at his side, listening to his father, not to the fairytales of some old Linois drunk.

Soon a wood-fire was blazing, the cool-box of beer and wine had been thrown open, and the evening took its usual course. Seabirds streamed in from the open sea, fruit bats crossed Passe Cabris in search of fruiting trees, frigatebirds quarrelled in the casuarinas, and Bernard drew their attention to the distant calling of feral goats. Goat meat was a great attraction for the Linois, and for a few moments Bernard and Timu were entranced. They began chattering excitedly, the word *cabris* prominent, Bernard presumably telling old goat hunt stories, now and then casting a glance in the direction of Gazza. Passe Cabris meant channel of goats, and the Prof had spent long periods here tracking and studying the feral groups out in the bush with Roland as boatman and guide. Goats had long ago been put on all these islands as a source of food for seafarers and the shipwrecked, and had proceeded to multiply and hammer the vegetation.

Besides barbecued grouper, Timu had made his version of octopus and coconut curry. This was a Papa speciality, and Stan managed to get a bit of it down so as not to show disrespect, but it had never been his favourite and his appetite wasn't great. It was an unappetising scene: the glaringly white artificial light, the loud music and louder voices, the beer bottles and fag ends on the beach, the pig trotting around in the firelight snaffling down scraps, careful to avoid the slower-moving robber crab which was doing the same. More objectionable still was Gianni's casual assumption of ownership. Ever since they'd arrived he'd treated the place as his personal playground. There was no respect, no humility. If it wasn't for the sharks they might as well have stayed on Prodigalson, and how he wished they had.

Had this idea of philistines in the temple concerned him before, when he'd been younger and less confused? The whole research station operation must have comfortably achieved more damage than the odd stray tourist boat. The Prof would argue that the knowledge gained helped protect places like Tsaramaso, and their natural history, better. But even he had grown equivocal after a time. In other words, was knowledge the same as understanding? Stan had been just another gormless young student, but he'd known something wasn't right. At the time he'd put it down to Roland's bad influence on the place.

Liza was still disturbingly quiet and contained. She had gone a little way off to sit on the beach, and Stan went over to sit with her. He scooped out a place beside her on the long pile of sea-smoothed shells and fragments of fossil coral which he knew were over a hundred thousand years old; but he'd retired from the tour guide thing. He put an arm around her broad shoulders, not knowing what to expect. After initial reluctance she settled against him, and he became aware of his heart pumping.

'All right Barra? You're not saying much.' He felt her take a deep, steady breath, and he tensed again.

'I could have been myself Stan, my full self, if I'd been stronger with you.'

'Oh?'

'It's not your fault, not really. One day life will bite you on the arse, then you'll see. But I only have myself to blame.' She took another deep breath, let it out slowly. 'I can still do it. When we get back.'

'We'll be OK Barra. Come on, drown your sorrows.'

'No. I don't feel right. It's this place.'

She spoke quietly, looking away, out over the rippling waters of Passe Cabris flowing in from the sea once again as the lagoon took in another vast breath under an immensity of glittering night sky. A late string of boobies curved in from the darkness, shadowy white, heading for the mangrove; but for the blaring reggae they would have heard the rush of air through pinions.

'I don't like it. I don't like it here Stan. You should never have brought us. What were you thinking of? You must know it's like this. Why did you bring us, if you knew?'

Good question. 'I must have forgotten. I thought it would be all right. I wanted you and Gram to see ... '

'We should have stayed at Prodigalson, we'd have been fine there.' She held a small piece of fossil coral and was using it to scratch remorselessly at the palm of her hand. 'We'd have been fine.' She sounded close to tears. 'It's not just me, is it? There's something in the air, I don't know, I keep expecting something awful to happen, and it nearly did. It's as though we're being watched - don't you feel it?' She turned to look at him, her eyes enormous. 'Don't you Stan? You must do. It's not just me, is it?'

No. 'You heard what Bernard said, Barra - it's a place of power. They all believe that, even the educated ones. Even the Prof believes it. Of course I can feel it. You're right. We should never have come.'

She turned her attention back to the piece of coral making its repeated track across her palm. 'At night, I'm having these really, really bad dreams. Last night I thought there was something on the roof - no, I didn't think it, there *was* something. We were all in bed, I'm sure we were, and it was over my head, I could hear it shifting about. Claws Stan, scraping on the roof - '

'You should have woken me up.'

'You were drunk, you'd have been useless. You were snoring, flat out, and I daren't move, in case it heard me. Don't laugh Stan, I've never been like this before. You know me. I thought I was losing my mind.'

'Gazza?'

Her glossy black head shook vehemently. 'Do me a favour. No, much bigger than the bloody pig.'

'Probably a frigatebird then. They sometimes do that, come to boats at night, like the boobies, only they prefer a flat surface, like a roof. They've got pretty major claws.' He'd never heard of a frigate doing this - they were generally wary of humans here. 'Bernard and Timu are out on deck at night, one of them could have - '

'Claws Stan, I know claws.'

'Maybe they were messing around.' If he asked Bernard, well, of course he would not be able to say.

'You think I'm stupid, you're thinking about that night at the house, the guy on the roof, here she goes again.'

'No, no.' Maybe a little, but this was Tsaramaso.

'I wish to God I was there now. I wish we all were, with Kato, just doing nothing, just in our house. Gram's totally wrapped up with Bernard and Timu here, hasn't got any time for Gina any more, I've never seen him like this, so, I don't know, so … not happy, but sort of at ease, as if suddenly he fits in. He doesn't though. Our Gram doesn't fit in here Stan.'

He stroked her hair. 'It's just a phase. He'll outgrow them.'

'I hope so. It's doing him good though, on the whole, I can see that. I'm not stupid. We're all changing though, all of us. That's what I don't like.'

'We'll be on our way soon Barra, and you'll just remember the good bits.' Like that straight right into Fabien's smirking face.

'I don't know Stan. Somehow I don't know.' She turned to him abruptly. 'And the guy on the roof – I know nobody believes me, but he was there Stan! Whatever you think, I know what I saw, just like I know there's something here now.'

As he stroked he began rocking her gently.

'It'll be OK Barra.'

'Why will it? How will it?'

'Because it will. I'll make it OK.'

'Will you?' She stopped his rocking. 'A hell of a lot depends on you here Stan, you know that don't you? I'll do my best, for Gram, of course I will. That's all I can say. But you have to promise to look after Gram properly – don't give me any of your lazy bullshit Stan! – and you have to make sure we get out on time. I don't care about Gianni and his bloody shark quest, we just go. Otherwise I'll do something about it. I'll hurt people Stan, if I have to, you know that.' She tossed away the coral fragment.

'You won't have to. I'll see to it, I said didn't I?' Bob Marley boomed out. It was hard to order his mind. Its edges were just outside his grasp. He needed tranquillity. 'OK?' She allowed him to resume the rocking. 'OK?'

'OK.'

He put his lips to her ear. *'Do you remember?'* he crooned, *'I held you so near.'*

A pause, then, huskily: *'Our love's glowing ember.'*

He waited, gave her a nudge.

'So precious and dear.'

We were young lovers, was the unspoken next line, *strolling near the fountain of love.*

'Uncharted waters though Stan.'

Yes. In due course he would announce the impending resurrection of the imperial, but not just now. Or should he simply appear, transformed?

Shells and coral fragments crunched, and Gram sat down at their side without a word. Liza put her arm around him. 'Here's my Grammy.'

'They're horrible, aren't they?' he whispered. 'Bernard says they have no respect.'

Another prickle of resentment.

'Dad, you should have stopped them coming here, somehow. Bernard says – '

'I'm fed up of hearing what bloody Bernard says, OK?' Stan looked quickly back to the fire, but no one was taking any notice. 'Look, they were planning to come here anyway, weren't they? At least we're here to tone it down a bit.'

'There is that,' said Liza. 'You two are policemen then. Let's make the best of it until we can get away from them. When we get back to Marga we'll have a party at the hotel, just the three of us, eh Grammy? You like a drink now don't you?' She hugged her son.

Stan had to get a grip. 'Sorry Gram, it's just all this bloody din ... didn't mean to snap.'

Gazza appeared, snuffling among the stones and pieces of coral. Liza aimed a swipe and he ran back up the beach, leaving behind the faint but definite smell of rotting turtle.

'And that bloody pig, it should never have come off the boat ... The world's full of people like this Gram, absolutely stuffed full of 'em. This is it, this is what people are like. Places like this don't stand a chance. All three of us feel the same, don't worry.'

'I know that, dad, I know what people are like, you don't have to tell me. Bernard says - ' Gram glanced at his father ' - he says Roland is here to protect the atoll, that's what he's here for.'

'Yeah. That's what he tells people.'

'Bern – Roland has power, that's what the Linois think. He's given power by the atoll, for him to use to protect it.'

Fabien was shouting something behind them and there was a burst of laughter.

'And you believe that?'

Gram looked confused. 'I don't know. It's a strange place, like you said. Fantastic, but a bit ... creepy. And when I was with Roland, in his boat, he's got these bizarre eyes, and he kept staring at me.'

'He does that. He can't help it.' An indelible face.

'Well, it made me feel really weird, even though I was a bit shaken up, you know? It was like I was being ... examined, I don't know.'

Stan shivered. Malicious old bastard had better leave his son well alone. No, wait, Roland had *saved* his son. He'd given him his son back. 'I know the feeling. As if you were being judged.'

'That's it! Is he always like that? It wasn't a bad feeling, just ... well, weird, like I say.'

Liza hugged him again. 'You're OK now, Gram. Look, the three of us are together, and we're like an indestructible rock, one granite rock. Like one of those corporate bonding exercises out on the moors, where they come back half dead and resign. Except the Blacksters will come out of it stronger than ever.'

She put an arm round each of them. Before them stretched the silvery lagoon, the reflections of moon and whirling stars, the patterns of the current; black shark fins rippled the silver surface.

From the flaming shadows behind them came an outburst of squealing and drunken laughter, triggering an eruption of frigates from the tall casuarinas. Long-winged black silhouettes circled slowly against the stars before gliding off into the night. The Blacksters rejoined the party.

By the end of the meal, despite the customary copious amounts of alcohol, Gianni and Fabien had talked one another into a night dive. There was no way Stan or Gram would be persuaded to take part. Bernard ferried them back to the catamaran, the zodiac's propeller at low throttle awakening flickers of green luminescence in the black waters of Passe Cabris. Then he went back to the beach where Timu and Gram were clearing up the debris.

An hour or so later the three Blacksters stood on the deck of *La Belone* watching two eerie, shifting blurs of light in the black sea which marked the underwater progress of Frenchman and Italian.

'How do you like watching two crazy drunks risking their lives then?' Stan wasn't exaggerating - there was no safety boat cover. In the drunken confusion of leaving the beach, Gazza had been left ashore, and Gina had pestered her irritated father into sending back the two Linois yet again in the zodiac to look for him, instead of standing by with the divers in case of emergency as they should have.

Liza snorted. 'As long as it's just those two. Maybe something horrible will happen and we can leave early.' There was nothing funny going on though, and it sounded forced. They were having to keep their voices down so as not to upset Aurora. After a minute or two more Liza gave Gram's arm a squeeze and retired below.

The catamaran seemed to be frozen with tension. From up here the dive torches looked super-powerful, but down there Stan knew the beam was so narrow, so feeble really ... the divers were down in a deep world of darkness, and out of the darkness, at any instant -

'Stan. Please.' Aurora's voice was soft, throaty, but it made him jump. He hadn't heard her come over. 'This tiger shark, the one who comes at night ... Gianni, he hates this shark, he is ... obsessed, no? Will he meet with this shark?' Aurora was an extremely private, self-contained person, unfailingly courteous, worshipped by her husband. She had somehow managed to stay apart from all the niggles and bust-ups. Just now, in the stark moonlight, she looked like a large-eyed ghost.

'Well, it's possible, but tigers are very rare, Aurora. And they would only react if they were provoked. And there are no records of attacks here. Not real attacks.'

'I know this, Gianni has told me. No records, but ... is this the truth Stan?'

'Well I don't know of any Aurora. Sharks get a bad press. People exaggerate. Your husband is more likely to be mugged next time he visits Stamford Bridge.' But it wasn't the evening for jokes. 'Really, there's nothing to worry about. He's very experienced, and Fabien.'

'Yes. Thank you. But you will not go into the water yourself. I understand. Gianni, sometimes it is *macho*, you know? If there is not a little danger, a little … violence, he has no interest. It is not nice to say this. At home, he likes to hunt. Many Italian men, they are the same.' Her eyes, no more than shadowy sockets, followed the spectral pools of torchlight.

The zodiac's outboard could be heard now, a distant droning, a man-made sound, as Bernard and Timu returned with or without Gazza.

'Yes, I understand. It's not only in your country, Aurora. And Gianni is very sensible. He will not take any unnecessary risks.'

Of course Gianni himself was down there now busily demonstrating the fatuity of this last statement, but never mind. Nothing in this world could have induced Stanley Blackster to go down to where the other-worldly light of the dive-torches glimmered. He cleared his throat.

'I'm just being ultra-cautious, Aurora, because of Gram. Listen, I lived here for a year and saw very few tiger sharks. And they never bothered anyone, as far as I know. It's the name, a lot of it – tiger, you know? It's misleading. They have bars on their sides, stripes, that's all.'

'*Grazi*, Stan. Gianni too should be more cautious. Still, he protects himself.'

'Oh?' How did Gianni protect himself? Prayers? Black Magic? His lucky tiger tooth? Remy Martin VSOP?

Gina had joined them and was peering anxiously at the zodiac as it advanced carefully towards the sunken lights. Timu waved and pointed down, and Gina clapped her hands in delight. 'Gazza! Gazza!' After an excited Italian exchange with her mother, she turned defiantly to Stan. 'They have found Gazza!'

'Good.'

The submerged lights gave a sudden lurch, and everyone gasped, but then two heads were up. Bernard and Timucu eased the zodiac forward and pulled the divers aboard.

Gianni was exuberant. 'We have seen it! I am sure we have seen it - a big shark, bigger than the hammerhead at Fiantsifer, right at the end, as we came to the surface!'

The Italian took a towel and wiped his face, then looked

challengingly at Stan. 'It was a tiger shark, what else could it be, eh Fabien?'

The Frenchman, looking uncharacteristically subdued, nodded, muttered '*Oui*' and disappeared inside.

'Could it have been another hammerhead, Gianni? They can get as big as tigers, five metres plus.'

'No no no! You do not understand, he was *big.*' He held out his arms, temporarily lost for the right word. 'He was *fat*, you know, around. And he was very close, five metres only, but he swam straight past, we could not follow, we could not see him well. But, at this time of the tide, the real shark enters the lagoon. Now that we know this, we will find him again, oh yes!' He remembered his wife and went over to her, still talking. 'And, Aurora, many other beautiful things, as I said, all the fishes of the night, the soldierfish, the morays, and the lobsters, the octopus, many, many. And a spanish dancer, you know, like the red one in the book, but this one is yellow, *bella, bella.*' These marvels were clearly of a lesser order though, entirely eclipsed by the shark.

Fabien had reappeared, breathing scotch fumes, to endorse his employer. 'A big tiger Stan. You should have come with us!' He lit up a gitane, took an impressive lungful and waved the glowing cigarette at Stan. The deck light emphasized the dusky remains of his black eye. 'You English, you are nervous always. If you are nervous, then *oui*, the shark will come for you, *mais certainement*. You must be strong, my friend!' His face was still white as he sucked at the cigarette.

Stan nodded, but was unable to manage a smile. What if the shark, certainly a tiger or a bull by the sound of it, both of them highly dangerous, hadn't carried on into the lagoon? What if it had circled round in an arc and loomed out of the darkness, jaws gaping? What protection would prayers, adrenalin and alcohol have been then? No safety boat, no way of treating major injuries anyway, Fiantsifer and its airstrip hours away ...

'I'm glad you enjoyed it.'

On his way in to join Liza he noticed a bucket, and inside it two large, brilliantly coloured lobsters, antennae waving uncertainly. Tomorrow's dinner, presumably.

Gram sat leaning forward, chin on tanned forearms, T-shirt wound around his head, watching his father write. By unspoken agreement, after the previous night's dramas, this was a day for relaxing. Sunbathing on the deck, a bit of swimming, snorkelling, a bit of reading. Everyone seemed tired and irritable. Tonight Fabien would go down again with Gianni to look for his shark, although his enthusiasm was hard to detect.

Things weren't working out the way they should have. Stan was determined to bring some order into the increasingly volatile situation, to take control. He wasn't here as a tour guide, he was much more than that, and Gram had to be made to see it. His visit to Tsara and to the Papalinas in general did have a professional purpose after all: he was sketching out ideas for his environmental article, and already he had a title to brandish: *Papa's Dilemma*. Not bad.

It was mid-morning hot, and the conversation of Fabien and the two Linois was already loud and argumentative. Where did they get the energy? Well, it wasn't exactly energy, and it was still coming out of a beer bottle. What would *Il Padrone* have to say? He sighed. This trip was almost enough to put you off the stuff.

Gram was by his side, that was the important thing. Stan had prised him away from the Linois, saying he wanted Gram's opinion, had something important to discuss. So far their conversation had been rather awkward. He wanted to shout I DIDN'T BRING THEM HERE – THEY BROUGHT ME. Instead he sucked at his pen.

'Why not use the laptop, dad? So much easier.'

'Oh. Battery's dead.' Which might have been true. He hadn't checked. The pen embellished a doodle of two stylised shark-shapes, chasing one another in the required circle.

'This is how you write Boscanion's stuff, when you're AB Defduf, no?'

'That's right. More satisfying.' The pen was sketching in a long, bookmark-shaped backdrop, framing the circling sharks with dark cross-hatching. Gram was fidgeting, starting to get up. 'Come on then, Gram. What are your impressions of nature conservation in Papa, from what you've seen so far?' Half-expecting Gram to stroll off with a contemptuous snort, back to the great Bernard.

But Gram eased himself back down. 'Well, from what I can see I think they're doing their best. I mean, look at Tsaramaso. Look where it is. The Papalinas government doesn't have the resources, does it?'

'They need help then.'

Gram's face wrinkled in a frown as he re-wound the T-shirt. His scalp was fuzzy again. 'From us you mean? From the so-called developed world? There'd be all the usual strings attached. It wouldn't be genuine help, would it?'

'But where else are they going to get the money to do it? They've only got the tuna and tourism.'

Gram snorted the Barracuda snort. 'Tourism! It's always tourism. Tourists are a bigger threat than oil. Nearly as big as global warming, which they're part of anyway. Why can't people just agree to leave places like this alone? They aren't wanted here, they aren't needed here. They don't fit. That's the help places like this need.'

'Yeah.' Gram had the passion. He didn't, even though he felt the same. He felt inadequate, even intimidated. He couldn't think of anything to say. His easy response mechanism had totally wound down, nothing left.

Gazza had arrived and was peering up at them with weak, blond-fringed eyes. His pink snout was shiny with mucus which shivered as he breathed. Stan used a foot to push him away up the deck. 'Bugger off Gazza.' How to make Gram stay for a while?

But Gram hadn't finished. 'The Linois are different though, some of them anyway. They have the right priorities. They fit in. Linois like Bernard and Timu. Roland even. Roland especially. I know you don't like him, but he's dedicated his life to the atoll. Bernard's been telling me.'

Bernard Bernard Bernard. 'Yes, I suppose he has, for his own inscrutable reasons.' And now Roland. The pen had gouged through to the page beneath. This wasn't what he'd had in mind. What about him, Stanley Blackster? Stanley Blackster fitted in better than anyone. He was glad when Liza sneezed and broke the silence.

She was sitting nearby under the canopy, wearing sunglasses and Aurora's slightly comical long-billed sun visor, which coloured her face green and made her look like a stork. She'd had another bad night; maybe they all had. When Liza was unhappy it was obvious, but sometimes she could paint her way out of it. She was concentrating on her sketch-pad, striking at it with her oil sticks, blocking and smearing in bursts of cerulean and turquoise, silver-grey and burning yellow: Passe Cabris, the Channel of the Goat.

'Gesundheit.' Stan always said this whenever a Blackster sneezed. The noble hound was a notorious serial sneezer who nevertheless managed to look bewildered every time. Nobody said it when Stan sneezed. He would stop saying it. Gram had mentioned AB.

'I expect you've been wondering about Boscanion – The Movie. How it will all turn out.'

All that seemed so far away now, all the movie aspirations, out of reach beyond a shimmering veil, just vague half-notions. The Badass, Hermann Hesse, Vanderhorst himself, all faded away now. And yet *Insidiator*'s essence, its elements, these were intensely here, pressing in.

Gram was frowning again. He used to smile all the time. There was no little silver shark swinging at his ear.

'Yeah, I suppose. It'll be good.' Now he was smiling. 'Louis Vanderhorst will make it dark, won't he? Not for kids anyway. He's good, isn't he? And Johnny Depp, that's so cool. Like in *Legend of Sleepy Hollow*. I've been telling Bernard and Timu. They love it. Depp as Boscanion will be a bit different to Charlie though, won't he?' He chuckled. 'You won't let them have American accents? Depp's OK at English.'

'Where's your ear-ring Gram?'

'Oh, I gave it to Timu. You don't mind, do you?'

'Why?'

'That's the way the Linois are, they share everything. It's so refreshing.'

Refreshing. 'And what did they share with you?'

Gram pursed his lips. 'Oh, all sorts of things. Knowledge, for a start. Company. It's like a brotherhood, so different from back home where everyone's scrapping to hang onto what they've got and grab some more, you know?'

'These are abstract things Gram.'

'You are pissed off, aren't you? I don't believe it!'

He was pissed off, yes. 'No, I don't mind. I gave it to you, it's yours. Maybe when Timu gets bored with it he can share it back to you.' More likely flog it on Marga. It was solid silver. He'd get it back one way or another.

Gram was staring at the deck, scowling.

'One thing though – what happens to your hair, when the Linois shave it off?'

'So far it's grown back again.'

'I mean the clippings.'

'I dunno. In the bin. Why?'

Futile question. Once would be enough, and the first time had been way back on Marga. 'Nothing, just wondered.'

'What happens to yours then? Do you collect it or something?'

'Forget it Gram.' He wasn't normally so ready with the backchat. 'Anyway, Johnny Depp. I think we can manage without American accents, don't you? As you say, these Hollywood types like a chance to do English these days. It's something I'll have to discuss with Louis.' Bloody Linois. Gram was still sulking. 'Who could they get to play Anakim, Gram?' There was an awkward silence. He knew he shouldn't have mentioned her, but he couldn't help it. She was pressing in. 'Louis mentioned the girl in *Lost in Space*.'

For a long moment it seemed Gram would not answer. 'Yeah, I suppose. She'd be OK. Bit old now though.'

Stan waited, staring at the scrawled, ripped page of his notebook.

'She's nothing like Kim though. Kim could never have been a film star. Not the way she looked, the way she was.'

No. Last night, after the night dive excitement had died away, and Liza was safely snoring, Stan had sat on his bunk with the cassette box again, watching the sleeping red face, waiting for the eyes to open, the too-fleshy red lips to part. He wanted to see Kim. He must see the final episode again.

'I expect they'll take some up and coming teen from USTV world and add a few prosthetics Gram, the way they do in all those Star Trek spinoffs. Big hair. Nothing too extreme – they won't want to lose marketability.'

Gram was grinning now. He had him! 'Yeah. OK, maybe the hairstyle's no problem, but the face, the teeth … '

'They'll cope.' He meant we'll cope, didn't he? 'Maybe the odd tooth cap, black contact lenses. They'll be going for quirky. Kim would only disturb them. They won't want disturbing.' *We*, we won't want disturbing.

Gram looked up, squinting into the glare, shading his eyes with a hand. 'Ah. For a minute I thought it was a plane, but it's just a frigatebird, way, way up. They're always up there, aren't they? Even at night there always seems to be at least one.'

We'll cope. We don't want disturbing. Who was we?

'You OK dad?'

'What?'

'You OK?'

'I'm OK.' He made the OK sign with finger and thumb.

The pen was completing a second pair of sharks. No one had ever seen a plane at Tsaramaso in the old days. Boats had been rare enough. The way one shark shape followed the other, pursued it, a perfect circle.

Gram cleared his throat. 'Yeah. In the movies they don't want things too real. People like to escape.'

'Kim was too real.'

Gram glanced towards his mother beneath the canopy, still sketching, green visored face fixed in concentration. He kept his voice low. 'Sometimes, from the side, when she was listening to you, she looked more like an animal than a person, you know? I'm not being mean. I didn't not like her, but she always seemed to be watching me, I remember that, I didn't like that.'

Someone switched on the radio, and there was a loud *tut* from Liza.

'What station can you pick up way out here, dad?'

A DJ rattled on in French.

'You liked her dad, I know, but mum thinks you … you know, loved Kim. How can she think that? I mean, you couldn't, not Kim. I mean, she was … '

Some fine cross-hatching to the background. Nearly done.

'Dad?' As he leaned forward Gram's shadow fell across the page.

'Mmm?'

'You love mum. You do, don't you?'

Stan smiled. 'Strange question. Of course I do. Why do you ask?'

'Dunno.' Gram stared. 'Just, with it being on telly again … '

The Italians were noisily preparing to go snorkelling. Gram no longer went with them; nor did Liza, and they were no longer asked. Three tribes on the boat now.

Strange question. It was only proper though to discuss family affairs, as father and son.

'And do you envisage keeping in touch with Gina, afterwards?'

Gram looked and sounded uncertain. 'I don't know. Maybe not. Mr Conti said I could visit them in Italy, but that was at the beginning. Things aren't going great, are they? Gina's all right, but she's incredibly spoiled. She has no idea. I mean, you've heard the way she talks to Bernard and Timu, as if they're servants or something. And Mr. Conti … he's not really a very nice man, is he, underneath? Bernard says he wants to kill sharks to show what a big man he is.'

Bernard again. Bernard says. He could hear his voice, *beeg man*. 'There will be no killing of sharks while I'm around Gram. Bernard knows that.'

Gram nodded vigorously, missing the point. 'He knows all

sorts of things. He's a serious guy, isn't he? He's been telling me all about life in Papa, the politics, the government, all sorts of other things. Hey dad, I can tie hooks like they do now, with my teeth!'

'You've got an unfair advantage, that Ronaldo gap in the middle.' He used to take Gram fishing with him when he was younger, for roach and bream, the odd trout from the Itchen, spinning for pike in the winter, before he turned against it. That had been the best, with proper winters, even snow sometimes, working their way along the river, teaching him what to look for, the fallen trees, the eddies, pools of slack water, places where food would accumulate, attracting unwary little fishes …

Gianni and Gina were climbing down off the transom into the sea. Fabien joined them with a whooping running jump straight past Liza and over the side.

'Pillock!' she shouted after him.

Gram exchanged an exasperated glance with his mother, waited until she went back to her painting, then turned back to Stan. 'He's been telling me all about this place, about Tsaramaso. He says that's why he came, to show me the atoll, to teach me about it. He says it's important. And to keep an eye on the others of course.'

Stan had stopped breathing. Bernard had come for money, beer and cigarettes. 'That's my job.'

Gram was shaking his head. 'I know, but you just have a different way of doing it, of looking at things, the way I know already. I need to know their way. You said yourself, the Linois see things we don't see.'

Had he said that?

'Dad, why haven't we seen the tortoises? There's supposed to be thousands.'

Good question. Ask Bernard.

'I asked Bernard, but he didn't know, or he didn't seem to want to tell me. Do you know?'

'Well, I cannot say.'

Gram looked puzzled. 'Really?' He thought about this for a bit, then he spoke in a lowered voice. 'Dad. Look. There's no way I'll be going to university, whatever mum says. I just wanted you to know.'

'I see.' He didn't see though. 'Sounds as though you've made a decision.' Decisiveness, this was his area too. Liza was showing signs of restlessness, but the radio had been left on and the tinny music stopped their words carrying. Otherwise she'd have been over like a shot.

Gram nodded, and leaned closer. 'I've been talking about it with Bernard and Timu. I want to come back out here, to the islands.'

What? What? He hadn't been prepared for this, not at all. 'And do what?'

Gram shrugged. 'Get a job. I could help Bernard fishing - he said I could. He says that with his help I could become as good a fisherman as him. Well, nearly as good. He says I can stay with him, at his house, with his family. He's teaching me Creole. I could even start off on a tourist boat, like this one.' He held up his hands. 'I know, I know what I said about tourists, but it would just be for a start, and I could teach them, maybe, how to do things properly. Timu knows all the tour operators. Then I could work my way to a good island. This one. You can live on very little out here, you don't need much. Bernard thinks I should go for it.' He was looking straight into his father's eyes. 'What do you think?'

Fabien clambered back aboard looking disgruntled. On his way past he offered a mock salute but said nothing. Stan was floundering, trying to gather his thoughts. He hadn't anticipated this. It was all suddenly impossibly appealing and perfect – for someone like himself. No, there wasn't anyone like himself, there could be only one. The perfect life for Stanley Blackster. But little Gram? His gravitation towards fishes was under way, an essential and overdue aspect of the maturing process. But fishing for a living? Out here? Abandoning his father? And his mother would never support the proposal. She would react. Life would be intolerable. He should issue sensible advice.

'Look, why not get your degree, then come out here? You'd get a better job - they desperately need qualified environmental scientists - and you'd be more useful to the country, to the environment. You'd never make it fishing.' Gram, fishing for a living? Inconceivable.

Gram chewed at his lip. 'What if we say to mum that I'm coming here for work experience, and to learn the language, just for a year, and then I'll go to university? Lots of guys do that. They hold the place open for a year for you.'

Craftiness was not a familiar aspect of Gram. He'd picked that up from Bernard Says. 'It's a thought, I suppose. Best not say anything just yet though, she's feeling a bit fragile.' In fact the Barracuda had diarrhoea, but there was never going to be a good time.

'She'll say no.'

'You might be surprised. She's a very independent-minded woman. Give her credit.'

'Yeah, I know. Fierce. Anyway, that's what I'm going to do, whatever she says.'

Bernard and Fabien were now arguing loudly in a mixture of French and Creole. He caught the word *respect*. The music had been turned up, and Liza had propped herself on one elbow and removed the visor in order to fire off a glare.

'Dad.' Gram had been about to go, but now he leaned very close, with an eye on his mother. 'About Kim. After all the TV stuff had finished, after mum banned her from the house ... I never said, but she came round. She came round, to our house. It was at night. She wanted you, but you and mum were out.'

Kim. Gram had his mother's expressive eyes, but where hers were too often on full beam, his often looked as they did now, gentle and bewildered.

'Go on Gram.'

'Dad, the thing is, she was black.' A pause. 'She'd painted herself somehow, makeup, I don't know. Her whole skin was black. Like mum.'

'What?'

'Really, dad. She said strange things. I was frightened. I wouldn't let her in. She made noises. I think she was crying, sort of. Then she went away.'

'What did she say?' Kim had come to him after all, and he hadn't been there. 'What strange things? Why didn't you tell me? Why tell me now?'

'I don't know. She's on my mind here somehow. I was scared, dad. I was just a kid, remember. And you didn't see. Then you said she'd gone, disappeared, and I was glad. I don't remember what she said. It was mad. She was mad, I think. Maybe all the time. You won't tell mum?'

No.

The drunken argument had ended, and a shadow loomed. 'Stan!' called Fabien at his shoulder. 'A cold beer, my friend, to give you *courage*.'

'No thanks Fab. Bit later, maybe. Cheers.'

A heavy French sigh. 'You must suit yourself. And the young soldier Gram. Perhaps a beer for you? Or a coke even?'

Gram smiled and shook his head. 'No thanks Fab, I'm fine.'

'*Oui*, you are fine, we all are fine. OK. But soon, no more beer. We must go to visit this guy Roland, to buy more beer.' Off he went.

'Fab,' called Liza, 'could we have the music down a bit?'

The skipper clicked his heels and snapped off one of his salutes. *'Mais oui madame, immediatement.'*

'Merci.'

A crumpled gitanes pack floated by, blue and white with its black dancing lady. Stan saw what had to be a red mist, threw his pad to the deck, pushed himself up and strode across.

'Fab! For chrissake, you French tosser! If you chuck any more of your rubbish overboard you'll be next! You're not in some bar. Christ!'

They stood eyeball to eyeball, watched by the two Linois and Gazza, who had been tied up on a very short lead while Gina was away snorkelling.

'Oui, mon colonel!' The Frenchman stood to attention with another mock salute, breathing beery breath, his eyes glassy.

Stan hit him smack on the jaw and he went over the side with a resounding detonation of seawater and spray. Bernard and Timu slapped hands and hooted approval in the Linois manner.

'About bloody time!' shouted the Barracuda. 'You just beat me to it.'

Fabien surfaced in a whirl of bubbles, kicking to maintain his position. He raised an arm, palm up, middle finger extended. 'You are English, so you are mad! You cannot help yourself, what you do!' He whooped and began smacking the water with both palms. 'Mad English, like your cows!' Then he was howling, like a dog. Timucu laughed and muttered something to his cousin Bernard.

'This French guy,' announced Bernard with authority, 'he is crazy in the head. And, he is the skipper.' *Skeepair.*

Fabien kicked off in a crawl, heading towards the snorkelling Italians.

Well to the north a succession of smoky blue-grey clouds moved westwards over an empty ocean. Bernard was calling softly. 'Stan, you must come.' As he followed he noticed Timucu in earnest discussion on deck with Aurora.

Inside Bernard indicated a narrow section of the polished wooden side-locker. A small brass key was in its lock. Inside Stan found the stainless steel rods and fitments of a powerhead, a bang-stick, which would discharge a shotgun cartridge when pressed against the head of a cow at an abbatoir or a shark in the ocean. Illegal here in Papa of course. He made to pick it up but Bernard was shaking his head, pulling him gently away, turning and removing the key.

'You cannot,' Bernard told him quietly when they were back on deck. 'It would make big problem for Timu. For me also.'

'Have they used it Bernard?'

'Well, I cannot say. Maybe no. They take it, when they dive at night, some other times. They tie it to the zodiac, so it is in the water, so you cannot see.'

'For sharks.'

'*Oui*. Certainly for sharks. I tell you before, this guy he kill sharks. Timu, he say this guy he want only the teeth, the mouth - you say jaw? - from a big *demzel,* and he must be the one to kill it. This give him power. But the skipper, he is afraid.'

Bastard. 'Right. First, we have to make sure he doesn't use it, disable the thing somehow. Then, back on Marga, we arrange for the police to meet us and have him arrested.'

Bernard shook his head impatiently. 'For this? This, it is no big thing. And this guy, they not arrest him, this guy. Mr Conti, he know all those big guy.'

He was right. The red mist was starting to lift. 'OK, I'll think of something else, some way round that. Don't worry, I'll make sure Timu isn't involved.'

The snorkellers were back aboard. No one mentioned the incident with Fabien, and the Frenchman restricted himself to a jaunty grin, but presumably there had been a full report.

Late in the afternoon Fabien took the zodiac back into Passe Cabris with Gianni, his daughter and her pig. The two Linois were not required, and no one else was invited. Stan had given up complaining about these jaunts of Gazza's. The atmosphere aboard the catamaran, with Aurora again in her cabin, was better for the absence of the two Italians and the skipper, not to mention the pig.

Through Bernard, Stan borrowed the brass key, disabled the bang-stick, and had just locked it back into its wooden compartment when a quiet voice surprised him.

'Stan. What is it you do there?'

Aurora looked paler than usual and dark smudges sat beneath her eyes. Another one not sleeping. She was holding her husband's red buoyancy jacket.

'Oh, Aurora, hello. I thought I heard something scratching about, thought maybe we had a rat aboard.'

'A rat?' She seemed distracted.

'I can't see anything - I'm sure there'd be droppings though, you know droppings?' He couldn't think how to mime droppings. 'Probably just a big cockroach. We've got a few of them, haven't we? You know, *cucuracha*?'

Aurora was frowning. 'A scratching sound? I have heard this, but at night only. Above us, when we are in bed. It is bigger than a rat, I think. Gianni says it is a bird.'

'Yes, he's probably right. A frigatebird, on the roof, roosting.'

She nodded slowly, staring into his eyes. 'Stan, the air, it is very strange here, no?'

'It's the climate, very humid. It's made us all tired, that's all. Maybe we've gone on a bit too long. Maybe we should think about heading back. Is there something wrong with Gianni's dive jacket?'

'Ah.' She had forgotten she was carrying it. 'I wish for Timu to clean it. There is a bad smell.' Aurora held it up, indicating a greasy-looking patch, and Stan took a step backwards from a whiff of dead turtle, rotten blood, carrion.

The evening was uncomfortable for a variety of reasons, not least that the drink had finally run out, except for a special reserve generally believed to be kept under lock and key by Gianni in his bedroom. Fabien began noisily advocating the long trip round to the settlement to buy beer or fermented palm sap or whatever Roland had to offer, but fell silent at a glance from his employer. Eventually it was time for the two of them to venture down once again into the submarine darkness, to await the Italian's shark; Fabien did not look keen, and had to be given encouragement. No one spoke as the Linois took them and their equipment onto the zodiac, then Bernard fired up the outboard and they moved off to the same spot as on the previous night.

When the divers had disappeared below Stan stayed on deck with Aurora, maintaining an aimless, one-sided conversation as she stared helplessly at the shifting underwater lights. It was like a bad dream now, one they were all sharing, and they all had to go on to the end. He hadn't spotted the useless bang-stick but he had no doubt it would be down there with them, providing Gianni with his 'protection'.

At intervals, out in the darkness, waves hit Tsaramaso's ancient coral limestone wall with sluggish slaps; every so often there would be a louder whooshing sound as seawater shot up through a blowhole in the rock. From the dark stand of casuarinas lining the channel approaches drifted the weird, warbling cries of frigatebirds, spirits of the atoll. On the black sea surface the dive lights twitched and flickered.

Forty unbearable minutes later Gianni and Fabien were being hauled over the side of the orange zodiac, without incident. The Italian was in a foul temper now, and no longer bothering to hide it.

'Nothing, Stan! No sharks at all! I am very disappointed. This place - it is not as you said it was. We have seen only one real shark here, in all our dives! Everyone tells me, go to Tsaramaso, there you will see the tiger shark. It is like Hawaii, there are many tiger sharks. But it is not like this at all, and you must know that I am very disappointed.'

Gram, Gina and Gazza were again watching the attendant school of trevallies under the catamaran's lights, trying to decide which of the jostling fishes was biggest, as food scraps trickled from *La Belone*. Gina gave a small yelp, and called for her father. There followed a brief exchange in Italian, then Gianni bellowed:

'Fabien! Gina says all the trevallies disappeared, then they came back. There is a big, big fish here! It must be our shark! Bring the dive torches!'

Everyone clustered at the rail, and soon the trevallies were blanked out again by an immense grey bulk. Unmistakable darker markings could be seen in the dancing torchlight.

'Tiger shark!' declared Gianni. He muttered to himself, then: 'This is my tiger! Fabien - ' A quick motion of his silver head sent the Frenchman inside. 'He comes for the waste food from *La Belone*.' His tone became urgent. 'We must keep him here until Fabien returns! Hurry, we must find food to throw in for him, or he will go!' Gianni glared from face to face, waving his arms impatiently. 'Quickly! Find something!'

Bernard and Timu ambled off at Linois pace while Stan and Gram stayed where they were: their attention was fixed on the prodigious, broad grey body which moved slowly alongside again, then turned away with the sweep of a long, long tail.

'Ah! He goes! He goes!' shouted Gianni. He then pointed astern. 'There, look! There!'

They all turned. There was a splash, and when they turned back there was a pale, struggling shape in the water, trailing a length of rope.

'Gazza!' wailed Gina.

Gianni addressed her impatiently in Italian, then bellowed for Fabien and began cursing.

All eyes now switched from the gamely paddling Gazza to the swirl indicating an abrupt change of course by the shark.

Gina became frantic, struggling with her English. 'Gazza! Timu, Bernard, you must go to save Gazza! Bring him to me!'

Gazza was only a couple of yards away now, making for the boat and safety, and Gram was placing himself to make a grab at the rope lead, when a massive, blunt grey and white head with a round black eye reared clear of the water, opened a gaping pink maw, made two convulsive gulping movements, then subsided from view. Timu arrived with the boathook, but by now there was nothing to see and the surface was once again calm. Aurora held her shrieking daughter.

Fabien bustled up, a cigarette clamped between his lips, waving the shotgun, to a volley of Italian abuse. The Frenchman's over-bright eyes suggested he might have a secret bottle tucked away somewhere. His comprehensive bawling-out was interrupted by a call from Bernard in the wheelhouse: the radar showed another vessel a few miles to the west, very close inshore so that the blip kept merging with the atoll.

'*Malgaches*,' muttered Bernard and Timu simultaneously.

No one could sleep. The air was heavy, and the fitful bursts of Italian coming from the master cabin were presumed to be Gianni promising Gina or Aurora or both that he'd buy another pig, ten pigs. A pig farm.

'Well, he did kick the bloody thing over the side, after all,' murmured Stan. 'Game little chap too. Nope. They'll never find another like Gazza.'

But Liza wasn't interested. She lay on her back, staring at the ceiling, her book abandoned beside her. For a while he sat on the edge of her bunk, stroking her long black hair and talking softly to her, but she seemed detached, not reacting to the muffled sounds of Gina's distress, or the bellows, or anything Stan could come up with. He couldn't get her to take her eyes off the ceiling.

Easing down beside her he focused inwardly, where there was only fog. There was a pressing need for equilibrium, for fixed points at which to grasp. Things were happening too fast, after years of not happening at all. He was being whirled along. Absently he flicked the pages of his Lieske & Myers, pausing at the illustration of the powder-blue while practising some deep breathing. He turned more pages, establishing calm, working backwards through the book: four pages of tiny gobies, then even more blennies, the mandarinfish *Synchiropus splendidus,* a 6cm long lover of silty reef patches, then the rapacious and familiar barracudas, the mullets, then six pages of fabulous parrotfish in all their rainbow glory. Here was the bumphead parrot *Bolbometopon muricatum,* the untypically drab, heavyweight chiseler of live coral they'd seen at the entrance to Passe Fregat on their first dive, which already seemed half a lifetime ago. There followed more than a dozen pages of sex-changing wrasses, an assortment of carnivores, planktivores and cleaners in a myriad of shapes, colours and sizes, from the 6cm minute wrasse *Minilabrus striatus* of the Red Sea to the giant napoleonfish *Cheilinus undulatus,*the wrasse world's answer to the venerable bumphead, over two metres long and still plentiful here at Tsaramaso. Then there were pages of damselfishes, angelfishes, butterflyfishes, goatfishes, emperors, the monocle breams and spine cheeks, sweetlips and fusiliers, and here the snappers whose Creole names Gram had learned from Bernard and Saba on the day he had suddenly become a fisherman: *zob, bourzwa, varvara.*

He came to a halt at the illustration of another snapper, his favourite snapper, one of his favourite fishes, the mangrove jack *Lutjanus argentimaculatus,* the predatory, brick-red snapper of the lagoon. This fish had something. In the old days Bernard had shown him a place in the mangroves where, beneath nesting boobies, the warm, green, guano-enriched waters held mangrove jacks over three feet long, attracted there by hordes of smaller fishes. Whenever they were in this part of the lagoon and time and tide permitted, and they needed a break from whatever was going on, they would come here to sit silently in the boat, the two of them, beneath the gurgling boobies, watching the big red snappers in the warm green water.

Stan closed the book. Suddenly he wanted to do that more than anything else, just take his son and go to sit in the boat and watch the mangrove jacks again. And Bernard should be there. They would see whose son Gram was.

18. **Kim**

Bernard switched off the outboard, cocking it to lift the dripping propeller clear of the water, then moved carefully to the front of the orange zodiac. Kneeling on the deck he steered them into the shallows with firm strokes of the paddle, first that side, now this. Mangroves crowded all around. They were in one of a thousand small, windless lagoon inlets, where the water beneath the keel measured less than a foot.

Dusty brown young boobies, out of the nest only a matter of weeks, perhaps days, perched in mangroves alongside the familiar white, red-footed adults; here and there, sheltered from wind and sun by glossy green foliage, sat untidy stick nests supporting woolly-white, black-faced chicks, one per nest. Gram squinted into his mother's camera. Flat brown crabs dotted the thicket of brown mangrove prop-roots curving through still green water into soft mud the colour of milky tea. From green and black shadows invisible birds fluted exotic notes, with now and then a sudden, scolding rasp. Away from the lagoon breeze the trapped air was heavy with heat.

There was no need for conversation. Stan's thoughts were turned inwards. Gianni had been reluctant to allow the three of them to take the zodiac for the afternoon - the biggest tides of all were coming and he planned to dive. The zodiac absolutely had to be back in time. The zodiac was needed, and Bernard to drive it, but it was fair to say that the Blacksters were now little more than an irritation. There had been some very awkward exchanges between Gianni and Liza, and just before they left Gram had stepped in to prevent her going for Fabien, who had placed an amusing drawing in her sketch book.

'I'll do my best Stan, you know that,' she'd said as she saw them off. 'I can't last much longer though, and it won't take much. I'm ready to bloody slotten somebody!' She made no effort to keep her voice down, and had no interest in coming with them.

Meanwhile Gianni would be preparing for a conclusive return meeting with 'his' real shark after dark - bait of some sort, the bang-stick, the shotgun. Nothing sophisticated. Now that the Italian's quarry was finally within reach patrician affability had been put aside, freeing his own predatory essence to follow its instincts. Stan had to decide what to do. This trip in search of tranquillity and order with the mangrove jacks had already run into problems.

Earlier, when they'd travelled only a little way inside Passe Cabris, Bernard had showed them a length of chain secured to a casuarina, covered lightly with vegetation, attached to a steel trace leading into a deep pool at the edge of the channel. The line was taut and moving. A ten-foot lemon shark had swallowed the hook and whatever was on it, and now held its position facing into the flow of water. Notched pink arcs left by deep bites mutilated the broad head. Stan had been overcome with fury and had ordered Bernard to make straight back to the catamaran. First the powerhead, then the shotgun, and now this - enough was enough. How stupid and gullible Gram must think his father was. Bernard had known all along of course, the way the damned Linois always seemed to know, but not Stan. Bernard had advised against going back:

'Stan-lee, this would not be good. This guy, he has power, many friends at Marga. He know all those big guy.'

'But – '

'Dad, Bernard's right, even I can see that.' Gram. 'Someone killing a shark hundreds of miles away, where there are still thousands. It's no big deal to them up there.'

'You're saying we should do nothing?'

'No, but not that. It has to be something that works.'

Bernard was nodding. 'Nothing will happen to him, this guy. Nothing. But for us, big problem at Marga for sure.'

'And we have to get back to Marga somehow dad.'

As though they'd already discussed it. How to handle him. Whether even to show him the shark in the first place, maybe. The shark. They would release the shark, that was the first thing. And then he would think. About this and the tiger.

Lemon sharks, as he knew from regrettable experience, were better able than most species to put up with this kind of thing. There was no chance of getting out the hook, which had gone right down, so he and Bernard had uncoupled the short final section of trace and the shark swam off slowly with it trailing behind. If the hook wasn't stainless steel it would rust away in time. Best they could do. They would carry on with their trip to find the mangrove jacks, and he would try to think things out.

Matters had taken several unexpected turnings, and must be placed under consideration. He'd learned from Gram that he, Bernard and Timu had known a tiger shark was visiting *La Belone* after dark, attracted by the waste, but Bernard had told them to say nothing, not even to Stan. This was difficult to believe. Bernard was here at his invitation. Bernard was, in effect, his back-up guide, his assistant. A secondary authority. Bernard had acted out of turn. And Gram? What of Gram? This place - he'd forgotten how easily it threw things out of balance, how it established patterns of its own.

If he closed his eyes, which he did now, he could feel the atoll breathing, here at its heart; as the pressure in his head slowly swelled, slowly faded. He opened his eyes to observe the richness of life around them in the milky shallows, where shoals of small fishes swarmed, most of them tiny proto-fishes, unidentifiable and anonymous; others had progressed, differentiated, becoming this species or that. Among them moved new-born sharks no more than a couple of feet long, the length of an arm, protected here from the predators of the lagoon and the open ocean; sunken coral rocks were slimed with soft aquatic life; young turtles the size of dinner plates grazed and drifted. The mangrove forest's network of interlocking root-branches, fully submerged twice daily, formed the atoll's giant nursery, the hub of its vitality, continuously replenishing itself, breathing in organic matter, re-configuring it, breathing new life out into the lagoon, from where it would feed out into the ocean itself. This was the true heart of the atoll, not Roland with his pitiful magic plants, his blood and hair and toenails.

At the edge of the inlet, where booby droppings clouded the water, swam sturdy red fishes: the mangrove jacks, still here as they should be, thank the heavens. Still here in Tsaramaso lagoon as they'd been every day since he'd last gazed on them with Bernard all those years ago, and for thousands of years before that. The knowledge gave him strength. They had not yet followed the gallant charco pupfish into oblivion, although surely it was only a matter of time.

For a while they watched in silence as the aggressive, paddle-tailed snappers patrolled the murky green margins of the mangrove forest, now and then dashing forward in a lunge to snatch at unseen morsels. With each lungful of hot air the three of them ingested the rich chemistry of rotting vegetation, sulphurous mangrove mud and guano, as boobies gurgled and water lapped. Overhead, as always, hung frigatebirds, black spiky shapes fixed to the sky.

Eventually they roused themselves and moved on, guided by the dipping strokes of Bernard's paddle. Soon they ran out of water and the orange zodiac grounded. Without a word the three of them climbed out into warm, muddy water, feet sinking down into sucking mud, slowly easing the boat back towards deeper water, alert for the outcrops of coral limestone which might rip the inflatable's thin, man-made skin. Beneath their feet, under the mud, lay the uneven rock of the ancient reef. Thousands of spire-shaped shells housed hermit crabs, smaller cousins of the giant, armoured robber crab which had conquered the land but still began its life drifting in the open ocean as part of the vast planktonic girdle. Sluggish clouds of creamy white sediment boiled up in the water around their legs and trailed away in their wake.

This activity was soothing, planting and unplanting feet slowly in the warm lagoon mud, pushing this lightweight boat, a mindless and undemanding process, an endless journey to a destination long forgotten, where the journey becomes its own end. The unhurried *sloosh* of legs pushing through shallow water provided a mesmerising rhythm. Distant birds called. With a small surge the boat lifted free of the mud to float again, weightless. Still no one spoke. Speech was not required. They sweated, they breathed, and were at one with their surroundings. How preferable to human speech were natural sounds and silence. Language, since its first grunt, a source of endless problems. Words had their place, which was elsewhere. Language could be lost, the way Roland had lost what little English he'd bothered to learn. Not needed. Water lapped warmly at his legs; soft mud sucked at his feet. He was ready to sink down, to fold into the soup, to be absorbed into warmth and tranquillity.

A human voice, far away. Bernard's voice, indicating that the diarrhoea which had sporadically afflicted them all over the past two days had struck again, and he had to absent himself for a brief period. They watched him slip easily, bare-footed, over the network of roots and into the forest shadows.

And so he found himself alone with his son in the mangrove forest of Tsaramaso atoll. Removing his straw hat he wiped away sweat then replaced it and set it at the correct angle. They exchanged easy smiles, Gram holding the rope of the orange zodiac. Gram had matured while they had been in these islands, and especially since they set out on this voyage, and this was only right. Gram was almost a man, about to slip out into the world. He sensed a propitious moment, a node in time.

'My son. Gram. You are now seventeen years of age, or very nearly, and stand upon the threshold of manhood. It is time for you to learn your identity, the origin of your name.'

The gap-toothed smile became broader. 'Come on, I know where my name comes from. Gram Parsons. GP.'

Stan was shaking his head. 'No.'

'It is. The Grievous Angel. Mum's choice. I know all that dad. What do you mean?'

'Your mother and I have a regard for Gram Parsons the Grievous Angel, her perhaps more than I, however that is not the origin of your name.'

'What *are* you talking about?'

'You are named in honour of an outstanding fish which I grew to admire during my period of study. A singular creature, showing some of the features of a grouper, but to my mind even more impressive.'

'A fish?' The smile faltered. 'I'm named after a fish?'

'You are named after a fish. *Grammistes sexlineatus.* The six-lined soapfish. It was my hope that we might come upon one here, but they are secretive and very shy.'

'But … mum told me when I was a little kid, I'm named after Gram Parsons. She told me, and you never said … '

'Yes. But this is better.'

'But … '

'This is an extremely resourceful fish, which is able to protect itself. *Grammistes* secretes a toxin into his skin, and if a predator approaches too closely, it will be discouraged. You will see this is no ordinary fish.'

Gram retained a faint grin, but it was a changed grin. 'But mum always used to say – '

'Your mother is not aware of *Grammistes*.'

'What? But, the Pink Panther and the Grievous Angel … Kato and me … the photograph … '

'Yes. The karate-chopping manservant. A misapprehension. The noble hound is named in respect for a second remarkable fish, albeit less dear to me than *Grammistes*.'

'Kato's named after a fish?'

'*Anomalops katoptron.* The great flashlight fish. A denizen of the deep, which we unfortunately have little chance of seeing. In its head is a rotating light organ powered by microbes.'

Gram was staring at him now, with renewed respect. 'Right. I see. So we're the soapfish and the flashlight fish. Good one dad.'

'Yes.'

'Maybe I'll keep this to myself. Mum would grab the wrong end of the stick, I can see that. Keep it as a private joke.'

As the boy's father he had felt the urge to share this with him many times before, but he had been wise to resist until this moment.

'Thanks for telling me, dad. Good one.'

Bernard had emerged and was making his way back across the mud in the casual Linois manner. Getting back into the zodiac required a small jump then a roll, one at a time, and when they were settled Bernard paddled them out of the inlet. There, far away across the reef flats and shining shallows stood *La Belone*, geometrically white at the seaward end of Passe Cabris, framed by blue sky, turquoise water and dark stands of casuarina. Gram gave his father a serious, unfathomable look. No doubt the boy saw what he saw: giant white *Xiphias*, the alien cruise-ship, overwhelming a tiny island of peace.

Bernard tapped Stan's arm, pointing in the opposite direction to two distant black figures, men, one at either end of a small white boat, one pushing as the other pulled. Roland's men, or interlopers? He nodded and Bernard began to pull towards the stranded boat with unhurried, purposeful paddle strokes.

Out here the sun filled the sky. Tsaramaso's lagoon at low tide was a vast, shimmering sheet of pools and channels, dried-out reef flats and dark islets, dotted black and white with egrets and other wading birds. The two distant black men strained and toiled in the grinding heat, pushing and pulling, rocking and heaving, desperately urging the fibreglass boat and its cocked outboard on through the shallows. Only twenty yards separated their *canot* from the deep blue channel which would lead them northwards through the lagoon and out to the open sea.

'*Malgaches*,' murmured Bernard.

At the sight of the orange zodiac there was a brief snatch of speech and the two men doubled their efforts, both sinking to their knees to set their shoulders against the back of the boat and heave, but the boat was stuck. One grabbed an oar, working it under the hull to free it from the mud while the other pushed, and it inched forward. They seemed frantic.

Bernard stopped paddling. The zodiac would ground again long before they reached the other boat. Slowly they drifted, watching as the two men finally reached blue water and, with a last push, sprang aboard, lowered the outboard and pulled at the starter. Once, twice, a third time and it fired. The small boat roared away up the channel trailing a foaming white wake. After so much silence the engine noise was a shocking intrusion.

The three watched the boat dwindle to a white point as it swept past *La Belone* and on out to sea. For minutes afterwards a faint engine noise hung in the air.

Something of a mystery. Stan looked back the way the Malagassies had come.

Bernard followed his gaze. 'Those guy. They have no turtle in their *canot*. No fish.' *Feesh.* His eyesight was phenomenal.

'They were in a hurry though.' Gram looked from one to the other, unsure. 'And they kept going. They didn't bother about *La Belone*, did they?'

Stan held his son's gaze. 'No. Their manner is best described as furtive, therefore they have something to hide. They could not await the turn of the tide, and lacked knowledge of the channels, not so Bernard?'

Those familiar with Tsaramaso's vast lagoon knew of the long, meandering channel, carrying water even on these spring low tides, which passed between and behind islets, linking part of the mangrove's tidal creek system with the oceanic Passe Cabris.

'We go back now.' Bernard sounded uncharacteristically firm. 'Mister Conti, he want his dive.'

A test. Stan held up a hand. 'A moment, Bernard. Time is not yet pressing. And Mister Conti has not behaved well. It will do him no harm to wait. We should investigate.'

Finding which of the winding, forest-lined creeks the Malagassies had emerged from was straightforward: a cloudy trail marked the passage of boat and men between the crouching mangrove roots. At the creek's entrance a familiar rock outcrop, and cut into its face, naturally, two barely-discernible curving torpedo-shapes: the broken shark circle of Bras Demzel.

Bernard looked to Stan, who held his gaze and motioned with his head. With obvious reluctance the Linois manoeuvred the zodiac between banks of wet mud, taking it into the narrow channel. They moved on slowly, cautiously, through swarming fish shoals, small turtles and sharks, as Bernard searched the cloudy water for rocks. Here he had hunted juvenile sharks with Julius, and with foolish, unlucky Alain. Foolish, unlucky Sleeper. The air here was hotter, heavier, the wind merely a distant hushing in the forest canopy.

The boat grounded. Ahead a frenzy of deep footprints had churned the mud. With a further glance at Stan, Bernard tied up the zodiac front and back to mangrove trunks. The water bottle was passed round in silence, then they slogged onwards. Around a bend they came upon a dirty white fibreglass boat canted over on the mud, secured to mangroves and surrounded by human trampling.

'Dad. That's Roland's boat. There's the frigatebird on the front.'

Bernard did not seem surprised, but then that was the Linois way. This was the boat which had carried Gram back to his father from his terrible adventure at Passe Fregat an age ago. Roland's boat, with its faded, child-like painting of a flying frigatebird. Stan became aware his innards were behaving most peculiarly, writhing like a separate entity, seemingly attempting to push downwards, trying to reach the ground.

One by one they stepped up onto the gnarled, fossil coral limestone of the atoll's rim. Following Bernard's example they found sparse scratchy grass to wipe at the clotted white mangrove mud plastering their legs and feet. They were sheened in sweat. Without haste or reluctance, Bernard led the way into the scrub, moving with care across the myriad teeth and daggers of the long-dead reef, stepping over or skirting man-sized cavities, avoiding fragile overhangs. Bernard knew where he was going, clearly. His eye caught something to one side on the pitted grey rock: a lightweight field stretcher, and beside it a coil of climbing rope. A feeling of unease had been steadily mounting. Now, as he saw Bernard fading into the scrub, there was a prickling of memory, of another time, a time when he had been deserted by his guide in the bush not far from here.

He had detected something subtly incorrect in the way Bernard had been behaving of late, and he was no longer visible. He must consider: for instance, if he and Gram were to return and find the zodiac disabled, or gone altogether, what then? They had very little water, and no means of communication with *La Belone*. He recalled that it had been concern over precisely this type of situation which had caused him to seek out the Linois back on Marga; and now here it was, and the man had disappeared.

'Gram. You must stay with the boat.'

'What? Why dad? It'll be OK.' Gram looked worried, in need of reassurance.

When he shook his head there was a curious creaking sensation, possibly audible. 'Perhaps. But in this place I have learned that caution is the watchword. Bernard has located the trail - I shall follow, we shall find what is to be found, then we shall return. You must guard the boat – our only way out of this place, remember. This is an important task.'

Gram nodded uncertainly. 'OK. I guard the boat. Right. Dad ... are you all right? You sound funny.'

'Funny? In no way.' A reassuring smile. Behind Gram water was creeping forward. A big spring tide was rolling in, the biggest. Could the boy not feel it? 'Be aware – such as Bernard and Roland are not alone in their knowledge of the area.' Although admittedly he, Julius and Alain hadn't come this far up Bras Demzel on their shark-catching trip. They'd stayed nearer the lagoon, where the water was deeper and there were more sharks. 'I suggest you settle down in a shaded spot, and rest.' He gripped the lad's shoulder, shook it. 'You are Gram.'

The terrain was difficult and demanded his full attention. There was no sign of Bernard on the trail ahead. After ten minutes of clambering, hopping, teetering and crouching under an archway of intertwined branches he came out into a small clearing. It was very quiet, and the glare was momentarily blinding.

To one side of the clearing stood a grove of takamaka trees, lushly dark-leaved, incongruous against the backdrop of scrawny scrub vegetation. In its shade he could see grey coral rocks piled in a wall, similar to the old, broken-down tortoise and turtle pens still to be seen at points along the coast where the great reptiles had once been imprisoned to await loading aboard boats for food and profit. And, just discernible in the shadows, surely there clustered a dozen or more tortoises, escaping their deadliest enemy, the day-long heat. How reassuring. They were smaller here, in this most remote, seldom-visited part of the atoll, where the harshness of Tsaramaso achieved its fullest expression; but this had always been where the greatest numbers lived out their long lives. There was a curious scent in the air, half-familiar. Where in damnation was Bernard?

He took off his straw hat and used a sodden T-shirt sleeve to wipe sweat from his face. Movement, in the deep shadows of the takamaka grove: a sensation rippled through his mind, a flickering shadow on a sandy sea bed; and an immense wave of yearning, momentarily overpowering. He'd taken a step towards the grove when something else caught his eye, a slivery glint off in the scrub to the side, and more movement. He walked across to it.

Lying a few feet inside the shade of the scrub were two bodies:

white men, lying on their backs, stiff and still. He studied the pale, still face of Julius Easterhouse, quite uncharacteristically and rather disconcertingly smeared with dirt, grey eyes open but unfocused, gazing up into the branches. Long, orange-pink filaments twitched in the vegetation by his outflung arm, ahead of the twin pebble-like black eyes and massive, dull red claws of a robber crab detecting organic decay. Around the bare white legs trembled a mass of small, intricately-patterned seashells, each containing a scavenging hermit crab striving with buzzing flies to get at the raw-red meaty mess behind either kneecap. Julius. His cap of many colours, symbol of times past, lay nearby next to the tranquilliser gun once used by Professor Dalyell to capture judas goats. The second man he had certainly never seen before: burly, middle-aged, heavily tanned, with a massive neck and a frozen pink block of a face with red-grey stubble, wearing army-style khaki bush-clothes and heavy boots. A barbed-wire tattoo encircled the rock-like muscle of an upper arm. The hands, fingers curled and rigid, with a single gold ring, were enormous even for such a powerful body. Crabs and flies massed where blood had oozed and pooled, where raw meat showed. Around the bodies the ground vegetation was torn, the thin soil gouged.

'Julius?' Curious. Easterhouse, here. For what purpose? And apparently dead. 'Julius.'

His hand reached down into the grass and lifted a gleaming, steel-silver and black pump-action shotgun. It was surprisingly light, like a toy. Also in the sparse grass he could see a backpack, the long black barrel and curved magazine of an assault rifle, and some sort of box. Pointing the shotgun carefully at the ground he leaned down, freed the box's spring-clip, and lifted the lid. His eyes moved methodically over the contents, most of them familiar: scalpels, scissors and probes, labelled tubes of clear fluid, syringes, packaging tape, needles in sterile packs, capsules, bandages, surgical gloves, cotton wool, tranquilliser and darts, a canister marked liquid nitrogen ...

The glade was silent but for fly-buzzing and the rustling and scraping of crabs, but he had become aware of two figures standing close by in the shadows. Sesil and another, vaguely familiar Linois man. Both avoided his eye. Each held a machete at his side. There was another glint in the grass: a chain and twin steel circles. Handcuffs. He must seize the initiative.

'Sesil,' he tried heartily, '*ca va?*' He could not recall the name of Sesil's comrade, possibly a brother, with the same squat, powerful physique, the same surly demeanour. Sesil flicked him a nervy glance, then returned his attention to the ground. Neither man spoke, nor did they move. The blades of the two loosely-held machetes showed silvery edges where they had recently been ground sharp, and some darker staining.

Flies buzzed, crabs rustled. He would try again.

'Sesil, these two men - they appear to be dead. How is this? What has happened here?'

No reply. No eye contact. A highly threatening situation. Action, then. He could account for one of them with the shotgun, on the assumption there was a shell in the chamber, but the second would be on him before he could pump in another. On the assumption there was another. One seemingly casual half-swipe of the machete - he'd seen it many times, to dispatch goats – just one, and he'd be disabled; a second, and if necessary a third, and he would take his place alongside Julius and his associate.

While smiling disarmingly he gathered himself, preparing to bring up the muzzle. This shotgun was so light it was hard to believe it would function. Certainly it would have little effect as a club. Sweat was cold on his back. Where in damnation was Bernard? Should he shout out? He'd give it one more try, then he would act on the instant.

'What has happened here Sesil? I do not understand. *Pa kompran*. Explain it to me please. This one is Easter House. You remember Easter House. How is Easter House dead? And the other one?'

They didn't even look up. Why did they just stand there? It was unnerving. What were they waiting for? Wait! Surely they had moved further apart?

'Come on now. Put down your machetes. I put down this shotgun. Then we can talk together. You know me. I know you. We are old friends.' In the same manner as Easterhouse. 'Bernard is here too. He will help us. We shall wait for Bernard.'

Still Sesil and his brother stood there, tense in that springy, Linois way, neither looking at him or away from him, saying nothing. Could he hear a new movement at his back? A stealthy tread? Or was it the confounded crabs? The two Linois showed no reaction. No, it would not be advisable to turn around. His head ached. It was time. He brought up the silver barrel.

There was a short, soft sigh behind him, an insect bite on his leg, his right leg. An excruciating sensation, which he willed himself not to slap at, but the barrel wavered. A mild burning sensation spread over his thigh, like the stinging of fire coral. Astonishing, he could actually feel it spreading along his veins. Slowly slowly, moving only his eyes, he looked down, to see sprouting from his thigh a short, dark spine, like some sort of monstrous bristle. A bizarre sight. Would it draw out, or was it barbed? He continued to stare, awaiting developments, as the burning spread. His leg had become very red. There was a sound, a muffled clatter. There at his feet, implausibly distant, was a silver and black rifle, a toy rifle.

Time had passed. Crickets had started up, *clink-clink, clink-clink*. The heat was draining from the air. Dusk, the brief tropical dusk, was at hand. His view of the world was restricted: he apparently lay full length on the shallow, compacted soil among coarse grasses and projections of hard coral rock. But he was unable to feel his body. Routine signals fired confidently off from the brain - leg, move; hand, show yourself - fizzled out somewhere en-route. The antennae of a brick-coloured robber crab waved a few feet away, testing the air, tasting the heady tang of wood-smoke and roasting meat.

From time to time there were murmurings, muted conversation, and he thought to hear the voices of Bernard and Roland. Without difficulty he narrowed the focus of his concentration, drew it tight around the spoken Creole ... *not this one ... pass between them ... delay ... must enter the sea ...* ' He could take pride in the precision of his awareness, but the words held no meaning for him.

Two pairs of strong brown legs went by, two strings of swinging fishes. Spangled emperor, *Lethrinus nebulosus*. Bluefin trevally, *Caranx melampygus*. Fishes held meaning. Fishes were full of it. A curious, heavy dragging brought silence to the clearing. Drag, rest. Drag, rest. The weary heaving of a great turtle, straining to return to the sea. At the limit of his vision a long, low, grey something moved slowly, in time with the sound. Very, very slowly. Difficult to delineate among the deepening shadows. Not a turtle.

He was up on his feet, being guided along the path. A milky glow bathed the tropical night sky: the full moon was rising. Ahead shone the waters of the creek, come to meet them. The rising spring tide had flooded the treacherous passage of jagged rock and mantrap holes, and continued to inch forward. Hands helped him into a boat which rocked with his weight, water lapping. Laid out before him on the deck were the unfortunate Julius and his unknown colleague, half-buried in shining fishes. A surreal image. Yellowlip emperor, *Lethrinus xanthochilus*. Lyretail grouper, *Variola louti*, one of his many favourites, flamboyantly red with an extravagant yellow-tipped, lunate tail and a bristle-toothed mouth. Tears sprang to his eyes. Julius's head rested against a brimming bucket, his dirty white face staring at the moon. And, in his dirty white face, his grey eyes were swivelling, peering around, while his head remained still. Not dead after all. The grey eyes looked right at him. I know you, they appeared to be saying. Julius wore his hat. A large piece of flesh had been sliced from his upper arm. Likewise with the other one, whose eyes also flicked helplessly in his head. Many times in the past he had watched the Linois slice meat from the carcase of a goat, holding down the haunch while stroking the machete blade away from the splayed brown hand. Effortless, as long as the blade had been well sharpened.

The small boat rocked twice more as Sesil and his brother stepped in. They pushed with long poles of mangrove wood, sending the loaded boat along the creek in silence under the starry tropical night sky.

He thought of Gram. Where was Gram? Gram was asleep, under the stars.

Out on the lagoon, in deeper water, they moved through a world of silver light and black shadow, gliding, rocking gently with each paddle stroke.

Hands helped him up onto a moonlit islet no different from a hundred other moonlit islets. The orange zodiac was already there. Gram? Where then was Gram? Bernard was there, and there was tiny Roland, wearing on his back gaping white jaws, circular white teeth with backswept cutting points, the distinctive and stylish teeth of a tiger shark. A cunning design. Nearby a small fire was burning; and again the smell of roasting meat sweetened the air. Above an inlet, Roland carefully placed a pair of human skulls.

His mind watched Sesil and his nameless brother wordlessly wielding their machetes, that casual chopping action which never varied; then his mind watched them dressing the two mutilated bodies with fishes. He suspected his face was smiling while his mind admired their work. The wiry black shape of Roland crept past carrying a rattling hoop of coconut half-shells. He knelt to anoint the two bodies from a small bottle. Concentration was pin-sharp, exhilaratingly so. He could see everything. The shark jaws shifted on Roland's back. The jaws of a real shark. Where was Gram? Asleep, he felt sure, sleeping and safe. Protected.

Chain rattled, secured to fastenings in the rock either side of the inlet. The bodies of Julius and the other one were in the shallows, held by chain. The two not-dead bodies. The nameless brother emptied the bucket of fish guts and blood over them and the air swarmed with the smell. Roland was shaking the hoop with its coconut shells in the water. Pale fish particles washed out into the inlet in a series of pulses on the tiny waves of the rising tide. The bucket had been emptied, leaving none for his own chaining and immersion. Surely he was next?

Four Linois now stood above the inlet, on the bare coral rock overhang: three men and one ancient child. One man grunted, pointing: the first fin, black-tipped, was already entering the little bay in the customary leisurely manner of the shark.

Abruptly the fin surged forward as the source was located, and the shark was grabbing and wrenching, threshing the shallows. Behind it came the twin dorsals of a lemon shark, then the single of another blacktip. Soon the bay was a threshing mass of coiling white undersides, fins and tails, mud and red foam, glinting fish-scales. Still more fins broke the lagoon's tranquil surface, all making for the inlet. The chain rattled and clanked as the waters slowly rose. Jaws gripped and twisted. One of the black figures was pointing again: a single fin approached the bay, a much larger fin, and behind it the tip of a long, sweeping tail.

'Demzel.'

The chain jumped, kept on jumping, as a great, square-snouted head shook convulsively back and forth, hurling water and smaller sharks aside. It backed off, drove in again, seized and shook, twisting over, a massive white length in the moonlight. Here she was, and his mind exulted. *Galeocerdo cuvier*. Magnificent. The Linois were now solemnly chewing. Fingers pressed warm meat to his lips. He chewed and swallowed. Roland cast meat down into the tumult of sharks. The remains of one body were finally torn free of the chain, dragged into the deeper water, gone. Smaller sharks fought on over what was left in a moonlit frenzy.

The small boat floated back across the silver and black lagoon. His body had not after all been given to the sharks. The looming black mangrove forest was reflected perfectly in the brimming silver channel of Bras Demzel.

Water now flooded the small clearing, a small clearing like a thousand other small clearings in the vastness of Tsaramaso. He stood in a foot of water. The four Linois were leaning over a low dark shape, easing it towards the channel. Another body? This cannot be his son! No, not Gram. Gram was destined to live on. The moon stood overhead, round and bone-white. Silvery ripples fanned across the flooded clearing. A lumpy fin thrust up from the dappled and barred grey hide of the man-sized thing in the water. The wide, half-submerged head moved ponderously from side to side, flexing the long body in awkward, sinuous curves. A tail fin stood clear of the surface. He had no name for this.

Gently, tenderly, four pairs of black hands guided the creature past him. He saw a round black eye in a sleek grey head. A round, lightless black eye. How could there be expression in such an eye? How could there be meaning? There, in the muddy shallows of the same creek long ago, with the sun blazing down and Julius and Sleeper beside him, he had seen the face of the shark before it hit the net, before Sleeper deliberately scared it away. The eyes of a shark, but no shark. He *had* seen limbs. An otter-like or cat-like thing, but no otter. No cat.

Roland was passed a cup made of dark and glossy leaves, the leaves of the takamaka tree. From it he took a piece of root, chewed deliberately, moving it around in his mouth, then spat saliva down onto the body in the water, kneeling to wipe it gently along a grey flank while the others watched in silence. On the night air his heightened senses caught the sharp tang of ginger.

The four figures stood back, watching. With a confident thrust their burden floated free of the land, moving ponderously out into the deeper water, the blunt fin sinking steadily lower, the tail swinging into the timeless rhythm of the sea.

He felt tears running down his cheeks. *Take me with you.*

The black fin vanished, the tail-tip swept back, forth, back, and was gone. The final ripples faded into the dark mass of the flooded mangrove forest. Hands touched him, turning him gently.

19. Confraternity of the Seas

The sea today was a fine and awesome sight, heaving itself ever onwards in a mountainous procession of irresistibility; and down there, beneath its roaring, hissing, glittering surface, a world-encompassing tumult of intertwined life grappled and fought and drifted forever: sight, sound and concept were a dizzying and hypnotic whole, worthy of an eternity's contemplation.

La Belone had started to roll as she cleared the shelter of the atoll and encountered the heavy swell coming in from the southeast. She was making for Fiantsifer, into wind and current, and it would be a long and gruelling crossing. The grimness of the atmosphere aboard was palpable: regrettable, but readily explained by the tragic and gruesome unfolding of the preceding night, which could now be reviewed.

Deprived of his zodiac, the Italian had been unable to perform his feat of underwater flying in Passe Cabris. This had enraged him, but had not deflected him from his foolhardy plan to make a rendezvous with the tiger shark which obsessed him. After dark, as the seas poured into Passe Cabris, he had directed his captain and crewman to set out heavy lines primed with raw slabs of meat taken from the vessel's refrigerated coffers - bait beyond the ambitions of lesser sharks. And, to the man's easily pictured jubilation, his monster had made its silent appearance, this assassin of pigs, to instantly set about the nearest hunk of half-frozen flesh. Soon the great predator wallowed at the vessel's stern, making sluggish passes at a side of pork trailed in the water by the apprehensive crewman, Timucu. The great man then brought himself into close proximity with the beast in order to detonate the warhead of his fearsome hand-held weapon, which had of course been interfered with and failed to respond. There had been an accident, a loss of footing, and events had taken an abrupt downward course.

At length the frantic crew gained purchase on a leg and were able to pull the body aboard, but staunching the flow of Italian blood had proved difficult and time-consuming. A series of urgent conversations had ensued with medical authorities in the distant main islands via a satellite whirling invisibly high above the world, while Aurora ministered to her stricken husband as best she could within the limitations of the facilities available. Her husband was soon unconscious. Even now a physician and nurse were aboard one of Air Papa's twin otters, hastening to the landing strip on the island of Fiantsifer, while a renowned Italian surgeon oversaw preparation of the operating theatre at a discreet and private hospital on Margaritifer.

Prior to this mishap the Barracuda, single-hearted and resourceful in the grand style, had naturally stalked the deck with increasing alarm over the course of the afternoon when they failed to return, and had finally assumed control of the shotgun, putting it to good use after Gianni's misfortune to prevent *La Belone* departing the atoll until her loved ones returned, however long this might take. Picture the scene!

In fact any delay had been trifling, as they had rejoined *La Belone* before dawn, fortunately just as even the Barracuda's fierce concentration was on the ebb, and they had hoisted anchor shortly thereafter.

An angled discharge of one barrel, aimed to curtail the captain's creeping advance when those amazon eyes at last showed signs of losing focus, had ripped an impressive hole in the wheelhouse roof. Sea-wind and spray had scattered and soaked charts and log-sheets which scuttled about the feet of the crew until they were trampled and useless. This captain, who always had been prone to recklessness, sported a piratical head-bandage dyed with blood and something darker, and complained endlessly of pains in his skull, while nonetheless striving heroically to hold *La Belone* to her course at best speed.

But that was inside. Out here on deck, out in the elemental world, he found the conundrum of his body of more immediate interest: it was clearly visible, which seemingly confirmed it was there, just where it should be. But it held no sensation for him, nothing of that tingle of life, as though it belonged to someone else entirely. He could move his head a little, or so he thought: he was secured in some type of rough harness, in the manner of deck-cargo - not, in his present situation, a particular inconvenience, but these stately rollers were increasingly impressive, and threatened to swamp the deck at any moment. No doubt it was all in hand, and someone would come for him if and when necessary. He had every confidence in his shipmates, and he was without fear. The vessel heeled over, and by angling his eyes downwards, just so, he brought into view a section of the wet, shining deck, and on it the greater part of this body, lurching from side to side within its restraints. The boy sat at his left side, while to his right he sensed his loyal partner in this great adventure. Emotion flooded through him and was gone. The boy leaned forward, looming into the field of his vision, at his neck a fetching string of crimson beads, the dried seeds of some manner of exotic plant, possibly familiar. The boy smiled, displaying the gap at the centre of his fine white teeth, and may have touched him. He fashioned in return one of his own most forceful smiles, one he had found to be an infallible confidence-builder.

One of the great, white-chested black pirate-birds now swung close alongside at eye-level, holding its position easily above the pitching seas, regarding this curious bale of flotsam and its anxious cargo. The span of its angled black wings exceeded the height of a man. Up struggled *La Belone*, up to the top of a giant swell, to poise there, and for an instant, off in the distance, there stood a long, low rim of grey rock and the rollers crashing white against it; then down plunged *La Belone*, down into the depths of a trough, and there was again only sea and sky.

It was proving something of a challenge to make a coherent whole of outside affairs ... surely there had been a time, not so long ago, when he had learned the technique? Something had gone away, he felt; something had, in some ungraspable way, gone out of him. Some vital essence. He had seen this in the eyes of the woman, thought to see it now in the eyes of the boy beside him, who no longer smiled. He performed the trick with his eyes and saw a brown hand holding the left hand of his body, a darker one moving shadow-like to grasp the right, and felt nothing.

A brace of deep, leisurely wingbeats carried the pirate-bird away in a long arc on the streaming sea-wind, back towards the vanished rim of rock.

He had listened as the estimable Bernard had explained, in that patient native way he knew so well, and with which he felt so at ease: this purple mark on the leg of Stan-lee, this is the poisonous sting of a very bad insect, you find it only at Tsaramaso. Like the scorpion, but this is not the scorpion. Like the centipede also, but not the centipede. This part of Tsaramaso, this is where live many, many of the bad insect. A very bad place, this place. The poison it is in the blood. There is also the poison in Stan-lee's head, from his ears. The poisons they work together. But soon it will go, he will be OK.

He had the impression it was somewhat uncharacteristic of Bernard to adopt such a positive viewpoint, but it was no doubt all for the best: various capsules and tablets had been handed over in silence by a woman with a haunted white face and averted eyes.

Yes, definitely this poison it will go. I have seen this many times.

Soon though? How soon? This from the strong black woman who shot a hole in the roof. His partner. How soon Bernard?

Well, Bernard could not say.

'We must assume a positive outcome.'

Had he spoken? He relished life and tomorrow, this was well known, but the serenity emanating from the hovering blue fish could not banish a nagging sensation that his exertions had somehow fallen short of the very highest standards. At his side, yes, there would certainly appear to be a handsome and loyal black woman and a strong brown boy, known to be the Barracuda and Gram; and yes, he had played his own part with vigour. But had he committed the whole of his heart? Had he?

This all now lay behind him however, beyond a threshold. A new day was dawning. A new adventure. And this time he would dedicate every atom of his being to this business of life.

His whirling blood had achieved its purpose: his brain, fully unspooled, pulsed in calm anticipation; all dimensions lay properly unfurled and in place. Deep within him, deep in the profoundest turquoise depths, the tiniest of glimmers trembled and grew: a glorious crystalline vessel, limbs beating in unison, driving up, up, ever up.

A familiar voice spoke a single word.

'Mandroso.'

www.ingramcontent.com/pod-product-compliance
Lightning Source LLC
Chambersburg PA
CBHW031059030726
47496CB00002BA/299